So Many Secrets, So Many Lies

Rosemary J. Fisher

Riverview Press

info@riverview-press.com
www.riverview-press.com

About the Author

WHILE GOING THROUGH some boxes in storage recently, Rosemary J. Fisher came across the rough draft for her very first novel, written over twenty years ago! She blew the dust off the pages and re-read the story. Attitude, experience, and growth all factor into a novelist's thinking as she writes, and Rosemary knows that she has changed a lot since she first penned this story. Yet she still feels it has a relevant message and is worthy of publication.

Rosemary lives in Columbia, MO, with her husband, John, and their two collies, Regina and Brynn. They have four children and eight grandchildren. Rosemary enjoys singing, reading, and dog training.

Other books by Rosemary J. Fisher

The White Dove Series
Under His Wings
Safely Abiding

And coming soon
Heaven's Waiting Room

Follow the author at
<u>Rosemary Gossell Fisher- Author | Facebook</u>
https://riverview-press.com/

Dedication

This book is dedicated to all women who are
searching for fulfillment and satisfaction.
You may take faltering steps down deceptive
roads, but don't be discouraged.
Keep searching! Be true to yourselves!
You are worth it!

Sometimes the things we desire are within ourselves.

Acknowledgement

I want to thank Kendy, Joyce Marilyn, Terry, Carol, and John who urged me to go for it!

Disclaimer

The events depicted within this novel are completely
fictionalized, although totally possible.
Any resemblance to people you may know
is simply a coincidence.
Or is it?

Table of Contents

PART ONE

EVERYBODY HAS A SECRET

Chapter One

Something's Missing

SUZANNE ROGERS PLACED the telephone near her on the bed. She laid her head down on the pillow and wrapped her body around the phone. Lying on her side, with one hand beside the phone, she closed her eyes and drifted towards sleep. She wouldn't stay awake, waiting for his call, for he might not be calling tonight at all. But if the phone did ring, she wanted to answer it quickly. Not because she was so eager for his call (even though she was). But her daughter was asleep in the next room. Suzanne certainly did not want Lindsay to wake up in the middle of the night. That would ruin everything.

Suzanne pushed a lock of her auburn hair off her forehead and thought about a few things. It was past eleven o'clock. Her husband had left for work, night shift at the county hospital emergency room. He was just a med tech. Not a doctor or nurse, but at least it was a job. He had had worse. The apartment door was locked. Her school papers were graded and packed in her briefcase. Lindsay's lunch was already packed for the next day, and she was planning to make oatmeal for breakfast.

Suzanne's thoughts were interrupted by noises outside in the hallway. She sighed and thought to herself, 'The neighbors must be having a party again, or doing some business.' Suzanne suspected there were drugs changing hands there, although no one had ever approached her. There was always a lot of traffic in the hallway, late at night. Suzanne vowed to stay clear of them. Hopefully, she could protect Lindsay from that for a while. She was just four.

So Suzanne fell asleep, wondering if he would call and hoping he would. She wanted to hear his voice again. She needed to talk to him. He had become a pleasant part of her life. A secret part, yes, but something she could look forward to. They would talk about their days, how things went at work, and what kinds of strange people he had met lately. What her daughter had been up to, and how she was growing. He was so easy to talk to. He seemed to really want to know about her. They were becoming friends. And Suzanne needed a friend right now.

*   *   *   *   *

Suzanne had been married for nearly six years. Everyone thought she was happy, though her mother had voiced her suspicions on a few occasions. But Suzanne had quickly dispelled any questions, and pretended that everything was fine. Her mother was not going to pry, but she kept her eyes open and observed what Suzanne thought she had hidden quite well.

Truthfully, it was not a good marriage, and seemed to be getting more unpleasant every day. Larry was a simple man. He had no goals except to make it from paycheck to paycheck. And he fell short of that from time to time, so they were getting deeper and deeper into debt. He had a college education, but seemed satisfied with low-paying jobs, which just about anyone could get. Suzanne always felt that if he would dress better, present himself better, and act a little more grown up, he could have actually done something with his life. But he did not see it her way at all. "If they can't accept me for what I

4

am, then I don't want to work with them anyway." So he never tried to improve himself, to better their financial situation. Suzanne found herself disliking his whole attitude.

In fact, if it weren't for her income as an elementary school teacher, they would not be able to afford the three-bedroom apartment condominium they had lived in for the past four years. It was a good thing she had a steady job and a decent, although modest, income. Larry was often "between jobs" and it was only Suzanne's paycheck that was dependable.

When she had found out she was pregnant and they had to move from their little one bedroom apartment, they actually looked at homes for sale in the area. But what a joke! Anything they could afford was in need of major repair, and Larry was certainly no handyman. So they settled for this condo, where Larry would never have to mow the lawn or fix the gutters or worry about any normal homeowners problems. It was easy living for him, and he liked it that way. He could watch ball games on television and sit back and take it easy every night. No responsibilities.

Suzanne had to admit that, under the circumstances, it was the best thing for her right now, too. If they had a house and a yard and all those normal household chores to do, she would certainly be the one doing everything, since Larry would be no help anyway. So at least living here, if there was a plumbing problem, or a leaky roof, she only needed to call the condo maintenance people and they would come right over to fix it. And when Larry threw a temper tantrum about one thing or another, and slammed his fist into the wall, she could just call maintenance. They would come to fix the hole, no questions asked. Suzanne had watched them repair drywall holes twice now, and felt that next time she would know how to do it herself, and would not need to call maintenance at all. She didn't like thinking that people at the condo office might be talking about what was going on in their apartment. How embarrassing.

But Suzanne longed for some space. She dreamed of having a house; it wouldn't have to be big. She would like to have a piano. She would like to have a garden, maybe plant some tomatoes and green beans. And flowers, lots of flowers. She would like to have a little swing set in her back yard, a place where Lindsay could play safely with some neighborhood friends.

Instead, they lived in a small apartment on the third floor of a development in a decent though not really desirable neighborhood. It was all they could afford, and she would have to be satisfied with it, for now. But deep inside, she was not satisfied, and felt cheated somehow.

She worked hard, and she was a very good teacher. She had a reputation at the school for being fair, fun and creative. Parents were pleased when their children were assigned to her class. She truly loved her work and her children. The school administrators acknowledged her dedication and her accomplishments.

On all fronts, Suzanne's life seemed pleasant enough. She had a good job, an apparently good marriage, a beautiful daughter, and a nice enough home. But it was deep inside her, hidden from all others, that she had this great turmoil. Something was missing, and she felt her inmost needs were not being met. Worst of all, she didn't know what to do about it.

Until that first phone call. After that, she began to find herself. She recognized what was missing, she slowly became aware of what was available to her, and she began to discover things about herself that would finally lead her toward total inner fulfillment.

So Suzanne Rogers had a secret life. It began after her husband went to work at his night shift job. It was a life of late night phone calls, whispered fantasies, and passionate conversations. She had never felt the tingle of sensuality like this before. It was a whole new experience, one that she planned to explore further. It would remain a secret forever. And it would change her life completely.

Chapter Two

The Way Things Were

ON THE NIGHT of that first phone call, Suzanne had cried herself to sleep. It had been a pretty typical evening. Nothing really out of the ordinary had happened that should have upset her so. But for some reason, hormones maybe, Suzanne just felt like crying. She needed to release her emotions somehow.

Suzanne had filled up the car with gas on her way home from work. The tank was nearly empty, and Larry did not like to get gas on his way into work late at night. Then she picked up Lindsay at daycare and headed for home. Lindsay had a lot to talk about, and Suzanne always made sure the car radio was turned off and she could give Lindsay as much attention as possible while driving on the busy beltway around town. The commute from work to home was nearly thirty-five minutes, but with a stop for gas, and then picking up Lindsay and chatting a little with her teacher, it made the trip closer to an hour. It was five o'clock when they made it home.

As Suzanne unlocked the apartment door, Lindsay said, "Mmmm Popcorn! Daddy made popcorn!" The delicious smell of freshly popped and buttered corn came at them as they walked through the door. Lindsay put down her backpack and ran to her daddy without even taking off her jacket. "Is there any left for me, daddy? Did you save me some?"

"There's a bowl sitting right here for you," Larry said, as he looked past her towards the television. A baseball game was just about over, and he needed to see the last two innings. He had some money riding on this game, and it looked like he was going to be a winner this time. Lindsay climbed up on the couch next to her daddy, while Suzanne busied herself in the kitchen. She had left some chicken in the refrigerator to thaw, and was planning to fix rice and green beans. She would really like a salad, too, but the lettuce was pretty wilted, and they didn't have any cucumbers or tomatoes anyway. Oh well, payday was coming, and then she could get some groceries. Hopefully lettuce prices hadn't risen again.

By the time the chicken was in the oven, the baseball game was over. Larry was in a good mood. He knew he would be collecting some cash tonight from some buddies at work. It was a good thing; he could use some extra cash. He wanted to buy some lottery tickets.

Now Larry could actually talk to his daughter. He looked over her art project from "school" and asked Lindsay if she had any new boyfriends. "Oh daddy, stop it!" laughed Lindsay. He asked her that every night.

Lindsay pulled a note from her backpack. There was going to be a special evening program at her school, and parents were invited. It was all about springtime, and Lindsay was going to be a yellow daisy. She needed a flower costume be next Thursday.

"Suz, you better read this," he called out to Suzanne. She came from the bedroom where she had changed out of her school clothes into jeans and a t-shirt.

Suzanne read the note over and wrote the date of the play on her calendar. Lindsay had told her about the costume she needed in the car coming home, so Suzanne was already planning how she might make a cute flower outfit. Fortunately, she was pretty creative, and knew how to make a lot of things look good, even if they were cheap. Elementary teachers were pretty used to that.

"Do you think you will be able to go to the program this time?" she asked Larry.

He shrugged and said, "You know how hard that is on me. I need to sleep in the evenings, or I can't make it through the night at work. I'd like to, but you know I can't. If I fall asleep at work, I'll get written up and maybe fired, and you know how hard it is to get a new job. I can't go; I have to stay home and sleep." Then he turned to Lindsay. "Sorry, kiddo," he said. "I'll buy you some ice cream to eat when you get home from the show. Chocolate chip, your favorite. We'll have a party to celebrate! Okay?"

"Sure daddy. I love chocolate chip! Can we have whipped cream on it, too?" Larry nodded and Lindsay threw her arms around him for a big hug. Suzanne sighed and wondered how long Lindsay would be satisfied with this kind of trade off. How long would ice cream remain as a good enough substitute for a father who was never really there?

Suzanne took the laundry basket off the table so she could set it for dinner. "I was hoping you would fold these towels this afternoon," she said to Larry.

"Oh, I didn't see them," he said with a shrug. Suzanne cleared away his coffee cup and a banana peel, which had been placed on the table right next to the laundry basket.

'Yeah, right,' she thought, but did not verbalize.

After dinner, Larry went to bed. He had to get up about ten, which left Suzanne with the evening chores. She had to do the dishes, pack a lunch for Lindsay and herself, make coffee for Larry to take to work, and a couple of sandwiches for him to eat in the middle of the night. Lindsay colored and worked on puzzles at the kitchen table while her mother buzzed around with preparations for the next day. At 7:30 it was time to give Lindsay a bath and read to her, say prayers with her, and tuck her into bed. Then there was the laundry to fold and school papers to grade. Actually, Suzanne did not mind this quite time to herself. She usually put on some soft classical music as she went about her nightly routines. She hardly ever turned on the television. It was too distracting, and she needed to concentrate on the papers she was grading.

At about 9:30 Suzanne heard Larry stirring in the bedroom. She knew what that meant, and sighed, resolved to get through it one more time. She hurried to finish grading the papers before he called.

"Hey, Suz, I need you," he called in a horse whisper. He knew that if he woke Lindsay, Suzanne would go to her, not him, and he would be left unsatisfied, or end up doing it alone again. But Lindsay did not wake up, and Suzanne walked into their bedroom and quietly closed the door behind her. She turned to him as he moved the open magazine onto the floor at his side of the bed. Suzanne glimpsed the centerfold spread, a blond with extremely large breasts. One of her hands was squeezing a breast, the other hand was lower. Her legs were spread wide, and she seemed to be enjoying the touch she was giving herself. "Undress in front of the window," Larry said to Suzanne. The sheers were closed but the blinds were open. There was light coming in from the parking lot below. Suzanne knew that probably no one could see into their dark bedroom, but Larry liked to think that someone was watching them.

She unzipped her jeans and let them fall to her feet. Then she kicked them free and raised her t-shirt up over her head. Now she was naked except for underwear. Larry had his eyes closed and was stroking himself quickly. "Hurry up," he said. "I'm just about to come." Suzanne removed her panties and bra and quickly lay on the bed beside him. Larry turned and mounted her, inserting his hardness into her roughly. She was not ready for this, and the entry was painful. She bit her lip to keep from crying out. With a few more thrusts, it was all over. He collapsed beside her, and only then reached out to touch her breasts and kiss her with any kind of tenderness. She responded, as she knew she must, but glanced at the clock to see what time it was. Pretending to be disappointed, she said, "Larry, it's after ten. You have to get going."

"Yeah, guess you're right," Larry complained as he lay back on the bed for a few seconds. Then he sat up. As he put his feet on the floor, he stepped on the magazine and tore the centerfold picture right across the crease. "Damn," he said. "And she was so hot. I was going to use her again." He kicked the loose pages and the rest of the magazine under the bed.

Suzanne pulled a sheet up over herself and lay quietly on the bed while Larry showered and dressed for work. Then he went into the kitchen, poured his coffee, and grabbed his sandwiches from the refrigerator. When she heard him lock the door, she got up from the bed. She needed a shower, but first she had to get that magazine. She found it under the bed and put it on the top of a stack of others in Larry's closet. She was careful to place a folded blanket on top of it all, just in case Lindsay would happen to get into the closet. She would have to think of some other way to hide these things soon. Lindsay was getting into everything these days.

The shower felt good, and took some of the strain and stiffness out of Suzanne's body. Her shoulders began to relax a bit as she let the hot water rinse away the shampoo bubbles from her hair. Now if she could only get her mind to relax. But that seemed impossible tonight. She was going around in circles, thinking, thinking, and thinking. How could she have gotten herself into this mess of a marriage? What could she do about it now?

Divorce? She just didn't feel right about that. Maybe it was her moralistic mid-west upbringing. There was Lindsay to think about, too. She had to consider what was best for her, and certainly having Larry for a father was better than having no father at all. And Suzanne knew she could not live here on just her teaching salary alone. Larry's income was not regular and dependable, but they did need that money to get by. How could she manage on her own? She would have to move, probably back home with her parents.

Suzanne's parents had been married for twenty-eight years. There had been some rough spots along the way, surely, but they always overcame the difficulties. That's what married couples do.

They pull together, work things out. For better or worse and all that. No, her parents did not approve of divorce for any reason other than physical abuse. Even adultery could be forgiven and trust could be restored. They would hardly condone their daughter's decision to leave Larry just because she was unhappy. That was not a good reason. Stick with it, grin and bare it, live up to your obligations. That's what they would say. If she left Larry, they would always be on her for breaking her marriage vows.

Well, yes, they would welcome her back home, but there would be strings attached. They would be supportive yet judgmental at the same time. They would be nosey and interfering. They would question her disciplining of Lindsay, and always be giving advice. She would never get away from their sideways glances and raise eyebrows. Living with them would not be easy, either.

She had suggested marriage counseling years ago, but Larry would hear nothing of it. He evidently saw no problem with their lifestyle. He was getting what he wanted, one way or another. He had food on the table, a place to sleep, and someone to cook and clean for him. He had sex whenever he wanted it, and a wife that kept her mouth shut and didn't complain too much. Everyone thought they had a fine marriage, why did she have to go and mess with things by bringing up counseling? Why couldn't she just leave well enough alone?

Suzanne fumed about it as she got out of the shower and dried off. Sure he was getting what he needed, but what about her? Did he even notice that she was unhappy? Did he even care? When was she ever going to feel satisfied and fulfilled? Or was she just destined to an empty lonely life? No! There had to be more to life than this. Yet she felt trapped, and didn't know what to do to free herself.

So the tears trickled quietly down Suzanne's cheeks as she towel dried her hair and put on her nightgown. When she closed her eyes and lay down in bed, the crying turned to sobs. She clutched her pillow close to her and buried her face into it. She did not want Lindsay to wake up and see her like this. And she had better get a grip, because tomorrow was another day, and life does go on, and all that.

That's how she planned to manage her life. One day at a time. Never get too distressed, never too involved. Get a good firm hold on each day, get through it as best she could, and go on to the next. No goals, no hopes beyond the next day. It was a pretty pitiful existence, but she would have to deal with it. What other choice did she have?

As Suzanne fell into a fitful sleep, she never imagined that the answer to her troubles was just a phone call away. And when the phone did ring a few hours later, she had no idea how her life was about to change.

Chapter Three

Lucky Numbers

GEORGE WILEY WAS filling out his report at the apartment office. He was the resident maintenance man on call for the night and had just returned from an emergency call. Broken pipes under the kitchen sink, what a mess. But once the water had been turned off, he had no trouble replacing the pipe. Plumbing and air conditioning were his specialties, but George could do just about any repair needed at the apartment. He stayed a while to have a cup of coffee with the residents. They were nice people and really appreciated George's help in the middle of the night. It was nearly two in the morning when he got back to the office to write up his report. When it was done, he made a copy, placed it in the account clerk's mail tray, and filed the original in the appropriate folder in the file cabinet. That done, he sat at the desk and lit a cigarette.

'Now for some fun,' he said to himself. He pulled a small notebook from his shirt pocket and flipped to the middle of the book. Scanning the page, he found what he was looking for. This was his phone book, of sorts. No names, just numbers in groups of five. Some had been circled, most had been crossed off. He picked up the phone and dialed the local exchange, followed by four numbers from his list.

A man's voice answered, and George clicked the phone's button with his finger. He crossed the number off on his list as he started to dial the next number. Another man answered and George hung up on him too. He crossed off the number and moved on to the next. No answer, so he skipped it and moved on down the list. 'Ahh, finally, a woman,' he thought as a sleepy female answered on the third ring. "Hey Sweetheart. What are you wearing tonight?" Sometimes this line worked, but not this time. She hung up on him without a word. 'Oh well, that's her loss,' he thought. But he really did like it if they got angry and called him a pervert or something. Hang-ups were no fun at all. He crossed off that number and moved on. He had a pretty good system, and quickly worked his way through a dozen numbers.

But George was getting a little frustrated. He took off his baseball cap and ran his fingers through his dark hair. "What the hell? Isn't there any woman who wants to talk to Georgie Boy tonight?" He spoke the words out loud as he hung up on yet another male voice. He thought about calling one of his regulars, but really wanted someone new tonight. He liked the challenge of breaking down a woman, and getting her to talk to him, even if she didn't know she wanted to at first. It was an art, and he was a very creative artist. "Give me a chance, Baby," he said, as he dialed another number.

The ringing of her telephone abruptly awakened Suzanne. She rolled over to reach the phone before it rang again and woke Lindsay. Maybe it was Larry, calling to apologize for his gruff behavior. She would accept his apology once again, of course. What choice did she really have?

She glanced at the clock as she answered her phone. Two forty-five. 'I just hope I can get back to sleep,' she thought to herself as she said, "Hello?"

"Hey Baby, what are you doing?" he asked with a lusty low voice.

Suzanne answered "I was asleep until the phone rang." But she wondered who this was, it sounded a little like Larry but not quiet. Maybe it was a bad connection. "Who is this?" she asked.

"My name is Paul, and I'm sorry if I woke you up, but I was wondering if you felt like talking to me. I really need somebody to talk to."

Suzanne knew what she should do. She had hung up on crank calls before. Maybe she was too tired to think clearly, but she hesitated just a second and that was the opportunity George needed to make his next move. "I just feel like, if I don't talk to you, I'm going to do something desperate." He wasn't lying, really. He was pretty desperate, and he did need to talk to somebody. Yes, he had lied about his name. But he had to do that. It was his first rule. Make yourself untraceable. And besides, he had done it so many times before that he sometimes actually believed his name really was Paul.

Something stirred within Suzanne. She felt a twinge of excitement race through her. She had never talked to a complete stranger on the phone like this before. His voice had sparked a little interest. What would be the harm in just talking to this guy? Other than interrupting her sleep for a bit, she could see no reason to hang up on him.

"Well, I really should be getting some sleep. I have to work tomorrow."

"Oh, well I won't keep you long. What do you do?" George was encouraged now. If he could get her to talk just a little more, he would have it made. He had a way of getting people to open up and share their thoughts and dreams with him. And once he knew a little about this woman, he would be able to bait his trap properly. Everybody responds to different things. If he could find out what makes this woman happy, excited, upset or nervous, he would be able to use that information to his best advantage. It had taken years of practice, but sometimes he could really get into a woman's head and play with her thinking. The first step was to keep her talking. He was on his way with this one.

"I'm a teacher," she said. "First grade."

"Oh, geez. First grade. That's a hard grade. You teach them to read and everything?"

"Well, yes. Reading is probably what we spend most of the day on. But there is a lot of social development and growing up in first grade. I think that's even more important than the academics, for most kids. I want them to know how to get along with others and be responsible and dependable and honest. Those are life skills they can't live without, whether they know how to read or not."

"Wow, you sound like a real teacher!" George chuckled. "I remember my first grade teacher. I really liked her. How long have you been teaching?"

"I'm in my eighth year. I've been at the same school for the past six years."

George didn't ask the name of her school. That was a bit too much information to ask for just yet, and he knew she might hesitate and feel uncomfortable revealing herself that way. Most women he talked to would go only so far. They didn't reveal information that would lead him directly to their home, or job, or anywhere he could actually encounter them face-to-face. Most women were afraid of stalkers and crazy men, but they were willing to play along with him from within the safety of their locked homes. And that was okay with him, for now. It was the second step.

"I bet you're a really good teacher. Sounds like you really like your job. You love kids a lot, don't you?"

"Yes, I guess I do. And I am pretty good with them. I think if you don't love kids, you should not be a teacher. It doesn't help anybody. Kids deserve the best I can give them. You have to go into teaching for the kids, not the money or the summer vacation or the prestige of the profession. That doesn't pay off. It is only for the kids, and improving their future."

"You sure are passionate about kids. Do you have any of your own?"

"I have a daughter. She'll be four soon."

"I bet you're a great mom, too, with all you know about kids."

"I try to be. It's hard sometimes, with work and everything else I have to do. I don't want to forget that she is my first priority. But sometimes I think I spend more time grading papers than playing with her."

George caught a hint of regret in her voice, and took a chance with his next question. "What about your husband? Doesn't he help you with her?" He was rather hoping she would say she had no husband, for one reason or another. That would give him a further indication into what kind of a woman she was, and what her needs might be. Of course, all women were basically the same. Married or not, they needed excitement and thrills and a little danger in their lives. He could give them that. He had done it plenty of times, with plenty of women, and they all appreciated what he added to their fantasy life. He was good for them, and he knew it.

"My husband," said Suzanne. "Well, yes, he helps some, when he can. But he works nights and sleeps most of the day, so he really isn't able to do too much while Lindsay is awake. She spends most of her time at daycare, or with me."

"Lindsay. That's a beautiful name. So your husband is at work now?" George wrote the name on a new page in his book of regulars. He was taking notes on things Suzanne had said, things he would want to remember the next time he called. Because there would be a next time, he was sure of that.

"Well, yes," Suzanne said, but hesitated. Maybe this wasn't such a good idea. What if this Paul was a real creep, what if he called her every night or something? What if somehow Larry found out? So she added, "He works most nights but not regularly. He is out of work sometimes, or changes his schedule." She was starting to feel uneasy. What was she doing, anyway? Was she crazy? Why was she talking to this man?

George noticed her hesitancy and tried to calm her fears. "Well, I guess I am lucky I called you tonight. Thanks for talking to me. I won't bother you again, if you don't want me to. But just hearing your voice and talking to you has been real nice. I was feeling really lonely and just needed to hear a friendly voice. I don't want you to get into any trouble because of me. I liked talking to you, though."

"Well, thanks. I guess I am glad you called, too, if it helped you some how. And I kind of like talking to you, too." It was true. Paul seemed really interested in her and kind and encouraging. Funny that she should feel that way, after just this short conversation. What was happening to her? Here she was, being friendly with a perfect stranger, and already wishing that he would call her again.

George knew that he had gotten lucky with this one. She was lonely, alone most nights, and already hooked on him. He could tell and it made him excited just to imagine what the next conversation would lead to. But he didn't want to press his luck. Better to close this call pretty soon. Just one more thing to ask anyway. "So, is it okay if I call you tomorrow night? Will he be working, do you know?"

"Yes, he is scheduled to work every night this week. But I might be really tired. I'm one of those people who need seven or eight hours of sleep every night or I just can't function the next day or two. So please understand if I don't feel like talking. I just can't mess up my sleep pattern too much."

"Don't worry. If you're tired or can't talk for whatever reason, just tell me. I won't be offended. And if your husband ever answers the phone, I will just hang up or do the "wrong number" thing. I wouldn't want you to feel uncomfortable talking to me, but I do hope we can talk again. I can tell we could be friends. And I'd like a friend like you. Just talking to you this little bit made me feel better."

Suzanne was sure now that she wanted him to call again. "Good, I'm glad you feel better. And yes, call me again. It's okay. I would like to talk with you again."

"Great! I hope you can get back to sleep now. I know you have a busy day ahead. So go to sleep and dream sweet dreams. And I will call you again. Goodnight."

"Bye," said Suzanne, and replaced the phone on the nightstand. As she settled back onto her pillow and pulled the blanket up around her chin, Suzanne felt an excitement and warmth she had not experienced in a long, long time. Was she crazy? How could this stranger get to her like this? Well, it was just an innocent, friendly conversation. And he probably would never call back anyway, and that would be the end of that. But secretly she wished and hoped that he would call. In fact, she was already looking forward to it.

George smiled to himself as he put away his phone book and notebook of regulars. He ran his hand over his chin, feeling the rough stubble of his beard as he thought about his success with this call. Yes, he had really gotten lucky tonight. This woman needed him. And he had just what she wanted. She may not know it yet, but he was the answer to this woman's dreams. 'I wonder how soon I can convince her that she really wants me?' he thought.

He locked the office door and walked across the parking lot to his own apartment. He was aware of his rising excitement rubbing against his blue jeans. In his bedroom he stripped naked and admired his profile in the mirror. His chest was firm, his stomach smooth, and most importantly, his manhood was thick and throbbing. He looked at his wife sleeping in the bed. She was stirring a little, so he rolled her over and kissed her hard on the lips. She opened her eyes a little and said, "God, what time is it?"

"After three," he said. "And I wanna fuck." He didn't give her a chance to respond. He grabbed her tits and squeezed them, forcing the nipples to become hard. Then he spread her legs wide and inserted his fingers into the dampness. When she began to moan, he climbed on top of her and drove his cock deep inside her. He was living out a fantasy. He was fucking his first grade teacher.

Chapter Four

Doubts and Determination

GEORGE CALLED SUZANNE the very next night. She was in a deep sleep and woke with a start. When he said, "Hi! It's Paul," she smiled and said "Hi. I didn't think you would really call."

He could hear the pleasure in her voice. "Did you want me to?" he asked, already knowing what her answer would be.

"Well, yes, I was hoping you would," she replied, and he was not disappointed.

"I just wanted to hear your sweet voice again," he said, and the words made a shiver run up Suzanne's arms. He didn't talk long. He asked if she had had a good day at school and if she had been very tired. He just wanted her to know he had been thinking about her. And when they said goodbye, he could sense that she had really wanted to talk with him more. That was the way he intended it.

Every evening for the rest of the week, Suzanne worked on Lindsay's daisy costume. It was coming along great, and would be ready for the kids' first dress rehearsals on Thursday. Paul called her again on Wednesday night and asked what she had been doing. She told him about the costume, and he seemed truly impressed and interested. He said he was sure Lindsay would be great as a yellow daisy, and she must be very excited to be going to watch her daughter perform. The play was Friday night, and he said he would call afterwards to see how it had gone.

The night of Lindsay's play finally arrived, and no little girl could have been more excited! As Suzanne sat in the small school auditorium, she found herself studying the room, feeling the atmosphere of excitement, and catching small bits of conversation here and there. She wanted to take it all in, to have a lot to share with Paul when he called. She was sure he would want to know all about it. He was so nice, and easy to talk to.

A quiet hush came over the room as the lights were dimmed. The curtain rose and fifty preschoolers danced, sang and giggled their way through a cute little play their teachers had written about springtime. Lindsay looked great in her costume, and she didn't forget any of her speaking parts. Suzanne was rightfully proud of her daughter. She clapped and cheered with the rest of the parents as the children took their final bows.

As they were leaving the school, one of Lindsay's teachers, Mrs. Jackson, came up to them and praised Lindsay for her great performance. Then she turned to Suzanne and told her how lovely the daisy costume had turned out. She said the teachers were wondering if Suzanne would be interested in designing costumes for their upcoming summer program, a simplified version of Snow White and the Seven Dwarfs. Since the show would be in the late summer, and Suzanne would be on a break from school, she agreed to help. Mrs. Jackson thanked her gratefully and promised to get back to her about the details.

It was late when they got home, but since it was Friday night, Suzanne didn't mind that Lindsay was up later than usual. Lindsay ran into her parents' bedroom to wake Larry. He got up and Suzanne served chocolate chip ice cream with whipped cream topping while Lindsay told her Daddy all about the show. He seemed proud of her and congratulated her for being such a beautiful flower and a great actress. Then he left for work.

Lindsay loved her costume and felt she should be allowed to sleep in it. Only after Suzanne pointed out that it might get broken or messed up did the little girl agree to take it off for the night. When she asked if she could be a flower at breakfast time, Suzanne agreed and Lindsay settled in to bed.

Although Lindsay was very tired, she was so excited she could not fall to sleep quickly. Suzanne stayed with her, sitting on the bed beside her daughter and stroking Lindsay's hair lightly while together they hummed one of the tunes from the show. Finally Lindsay drifted off to sleep. Suzanne kissed her on the forehead and tiptoed out of the room.

It was nearly midnight when Suzanne finished cleaning up the dishes and straightening up the apartment. She took a quick shower and climbed into bed. She was exhausted, but like Lindsay, too wound up to fall right to sleep. Besides, Paul had promised to call. Although she didn't know what time the phone might ring, she did think that he really would call. He had as much as promised.

Questions and doubts paraded through her mind as she drifted off towards sleep. What had come over her, to talk to this man she knew nothing about? Why did she feel compelled to tell him things and open up to him? Sure he seemed nice, and interested in her just as a friend, and there was no harm in that, yet there was something dark and mysterious about these late night calls. 'The whole thing could be right out of a murder mystery,' she thought. Where was it headed?

'Well, one thing's for sure,' she formed the words in her mind. 'I'm never going to meet this guy, so it will never go any further than a secret relationship with a man on the phone. That can't be too bad. Nothing dangerous or risky. Nothing that could get me into any real trouble. Unless Larry finds out. So I'll just have to make sure that he never does.'

So, with determination firmly settled in her mind, Suzanne fell asleep.

Chapter Five

Part of the Game

GEORGE TURNED OFF the TV in his apartment and looked at the clock. It was nearly one o'clock. His wife was asleep already. She had had several glasses of wine with their dinner, and that always made her sleepy. She fell asleep on the sofa shortly after dinner and about eleven he had convinced her to just go to bed. Of course, the dinner dishes were still on the table, along with leftover spaghetti and salad. 'Oh well,' he thought. 'Let it just stay there. It's not my job. She doesn't do anything else all day anyway. Let her clean up this mess in the morning.'

He picked up his work phone, and dialed his home number. As the phone in the kitchen began to ring, he turned the power off on his cell. He walked to the kitchen and answered the phone. Speaking to the silence, he said, "Sure, I can be over in just a few minutes." He hung up and walked to the bedroom. "Ruth, I've got a call. Be back in a couple of hours." She made a groan of acknowledgement and fell right back to sleep. He knew she would.

George left his apartment and strolled across the parking lot to the office. The night was a little chilly, and he felt like there might be a storm coming. He shivered a bit and zipped his jacket.

Most of the apartment residents were home and tucked into bed by now. Only a few lights were on in the buildings, and George could see the glow of a few television sets. A middle-aged man came down the sidewalk, walking his dog. George noticed the man was carrying a little baggie of doggie poop and nodded as they passed. 'Good. One less pile for me to clean up tomorrow,' George said to himself.

A car whizzed past him in the parking lot and the driver waved. It was Tim Simpson, and a bunch of his friends from the High School. George knew just about everybody that lived around here. He knew that Tim played basketball on the varsity team. And he knew that he had seen Tim and some cute little blond making out in the back seat of Tim's Camero. He remembered watching them, remembered how excited he had gotten, remembered how he had described it to one of his regulars, and remembered how she had been turned on by it too. That had been a wild night, one of his best as far as phone sex went. Not as good as the real thing, of course, but still pretty damn good. And lots better than he had been getting at home.

He let himself into the office with his key. He turned on his work phone, in case he should happen to get a real call from the answering service, sending him out on a real after hours maintenance call. Then he automatically dialed her number. He no longer had to scan his phone book for the last four digits. He had that memorized. He opened his notebook and jotted down the date and time of this call. He really was good at keeping records.

George was going to try to get a little closer to this woman tonight. He needed to know her name, and hopefully get her to describe what she looked like. That way, when he fantasized about her later, he would have a better picture of her in his mind. He was pretty sure she was ready to open up to him in that way. But as always, he would have to be cautious and take it slow. Rushing a woman like her could scare her off completely.

Suzanne answered the phone on the first ring.

"Hi. You answered the phone fast! Were you still awake?" he asked.

"No, I've been in bed for about an hour" she said as her eyes adjusted to the dim lighting and she noticed the time on the clock. One-fifteen.

Just the thought of this woman being in bed got George's juices flowing. He wondered what she wore to bed, if she wore anything at all. But it was too soon to ask. That time would come, and he hoped it would not be long.

"So, tell me all about the play. Was Lindsay great? Did she have fun?"

Suzanne proceeded to tell him how the evening had gone. She mentioned with pride that Lindsay had done her part very well. She also told him about the request from the teacher to make costumes for the summer program. He could tell she was excited by the new opportunity. He congratulated her and said she must be very good with costuming, or they would not have asked her to help out.

"I know what Lindsay wore tonight, but what about you? What did the star's mother wear to opening night?"

"Me? Well, I wore a dress, pale pink with flowers. It isn't new or anything, but it was okay. I made it a long time ago, before I even got pregnant with Lindsay. I used to think I couldn't wear pink, because I have reddish hair, but I loved this material and decided to try it, and so many people commented about how nice it looked; I just figured it was all right after all. I guess the notion of redheads not wearing pink is a little old fashioned. I haven't been brave enough to try red though!"

George jotted 'red head' in his notebook. "I'll bet you looked great," he said, and Suzanne got that tingle up and down her arms again.

"You know what?" he asked. "We have been talking for a couple of weeks now, and I don't even know your name." He left off there, hoping that she would feel comfortable enough to offer the information without him having to beg for it.

For some reason, Suzanne felt it necessary to put up her guard. If he knew her name, it would be just one step closer to trouble. So she asked, "Why do you need to know my name?"

George was a little surprised by this reaction. He figured she would fall in line without questioning. But this was new; she was resisting more than he had expected she would. 'Just makes it a bigger challenge,' he said to himself.

To her he said, "I think of you as a friend, and friends should know each other's names. You know mine." He smiled to himself at the lie.

"Well, I guess it's all right. My name is Susan."

"Susan," he said, as he wrote the name in his notebook. "Well, Susan, it is nice to talk to you. I think you are a pretty special lady."

"Special? What do you mean by that?" She was feeling safer now. He didn't really know her name, so he couldn't stalk her or murder her or anything. 'Besides, he doesn't know where I live either,' she thought.

"Special because you are nice, and friendly, and seem like a great mom and teacher. And you are talented and dedicated to your job and daughter. And you are adventurous and try to wear pink even though you think you shouldn't. And you let me call you in the middle of the night. I really like talking to you. Besides, you have a really sexy voice!" He couldn't resist. He knew it was risky, but he just had to try this out with her. Would she be interested? She could just hang up.

But Suzanne just giggled a little, and said with a Southern drawl "Why Paul, you shouldn't say such things!"

"Hey, that was a great Scarlet O'Hara impersonation!" he laughed. "Now I can tell where Lindsay gets all her acting talent!"

This made Suzanne laugh and she relaxed a bit. "Hey, Paul, tell me about yourself. I don't know anything about you except your name. You keep asking about me, but if we are going to be friends, I ought to know about you. So tell me."

"Okay. Well, I'm 28. I've got dark brown hair and brown eyes. I'm six-one and weigh about two hundred pounds." He almost stopped to ask Susan what she looked like but didn't want to push her. And it was a good thing, because her next response surprised him.

"Oh, I don't need to know what you look like. Looks are not important in a friendship. I want to know who you are a person. What you do. What you believe. Those are the important things. Looks can change, but a person's personality is much more important."

George adjusted his conversation to match hers. "Okay, well, I drive a delivery truck for Kastner's Bakery. I also volunteer with the fire department on weekends and some nights. Usually when I call you, it is after a night call, when I have my adrenalin flowing and can't settle down to go back to sleep. I just need to talk to someone awhile, to get my mind off the fire call, so I can relax a bit." He was making this all up, but it sounded convincing enough to Suzanne.

"So that first night when you called me, it was after a fire?" she asked.

"Yeah, and it was a real bad one," he lied. "Maybe you heard about it. A little boy was trapped on the second floor. We didn't think we would get to him on time. But thank God my partner got him out. Pretty scary for a while there though."

"No wonder you needed to relax some. I guess I didn't hear about it. I don't get much chance to watch the news or anything. Was the little boy okay?"

"Yeah, he's okay now. He stayed in the hospital overnight and they treated him for smoke. My partner went to visit him while he was in the hospital. He's going to be fine."

"Do you ever get scared, going in to a fire?"

"Sure. Every time I go in I know that I might not come out. Its just part of what I do. But it's not much different from driving a car, or a delivery truck. Any day could be your last. Just walking down the street these days, you never know what can happen."

George loved this part of the game. He told the same story, with minor variations, to all of his regulars. He wasn't about to tell them anything true about himself. Rule number one, make yourself untraceable.

So they talked on into the night. It was nearly three when Suzanne finally looked at the clock. She could hardly believe they had talked that long. They both said they had enjoyed getting to know each other better. And when George said "Goodnight Susan. Dream sweet dreams," Suzanne said, "Thanks, Paul, I think I will." They hung up with smiles on their faces.

George knew he didn't want to go home and try anything with his wife. She was too drunk to respond, anyway. So he stayed in the office stroking himself as he played out one of his favorite fantasies in his mind. He was a fireman, rescuing a naked woman from a burning building. And this time the woman was a redhead.

Chapter Six

Despondency

LARRY WAS IN a bad mood when he got home from work the next morning. He had made a mistake at work and been called into the supervisors' office at the end of his shift and told in no uncertain terms that if he screwed up one more time, he would be looking for another job. Larry had stormed out of the office and stalked out to the parking lot. 'The hell with them anyway. I am sick and tired of working with these jerks. They think they are so much better than me. They think they can just tell me what to do and how to act. Well, I don't need this rotten job anyway.'

But of course he did. He needed some kind of job, that's for sure. He had a gambling debt that he needed to pay off. Some pretty tough looking guys were pressuring him. If he could only make it big at the track, get some real money to bet on the horses. That's where the big money was, not in little bets with co-workers about ballgames. But to make money you had to have money. And Larry didn't even have a substantial amount to place a decent bet at the track.

No, he would have to just mind his manners and stick with this rotten job. At least it was some sort income. And the wife would be pretty pissed off if he came home unemployed again.

Larry got into his car and turned the key in the ignition. The engine made a grinding sound before it finally sputtered to life. "Piece of junk," Larry muttered under his breath. The car was nearly eleven years old. Well, they sure couldn't afford a new one now. That would really kill them. Probably couldn't get credit for it anyway.

He knew he was a big disappointment to his wife. He could see it in her eyes, every time he lost a job. He didn't like getting fired either, but usually it wasn't his fault. Seems like everywhere he worked, somebody had it in for him, and he got in trouble or at least raked across the coals. Why couldn't people just get off his back? Let him do his job and leave well enough alone. But no, somebody was always hassling him about something.

And it was hell every time he had to tell Suzanne the paycheck had come to an end. It was bad enough that he couldn't afford health insurance or retirement benefits or any of that other financial stuff he would like to provide her with. And now that they had Lindsay, it was extra tough. No chance to put away money for her future either.

That would change, once he got a chance to make it big at the track. They could move out of that apartment, get a decent car, maybe two. They could save money for Lindsay's college. They could take a real vacation. There was only one problem. He never made more at the track than he spent. Seems like every time he won a little, he lost a little more.

But someday, he would get a break. The odds were in his favor. He couldn't be a looser forever. Someday he would come home from the track with his pockets bulging. They would go out to a fancy restaurant to celebrate. Then they would go out and buy whatever they wanted. Clothes, cars, furniture, furs, diamonds. Whatever Suzanne and Lindsay wanted, he would get for them. He would finally be the king of his castle. He wouldn't ever again have to dodge creditors or heavy-handed debt collectors. And he wouldn't have to depend on Suzanne to bring in the money. He would have it made. Finally. It was about time things turned around for him.

Larry was surprised by the silence when he walked into his apartment. Usually on Saturday mornings, Lindsay was up watching Sesame Street or cartoons and Suzanne was busy fixing them breakfast in the kitchen. Then he remembered that Lindsay had been in that play last night, and they probably got to bed really late. 'Better just let them sleep,' he thought. 'I'm not too hungry anyway. I can wait till Suz gets up.' He noticed two laundry baskets sitting by the door. 'She must be going down to do the laundry this morning,' he thought. He saw the pile of quarters sitting on the end table and picked up four of them. Then he went back out of the apartment. He was going to walk to the nearby Seven Eleven to get a cup of coffee. The fresh morning air would do him good, anyway. He kinda needed to clear his head.

Suzanne woke when he closed the door. At first she was startled, thinking it was the middle of the night. Her first thought was that someone in the building had slammed a door. Probably those druggies across the hall. 'Hope they are not having another loud party,' she thought. Then she realized that sunlight was filtering through the bedroom blinds. She looked at the clock and couldn't believe it was nearly eight o'clock already.

She lay back on her pillow and listened. The house was quiet. 'I thought that was Larry coming home. I wonder if he went out again. Oh well, I'd better get up and get going on the laundry.' Saturday mornings were about the only time Suzanne had to do the laundry. The washers were in the basement, and she did not feel comfortable going down there in the evenings. You never knew who would be in the hallways, and she would rather not take a chance. But she had also learned that if you wanted to do laundry on Saturday, you had to get an early start. If she waited much longer, other residents would be using the machines and she wouldn't get to do her wash until who knows when.

She sat on the side of the bed and began to brush out her hair. It was shoulder length and thick. Sunlight coming through the window made her hair glow with an auburn shine that was the envy of some of her co-workers at school. She was thankful to be blessed with this color. She knew several women who tried to get this color out of a bottle, but Suzanne's was completely natural. 'Thanks again, Grandma!' she said to herself. She had inherited the color from her maternal grandmother.

Suzanne went to the closet to find some sweats to wear while she did her laundry and house cleaning chores. She saw her pale pink dress lying on the chair beside the closet door and remembered telling Paul about wearing it to Lindsay's play. She played back the evening's conversation in her mind, and smiled at the thought of him. 'He said I have a sexy voice!' she thought with a surprising thrill. But then she stomped her foot and put her hands on her hips. 'This is so silly,' she thought. 'I feel like a starry-eyed teenager again. It's crazy. I better snap out of this, now!'

The coffee was perking and bacon was cooking in the microwave when she heard Larry come into the apartment. "Good morning," she called out from the kitchen. "Coffee's almost ready. Want some?"

"Not right now," he answered, settling down on the sofa with the morning paper. "I just got some at Seven Eleven." He turned the paper to the sports section. He hadn't heard how last night's double-header had turned out. And he wanted to scan the racing results, just in case any horse's names jumped out at him. You never knew when that big break might come along.

"I'm gonna run down to the basement and get some laundry started," Suzanne said as she picked up the quarters and juggled the two laundry baskets. She saw right away that some of her quarters were missing, and just sighed. It would do no good to confront him with it. He would just deny it, or shrug it off like it was nothing. She would just have to get some more quarters out of her secret hiding place. She had been trying to save up money for Lindsay's birthday, which was just six weeks away. But she had had to dip into the birthday fund just yesterday, for chocolate chip ice cream and whipped cream. And now this. It was beginning to look like Lindsay was not going to get her first Barbie doll after all. She might have to settle for a generic look-alike.

Suzanne was glad to see that she had beaten the Saturday rush to the washing machines. She started two loads of laundry and went back upstairs. As she prepared the batter for French toast, she heard Lindsay waking up. She smiled to herself as she imagined her daughter taking off her pajamas and getting dressed in the daisy costume. Her mind drifted again to the conversation with Paul, as she told him about making costumes for the summer program. She hadn't even told Larry about it, and yet this stranger knew about it already. He was so easy to talk to. And supportive. Suzanne doubted that Larry would have been supportive. He probably would have just wanted to know how much she would be getting paid for her work. Well, Mrs. Jackson hadn't even mentioned payment. As far as Suzanne knew, she was doing this on a volunteer basis. And that was fine with her. It would be fun, and something creative to do during the summer. She didn't need to be paid.

"Mmmm! French toast!" exclaimed Lindsay as Suzanne put the breakfast things on the table. Larry and Suzanne ate in relative silence, as Lindsay talked excitedly about the play. It seemed that she loved performing and was already hoping to be chosen as Snow White in the summer production.

Suzanne could tell that Larry had something on his mind. He was more withdrawn than usual. 'I wonder what's going on now. I hope he's not in some kind of trouble at work again.' Suzanne really didn't think she could handle another bout with unemployment. Larry got so depressed during those times, and would often sit around the apartment for days and days, without even trying to find another job. He would wallow in self-pity, blaming others for his misfortunes. It was never his own fault. And he always got so angry. It was frightening sometimes. But he had never done anything to actually hurt his family physically. No hitting or pushing. Just tension and despondency. And occasionally a fist thump on the wall, harsh enough to crack the drywall and require repairs.

After breakfast, Suzanne took some more quarters out of her savings jar and ran down to the basement to put the clothes into the dryer. When she came upstairs, she noticed that Lindsay had started clearing the table. "Daddy went to bed," Lindsay said matter of factly.

She thanked her daughter for being so helpful and asked what she would like to do since it was such a nice day. It had rained a little in the night, just enough to settle the spring pollens a bit. The day promised to be warm and sunny.

They decided to go to the big playground in the apartment complex. Lindsay changed into play clothes while Suzanne brought the clean laundry up from the basement. Together they folded and hung the clean clothes. Lindsay was pretty good at matching socks and folding towels. Then they loaded the dishwasher and swept the kitchen floor. Next it was on to dusting in the living room. Suzanne would have to wait and do the vacuuming in the late afternoon, when Larry was awake. Soon the chores were done and Suzanne quickly and quietly changed into blue jeans and a plaid button down shirt. They headed out to the playground. It was a beautiful spring day.

Chapter Seven

Discovery

GEORGE SAT HIS toolbox down in the grass and surveyed the damage. Someone had evidently driven his car right into the wooden fence that separated the playground from the parking lot. Broken boards were strewn for about twenty-five feet and there were tire tracks in the grass. A whole section of the fence would need to be replaced. 'No use calling this in to the police,' he thought, as he began gathering up the trash. 'They would never find who did this anyway. Just collect the insurance and replace the fence.'

He really didn't mind this type of work. It was a beautiful day, and it was good to work outside. Better than fixing somebody's toilet, that's for sure. Besides, spring was in the air, and lots of residents were out enjoying the day. Many spoke to him as he worked. George enjoyed knowing so many people. But he especially enjoyed seeing that several women were at the playground with their children. He recognized a few and stopped to talk a minute as he hauled broken boards to the nearby dumpster. He noticed a redhead pushing a little girl high on the swings. He didn't remember the woman's name but was pretty sure he had been to her apartment once to fix a damaged wall. George made it a policy never to get involved with women at the apartments. It was too risky, and he could wind up loosing his job. So no matter how attractive a woman might be, he kept his distance. Friendly, efficient and pleasant, sure, but never aggressive or forward or personal. But this redhead did grab his attention. Probably because of his fantasy last night, but she really was good looking.

George continued to work on the fence repairs, all the while casting sideways glances at the women on the playground. The sleeves of his uniform shirt were rolled up to his elbows and his biceps were straining as he lifted and hauled pieces of fencing. At five foot ten, he was not a big man. But his job required strength, and George worked out frequently. He was in good shape physically.

His doctors had warned him about the hazards of smoking and drinking. George wasn't willing to give up either. What fun is life without a few pleasures now and then?

A group of teen-agers came along, with their boom boxes cranked way up. Several of the girls were wearing shorts. 'Geez, I love this time of year,' George thought as he watched them as they sort of danced across the parking lot. 'Look at those little girls move! I'd sure like to be a part of some of that action.'

The group stopped in front of an apartment building and Tim Simpson came out to join them. He had a basketball, as usual, and they all moved over to the basketball courts. As they walked past George, Tim stopped to ask when the pool would be opening. George answered, "Memorial Day weekend." That was only three weeks away. One of the girls said, "I can't wait! I love summer!" and the rest of the kids agreed. George was mentally agreeing that summer was his favorite time of year too, especially since his apartment windows overlooked the pool.

The teens went on to the basketball court and George let his eyes wonder back to the women at the playground. The redhead was sitting on a park bench with another lady. They were talking while all the children played together in the jungle gym. George could barely keep his mind off her. 'I wonder what she looks like in a bathing suit,' he thought.

It was a little past noon when George finished with the fence repairs and began to gather his tools. As he walked past the play-ground, he heard the redhead calling to her daughter. "Five more minutes, Lindsay. Then we have to go home for lunch."

George was stunned. He nearly stopped short in his tracks. 'No, it couldn't be,' he thought. But the voice, the red hair, the daughter named Lindsay. This seemed to be more than a coincidence. This was too weird. He never guessed that by dialing random numbers he would end up talking to a neighbor. That might just change everything. He had never had an affair with someone from his own apartment complex. That was not only risky, it was just plain stupid. He wasn't quite sure how he was going to handle this. He ought to just end it, cross out the number and move on to another. But see-ing Susan just now, he already knew he wanted her more than ever. Maybe it was time to add a little element of danger on his part. A bigger risk might even make their affair more exciting. Maybe. He had a lot to think about.

Chapter Eight

Risky Business

ON SUNDAY AFTERNOON, George left his apartment, got into his truck, and headed out to the river. He had his fishing equipment and a six-pack of beer in the back of the truck. It took about half an hour to drive out of town to the reservoir. George was glad to see that his favorite fishing spot was available, so he sat on the riverbank, opened a beer, leaned against a tree, and began to think.

George really did need to think this thing through. He would have to choose his next steps very carefully. It was one thing, knowing who she was and where she lived. But it was another thing altogether knowing that she was about to find out more about him than he wanted. George put his elbows on his knees and held up his head with his hands. He hadn't shaved and the stubble on his face scratched his palms. 'Better think this trough carefully.' he thought. In his past relationships, he had been in control of just about everything that happened. The women never knew his real name or his real job or where he lived. That was all part of the game. Everything on his terms, just the way he liked it.

But if he continued with Susan, and became intimate with her, he was taking a big chance. Bigger than at any other time in the past, with any other woman. Susan would put all of the pieces together eventually. She might recognize him the very first time they got together, and that would blow his cover for sure. Even if he got away with it for a while, it was only a matter of time till she saw him around the apartments and figured it all out. She might run into him out in the parking lot. She might notice his work shirt with "George" sewn above the pocket. She might even have a maintenance call and need him to fix something at her apartment. He would not be able to hide behind his "Paul" image forever. She would know he had been lying all along. She would probably be angry and notify the office. They would not tolerate a pervert like him working around the buildings. He had a good reputation for being dependable and a hard worker. But the management wouldn't want a scandal right here on their property. He was replaceable. No, he couldn't risk that.

George baited his hook with a long night crawler. He stood and walked a few steps toward the water. Then he reached far back with his right arm and cast his line out into the river. He watched his bobber settle into the water and walked back to rest against the tree. He popped open another beer and took a long satisfying drink. Now, to think.

The safe thing to do, he knew, was to forget this woman altogether. But there was something about her that really made him hesitate to let her go. What was it? Her looks? Well, she looked good enough, but nothing spectacular. Her desperate need for hot, exciting sex? True, but she didn't even know how good he was yet. Maybe the most enticing thing about her was her innocence. She seemed inexperienced and pure. Maybe he was wrong, but George was pretty certain that she had not been with a lot of men. There was probably a lot he could teach her, and a lot of "firsts" he could experience with her. That was exciting to him. He could really have some fun with being the teacher!

That thought led George to another possibility. If he could make Susan so grateful, so satisfied, so appreciative of him, then she would keep quiet and not blow the whistle on him. He could keep the woman and his job, as long as he kept her happy and quiet. But in some ways, that meant that she was in control of the situation. She could run the whole show. It would make him feel like he had to perform and behave just so, or she had something to blackmail him with. Did he need that kind of pressure? He knew he could satisfy her sexually, but how long before he tired of her and started dialing up someone new? His affair with Susan certainly wouldn't last forever. How would she react? Would she feel rejected and angry enough to report him?

And was she even worth it? That was the big question right now. He hadn't made any progress in the phone sex department. It was early yet; it usually took half a dozen phone calls before he got to do that with a woman on the phone. But what if she turned out to be an ice goddess? Sure, she had the looks, and the sexy voice (he hadn't been lying about that). And she did seem lonely and probably desperate for some good lovin'. But he didn't really know for sure yet if she would respond to him physically. And if she wouldn't have phone sex with him, then she surely wouldn't allow him to screw her, so why should he waste his time and risk his job?

George reeled in his fishing line and laid the pole in the grass beside him. He hadn't caught any fish, not even a nibble. But he wasn't really in the mood for fishing anyway. He opened another beer and settled in to relax and think some more.

By the time George had finished this long conversation with himself, he had made a decision. He had a plan; a method that he thought would eventually work out to his advantage. First of all, he would continue with the phone calls as usual for the next few weeks. He would follow his normal routine as far as that was concerned. He would work Susan up to the point that she would have phone sex with him. But this is where the game changed. If she was good at it, and seemed to really be responding to him, and had a lusty desire for this sort of thing, then he would pursue it further. He would have the phone sex with her for as long as he could, testing to see if he could win her over completely. He would fine-tune their relationship to the point that he could anticipate her reactions and read her mind. He would string her along, bait his trap, until she was practically begging him to have sex with her.

At that point, if he felt certain that she was really his, that he had woven his web around her so that she would not even want to get away, then and only then would he push for a more intimate relationship. He was certain he would know how she would react to seeing him, to hearing the truth. And if he felt that his trap was secure enough he would continue.

And then, before he had her for the first time, but while she was dripping with desire for him, then he would have to reveal his true identity. He would break his normal pattern; he would make himself more vulnerable than he had ever been before. But he would have to tell her the truth, at least in part, because she would feel used and cheapened if he didn't. He would have to go about it gently, too. That he knew for sure.

So he would take it one step at a time, never venturing towards the next level until he was certain he stood on safe firm ground and the next step would be safe as well. And if he felt safe moving on, it would be a slow, deliberate process.

He would move forward only if he was absolutely certain that she was going to be worth the risk. All indications were that this woman was going to be very receptive to him, and quite a find. He had to be careful, though. He wanted her badly, but he had to take it slow.

George was beginning to get hungry. He glanced at his watch and decided it was time to head home. Hopefully Ruth would have something good made for dinner, but he doubted it. She had been drinking a lot again, not just wine with dinner, but drinking all day long. He often came home to find her passed out on the couch or in the bedroom. She was beginning to disgust him. When they were first married, she was really wild in the bedroom. She was willing to try anything with him, and even had been agreeable to threesomes. She was uninhibited and free. But things started to change after she had a miscarriage. She went into a tailspin of depression, and started drinking to forget the baby she would never deliver. Most of the time now, her mind was blurred with alcohol.

George had suggested she get some help, years ago, and she had gone to a couple of meetings but always slipped back to the drinks. George could hardly recognize her now; she had changed so much from the happy and free woman he had married. She had gained over one hundred pounds in the last five years. She was never clean and dressed nicely. She hardly ever went out of the apartment. She had no friends but the empty bottles that littered their apartment.

Yet George stayed married to her. He wasn't quite sure why. It was surely not because of any vows he had made or religious commitment he felt. It was more that, with Ruth, he could get away with so much. She was usually so drunk she didn't know if he was home or not. He could come and go, anytime of the day or night, and she really didn't know what was going on. So he was safe with her. He hardly ever worried about getting caught, although he did take precautions.

George was not surprised when he arrived home and found Ruth asleep. There was nothing cooked for dinner, but she had apparently ordered a pizza delivered because the half empty box sat on the kitchen table. George warmed a couple of slices in the microwave and went to the video cabinet to choose a movie. He was in the mood for something sleazy, something erotic. 'Ummm, here it is. "Body of Innocence." Madonna at her sexy best.' George had the uncut version, and it did have some juicy scenes. Just what he needed tonight. He would not be making a phone call to Susan tonight, since it was the weekend and her husband might be home.

George unbuttoned his shirt and removed his jeans. The pizza could wait. He had something else to attend to first.

Chapter Nine

Developing a Friendship

THE NEXT FEW weeks went by routinely for Suzanne. She filled her days with caring for Lindsay, keeping up with her school lesson plans and paperwork, and efficiently running her household. She balanced her time wisely, and although she was usually tired when she went to bed, she was also satisfied with what she had done throughout the day. Her only point of discontent was with her husband. Something was brewing with him, and he was out of sorts most days. She didn't ask him about it. Maybe she didn't really want to know. It was his problem; one she didn't care to share. When it came right down to it, there were times she wished he would just pack up his troubles and take a hike. A long hike.

Several times Suzanne had been awakened with a phone call from Paul in the early morning hours. She never seemed to mind this interruption to her sleep. In fact, it was almost invigorating. The conversations were stimulating and usually left her with an exhilarated feeling. Aside from other teachers at school, Suzanne had few friends. And even so, the teachers were friends primarily on a professional level, not socially. She really didn't have time for socialization anyway. But she did long to have someone to talk to. Larry was so distant most of the time. Since Paul's first phone call she was depending on him more and more.

So they talked. They talked about school, and some of the funny things the kids said. She told him about the little boy who lost his first tooth during math class. She told him about the two girls who were flirting in six year old fashion with one little boy. She told him about some of the pictures and love notes she got from the kids and kept in a loose-leaf notebook.

Paul told her about events on his delivery routes. He told her about some of his customers, how bad the traffic had been and a bad accident he had seen. Sometimes he told her about fire calls he had been on, or something funny that had happened at the firehouse.

Suzanne thought she was learning a lot about Paul. And she knew she liked him, as a friend. He was funny and could make her laugh. He cared about things she was doing and how she was feeling. He seemed to have a real insight into her, like he could almost guess what she was going to say. Usually he could pick up hints from her voice, so he knew if she had been having a good day or a bad day at school or at home in the evenings.

Suzanne did not usually talk about Larry, although Paul tried to turn the conversation in that direction a few times. All she would say was that he had been acting strange, more withdrawn than usual, and she did not know what was going on with him.

They talked about the fact that Memorial Day was coming, and Suzanne was glad to be having a three-day weekend. Paul mentioned that most of the local pools were opening that weekend. He asked Susan if she liked to swim. She said that she did, but that in the last four years she had spent most of her pool time in the baby pool with Lindsay. She was hoping to get Lindsay enrolled in swimming lessons this year, and that would make her more confident in the deep water. "And that reminds me," she said. "I have to get over to the apartment office to get pool passes for Lindsay and me. I guess I will do that Friday after work." George made a mental note to be somewhere near the office that evening, so he could see her but not be observed. He would like to get a better look at her.

Suzanne talked to him about Lindsay's birthday, which was rapidly approaching, though not fast enough for Lindsay! She told Paul she had wanted to get Lindsay a Barbie doll, but didn't seem to be able to get enough money saved up for it. Instead she was going to buy her some Barbie clothes and accessories. The Barbie doll itself would come from Suzanne's mother and father. They were always happy to buy nice things for their only granddaughter.

In the course of these few weeks, George solidified the feeling of friendship he was developing with Susan. He wanted her to be very comfortable with him, to trust him, to eventually be able to open up to him in ways that she probably didn't even know were possible.

So the weeks passed. Suzanne did her job, kept up with her mothering responsibilities, and continued to keep the house clean and put decent meals on the table. In the evenings, after Larry had gone to work, Suzanne lay in bed, hoping that the phone would ring and she would have another chance to talk to her new friend. She didn't lay awake, waiting for his call; she knew that he would not call every night. But she did fall asleep with the phone near her, hoping. She needed a friend.

On Friday evening, when Suzanne and Lindsay went to the office to get their pool passes, George was watching from his balcony across the street. He picked up his toolbox and left his apartment, headed to the office on the pretext of doing some paperwork. As he entered the building and walked past them in the hall, Suzanne noticed that he gave her a pleasant smile. She then recalled that he was the maintenance man who had fixed one of the dry wall holes Larry had made in their apartment wall. She smiled back at the man in recognition but said nothing. George went into the back office and busied himself with filing papers. He left the door open so he could listen to her voice as she paid her pool fee and asked about swimming lessons for Lindsay. He smiled. Hearing that voice in person was even nicer than hearing it on the phone.

Chapter Ten

Life is Full of Disappointments

THE POOL OPENED on the Saturday before Memorial Day. The weather was not perfect; it was a little too cool and threatened rain showers. Suzanne convinced Lindsay that they should wait until the weather was better before they ventured out to the pool. They had a long three-day weekend to be together, and they needed to finish planning the birthday party, which was just three weeks away. Lindsay was inviting four friends from daycare, Jenna, Katie, Allison, and Abby. Jenna Anderson was Lindsay's very best friend, and the two girls were nearly inseparable at daycare. Jenna's mother was also a teacher, though not in the same school as Suzanne.

After the regular Saturday chores were done, and while Larry slept, Suzanne and Lindsay worked on the invitations. Suzanne wrote all the important information inside the cards and Lindsay wrote the names of the girls on the outside of the envelopes. She printed quite well, for being just four. Suzanne had encouraged her daughter to learn to form letters as soon as she was able to hold a pencil correctly and showed an interest in writing. The result was that Lindsay did very well, and tried to please her mother with neat lettering. She still needed help sometimes, and preferred to use all capital letters, but that was fine with Suzanne, for now.

After the invitations were finished and put into Lindsay's backpack for delivery on Tuesday, they started on placemats. Lindsay had a Barbie coloring book and had chosen her five favorite pages. She was going to color the five pictures, and Suzanne would cover them with contact paper. They would use these for place mats at the party, and afterwards the girls could take them home afterwards. For other party favors, Suzanne had found Barbie window clings at the Dollar Store, and stickers and hair barrettes. She hoped that would be adequate. It was the best she could do, and Lindsay seemed happy with her choices.

George sat on his balcony watching people arrive at the pool. A few families had ventured out after noon. He was looking for a pretty redhead with a cute daughter, but she never appeared. The pool was virtually empty. A group of teenagers had staked out the lounge chairs at the deep end, but few of them were venturing into the water. It was just a bit overcast and chilly. Most of the kids kept their shorts and t-shirts on, never even stripping down to suits. George hoped that the rest of the weekend would be warmer and sunnier. He longed to see the teen girls in their little bathing suits, to watch them splash around in the water, to see them as they climbed out of the pool. He loved to watch them as they applied sunscreen to their lush little bodies. Better yet, to watch as the girls put the lotion on each other. He got great pleasure from watching them touch each other, and just thinking about it now sent a longing through him.

George decided there was not much to watch at the poolside, so he went into the apartment. He turned to Ruth. She was sitting in the recliner, watching some sappy movie on the woman's channel. She was wearing nothing but an extra large sweatshirt. She didn't have any jeans that fit her anymore, and since she hardly ever went out of the apartment, she usually dressed as loosely as she could.

Today George didn't even care what she was wearing or how she looked. She was there, available, and he did need somebody.

He pulled her up out of the chair and raised the shirt. He rubbed his hands along her hips and up to her breasts. She moaned and yielded herself to him. Sex with him was always good. He had a power, a strength, which could turn Ruth to butter. She did long for the old days, when she was on fire for him all of the time. Things had changed, and usually she felt nothing for him one way or the other. But today, she closed her eyes and enjoyed his attention. On the living room floor they made love. George's eyes were closed too, and in his imagination, he was at the pool with a sexy young thing. They were in the water, and his hard cock slipped easily into her. He pumped hard and deep, and within a short time he exploded inside Ruth with a power that knocked her breathless. Ruth shivered with pleasure. He sure knew how to fuck.

George got up and looked at his wife. He smiled at her satisfaction and went into the bathroom. 'Woman, it's nice to know you are still good for something,' he thought to himself as he stepped into the shower. He turned on the water and rubbed himself with soapy hands until it responded again and he released his hot juice against the shower door. He watched as the force of the water cleaned the door and washed everything down the drain.

It rained on Sunday, a downpour complete with thunder, lightning, and high winds. The pool was closed. Suzanne and Lindsay stayed home all day, playing games and reading. Suzanne's mother called, just to see how things were going. Lindsay told her about her upcoming birthday party. They talked a few minutes, then the thunder banged loudly and Suzanne felt they had better get off the phone.

Larry came out from the bedroom. He had been awakened first by the phone and then the thunder. Since he didn't have to go to work this evening, he didn't really care that his sleep had been interrupted. He went to the kitchen to get some iced tea, but found that the empty pitcher was draining in the dish rack. "Darn it, Suzanne. How many times have I told you that you need to make more tea when you empty the pitcher? Now I don't have anything cold to drink. It's such a simple thing. I just want iced tea. But no, you can't seem to get that through your head. So now I suppose I'll have to make it myself?"

Suzanne came into the kitchen and quietly began making a pitcher of iced tea for him. She didn't say a word. She knew better than to confront him about anything, especially when he was in a bad mood. And he seemed to be in a bad mood a lot lately. Suzanne heated the water and poured it over the tea bags. She let it brew while she filled a glass with ice. Then she poured the tea over the ice and served it to Larry, who was standing in the kitchen doorway watching her every move. "We got any lemon?" he asked. To Suzanne, it seemed more like a demand. She found half a lemon in the refrigerator and cut a wedge, which she added to his glass. Larry turned and left the room.

'A thank you would have been nice,' she thought with a sigh.

Lindsay had been watching a Disney video on television, but when Larry came in to the living room he turned the movie off and switched on a ball game. Silently she got up from her chair and went into the kitchen to join her mother. Lindsay had learned well from her mother's example not to upset her father. "Hey, honey, why don't we make some rice crispy treats?" Suzanne suggested, and Lindsay brightened at the thought. Soon they were busy measuring cereal and melting marshmallows. The gloomy mood lifted slightly.

"How about pizza for dinner?" he called out from the living room. "How much money do you have?" Suzanne had a few dollars set aside for milk, which they would need before the next payday. But she didn't tell Larry she had it, saying instead that she was broke except for some change. Larry emptied his pockets and counted his money while Suzanne went to her desk drawer. She found a coupon for three dollars off on the price of a large pizza. With the coupon and what Larry had come up with, they could cover the cost. Larry picked up the phone and called in the order.

In twenty minutes there was a knock at the door. Lindsay pushed a footstool up to the door so she could see through the peephole. "It's the pizza man!" she exclaimed, and Suzanne unlocked the door for him. Suzanne gave him the money for the pizza and then presented him with a two-dollar tip. She had taken it from Lindsay's birthday money, but she had to give the boy something. After all, he had to come out in this terrible storm to deliver this pizza for them. She appreciated that, and wanted to treat him nicely.

As she was conducting business with the delivery boy, who was really just a teenager, Suzanne realized that she had seen him before. "You live around here, don't you?" she asked. "Yes ma'am," he answered politely. "I live in a building near the playground. Name's Tim."

"Oh yes, now I remember. You play basketball don't you?"

"Sure do," he answered. "Well, thanks for the tip. I have to get going, have another delivery to make. Enjoy your pizza." Tim left their apartment but did not exit the building. He walked across the hall and tapped on the door. It was a code they had developed, two quick knocks, a pause, and then one more knock. The door opened and Tim quickly walked in. He was handed a small package, and a slip of paper on which was written an address and a name. Yes, he had another delivery to make. But this one would make him lots more than a two-dollar tip.

Chapter Eleven

Pool Time

MONDAY MORNING DAWNED brightly although traces of yesterday's storm could still be seen. Puddles stood in the low spots of the parking lot. A couple of tree branches had fallen near the playground. The weatherman on TV said they had received over three inches of rain. There had been some flash flooding in the area. And to the north of them, a tornado had been on the ground for five or six minutes, causing severe damage to several homes and destroying a barn. No one had been killed, but there was a lot of cleanup to be done.

As Lindsay watched the report of the tornado, she saw a little girl about her own age, sitting with her family in a Red Cross shelter. Her father was talking about how they had lost the roof on their house and many of their possessions were gone, but they were fortunate to have escaped unharmed. The television camera panned across a scene of devastation. There was a little girl's bedroom, with the dresser tossed to the floor and clothing strewn all over, soaking wet and covered with debris. The camera settled on the girl's coloring book, torn and wet.

Lindsay looked at her mother and said, "Mommy, I want to help that girl. She is sad. Her room is a mess and her roof is gone. She can have my coloring books. That will make her happy." Suzanne's heart filled with joy when she heard her daughter's willingness to share her own things with those less fortunate.

"What a good idea, honey. In fact, we could go to the Dollar Store and buy her some new coloring books. Would you like to do that?"

"Oh, yes, Mommy! Can we take Jenna along, too? She would like to help the girl, too, I know she would!"

Suzanne agreed to take Jenna along, if it was okay with her mother. She looked up Anderson's phone number in the daycare directory and spoke to Jenna's mother Melissa about the little project. Melissa was in agreement but had a suggestion that took the project a step further. "Why don't we make this a daycare project? We could make some signs, and have a clothing and toy drive at the daycare, to benefit those suffering from the tornado. We could make it a service project for all the kids at the daycare."

Suzanne liked the sounds of this, and agreed to help in whatever way she could. She suggested that they call the director of the daycare, to clear it with her first. Melissa said she would do that and would then meet Suzanne and Lindsay at the Dollar Store.

Melissa got the go ahead from the daycare director. Then they all met at the store. The girls were happy to see each other, and excited about helping the little girl who didn't have a roof on her house. Suzanne and Melissa bought some poster board and paints while the girls each picked out an item to send to the little girl. Lindsay picked a set of three coloring books and Jenna chose a pop-up storybook.

Suzanne was embarrassed but honest when they went to the checkout counter. She told Melissa she only had enough cash to cover the cost of Lindsay's coloring book purchase. Melissa was kind and said, "No problem. It's not much. I'll cover it this time." Suzanne smiled her thanks.

Melissa suggested that they all go back to her house to work on the posters. Suzanne followed in her car although she knew the way. Lindsay and Jenna had been friends for several years, so she had driven to several birthday parties and other get-togethers at Anderson's home. They lived in an older section of town, with tree-lined streets and houses with big front porches. The Anderson's home had a large fenced-in back yard, with a swing set and sandbox. The girls played in the backyard while the moms got busy with paints. They made several clever posters to take to the center the next day.

Melissa invited them to stay for lunch, which Suzanne gratefully accepted. While Melissa made a salad and tuna sandwiches, the girls washed their hands and Suzanne cleaned up the paints. The posters were drying in the family room. Lindsay and Jenna studied them carefully. They liked the bright colors and sketches.

Suzanne helped with the cleanup after lunch and then she and Lindsay drove home. It had been a good morning. Lindsay and Jenna were excited about helping the tornado victims. Suzanne was pleased to be working on the project with Melissa, who had a lot of enthusiasm and creative ideas. In addition, she offered a non-judgmental friendship. Even though her house was bigger and nicer than Suzanne's, Melissa didn't act like it mattered.

When they got to their apartment, Suzanne and Lindsay were quite surprised to see that Larry was not at home. They had expected he would be sleeping, to get ready for work that evening. "Well, Daddy must have gone out to Seven Eleven," Suzanne said to Lindsay. "You go ahead and get ready for the pool. We can go over for a couple of hours." Lindsay skipped into her room to get into her suit.

Suzanne gathered up towels and sunscreen. Then she went to her dresser and brought out her swimming suit. It was a bit faded and old looking, but it would have to do. As she stepped out of her clothes and got into the suit, she was pleased to see that at least it still fit. She had never been model thin, but she had tried to keep in shape somewhat. She smoothed her hands down her stomach, and was content that her muscles were fairly tight and flat. Her suit was modest, not cut up high on the thigh as many women were wearing today. Her breasts were properly covered and supported, yet there was a bit of cleavage showing, as would be expected in a bathing suit. She slipped into a pair of shorts and flip-flops.

Lindsay was having trouble finding her water wings, but Suzanne knew right where they were. Larry still wasn't home, so she left a note on the table saying they had gone to the pool and would be back home in time to fix dinner. Then they gathered their pool passes and headed out the door.

Crossing the parking lot a few minutes later, they were met with the sounds of summer. Laughing and splashing sounds came from around the pool. Radios were spinning tunes. The diving board sprang into life every few minutes, as swimmers boldly took to the air in graceful arches. An occasional lifeguard whistle cut the air as pool rules were enforced. It was a wonderful beginning to the pool season.

Another more unusual sound met Suzanne's ears as they neared the pool. It was the whirl of chainsaws. Last night's storm had damaged tree branches from two trees near the playground. A small crew of maintenance men was cutting branches into manageable pieces. One of the men stood to wipe the sweat from his brow. He noticed the pretty redhead and her daughter checking their pool passes at the gate. He followed them with his gaze as they found seats near the shallow end of the pool.

George called out to the rest of the guys on the crew, "It's hot, fellas. Let's take a ten-minute break. Get something to drink. Then we'll get this job finished and we can call it a day."

George walked over to the pool and got a soda from the machine. He stood and leaned against the fence and watched as the redhead put sunscreen on her daughter and adjusted the water wings to fit properly. Then he felt himself shudder with pleasure as the woman removed her shorts and began to apply lotion to her own body. He stood silently watching, and ten minutes stretched to fifteen.

Chapter Twelve

Keep Your Eyes Open

LARRY HAD GONE to Seven Eleven all right. He bought a coke, a hot dog, and a lottery ticket. Since he didn't have any cash, he used his credit card for the purchases. As much as he knew Suzanne wouldn't approve, he just had to get that lottery ticket. He was hoping to get lucky on tonight's Big Money Ball game. As he stood wondering what numbers to play, he overheard a conversation going on between several teens by the soda machine. One kid he knew, Tim Simpson. He was a jock for the local high school, had had his picture in the paper several times for his great basketball playing. He was supposedly the school's ticket into the state championship next year.

Tim and the other guys were holding a boisterous conversation. Evidently Tim had volunteered to buy the others whatever they wanted, sodas, sandwiches, chips, or whatever. One of the boys said, "That's why I like you, Tim. You always have money and you know how to treat your friends right!" They all laughed and gathered up their goodies. Still joking and carrying on, they walked to the counter with their items. Tim pulled a fifty-dollar bill from his wallet and the group of teens burst into whistles and hoots. "Whee Haa! A fifty! Le'me see that! God, where'd you get a fifty? You make money like this delivering pizzas? Can you get me a job there too?"

Larry looked on with interest. Now he remembered seeing Tim deliver the pizza to their apartment. But he doubted seriously that this kid got paid this well, and tips sure didn't amount to much. Well, maybe he had just cashed his paycheck for two weeks or something. That might make a little more sense. And kids his age don't have anything to do with their money but spend it on snacks for friends anyway. 'What a fool!' thought Larry. 'Just wait till you grow up, kid. Wait till you have a wife and a child and a broken down car and bill collectors breathing down your back. You might be sorry you blew that fifty.' As Larry finished eating his hot dog, he added to himself, 'Sure wish I had a fifty though.'

Over by the chips and other snacks, a short balding man stood. He seemed to be deciding what kind of chips to buy. Detective Randall Larson glanced over at Tim and the other boys. He listened intently but went unnoticed by the teens. Detective Larson was dressed in jeans and a light blue short-sleeved shirt. He looked like just an ordinary man, no one that mattered to them in the slightest. But Tim mattered to the Detective. Tim was going to lead him right up the department ladder. Tim was the key to Detective Larson's reputation, the hope for his long overdue recognition with the department. Tim was the key, all right. Larson knew he just had to lay low, keep his distance, gather his information, and eventually, when the time was right, he would get the collar on the big man. Tim was not that man, Larson knew. But Tim could lead him to the man, or at least a step closer. Detective Larson would stay with this kid. Kids make mistakes. Even cocky kids like this one.

The teens left the convenience store and all piled in to Tim's Camero. Larry shook his head and shrugged his shoulders. 'Oh, to be young again.' he thought. The balding detective bought a bag of potato chips and left shortly after the Camero.

Larry finished his business at the lottery machine and headed for home. He was walking because Suzanne had the car. Anyway, it was only a couple of blocks till he was home. It was getting quite warm, though, and Larry was glad he still had some of his soda left to drink as he walked along. As he approached his building, he noticed that Tim's car was parked out front. The car was empty. 'I wonder who they know in this building?' thought Larry. 'As far as I know, there are no teenagers that live here.' Just then, Tim came out of the building alone but carrying a duffel bag. He got into his car and pulled away. 'Now, isn't that strange? Wonder what he was doing here? Not delivering pizzas, I bet.'

Down the parking lot, parked between a minivan and a station wagon, Detective Larson sat eating his chips. He watched as Tim put the duffel bag in the back seat of his car and pulled away from the building. He watched as the Camero turned the corner and headed towards the swimming pool. Detective Larson started his own engine and followed at a distance. When Tim stopped his car, Larson pulled into another spot and waited. He jotted some notes in his logbook and finished the chips.

As Larry climbed the stairs to the third floor, he heard music coming from the apartment across the hall from his own. 'Oh, great,' he thought. 'I was going to try to get some sleep before I go to work. Now they go and turn this loud stuff on.' Then Larry did something rather uncharacteristic. He knocked forcefully on the door.

Someone walked to the other side of the door. 'Probably looking through the peep-hole,' Larry thought.

"Who is it?" called a man's voice.

"I'm Larry, your neighbor across the hall," he answered. The chain was loosened and the deadbolt was unlocked and a man came out into the hall, closing the door behind him.

"Hello, Larry. Nice to meet you. I'm Mike. What can I do for you?"

The men shook hands and Larry spoke. "Well, I was just hearing your music, and I don't suppose you know it but I work nights and sleep much of the day, and I was just getting ready to get some sleep and I hear the music so I was wondering if you could maybe turn it down a little? I mean, it is hard enough trying to sleep in the daytime anyway, with the sunlight and all, but if you could turn down the music, it would really help me a lot."

"Sure, man," said Mike. "No problem. I wouldn't want to be a trouble to you. Anytime, you just let me know, and if I can help you out, I sure will. We'll turn this down right now." Mike opened the apartment door just enough to stick his head in and yell, "Hey, Robin, turn that stereo off, will you? Larry here needs to sleep and the music is bothering him." Right away the stereo was turned off. Then he closed the door and turned back to Larry. "So, you work nights? What do you do?"

"I work in a hospital."

"Oh, yeah? Are you a doctor or something?"

"No, I'm a med tech in the ER. For now anyway. The job sucks, but it pays the bills. Just barely. I'd sure like to walk away from it, get something that pays better. What do you do?"

Mike hesitated just a bit. "Me? I'm in business for myself. Sales. You need something, I can get it for you. At a good price, and good terms. I'm sort of a financial entrepreneur." He chuckled at his wit.

"Oh, really? How about a million dollars? Can you get me a million dollars? That would sure come in handy!" The men laughed at this thought, but Mike could sense that Larry was at least partly serious.

"You need money, huh? Don't we all? Well, like I said, I can get you anything, for the right terms. A million might be a little tough though!"

"Yeah, well, a million would put me on an easy street. A couple thousand would get some goons off my back. Another thousand and I would play the horses and get lucky, and *then* I'd make my own millions and have it made!"

"I like a man with goals!" laughed Mike. "But seriously, you need a loan? I'd be happy to loan you some. You could at least buy some time with those goons."

"You'd do that? You don't hardly even know me. Kinda risky, don't you think?

Mike answered, "I know people pretty well. I know I can trust you. Besides, I know where you live! I can always come and collect, one way or another!" The men laughed again. Mike flashed a smile that oozed confidence. It put Larry at ease.

"Well. Mike, the truth is, I don't have a real good credit history. I would not be able to guarantee you'd get paid back right away."

Mike looked at Larry and just shrugged. "I can wait till your horse wins big!"

Larry didn't say anything; he didn't know what to say. So Mike asked, "What time do you go to work? Maybe you could come over and we could talk about it some more."

I usually leave at about 10:30. Gotta be there by 11," Larry answered.

"Well, I'm busy tonight, but why don't you come by tomorrow night, say about 9:30 or so. We could talk this through. I've already got some ideas for you!" Mike seemed very confident and willing to help Larry out of his financial bind.

Larry was both surprised and relieved. 'Whatever it takes,' he thought. 'I've got to at least pay those thugs back the two thousand I own 'em.' He agreed to stop by on Tuesday night about 9:30. They shook hands again and Larry unlocked his apartment door, lay down on his bed, and fell right to sleep. It was the best sleep he had gotten in months.

Chapter Thirteen

More Risky Business

TIM PARKED HIS car near the swimming pool gate. He grabbed his duffel bag out of the back seat, showed his pool pass at the gate, and made his way over to a group of friends gathered near the diving board. It wasn't long before a small group of guys broke off and went into the men's changing room. One guy watched the door while Tim made his sale. Tim took four little plastic bags of white powder from his duffel bag. Quickly and with barely a word spoken among them, Tim exchanged the drugs for his payment. He placed the money in a concealed zippered section of his bag, thanked the guys for their business, and left the locker room. The four guys exited a short time later, returning to their friends at the pool.

Tim had other customers to attend to. Usually he was only able to work during the evenings, under the cover of his pizza delivery job. Sure, he did a little business at school, but found that more of a hassle than he needed. You never really knew when someone was listening, and now since the school had installed more surveillance cameras, there were few places around school he considered safe. It was better for him to wear his pizza shirt, and go in and out of homes basically unsuspected.

If it weren't for finals coming up at school, he probably wouldn't even have done this business at the pool today. But everybody seemed pretty stressed out about the big end-of-the-year tests, and needed something to keep them awake while they were studying. Or to take away their fear of failure. This time of year always brings out the worst fears in teenagers, especially juniors and seniors taking PSAT's and sending out college applications and waiting for acceptance/rejection letters. 'Oh well,' Tim thought to himself. 'If I can help kids get through this stressful time, then I have done a good thing, right?' Not to mention the financial security he was building for himself!

Tim had been running drugs for Mike and Robin for just less than a year now. He had started using marijuana when he was a freshman, to get loosened up before basketball games. He added speed when test time came around, especially in the last couple of years. Then last year, before finals, he started buying stuff for friends. When Mike found out about it, he offered Tim a job running for friends at school and some other customers Mike had.

Except for a few deals at school, Tim did most of his drop offs under the guise of a pizza delivery boy. Not that the boss at Pizza Palace was wise to it. That guy was spaced out most of the time anyway and seldom even noticed that Tim was gone out on pizza deliveries longer than he ought to be. So Tim made a run with pizza and delivered drugs to others in the vicinity. Mike would give him addresses, and Tim would deliver the drugs and pick up payments. And every evening he worked, about midnight or later, Tim would give the coded knock on Mike's apartment door. Then he would present Mike with the evenings' income. Mike would pay Tim a generous cut, plus give him whatever he needed, speed or coke or whatever.

It was a pretty good arrangement. Money was rolling in for Tim; Mike was happy with his services and his discretion. Tim was actually considering quitting the pizza job altogether, as long as he could figure out a way to keep a uniform to use in his undercover work. It was a good plan for Tim. He was doing well enough at school and with basketball. He figured he would sail through his last year of high school and then go on to a big university on a basketball scholarship, maybe even take the team into the NCAA finals. Yep, things were gonna work out just fine for him. He had drive, and guts and brains enough, not to mention charm and sweet-talkin' ways. And money, don't forget the money.

So as Tim left the pool that afternoon and began his deliveries, he was very confident that things were going smoothly in his life. You had to have confidence in yourself. It helped with the image he tried to carry off. Sure, guys were busted all the time for drugs, but none of them were as cool and clever as Tim Simpson. He had this all worked out. He had never been in trouble with the cops before, and even if he did get caught, they wouldn't do much to a first time offender, and he could get out and get on with his life in no time. You couldn't keep him down for long.

Chapter Fourteen

Dreaming

MONDAY'S DINNER WAS hamburgers, potato chips, deviled eggs, and baked beans, perfect food for a summer's day. Lindsay was very tired after all of the activities of the day. She fell asleep for a late afternoon nap while Suzanne fixed the picnic goodies. Suzanne set the card table and three chairs on the deck. She used paper plates and plastic silver ware to complete the picnic atmosphere. It was a beautiful evening, perfect for a meal on the deck.

When Larry got up from bed, he seemed more rested than usual. He was also helpful and a bit talkative. Suzanne told him about the plans for the daycare's tornado relief project, and Larry said he was proud of Lindsay for thinking of such a good idea. He wondered how the donations were going to be delivered to the displaced families, and Suzanne admitted that they had not planned that out completely yet. She wondered if the Red Cross would distribute the donations, which Larry agreed would probably be the case.

After Lindsay had napped about an hour, Larry went into her room to wake her. She was still a little groggy when they came out onto the deck, but woke up when she realized they were having a picnic. This was going to be fun! She told her daddy about playing at Jenna's yard, and about the tornado, and helping with a little girl with no roof on her house. Then she talked about the fun she had had at the pool. She was really looking forward to starting swimming lessons in the summer.

The evening passed pleasantly enough. The whole weekend had been both productive and restful for Suzanne. And Larry was certainly in a better mood than he had been recently. 'Maybe he needed a little break from our usual routines, too,' she thought. When Larry left for work that evening, he actually kissed Suzanne good-bye.

When the phone rang at two, Suzanne happily answered. She told Paul all about their nice weekend, the tornado project, and Lindsay's fun at the pool. He listened with interest, and didn't let on that he had seen her at the pool. But in his mind, he was envisioning her, in her modest but becoming one-piece suit, smoothing lotion on her arms, legs, neck and chest. He imagined he was rubbing the lotion on her back and shoulders. He fanaticized about touching her neck, letting his fingers explore downward to her breasts as he spread lotion on her delicate skin. He dreamed of her leaning back into him. Yielding herself to his desires. He would kiss her neck, nibble on her ears, and then kiss her firmly on the lips, letting his tongue twine with her own. She would sigh and relax, totally yielding to his touch. His hands would completely engulf her breasts and she would move into his embrace. He would reach around her, pulling her as close as possible. She would wrap her arms tightly around his neck, and he would lift her feet from the ground and hoist her up to his waist. She would wrap her legs around him and feel him hard and firm against her.

But he spoke none of this to her. He kept the thoughts buried deeply in his mind. She was not ready to hear this type of talk yet, but he could not stop the lusty feelings from surging wildly through him. He gave a little moan, only slightly audible, and told her good-night. Suzanne caught the slightest hint of something distracting in his voice and wondered if he had something on his mind. She hoped everything was all right with him.

As Suzanne fell back to sleep, she smiled to herself and thought about her new friend. He was so interested in the things she did every day. He actually made her feel like she was a woman of worth and purpose. That was something Larry seldom communicated to her. No, Larry was usually judgmental and totally uninterested in the things that occupied her days. But Paul was different. He always asked questions about her life, her dreams and ambitions. He made her feel like what she did day in and day out was the most important business in the whole world. He was so easy to talk to, so accepting of whatever she said. 'So I wonder what that little sigh sound was all about?' she thought. 'I hope there is nothing wrong. I do like talking to him, and so seldom get to talk about my days. I hope he doesn't stop calling because I'm so boring! Maybe I'll ask him next time he calls.'

When the alarm clock woke Suzanne in the morning, she was deep into a dream. In her dream, she was in a room filled with sunlight. Soft warm breezes were billowing gauzy white curtains at the windows. It seemed like some tropical beach, warm and sunny, quiet and peaceful. She lay naked on a white bed, and a man, dressed in a white shirt and white pants, stood beside her. She could not see his face, but she knew that he was a stranger. She was asleep and he just stood there, watching her, as the white curtains blew behind him in the breeze.

Chapter Fifteen

Surprise!

SUZANNE AND LINDSAY arrived at the daycare center earlier than usual that morning, but Melissa and Jenna were already there. Melissa was setting up a display in the entry foyer. One of Suzanne's posters was hung on the wall above a small table. On the table there were letters explaining the project to other parents. On the floor near by, Mrs. Williams, the daycare director had placed a large box for donations.

Lindsay and Jenna helped their mothers hang more posters throughout the foyer and in the halls. Then the girls skipped down the hallway to their classroom. Lindsay was looking for her other friends, Katie, Allison and Abby, so she could give them the invitations to her birthday party.

Several parents stopped in the hall to ask Melissa and Suzanne questions about the project and express their willingness to help. Mrs. Williams came out of her office to greet the women and thanked them for organizing this service project. She was sure most of the families would want to get involved with the relief effort. She looked forward to seeing the donations as they came in. She also said she had lots and lots of boxes in the back storage room, so as the one here in the foyer got filled up, she would be sure another empty box would take its place.

When Suzanne was leaving the daycare center and driving on her way to work, she was pleased with how the morning had started for her. The tornado relief project was being well received. The girls were happy and excited about their involvement with the project. Melissa was a pleasure to work with, and Mrs. Williams seemed truly appreciative of their efforts.

School went well for Suzanne that day. Always after a three-day weekend or any vacation from school, the children were a little out of sorts and off schedule. Some had stayed up too late, most had been quite busy with family activities, and some were just plain unhappy to be back to school and wished for a much longer vacation. But Suzanne knew this would be the case, and had planned some exciting and varied activities for the day. She was able to pull the children back in to the routine of school, yet at the same time allowing for their individual needs to be met. This was one of Suzanne's strengths as a teacher. She really knew her children, and loved them individually. She understood group dynamics and individual personalities. She could anticipate and therefore ward off disturbing or troubling situations. She was experienced with children of this age, yet not so routine as to forget the uniqueness of each child.

So most days went smoothly in Suzanne's classroom. Things were not always perfect, of course. But for the most part the children were happy, were in a safe and warm environment, they were developing respect for others and appropriate self-esteem and they were learning. It was all Suzanne could hope for, and she was providing them with the best school experience she possibly could.

Every Tuesday afternoon there were staff meetings at the school. After the children were on their buses and safely headed home, all the teachers would meet together in the library. There the principal would discuss items of importance to them all. Usually afterwards, the teams would break up for a small group agenda. The teachers would meet by grade level to make level appropriate plans.

This Tuesday afternoon meeting took on a different format. Suzanne and the other teachers noticed it as soon as they entered the library. There was a large bouquet of spring flowers on the principle's podium. Video equipment was set up near the front of the room. Blue and silver streamers were hung from the ceiling. Helium filled blue and silver balloons were tied in bunches behind several chairs scattered around the room. "What's going on?" one of the teachers asked Suzanne as they entered the room and took their seats. "I don't know, it must be something special," said Suzanne.

The principal took the podium and conducted the business as usual. There was no mention of the special decorations until the end of the meeting. Then he said, "I'm sure you are aware of the decorations in blue and silver, our school colors. We wanted to do something special today, in recognition of a very special person on our staff. Several weeks ago, all the elementary principals in the county were asked to submit the names of the teacher they recommended for "Teacher of the Year." I am pleased to announce that this year, our school has nominated Mrs. Suzanne Rogers! Suzanne, would you come up front please?" Suzanne's co-workers cheered and clapped their hands for her as she rose and walked to the podium. She was stunned and tears welled up in her eyes. The principal shook her hand warmly and said, "Mrs. Rogers, for your dedication to your profession, and your commitment to the children you have had in your classes, for your untiring enthusiasm and your amazing creativity, the administrators of Dickinson Elementary School have nominated you as teacher of the year. We have submitted your name to the Linn County Board of Education for consideration as Elementary Teacher of the Year. If you win at the county level, your name will also go into nomination for the state award. We present you with these flowers and this plaque, which reads:

Suzanne Rogers
Teacher of the Year
Dickinson Elementary School
1980

Teachers throughout the room rose to their feet and applauded the nomination. Suzanne spoke softly, yet all could sense her heartfelt emotion. "I just don't know what to say." People took their seats and waited for Suzanne to continue. "I do appreciate this nomination and I certainly did not expect it. This is such an honor." She paused for a minute and then smiled. "You know, I love teaching. I've always felt that if you can love your job, if you get great joy and pleasure and fulfillment out of what you do for a living, if you are satisfied that you are doing a job well, and making a difference in the world, then you are in the right place. You are where you were meant to be. You are living a destiny that was intended for you. And that is how I feel about teaching. I love it, maybe not every day, but I do feel like this is the place I am intended to be. I am grateful that the staff here at Dickinson feels that I have done a good job. But I know that I would continue to love these children and this job, whether I get this reward or any other. Being here, doing what I love, and making a difference in the lives of my children, that is reward enough for me. But thank you, thank you very much, for this recognition, and your support. Thank you."

Suzanne accepted the plaque and walked back to her seat. The other first grade teachers sitting near her smiled and nodded as she wiped tears from her eyes. After the meeting was adjourned, many co-workers congratulated her on the nomination. She was beaming with happiness. The video camera had captured her acceptance speech, but now they wanted still photos for the school newsletter. Smiling brightly, Suzanne posed for a few photos with the principal and other administrators.

A few minutes later, driving towards Lindsay's daycare, Suzanne breathed a deep joy-filled sigh. Yes, it had really been a good day, better than she could have ever expected. She glanced back at the beautiful bouquet nestled safely on the back seat. She could smell the lilacs and other spring flowers. They were certainly going to brighten up the kitchen table tonight while they ate dinner.

She was running a little late in picking up Lindsay, but she did take a minute to glance at the relief box. Some parents had already started to bring in donations. She saw quite a few used toys, some blankets and a couple of unopened packages of sheets. 'Very nice beginning,' she thought.

As soon as Lindsay got into the car, she noticed the flowers in the back. She asked her mother about them, and was happy to know the reason her mother had been given them. When they got home, Lindsay carefully carried the flowers all the way up the stairs and then put them on the kitchen table. Larry was just getting up. He asked, "Where did those come from?"

"Mommy got them at her school, cuz the principal said she is a good teacher." She smelled the pretty purple flowers and asked, "Daddy, do you know what kind this flower is?" He said, "No, but your mother probably does. She likes flowers and knows them a lot."

When Suzanne came back to the kitchen from changing her clothes, she told Lindsay they were lilacs. She told her that lilacs were one of Grandma's favorite flowers. When she was growing up, on the farm in Kansas, Grandma had lots and lots of lilac bushes. Some had purple flowers, some had white, and some even had double flowers.

"Can we have a lilac bush sometime?" Lindsay asked.

"We'll see, honey. Someday, if we get a little house with a yard, we can plant all kinds of flowers. And if you want a lilac bush, then we will just have to get one! Now, you run on to your room and change your clothes. Then come help me set the table, please."

Larry was listening from the living room. He smiled to himself, thinking that if all went well at Mike's place tonight, he might soon be on his way to making enough money to buy them that little house and that lilac bush.

At dinner they talked about the reward Suzanne had received. Larry wanted to know if there was any monetary bonus involved, but Suzanne didn't think so. Although if she won at the state level, there might be, she wasn't sure. Then Larry said that he had to go in to work early, leaving about 9:30. He didn't seem unhappy about it, not like he was worried about something, so Suzanne didn't think anything of it. 'Probably a staff meeting,' she thought.

After Larry left for his meeting, and Lindsay was asleep for the night, Suzanne decided to reward herself with a quiet, relaxing, self-pampering evening. First she opened a bottle of White Zinfandel wine she had saved for a special occasion. She poured herself a glass and took a sip. Then she carried the glass into the bedroom. She lit three candles and placed them on the vanity in the bathroom. Next she ran hot water into the tub, and added lilac scented bubble bath. While the tub was filling, she went back into the bedroom and drank some more wine. Then she took off all of her clothes, and studied herself in the mirror. Her hair was thick and hung around her shoulders in waves. Her skin was smooth and white, with just a hint of color from being at the pool yesterday. Her stomach was fairly flat, her bottom tight, legs firm, and her breasts were full. Suzanne had never been especially proud of her body, and had always dressed modestly. But now, studying herself in the mirror like this, she realized that most men would find her attractive, maybe even sexy. She was a little surprised to find herself even thinking like that! Still nude, Suzanne carried the wine glass back to the kitchen for a refill, and returned to the bathroom. The air was steamy and the mirrors were already fogging over. She turned off the overhead light, took another sip of wine, and set the glass carefully on the edge of the tub. After testing the temperature of the water, she reached to the faucets and turned them off. Then she stepped into the tub, slowly sat down and let her body relax. She sank deeply down into the hot bubbly water and was soon overcome with an intense peacefulness. She felt relaxed and stimulated, all at the same time. She so seldom had the opportunity to pamper herself like this. It felt wonderful. In the semi-darkness of the room, she reached for her glass of wine and drank deeply. It was sweet, cold and provided her with just the right amount of self-indulgence she needed after today. It was a delightful experience.

Rubbing a bath sponge over her body, Suzanne let her hands linger on her breasts. She felt their fullness, and noticed that the nipples were hardening a bit. She pulled the nipple of one breast and felt it stiffen even more. She remembered the times when Lindsay was a baby. Nursing her had been such a joy. And her breasts had become so heavy with milk, she remembered sometimes imagining they could stay that large forever. But they didn't, of course, and she was quite satisfied with what she had now! They were big enough, filled her hands nicely, and looked so good when she squeezed them upwards together. And they felt good, too.

Suzanne took the bath sponge down to her feet and raised one leg slightly out of the water. She rubbed the sponge along her leg as water and bubbles dropped back into the tub. She moved her hands up her leg, past her knee, up to her thigh. She covered every inch of her leg with her hands and soapy sponge. Then she did the same with the other leg. But this time, when she reached the top of her leg, she sank herself even more deeply into the water and began to wash her pelvic area. She dropped the sponge back into the water and used only her hand. Suzanne closed her eyes as she let her fingers massage her vaginal lips. She had never really done this much before, and she was rather surprised at how good it felt. She was beginning to understand why the women in Larry's magazines always had a far away look in their eyes. Suzanne was beginning to feel she herself was another person, someone uninhibited, someone who knew how to pleasure herself intensely. Suzanne took another big drink from her wine glass and then put her hands back to her pubic area. She moaned as her fingers reached the opening, and she inserted them deeply inside. The palm of her hand touched the top of her pubic bone, and the fingers rubbed the clitoris. She had never done this to herself, and was enjoying the discovery of self-stimulation to its fullest. Her fingers began pumping in and out rapidly, and bath water was sloshing over the side of the tub. But Suzanne did not care. She was not aware of anything but the new feeling she was experiencing. She brought herself to a climax and sat quivering in the tub of hot water. She could barely breathe, she was panting and near exhaustion. The combination of hot water, cold wine, and sexual pleasure was overwhelming.

Emotion after emotion rolled over her and suddenly tears formed in the corners of Suzanne's eyes and overflowed down her cheeks. Suzanne began to cry. She cried for the joy of her new discovery, the release of pent up sexual tension, for the longing for more intimacy than she had with her marriage. She cried for the shadow of unhappiness that settled over her, the lies she'd been telling herself and the feeling of entrapment she was living under. Despite all the positive and good things that she tried to always focus on, she was not happy with her life. Something was missing. Her self stimulation, pleasurable as it was, had exposed a big hole in her life. She was not sexually satisfied in her marriage. But she felt powerless to do anything about it.

Chapter Sixteen

Money Problems Solved– Maybe

WHEN LARRY KNOCKED on Mike's door at 9:30 that night, he was hopeful. He thought this new friendship with Mike might just lead him to a debt free life. He had reason to believe that Mike was the answer to his troubles, most of which were financial. Mike had certainly been friendly the other night. Larry was ready to seal some kind of a deal, one that would keep him out of debtor's prison, he hoped.

Mike answered the door right away. His wife Robin was in the kitchen and came out with coffee for the two men. Larry had never really noticed Robin before, and was stunned to see how beautiful she was. Her figure was just about perfect, as far as Larry could see. She was wearing cut-off blue jean shorts, very short and tight around her little firm ass. She had long straight jet-black hair that shimmered in the evening light. As she leaned over the coffee table to set down the tray with coffee and sugar, Larry couldn't help but notice that her blouse opened before him and he was given a quick view of two full and firm mounds of female flesh. Instantly he felt a twinge of excitement, and was rewarded with a bright smile from Robin, who seemed to know exactly what her actions had provoked in him. Then she went into the back bedroom, to give them some privacy.

Larry sat on the sofa and looked around quickly. The apartment was clean and nice enough, but nothing out of the usual. Furniture was modern and new looking, but not expensive. Pictures on the wall were mostly posters of movies and actors. It was a decent place, but nothing extravagant or elaborate. Yet Mike gave off an air of financial stability, like he had plenty of money.

"So Larry," Mike began. "You need money, right? I believe you mentioned you owe someone two thousand dollars. Is that right?" Larry nodded and Mike continued. "Okay, so here's the deal. I am in the process of expanding my business. I need someone to make deliveries for me two nights a week, either Friday and Saturday or Saturday and Sunday. If all goes well, I will be looking to increase to possibly four, maybe five, nights a week. The hours are some-what flexible. Starting time could be as early as ten o'clock, or as late as midnight. Work until the deliveries are made. Usually five or six hours a night. It does involve some driving, so a dependable car is a must. I am prepared to give an advance of two thousand dollars. We could call it even after say ten deliveries. After that, the salary is on a commission basis. More productivity means more money; it's that simple. A good man could average easily four hundred dollars a night. Quite possibly more. To start, when I only need help two nights a week, you could still be working at the hospital. But I think, after you get started and see what a great opportunity this is, you will soon want to leave that old job behind, and come on board with me all the way. Imagine making four or five hundred dollars a night, Larry. What is that, triple what you make now? And less hours, too. More time to spend with your family, and more money to spend on them! So how does that sound, Larry? How can you not love it?"

Larry took a drink of coffee and started in with some questions. "You would give me an advance of two thousand dollars, and I would make ten deliveries and we would be even?"

Mike nodded. "Yes. That's right. Two thousand dollars up front, to do with as you please. You just agree to make ten deliveries, and when you do that, we are even."

"I could work for you on the weekends, when I am not scheduled to work at the hospital? And after a while, you might need me more nights a week, so I would have to quit the hospital job, or at least change my hours, to work more nights for you?"

"You got it. I don't expect to start needing more nights right away, but maybe in a couple of months. Couldn't pinpoint it exactly right now, but probably mid-summer. Till then, you can work at the hospital for your meager wages, and roll in the big money with me on the weekends. How would you like that?"

Larry hesitated just a bit. "You mentioned needing a good car. Well, mine isn't always dependable. It's pretty old."

Mike had an answer for that, too. "Listen, Larry, with all the money you will be making, you will be able to get yourself a better car in no time. You could pay cash for it even! And honestly, if you were in a bind one night, and really couldn't use your car, you could probably borrow Robin's or mine for the evening. Just fill up the tank afterwards, and I see no problem."

"Oh, okay, that would work, I guess. And how far would I have to drive on these deliveries? I'm just wondering how many miles I will put on the car every night. There is going to be the expense of gas, you know. Unless I submit vouchers for reimbursement or something?" he added hopefully.

"No, no reimbursement, Larry," Mike laughed. "The gasoline is on you. But look at the money you're gonna be making. Gas expenses are trivial. And you can count on probably two, maybe three hundred miles a night. Shouldn't be more. Maybe after we expand our territory it would increase, but you will have your new car by then." Mike was so confident. He had a solution for everything. And Larry did see this new job offer as the answer to his money troubles. He was ready to jump at the chance.

"Sounds good!" exclaimed Larry. "Can I start this weekend? I could work Friday and Saturday nights. Where do I report? And who do I report to?"

"Hey, man, slow down!" chuckled Mike. "To begin with, report to me at let's say Friday night at 10:00. I will have your list of delivery addresses. I will give you all your instructions then. How soon do you need the two thousand? Will the goons get you before Friday? I could actually give you half now, the other half on Friday, if that works better for you. What do you think?"

Larry thought walking out of here with a thousand dollars would be a terrific feeling. He sure would like to see those guys' faces when he paid them off. Bet they never expected it. "Yeah," he said, "It would be good to pay them half tonight. Take some of the pressure off, that's for sure."

Mike walked to the side of the sofa and opened a door on the end table. Inside there was a safe deposit box. He twirled the combination lock until it clicked open. Then he withdrew ten one hundred dollar bills and counted them out to Larry, who tucked them away inside his wallet gratefully. Mike closed the box, spun the dial, and replaced it back inside the end table. Then he stood, shook hands with Larry, and led him to the door. "So, I'll see you Friday night at ten. I will give you the rest of the advance then, and also your delivery instructions. See you then."

The door closed and Larry heard it lock behind him. He patted the money inside his wallet and walked briskly down the stairs and into the cool evening air. He looked at his watch. Ten–fifteen. He had just enough time to stop at seven eleven, make a phone call and get on to work. He would arrange a meeting time for the goons to come pick up their money. Well, half of it. He was sure they would be happy to get what they could tonight, with the promise of more on Friday.

He jumped in the car and headed out to the pay phone at seven eleven. "Darn it," he said out loud. "We're nearly out of gas. Now I will have to take time for that too. Why doesn't she ever remember to get gas before she gets home? And I don't even have enough money for a fill-up, except for these hundreds. Guess I'm gonna have to break one to buy gas. What a bunch of bull. Why can't she get this right?"

Larry pulled up to the gas pump in front of the convenience store. He went in and said, "Fill up on number two, regular." Then he gave the man behind the counter a one hundred dollar bill. "Hope you've got change for this," he said rather proudly. After he pumped his gas and got his change, Larry made a phone call. A meeting was arranged. Larry's troubles were almost over. Or so he thought.

Chapter Seventeen

New Adventures

SUZANNE WAS STARTLED to realize that she had drifted off to sleep while she was still in the bathtub. When she woke up, the bath water was getting chilly. Wrapping a towel around herself, she walked into the bedroom and looked at the clock. It was nearly one o'clock! 'Oh geez, I haven't even gone over my lesson plans for tomorrow. I mean today. Oh well, I guess I will do okay; I can skip the review just this once. Other teachers do it all the time.' Somehow that didn't really make her feel better, but Suzanne was very tired, and knew she would fall asleep anyway, if she tried to go over the plans. 'Must be all the wine, making me so sleepy,' she said to herself. Then she lay back on the bed and nestled up on the pillow. Her damp hair fanned out beside her, her nude body stretched out on top of the sheets and Suzanne closed her eyes. Suddenly she opened them with a quick blink. She had remembered what she had done in the bathtub. She remembered how excited she felt, how aroused she had become. She felt both guilty and elated. That was not something she usually did, hardly ever, in fact, and never with an overpowering sensual reaction that had come over her like this time. 'It's got to be because of the wine,' she said, making an excuse for herself. 'I would never have done that otherwise. Or felt so good about it anyway!'

She settled back down on the pillow, and as she returned to her slumber, her left hand reached up to feel her breasts, and her right hand slowly but intently reached between her legs. Again she felt a quiver of excitement, for she now could anticipate the surges of pleasure that she knew were soon to course through her body. Now that she knew she was capable of giving herself such pleasure, she wanted to try it more and more. Within a few minutes she brought herself to a climax, and collapsed weakly on the bed. That's when the phone rang.

George noticed a difference in her voice right away. It was a sort of breathless, raspy "Hello", a little deeper than usual, a little slurred maybe. "Susan, is that you?" he asked.

"Mmmm, hi Paul," came the response. Yes, it was definitely a deeper tone, definitely sensual.

"Are you alright?" he asked.

"Yes, I'm fine. Why?" she replied.

"Well, you just sound different. Your voice is even more sexy than usual. I hope I'm not interrupting anything!"

"Interrupting? Well no not really. But that reminds me; I wanted to ask you a question. The last time we talked, just before we hung up, I got the feeling something was on your mind. Was everything okay? Or did I say something that upset you or bothered you or something? Because if I did, I sure didn't mean to. And I don't want you to stop calling me because of something stupid I might have said. I must really bore you, anyway, with all the dumb stuff I talk about all the time. But you are such a good listener. And I like talking to you, and I even kind of miss it on nights when we don't talk. I wake up in the mornings and feel sort of sad, like something has been missing. You know what I mean?"

"Yes, I do know what you mean. I like talking to you, too. And no, you didn't say anything to upset me last time. It's just that, I, well, I was thinking about you and maybe I kind of let my imagination get the best of me. We were talking about you going to the pool, and I got to thinking about that, and how you might look and, well, I knew I shouldn't be thinking about you in that way. So I just decided I had better get off the phone before I said something I would regret later. I'm sorry if I seemed abrupt or anything. I just didn't want to say anything that might make you not want my phone calls anymore. You know?"

"Okay, as long as you weren't upset or anything. I just was afraid you were getting bored talking to me."

"Bored? No way. You are a very interesting person, and I enjoy talking to you very much. So tell me, what happened with you today?"

"I'm glad you asked!" Suzanne giggled. "Because it was a terrific day, and I can't wait to tell you about it!" She proceeded to describe the staff meeting and her surprise at being nominated as Teacher of the Year.

"Oh, god, Susan, that is terrific! I'm so happy for you! You need to really celebrate this! It's great! What are you going to do to celebrate?"

"Well, actually, I already celebrated! Larry left for work early, and I drank almost a whole bottle of wine, and took a long hot bubble bath!" Suzanne felt very comfortable telling him this, probably because the wine was still affecting her normal thinking processes and she let her guard down a bit.

"Oh-oh, there goes my imagination again! You drank a whole bottle of wine? I would not have thought that was in your character. So that really was a celebration!"

"I don't usually drink much at all, and then just wine, but really not much. I just started and one glass led to another, and before long I was really relaxed and doing things I don't usually do." She giggled a little again, and even blushed as she remembered. Her mind was still foggy, and she was walking into unfamiliar territory, talking to a man like this, and thinking what she was thinking. But what could it matter? How could it hurt? Just innocent flirting and fun.

George was definitely getting the feeling that Susan was a little bit drunk. He wanted so badly to take this conversation to the next level. It sounded like she was ready, now more than ever. She may not remember the conversation in the morning, but for tonight, he would get what he needed from her. It was definitely worth a try.

"Doing things you don't usually do? Now that has sure got me interested. Would you tell me what you did?" George wondered just how far he could get with this woman.

She hesitated a second, and George knew he would have to pull it out of her. "Did you have the tub filled with lots of bubbles? Was the water hot, really hot?"

"Mmmm, yes, really hot." Her voice was drifting off, as if remembering how it all felt. "And lots of bubbles. And candles, I didn't tell you I had candles. The lights were off, except for the candles. It was so nice."

"And did you touch yourself? Did you touch your breasts?" George was breathing deeply now, trying to stay in control, but letting his mind shift into fantasy mode.

"Well, yes I did. Were you watching me?" She giggled again, playing a game now, delving into a fantasy of her own. Why not? What could it hurt? The wine was affecting her thinking, for sure, but she didn't even care. This was her night, her chance to celebrate, and she did deserve to have some fun, after all.

"Watching? Mmmm, I sure would like to have been watching. I bet you are beautiful. You are sure exciting me now, just thinking of you in that bubble bath. I bet your breasts are big and beautiful. And your hips are full and your legs are long. I imagined you in a bathing suit the other day. And now I'm imagining you in a bubble bath, totally naked. Oh, god, I want to see you covered with bubbles, touching your breasts, squeezing them. Ohhh! But do you want me to stop? Because now that I've started, I don't know if I could make myself stop. But if you are uncomfortable, I won't talk about it anymore. It will be hard, but I will stop if you want." He wanted to give her a chance to think she was in control, to think she could say just how far this was going to go. He knew that she was already going further than she normally would, without the wine to loosen her up. But he also knew he wanted to go further still.

"It's okay, really. I kind of like it!" Suzanne said, surprising herself a bit. "You want to know what else I did in the bathtub?"

"Oh, yes, tell me more." George was loving this. At last, a little sex talk. His hopes were soaring. His cock was already hard. He had it out, and was stroking it gently. It was going to be a good night.

"Well, I don't usually do stuff like this, but I guess it was because I drank all that wine, but anyway, I touched myself, between my legs, you know. And I liked it." Suddenly she seemed a little shy; this was kind of hard to talk about after all.

"You liked it, huh? It felt good? Did you put your finger up inside your pussy? Did you fuck yourself with your finger?" George was very used to this kind of talk, and he knew that she would open up to him more if he taught her the words. She didn't know how to describe the things she had done, and he could help her.

"The water was really hot, and it surprised me how it felt going inside me. Very hot."

"Did you play with your clit? Did you make yourself come?"

"Mmmm, yes, it felt so good. I put my fingers inside, and moved them around, and then I just couldn't stop myself. I haven't ever done that before. I liked it. I liked it so much I was doing it again just when the phone rang."

"Oh, that's why you sounded sorta different. You were rubbing yourself, and I called right in time to help you. Would you like that? Would you like to come again, while you are talking to me?" He was rubbing his shaft faster now. It was thick, hard, and ready for some action.

"Oh, yes, I think I would like that a lot. But I have sure never done anything like this before. This is all new to me. What do you want me to do?"

"First tell me what you are wearing," he demanded. He wanted to picture her just as she was at that moment.

"Nothing," she answered shyly.

"Sounds good to me. Touch yourself between your legs. Rub yourself." George's eyes were closed. He was imagining her lying naked on the bed. He was watching her touch herself shyly, exploring new places. He wanted to touch her himself, smooth his hands over her soft silky skin, kiss her breasts, pull her close to him.

And so the conversation continued, long into the night. While George led her to new levels of self-exploration, Suzanne allowed herself to be totally overcome with sensual passions. At last she lay exhausted on her bed, body quivering with pleasure, sweat droplets trickling down her neck. George himself was drained. His emotions were spent, his fantasy fulfilled, and his manhood lay in his hand, limp and dripping. George had always enjoyed the first time with a woman on the phone. It was like a conquest, and gave him a power and sense of manliness. George reached for some tissues to clean up, and whispered to her, "Oh baby, that was sooo good. I know you must feel great. Your moaning about drove me crazy. How do you feel?"

"Unbelievable," Suzanne said softly. "I can't believe I did that with you. And it felt so good."

"You really needed that. I could tell from the first time I talked to you that there was a side to you that hadn't been explored yet. I just knew you were hot and sexy, and needed someone like me to help you enjoy some sexual pleasures. You are really a turn on, you know that?"

Confused by wine, the late hour, and a surge of unfamiliar hormones, Suzanne felt a sudden twinge of guilt. What she had done this evening seemed a little twisted, not really normal, probably not good. She was married, and yet she had just had a delightful sexual experience with another man. She knew it wasn't really cheating, but she also knew where it could lead. Well, she just couldn't let it go that far. This was fun, kinda risky, but still safe enough. And it felt so good. So good. Didn't she deserve some real pleasure for a change?

When she finally responded to Paul's question, her voice was a little shaky and weak. She was tired, her mind was still in a fog, and now, to make matters worse, she was dabbling with guilt as well as sexual satisfaction. It was an unsettling combination of emotions. "I turn you on? I might, but you don't know anything about me. I could be 500 pounds and dirty and smelly. I could be faking this whole thing, you don't know. You're just turned on by the idea of a woman doing this with you on the phone."

"Okay, you are absolutely right. But you do turn me on. Tonight was good for me, as I think it was good for you. We just happened to really need this release tonight, and we happened to be there for each other. And I wouldn't mind at all if we did it again sometime. What do you think?"

"I don't plan to drink another bottle of wine anytime soon!" she laughed.

"You are avoiding the question, Susan. Do you think we could talk like this again sometime?" He was being persistent.

"I can't make any promises, Paul, but under the right circumstances, I have a feeling I would enjoy doing this with you again. I must admit I feel wonderful, and part of that is because of you. But you know what? It is really late, and I have to get some sleep. I have an awful feeling that I will not feel so well in the morning. Hopefully I can get through the day without falling asleep. So I better go now. Do you think you will call me tomorrow night?"

"I'd certainly like to, if that's okay with you."

"Sure, but I might be really tired. Call if you can, and we'll take it from there."

Suzanne pulled a sheet up over her nude body and fell right to sleep after they said good-bye. She slept well, even though it was for only a short time. When the alarm rang, she awoke easily and was pleased to find that she was alert and didn't even have the slightest headache. She realized that she had slept all night with no nightgown on, and then remembered the wonderful feelings she had experienced the night before. It had been a pretty wonderful evening, one she would not mind repeating.

Chapter Eighteen

Questions

LARRY WAS HAVING a pretty good evening, too. He had decided that he would keep one hundred dollars for himself, for incidentals. It felt great to have some spending money for a change. Just knowing he had something in his wallet to fall back on to if he happened to need it. The guys he owed money to would be happy to get nine hundred paid back to them tonight. This weekend he would get another thousand, then after he made it past the first ten deliveries, the money would come rolling in to him and he could get rid of these guys once and for all. That would be the end of his troubles, as far as they were concerned.

So the evening went along well enough. No big traumas came in to the emergency room for a change, and it was a rather uneventful evening. He had arranged to meet the goons at 7:15, right after he got off work. Then he would have to hurry home, to get the car to Suzanne so she could go to work.

He was waiting beside his car in the parking lot when the Lincoln drove up. One of the guys got out on the passenger side and walked over to Larry. "Good thing you came up with this tonight," he said threateningly. "We were just about to pay you a real painful visit." He looked inside the envelope Larry handed over to him, and counted out the hundreds. "Hey, what'cha try'n to pull here? I thought you said you had a grand. You're short, little man." He pushed Larry in the shoulder and knocked him back against his car.

Larry recovered and straightened up. He put his hands up to indicate that he was not going to fight and said, "I know, I know. Something came up and I had to use part of it. But don't you worry. You will get it all, and real soon. The other grand, plus this hundred I still owe you. My word is good. I got you this much, didn't I? Just give me a little more time. I'll have this all paid back within a week. You'll see. You can trust me."

The guy moved at him again and grabbed him by the collar of his shirt. "You better, you little punk. You have one week, not a minute more. And we want it all. One thousand, one hundred dollars. No more playing games with us. You'll see. This is the end of the line. Pay up or things get serious." With that, he tucked the envelope inside his black suit jacket and walked back to the Lincoln.

When Larry got into his car, he realized he was shaking. He didn't like being threatened and pushed around. 'Oh well,' he thought as he started the car. 'One more week and my business with them will be over. And not a day too soon.'

Driving home, Larry decided to take one quick detour. He didn't have much time, but he ran into the all-night grocery store and hurried to the florist department. He wanted to pick up something for Suzanne, something that would say he was happy for her and proud of her. He didn't want to get her flowers, since she got that bouquet yesterday at school. A big helium balloon would be just the thing. He chose a shiny metallic balloon that said "Way to Go!" in bright purple letters. Yes, she'd like that. He thought about getting her a card, too, but he really didn't have the time to pick one out. Besides, no sense in totally wasting his money. It would be gone soon enough, he knew.

When he walked into the apartment, he heard Suzanne talking to Lindsay in her bedroom. 'Ah, the morning debate of what to wear to school,' he thought, as he walked to the kitchen. He quickly tied the string of the balloon on the back of a kitchen chair. Then he turned to the refrigerator and took out the jug of milk. It was nearly empty, but there was probably enough for a couple bowls of cereal. He noticed the almost empty bottle of wine in the back of the refrigerator. 'Good grief, she drank all of this last night?' Larry was quite surprised; Suzanne had never had much more than one glass at a time, that he knew of.

Suzanne and Lindsay came down the hallway to the kitchen. Larry took a good look at his wife as she walked into the kitchen. Her red hair was bouncy around her shoulders. She looked very teacher-like in her light tan colored suit and a green shell top. She wore comfortable tan flats and was carrying her brief case and Lindsay's backpack. Her eyes were gleaming as she noticed the balloon. "Oh, Larry, how sweet of you. Thanks," she bubbled, and then kissed him on the cheek. He smelled her perfume and pulled her closely to his chest. He kissed her neck, nibbling a little on her ear, and she giggled and pulled away. "We're running a little late" she said, and helped Lindsay pour milk on to her cereal. "Eat quickly, honey," she instructed.

Just then the phone rang. Suzanne jumped a little, startled to hear that sound at this time of the day. 'That's odd,' thought Larry. 'She looks a little nervous.'

Suzanne did have a fleeting fear that it might be Paul, though she couldn't imagine what would possess him to call at this time of the day. She breathed a little sigh of relief when she heard Melissa's voice on the other end of the line. "Hi, Suzanne. How are you this morning?" she asked pleasantly.

"Oh, fine. Running a little late, but we'll make it. What's up?"

"I was wondering if we could meet for a few minutes at the daycare center sometime today. Maybe not this morning, if you're running late. We need to look over the donations, and try to figure out just how we are going to get them to the tornado victims. How about 4:30 this afternoon? Would that work for you?" Melissa was quite organized.

"Sure, I can do that. The afternoon is definitely better than this morning. We've got a late start, and I still have to get some gas in the car or we'll never make it there at all. But 4:30 should work fine. I'll see you then." Suzanne finished the call, Lindsay finished her breakfast, and Larry started some toast in the toaster.

"Hey, Suz," he said. "We're almost out of bread and milk. Here, take this money and stop at the store on your way home. Pick up whatever you want. Do you think twenty will do it? Oh, heck, here. Take forty." He reached into his wallet and handed Suzanne two twenty-dollar bills. Her jaw dropped as she asked, "Where did this come from?"

"Don't you worry yourself about that, girl. Just get some groceries and be happy about it." He turned back to the toaster and that was the end of the conversation. Suzanne wondered about what was going on, but was used to his moods when it came to money. She didn't know how he got this money all of a sudden, but they did need milk and a few other things. And with Lindsay's birthday coming up, there would probably be some things she should get for the party. This would sure come in handy.

With Lindsay safely buckled into her seatbelt, Suzanne started the car. She checked the gages and was surprised to see that the gas tank was almost full. That meant that Larry had gotten gas last night. 'What is going on here?' she asked herself. 'Presents, extra grocery money, gas in the car. Where did he get that kind of money, when payday is still a week off? I don't get it.'

Before long, Lindsay was settled into her daycare classroom and Suzanne was pulling into the parking lot at her school. As she walked up the sidewalk in front of the school, she saw a poster hanging on the front door. Getting closer, Suzanne could see it was a picture of herself accepting the plaque from the principal at yesterday's staff meeting. Blue and silver stenciled letters gave her name and new title, Dickinson's Teacher of the Year. Throughout the day, teachers, students, and parents congratulated Suzanne.

Despite her lack of sleep, Suzanne felt the day had gone well. She had managed to keep order on a slightly unusual day. She taught her lessons with enthusiasm and the children were interested and attentive. After school, she got things in order for the next day, wrote a few morning exercises on the blackboard and locked her classroom door. There was still a lot left to do in her day, both at the daycare and at home. And then, there was the hope of a phone call to look forward to.

As she headed to the daycare, Suzanne was aware that traffic was moving slower than usual. The four lanes of the beltway merged down to three, and then two lanes. On the car radio the traffic reporter was talking about a traffic tie-up, involving two cars and an overturned bakery truck. Suzanne inched her way along the highway and eventually arrived at the accident scene. Several fire trucks and police cars were there and an ambulance had just pulled away, sirens screaming. There was a red car upside down in the ditch, another car badly damaged, and a white delivery truck lying on its side, halfway off the road. She caught her breath sharply as she read the lettering on the side of the delivery truck. 'Kastner's Bakery.' Her heart began to beat rapidly. 'Paul drives a delivery truck for Kastner's Bakery. Oh my gosh, I hope that wasn't him in the accident.'

She tried to listen to the car radio for more details on the accident, but there was no additional information available yet. 'I'll just ask him about it when he calls tonight. What's the chance he was in that truck, anyway? There must be dozens of delivery trucks for Kastner's. Couldn't be him." Yet Suzanne couldn't shake the memory of that overturned truck. She was visibly shaken when she finally got to the center, about twenty minutes late for her meeting with Melissa.

"Oh, my god, Suzanne, are you alright?" Melissa asked right away. "You look white as a ghost. What happened?"

Suzanne couldn't tell her about her fears, so she just said, "Traffic was awful. I'm sorry I was late. There was a real bad accident on the beltway, and I guess it rattled me, all that traffic and stuff. Anyway, let me just get a drink of water, and I'll be with you in a second."

The meeting was short and went well. They sorted boxes, making one box of toys, one for boy clothes, one for girl clothes, one for adults, and one for household items. Melissa said she would call the Red Cross to get their suggestions about how to transport the things to the tornado site.

Lindsay was happy to see her mother, who was not usually late. She talked about her day, and said that all of the girls were coming to her party. It was just nine days away! She had it all figured out, and had even made a calendar chart so she could mark off the days. Suzanne smiled at her daughter. So sweet, so happy to be alive, so sure that life was good. 'Keep your cheerful, optimistic outlook, little one. It'll take you places,' she thought.

She turned the car into the parking lot of the grocery store, and they went inside. She picked up milk and bread, then went to the frozen food section and picked out frozen lasagna. Usually she liked to make it from scratch, but tonight she was running late and she was sure Larry would not have started anything before they got home. She even got a large salad from the salad bar, to save time once she got home. Quickly they paid for the groceries in the express lane and hurried on their way. There was plenty of money left over from the forty dollars Larry had given her that morning. She saved the rest of the money, planning to use it for Lindsay's birthday.

Larry had the television on when they got home, and turned to her as they walked in the door. "Did you see that big accident on the beltway? I figured that was why you were late. Looked pretty bad on the news. One guy was killed, they said. Couple of others injured." Suzanne sent Lindsay out of the living room, to change her clothes. She didn't see any reason to expose a four year old to all of the tragedies of the world. She would face enough of that later on.

"Yes, I saw it. Really bad. The red car was upside down. I don't know how it happened, did they say on the news? And who was killed? The driver of the red car, I would bet." Suzanne put the lasagna in the oven and tried to sound just slightly interested in the accident. But she really needed to know if the truck driver was okay.

Larry's answer put her at ease. "Yeah, they said the dead guy was a passenger in the red car. And the driver was driving drunk. What an idiot. Now he killed his friend, and he'll have to live with that memory forever." He went back to watching the television. Sports scores were on.

Suzanne went to her bedroom to change. She sat on the side of the bed and breathed a sigh of relief. At least it wasn't Paul who was killed. But he still might have been involved. But probably not. She would just have to wait and see.

That night, the phone did not ring. Paul did not call. With a heavy heart Suzanne prepared for school the next morning. To make matters worse, it was raining. Not a downpour, just a light drizzle that dampened the streets and her spirits and made the day gloomy and dark. She would have to try her best to get out of this mood, to get over this feeling of dread. She had school to teach, Lindsay to care for, and a million things on her mind. But why didn't he call?

Chapter Nineteen

Rainy Days

IT RAINED ALL day Thursday. All day the sky was overcast. The sun never came out of the clouds. The wind would blow, bending the trees with their young leaves, twisting the trunks and gusting, then quieting. All day rain fell, sometimes in a light drizzle, sometimes heavier and loud. Occasionally thunder rolled, and a few times the sky was lit with lightning high up in the atmosphere. But all day the air was heavy with moisture and sky was dark.

In the third floor apartment, with curtains drawn to block out the occasional lightening flash, Larry slept. Larry liked rainy days, as long as the storm didn't get too wild and windy. He was able to sleep much better when it was cloudy. He did wake up once and look out the window. Few cars moved through the parking lot. A maintenance man hurried from his van to a building over by the pool. Holding an umbrella and splashing in the low puddles, the man looked chilled and soaked to the skin. Larry was glad to be inside, and hoped the storm would be over by evening. Driving in this, at night, would not be fun. Larry went to the closet and pulled his latest magazine from the top of the stack. "Why does she have to keep moving my stuff?"

he murmured to himself. He lay on the bed, turning page after page until he came upon a blond that appealed to him. Within a few minutes, she had aroused him sufficiently and he was able to bring himself to complete satisfaction. He rolled over, wrapped a corner of the bed sheet around himself, and fell back to sleep.

Lindsay liked the rain. On rainy days the daycare children did not go out to the playground. They got to have inside recess and play in the big playroom at the daycare center. The teachers played with them on days like this, huge games of Farmer in the Dell, and Duck, Duck, Goose, and sometimes Red Rover. If they were outside, the teachers usually just watched the kids play, swinging or sliding or chasing. But in the big playroom, the teachers actually played games with the kids. Lindsay liked that.

Suzanne wasn't having a very good day. The children were noisy and felt penned up. When the rain beat especially hard against the classroom windows, all little eyes would turn to watch the storm. She lost their attention, and it was a struggle to pull them back. They gave exaggerated shrieks whenever thunder rolled loudly or lightning cracked. One of the little girls was actually in tears over the storm, and needed special calming. Suzanne felt her patience running short. She just wanted to do her teaching, without all these interruptions.

George didn't like the rain much either. He was getting soaked running from building to building doing his maintenance duties. His feet were cold and wet, even though he was wearing boots. His uniform was wet from the ankles to his knees. His hair was dripping little rivers of rainwater down his back, saturating his t-shirt and giving him a chill. Not a nice day to be out working, but that was the job. He tried not to drip too much water through the apartments where he was making calls. He gratefully accepted a cup of warm coffee here, a hot tea there, and even some fresh baked oatmeal cookies from a little old lady with a sliding door off the track. There were rewards to this line of work; he did have to admit that.

Tim liked the rain. It gave a little variety to the day. School was almost over; the kids were looking for some way to add a little interest to their last days. Finals were intense, and the thunder and lightening of the storm added a little excitement and relief. Of course, it didn't hurt when some of the girls ran in from the parking lot, shrieking with laughter, hair dripping and wet blouses clinging to their bodies like saran wrap. 'Nice on the eyes,' he thought. 'A hell of a lot better than looking at Mr. Bramley and thinking about U.S. Government.' But as the storm continued well into the afternoon, Tim wondered about his deliveries that evening. Not that he minded driving in the rain. But it would be slower going than usual, and that would probably cut into his rate of profit. Oh well. He would just have to hope Mike gave him some really big orders, so he wouldn't have to make as many stops but still make as much commission as usual. He could hope.

Mike got off the phone with his supplier just as a loud crash of thunder rumbled overhead. "Everything is all set for Saturday afternoon, Robin. This just might be it, sweet thing. The chance we have been waiting for. Everything is falling into place. Won't be long, we will be on that cruise ship to the Bahamas, and nobody can stop us. Just a few more months and we will have enough money in the bank to ditch this place. Then we're out of here." Robin smiled, threw the sheets off the bed revealing her perfectly shaped body. "Come here, baby," she said enticingly. "Let's celebrate."

Detective Larson sat in his unmarked car with the engine running. It was chilly and he had the heat turned on low. The wipers made a swish-swish sound as they attempted to clear away the raindrops, which had been falling all day. Larson was watching the entrance to the building to the left of him. If he had this right, Tim Simpson should be pulling up soon. School would be out, and he would be meeting Mike Santini for his instructions and delivery packages. Tim would probably lock the packages into his trunk while he went home and changed into his pizza delivery uniform. 'I sure wish it would stop raining,' the detective said to himself. It was a lousy night to be following a kid delivering pizzas. But it was a job, and this was going to take him places in the department. He would do what he had to do.

The rain continued through the afternoon, through the dinner hour, and long into the night. Larry drove to work in it. Suzanne graded spelling pre-tests with rain beating hard against the roof. Lindsay slept through it. George stayed home, waiting for emergency calls that never came. Tim made his deliveries but didn't have much business in this weather. Detective Larson followed at a distance.

Chapter Twenty

What a Relief

'**ANOTHER NIGHT WITHOUT** a phone call. So what does this mean?' Suzanne wondered the next morning. 'Could mean a lot of things. He was hurt in the accident Wednesday, and he can't call because of that.' She paused as she thought of another possibility. 'He never wants to talk to me again, after our last little adventure. He got what he wanted from me once, and isn't interested in it any more with me. Or maybe he just can't call for some other reason.'

Suzanne looked at herself in the bathroom mirror. 'So, how do you feel about that, girl?' she asked herself. 'Well, I miss him. Strange but true, I miss talking to him. I miss that little thrill when the phone rings. I miss the excitement and mystery he adds to my life. And I wouldn't mind having phone sex with him again. I did rather enjoy that, something new, something totally un-Suzanne. Fun, risky, kinky, and pleasing. But it's also probably not a good thing for me. This is taking entirely too much time out of my normal life. And where is it going to lead? Nowhere, that's where. But why does it have to lead anywhere? Why can't I just live for the moment, enjoy what I have, get a little pleasure from wherever I find it?' And so this internal reflection continued as she got ready for work. Nothing was resolved by it, of course, except that her longing for a call from him was heightened and her mood was set on edge, wondering if he ever would call again. She wished with all her heart that he would call that evening.

Friday night at dinner Larry announced that he would be working overtime for the next few weeks, which meant working every Friday and Saturday evening. He didn't know how long it would last, but maybe a couple of months, maybe more. He would take all the extra hours he could get; they could sure use the money. And maybe they could get enough ahead that they could get a better car pretty soon. The one they had was on its last leg.

Suzanne wasn't crazy about the idea of getting another car. Even though she knew that their current car could not last a whole lot longer, she was hesitant to take on another debt. The overtime would eventually end, and how could they be making car payments on Larry's regular salary? But she knew better than to say anything about that now. He was feeling pretty good lately about the way things were going, and he would just get all upset if she threw cold water on some of his hot plans. Besides, she was happy to see that he was trying to make some extra money, at least. He could have turned down the overtime, but he did realize that the extra hours would really help to meet their bills. So that was a good thing, and Suzanne certainly didn't want to say anything that would seem like she didn't appreciate it, or support his judgment. The whole thing might backfire if she did that.

Another consideration… If Larry were at work more often, she would be alone more often. That could mean more phone calls, more phone sex, and more time that she could spend exploring her own sexuality. That thought intrigued her more and more.

So when Larry left for work that night, Suzanne just assumed that he would be working at the hospital. She had no way of knowing that he left their apartment to walk quietly across the hall to Mike and Robin's place. She had no way of knowing that he stayed only a few minutes, long enough to get a list of addresses, directions, several small packages, and ten one hundred dollar bills. She had no way of knowing that Larry's eyes had lingered a while on the shapely form of their neighbor. She had no way of knowing the thoughts going through Larry's head just then. Totally unaware of the new pathway her husband was taking, Suzanne went about her evening chores and went to bed. Her last thought before falling asleep was that she wished Paul would call.

*   *   *   *   *

Very, very early Saturday morning, Suzanne got her wish. She was so relieved she actually started to cry when she heard his voice. "Oh my god, Susan, what's the matter? Are you alright?" he asked her. And he was truly concerned.

Between her sniffs and sobs, Suzanne told him about her fears, that he was hurt in the accident, or that he just was never going to call her again. He was touched by her sweetness, and excited by her emotion. Not only did this woman care about him, she was also getting emotionally attached to him. That could be both good and bad, he knew. It was fine for now, but could lead to a real dependence and that could be quite restricting. It was kind of flattering, too. Had he made such an impression on her that she was actually in tears over the thought of 'loosing' him? Or more likely, she was so desperate for some sexual excitement that she would be lost herself if he were no longer in her life, in her fantasies. George felt a power surge through him. This woman really wanted him.

So he put her fears aside with one simple sentence. "Oh, baby, I've wanted to call you every minute of every day and night since the last time we talked."

Suzanne caught her breath and barely whispered, "Oh." Then she spoke a bit more bravely, more in control now, more restrained. "I was just so worried. And when you didn't call, I let my imagination take over and it all got out of hand. I'm glad you are okay, and I'm glad you called me."

"I've let my imagination get away with me a little bit in the last two days, too," George said. "I've imagined you a lot of ways. You really enjoyed the other night didn't you? Before I called, and while we were on the phone together. I could tell you were really turned on. Have you ever done that before, the phone sex I mean?"

"Gosh, no!" she exclaimed. "I've barely even touched myself before, and never while I was talking to someone on the phone. Never. But I would do it again, right now, if you wanted to." Suzanne didn't know it, but she was already becoming aroused, just talking to him. She had enjoyed the feeling she had discovered the other night, and she wanted more of that good feeling now. She liked to hear his voice, to know that the things she was doing turned him on, too. And just the thought of Paul touching himself while he was thinking about her gave Suzanne a shiver.

Suzanne cradled the phone with one hand, and let the fingertips of the other gently brush her chin and move down her neck while she leaned her head back. Slowly, and very lightly, her fingers inched towards her breasts. She smiled.

Chapter Twenty-One

How It Works

MILES AWAY, LARRY was driving. He had made four stops already tonight, and had only one delivery address left on the list. Glancing to the seat beside him, he couldn't help but wonder a bit about the package he was about to deliver. It was the biggest of all the packages Mike had given him, but yet it was no bigger than a shoebox. The other packages had been smaller, one even almost flat. His instructions were to collect envelopes of cash before each delivery. "Count the money, hand over your package, and leave. No small talk, just collect and go." Whatever. Easy work, that's for sure. Except one place he had been tonight was in a real nasty part of town.

Larry turned up the radio and sang along with Jan and Dean. 'Two girls for every guy, oh yeah, wouldn't that be sweet.' His thoughts wandered toward Robin, and he thought again about that glimpse of flesh she had given him. And the smile that said so much. Now that was sweet!

He turned the car onto the beltway and headed for a better section of town. The road was nearly deserted, which was just fine with him. He could skirt around town quick as a wink, with no traffic.

But he knew he could not be caught speeding. Mike had been very clear about that tonight. "Don't call attention to yourself. No trouble with the police." Larry scanned the road for police cars and thought. 'Don't you worry, Mike ole' buddy. I am not going to mess up this job. You can count on me.'

Larry signaled and slowed to make the exit. 'Now this is some kinda neighborhood,' he thought as he cruised slowly down the wide street. He drove past stately homes, most lit brightly with exterior landscape lighting. 'Must be million dollar homes here,' he said to himself and whistled as he drove past a huge Mediterranean style mansion. Every house on this street was surrounded with tall fences and guardhouses at the gate. Larry glanced again at the address. Yes, he was on the right street, just a little further, according to the house numbers.

He crested a hill and caught sight of a monstrous house sitting far back from the road. He neared the guard gate, checked the big brass numbers, and slowed to turn in at the drive. 'Probably ten acres for a front yard,' thought Larry. The driveway curved in a half circle. At the top of the circle stood the guardhouse, manned with at least two guards and one Doberman. One of the guards stepped forward as Larry slowed the car and put it in park. He left the engine running and rolled down his window. "I have a delivery for someone at this address," he said. The guard said, "I will handle the delivery." He reached into his uniform jacket and withdrew a long white envelope. He handed it to Larry, who took it, counted out the correct amount of cash, and placed the envelope on the seat beside him. He picked up the package, gave it to the guard through the window, and said, "Thank you." Then Larry put the car into gear and eased it around the circle, back out onto the main street.

He drove a short distance down the street and stopped the car. His hands were shaking as he gathered four white envelopes from under the car seat and placed them with the one he had just gotten. 'Oh my god, this is a lot of money. No wonder Mike is willing to give me a nice cut, if he is pulling in this much every night.' A quick thought entered his head. If he were to take off now, he could get half way around the world with this money, and live pretty well for a long time. But no, Mike trusted him. And who would want to live looking over your shoulder all the time, anyway?

Larry reached behind himself and grabbed a large brown mailing envelope off the back seat. Mike had given it to him, along with a key for a locker at the bus station in a town about twenty minutes away. He was to take the large envelope, with the five smaller envelopes of cash inside, to the bus station and leave it all in locker number C174.

The bus station was almost empty. A few travelers sitting with suitcases waited at one gate. The ticket agent was washing the glass windows around his counter. Over in the corner away from what few people were in the station, an old man lay stretched out on the bench, sleeping. A couple of teenage travelers stood by the vending machines, getting candy bars and sodas for the trip ahead.

Larry found the locker with no trouble and opened it with the key Mike had given him. He placed the brown envelope inside, closed the door, and locked it again. Pocketing the key, Larry fumbled for some change and got a candy bar from the machine for himself. Larry went to a trash can sitting next to the vending machine. He threw the candy wrapper away, and then, as instructed, tore up the address list and threw it away too. He walked confidently back to his car. His first night was almost over. Now he needed to find a gas station, head for home, and maybe stop somewhere and get some breakfast. It was only four in the morning, but he had nearly an hours drive before he got home. But since Suzanne wouldn't be expecting him till after seven, he had some time to kill anyway. Breakfast would be good.

Truck stops always have the best food, and the best coffee, Larry had always believed. He had passed signs for one just down the road a bit. He decided to get gas there and breakfast, too. As he sat at the counter, sipping coffee and waiting for his ham and eggs to arrive, he had time to take stock of the evening. It sure had been easy. And he had earned one thousand dollars! Just five, well maybe six, more deliveries to go, and he would have his big debt paid. Then he would be able to put a bunch away. It was true; he really was going to need a better car. But he also wanted to get some money ahead for other important things. Like Lindsay's college. It was never too early to start saving for a big thing like that. And maybe he could start investing, and get some fast growth from his money. Then there was always his big dream, to make a bet at the racetrack and walk out a big winner. Yes, he could sure use this money. Luck was sure shining on Larry now!

Breakfast finished, Larry made a stop in the men's room, then placed a call from the phone booth. He would be meeting with the goons in the Lincoln at the hospital parking lot at six-thirty that evening. He would pay them one thousand dollars, and yes, he did know he still owed them one hundred. They would have it just as soon as he got his next paycheck from the hospital. Next week.

Business taken care of, Larry pulled into a parking space in front of his apartment building at about seven-fifteen. He sat in his car for a few minutes, listening to the radio and looking up to the third floor. He wondered if they were asleep together, the woman with the perfect body and his new boss. He wondered if they were good in bed together. He wondered how she liked it. He had a feeling she liked to be in control. She sure was controlling his thoughts right now.

Eagerly Larry flipped the radio off, jumped out of his car, and bounded up the stairs to his apartment. He unlocked his door and walked quietly into the apartment. Everyone was still asleep. He went to his bedroom and closed the door. Suzanne lay curled up in the middle of the bed. He went to her, dropping his shirt on the floor. She stirred and moved her hand to her breast. Larry watched as a slight smile formed on her lips.

Chapter Twenty-Two

Party Plans and Potential Problems

"ONE MORE WEEK till my birthday," Lindsay sang joyfully. She and her mom were cleaning the apartment after breakfast. Larry was asleep, so Lindsay sang softly. They had a lot of fun stuff to do today, so they were hurrying to get the routine chores done. Then they would go shopping and get everything they needed for the upcoming party. Lindsay had decided on a Barbie theme weeks ago, and Suzanne was going to make a beautiful cake. She had seen the directions in a party book. The cake would be layered in tiers, with a doll's body stuck in the center. Once frosted, it would look like the doll was wearing a beautiful gown. Although she had never made one like this before, Suzanne was confident that she could do it. They would buy all the ingredients today, and she would make the cake later next week.

The girls were going to love this party, she hoped. She was not able to go all out, the way some parents did, with birthday parties at McDonald's or Chuck E Cheese's, or by hiring a clown or magician or having pony rides. No, this would be a simple, basic party. Five little girls getting together to laugh, play, eat cake and ice cream, and share in the joy of the celebration. Suzanne felt she knew kids pretty well. These girls would be quite satisfied with the party. You didn't need to impress children with all the bells and whistles. Only after exposure to those things would they come to expect, even demand, that more be done for them. For now, four-year-old girls would be content with a cake that looks like a doll in a beautiful gown.

Chores done, they headed for the store. Cake, frosting, ice cream, pink plates and cups and Barbie napkins. Suzanne was grateful for the extra money Larry had given her. There was enough for a few special touches for this party after all. Next they went to a craft store and got the doll form for the cake. Suzanne also found some inexpensive strands of beads, to use on the cake and as bracelets for the girls. Everything was falling into place.

Back home, they had lunch and decided there was time to go to the pool for a little while. Suzanne wanted Lindsay to take a nap first, and she took that opportunity to finish up her schoolwork. Report cards were due in the principal's office by Tuesday, and she wanted to get hers done this weekend. There was always so much to do at the end of the school year. Friday would be the last day of school for the children, but teachers were expected to return for two days the next week, to do inventory and organize and clean their rooms.

So with school festivities and final preparations for Lindsay's party, the week flew by. In addition, the tornado relief project was completed, with a pick-up by the Red Cross truck on Wednesday afternoon. Both Suzanne and Melissa were there to see the donations loaded and on their way to the tornado victims. Mrs. Williams had called the local newspaper, and a reporter was there, with a cameraman, to make a little plug for the daycare center. It was always good to have your name in print, and this was free advertising for the center. Mrs. Williams understood the importance of good public relations.

There were several phone calls from Paul throughout the week. Sometimes they simply talked about events of the day, and twice they talked of fantasies and secret pleasures. Both of them enjoyed these conversations, Suzanne because it helped her to express herself in new ways, and George because he felt the power of control over yet another woman. And for the time being, he was content with the phone sex. She was getting really good at it, and could turn him on with a phrase or just the tone of her voice. Sure, he hoped for more eventually, but for now he was satisfied with the phone sex as often as he could get it. Besides, he had seen her many times now, around the apartment buildings and at the pool. She didn't know him, of course, but he was able to see her and sometimes hear her voice. Once, in the hallway of her building, he came out of a first floor apartment just as she was going up the stairs to her own apartment. He stood at the base of the stairs and watched her climb agilely to the top floor. She had no idea he was there, but he had been so close to her, he could practically smell her perfume as it lingered in the stairwell. And the view he got of her slender legs in their silken stockings was amazing. He was so glad she was wearing a skirt. It was a thrill he would not soon forget.

The week went fast for Larry, too. He made his four deliveries on Saturday night, following instructions completely. He worked at the hospital as usual the rest of the week. Friday night, the day before Lindsay's party, he was ready to work for Mike again. As he knocked on Mike's door at a little past ten, he was actually humming to himself. This was the night he would start making commission money. He had one more delivery to make to break even, and then he was on his own. 'Oh, well, except for that one-hundred I still owe, but that will be taken care of tonight too.'

Robin answered the door. The sight of her made Larry's heartbeat quicken. What a looker. And especially tonight. Evidently she had been working out because she had on one of those athletic t-shirts that left little to the imagination. She sure had some full breasts. Larry could hardly take his eyes off them but did avert his glance just as Mike walked in from the bedroom. He also had been working out, for his tank top was wet with perspiration and his chest was heaving as he caught his breath. He gave Larry the list of addresses and five small packages. Then he asked Larry for the key to the bus locker, and exchanged it for a different key. He explained, "Every week or so, we change the location of the drop-off point. When we do, I give you a new key, and new directions. Simple as that. Now, you make these deliveries tonight, and you will get paid commission on all but one. That's the one you still owe me. But after that first delivery, you start making cash for yourself. Tomorrow night, I will have your cut ready for you when you come over for the next list. Okay?"

"Sure, Mike, no problem," said Larry. He was trying to concentrate on what Mike was saying, but it was sure hard, with Robin in the room. She had gotten back on the treadmill, and was walking at a quick pace. With every step, her body bounced a little, and those big breasts just quivered. Beads of sweat were forming around her neck, and began to make a little trickling river downwards, moving slowly but surely towards the deep valley of her cleavage. The t-shirt was already tight, but with the addition of each drop of sweat, Larry could see her breasts becoming more and more pronounced. He had to turn his eyes away. Wouldn't do for Mike to see him ogling his wife.

So Larry left quickly, and as he headed down the first flight of stairs, Mike locked the door and turned to Robin. He reached over to turn off her machine, and gave her rump a pat. "You like that tight thing, baby?" she asked, and pulled him even closer to her. "Pick me up. I want to feel your strong hands on me. "

Mike lifted her with both his palms cupping her cheeks. She smothered his face with kisses, and their sweat mingled as he carried her to the sofa. She moaned with pleasure as he stripped off first his clothing, then what remained of hers. She knelt on the sofa, facing the wall and commanded, "Take me this way." Gladly, Mike did as he was told.

Across the hall, Lindsay was supposed to be sleeping. "But I can't Mommy, I can't fall asleep. Can I watch you do the frosting? Please?" Her pleading was hard to resist, so Suzanne let her stay up and watch as the cake layers were transformed into a beautiful pink and white ball gown. The doll body, stuck securely deep into the middle of the cake, was also covered with pink frosting, to resemble a bodice. Then the jewels and beads were added. Suzanne showed her daughter where to place them, and before long they were gazing with wonder at their creation. "It looks better than the one in the picture book, Mommy!" Lindsay exclaimed with joy.

They placed the cake in the center of the table and went to the kitchen to clean up the frosting bowl and utensils. That's when Suzanne noticed that it was after midnight already. "Sweetie, you'd better get to bed. Or else you might be so tired for your party you will sleep all day and miss the whole thing!" Lindsay giggled at that thought and said "Mommy, I won't. I couldn't!" But she was stifling a yawn, and Suzanne ushered her down the hall and tucked her into her bed. With a kiss on the forehead and a wish for sweet dreams, Suzanne returned to the kitchen with a tired but happy smile on her face.

The phone rang and she caught it on the first jingle. Speaking quietly so as not to wake Lindsay, if she was asleep even, she said, "Hi!" It was earlier than usual, but she just knew who it was!

He said, "Hey, you sure did answer quick. Were you waiting for me?"

She chuckled, and said, "Honestly, I was just walking into the kitchen. Would you believe Lindsay just went to bed? She might not even be asleep yet. So I can't talk long, if you know what I mean. Besides, I am absolutely exhausted."

"Schools out, right?" he asked, but he already knew. "So you are on vacation!"

"Not exactly! There's two more days for teachers next week. But the first hurdle is tomorrow, Lindsay's party. We just finished decorating the cake, and it did turn out nicely, if I do say so myself."

"What time's the party?" George asked.

"The girls arrive at three. I am hoping to take them to the playground for a while, to give Larry a little extra time to sleep. He's been working so much lately. Then we'll come back up here for cake and ice cream and presents. I have some party games planned, too. And I brought my dress-up clothes from school, with hats and boas and other girlie stuff. I think they'll like that. A Barbie dress-up tea party. The moms come back to get their girls at 4:30. Except for Jenna, who is going to spend the night with Lindsay. It will be her first sleepover, but I think she'll be fine. She knows me, and is actually pretty mature for her age. I don't think she'll get homesick. But I think it would be best if you did not call tomorrow night. Do you mind?"

"Do I mind? Well, I understand, if that's what you mean. But I will sure miss talking to you. I'll be thinking about you tomorrow, with all those little girls! You must have the patience of a saint! You amaze me!"

"You amaze me, too! I'm amazed that you call me, and don't mind if I tell you I'm tired or just not 'in the mood.' You know? You're amazing, all right, and I like you that way!"

"Hey, that's what friends are for." George was already getting ready to hang up and go home. "Anyway, why don't you put your sweet little self into that bed of yours, and get some sleep. But don't forget to dream sweet dreams. Maybe I will see you there, in your dreams."

"You are there, more often than you know," she said seductively. And George smiled as they said goodnight and he locked the office door. It would have been nice to do it with her on the phone, but sometimes you just have to give in to the woman. Makes them feel like you really care, like you are not after just one thing. Of course, George knew better.

Chapter Twenty-Three

Summer Surprises

"WHERE DID THE summer go? How could it possibly be time to get back to school and back to work and back to routines? Are you happy you will still be teaching first grade this year?" Melissa was full of questions. "I've been switched from second to third, so I have that entire new curriculum to learn. And it's like starting from scratch with lesson plans. Everything is new! But actually, I'm really looking forward to the new age level. I guess it's probably good to switch sometimes, keeps us on our toes, you know?"

"I'm happy to be sticking with my first graders again this year. I might switch someday, but not this year. I am very happy with things the way they are, thank you!" Suzanne was busy cleaning out the wardrobe room at Lindsay's daycare center. Summer was just about over. The summer play had been a great success, due in part to the wonderful costumes Suzanne had created for the children to wear. Now it was time to straighten the closets, wash the costumes, and store them carefully for use another time.

Melissa went on, "Of course, you are always on your toes any-way, Miss First Grade Teacher of the Year for Linn County. That school is lucky to have you. If you ever want to get transferred, I could recommend Lincolnwood. We would see each other every day. What fun!" The two did enjoy working with each other, and had become even better friends through the summer.

"It's good that I like you so much, since our daughters think they are actually sisters and spend just about every waking minute with each other or wanting to be with each other! I think I could put my car on auto-pilot and it just knows how to get to your house without any help from me!"

Melissa closed the closet door firmly. She put a tanned arm around her friend. "The girls may think they are sisters, but I'm inclined to think of you as my sister, too." Yes, they had become better friends over the summer. The Anderson's spent many days at the apartment pool, and Suzanne and Lindsay were often at Melissa's home for picnics, or just to let the girls play together. Neither Lindsay nor Jenna had been enrolled in the daycare center throughout the summer, since both moms had summer breaks from school. So they saw each other as often as they could. They were both looking forward to the start of another school year, so they could be together at daycare again while their mothers were teaching.

"I never had a real sister, you know," Melissa went on, "Just brothers. I always wanted someone to tell my deepest secrets to, someone to share clothes with, and giggle with at night."

"We might be a little too old for some of that stuff!" laughed Suzanne. 'Besides,' she thought, 'There are some secrets I won't be telling anyone.'

The two women gathered the bags of laundry and walked together out of the building. Suzanne opened the trunk of her new car and they gently set the soiled costumes inside. "I think it's great Larry got you this new car." Melissa smiled, happy for her friend.

"Well, it was sure a shock to me!" Suzanne said. True, the car was a couple of years old, but it had low mileage, dependable tires, and a few nice extras, like a tape deck. "Larry has been working so much overtime all summer. We hardly ever saw him; he was working almost every night. But we were able to get this car, and we really did need it. I wasn't too happy about the idea of car payments again, but it does look like things are beginning to lighten up for us financially. It's about time!" It was easy to talk to Melissa, about this anyway.

They called the girls in from the playground, where they had been happily chattering with Katie, Allison, and Abby. It seemed like those five girls had become quite the social team. "Just look at them," Suzanne said to Melissa. "This time next year they will all be headed for Kindergarten. Our little babies are really growing up fast."

"I hope they can deal with the separation once they start school." Melissa reminded her. "Since Jenna and Lindsay won't be going to the same school, it's going to be rough on them. They have been together since they were babies!" Suzanne nodded and watched the two girls as they skipped together across the playground, waving good-bye to their other friends. Melissa continued, "You know, maybe you really should consider a transfer to Lincolnwood for next year. Then Lindsay could be enrolled in school there, and the girls could stay together. You really should think about it."

"Or you could transfer to Dickinson!" Suzanne laughed. "Change is hard for me, too, you know!"

The girls got in their cars and settled into their seat belts. Suzanne spoke to Melissa over the tops of their vehicles. "So, you're coming over around three tomorrow? We'll do the pool for a few hours, then take the girls out for pizza, right?"

Melissa nodded as she opened her car door. "Our last free Saturday of the summer! Oh geez. How did it go by so fast?"

"They say time flies when you're getting older!" Suzanne laughed as she got in her car. They waved and headed out of the parking lot, turning in different directions at the exit.

Oh, yes, it had been a good summer. Lots of time for relaxing and fun. A chance to try something new and creative with the costumes. A happy, healthy daughter. A husband who finally seemed to be getting himself settled and serious about providing for the family. And an experience in sensuality that would remain a secret forever.

Yes, Suzanne had had a good summer. She had learned a lot, experimented a lot, and gained some self-assurance and an open mind. Oh, yes, it had been a good summer.

As they parked the car, Suzanne saw a nicely dressed man coming out of their building. He was wearing dress pants and a shirt and tie. 'Unusual to see someone so nicely dressed this time of year. Probably some kind of door to door salesman,' she thought. He was carrying a briefcase. The man smiled politely as they met on the sidewalk.

"Mrs. Rogers?" he asked. When Suzanne stopped and nodded, he held out his hand to shake hers. "I'm David Thompson, with Investor's Mutual Life Insurance Company." He handed her his business card. "I was just upstairs doing some business with your husband. I recognized you and your daughter from the photos in your apartment. Nice to meet you."

"Mr. Thompson," she acknowledged. "Did you say life insurance? Larry hadn't mentioned getting any life insurance."

"Well, he called me in to discuss a policy. I'm sure he will tell you all about it when you get upstairs. He seemed very pleased with some of the retirement programs I suggested. Well, I won't keep you. Nice to meet you." With that, Mr. Thompson got into his car and drove away, leaving Suzanne standing on the sidewalk, puzzling over the events of the last few minutes.

'Insurance policies? Retirement programs? I never would have imagined that Larry would be talking to someone about those things. Planning for the future? What a change!' She walked slowly up the stairs to their apartment, giving herself time to think.

As soon as Lindsay was in the apartment Larry scooped her up and danced her around the room in his arms. Her legs were dangling and she was shrieking with laughter. Suzanne had to smile. This was fun to watch, the father playing with the daughter. It didn't happen often, so she wanted to take it all in, savor the moment.

Larry put the little girl down on the sofa and went to dance with his wife. Her arms were full of laundry from the center, so first he took one plastic bag, then the other and waltzed them around the room, only to be dropped on the sofa beside his still laughing daughter. Then he took his wife in his arms and began a silly dance, kind of like a tango, up and down the hall. Back to the sofa they danced, and collapsed in a laughing heap, man, wife, and child tumbling together with costumes and sofa pillows. It was a delightful time!

"So, you're in a pretty good mood, I would say," Suzanne said as she struggled to free herself from the costumes tangled around her legs. Larry helped her pack the clothing back into the plastic bags as he explained to her about the insurance policy he planned to take out so that she and Lindsay would be provided for, if anything should happen to him. There was a cash value in it, too, which they could use for Lindsay's college expenses when the time came.

Suzanne didn't know what to say. She was filled with a mix of emotions. She was stunned, to say the least, and grateful, and proud, and relieved, and so happy. Finally Larry was taking an interest in the family, in bettering life for them all. She didn't know how this all had come about, but she was happy, very happy.

Oh, yes, it had been a very good summer.

Chapter Twenty-four

It's Getting Hot in Here

EARLY SEPTEMBER IN southern Maryland can be warm. Temperatures in the upper 80's are normal, and this had been a really hot summer. When Suzanne and Lindsay got home from school one afternoon, they were in for a surprise, and it wasn't a very pleasant one. The temperature in their third floor apartment had reached close to one hundred degrees. It was sweltering. Evidently the air conditioning unit had broken.

Larry had left a note on the table. "Too hot in here. Went to the pool to cool off. Maintenance should be here soon." Suzanne let Lindsay have some cold fruit juice and watch a video. At least that way she was relatively still and not exerting too much in the heat.

Suzanne got herself a glass of ice water and went to the bedroom to change clothes. She put on shorts and a sleeveless shirt and put her hair up in a bouncy ponytail, which was much cooler than having her long hair hanging down her neck. She had just started fixing a salad for dinner when there was a knock at the door.

George had been waiting for this opportunity. When the maintenance call came in from her husband, George knew right away that he would take the call, and that he would wait until she was home from work before he went to the apartment to see what was wrong with the air conditioner. He hadn't counted on the husband leaving an hour before, leaving George alone with the woman he still thought of as Susan. All he knew for sure was now he would finally have a chance to see her up close and talk to her a bit. It made him more than a little excited.

When Suzanne answered the door, it was all George could do to control himself. He thought for sure she would be able to hear his heart beating wilding in his chest. Did she wonder about the beads of perspiration that formed on his brow? He knew she surely must have noticed the bulge in his pants.

With a little quaver in his voice, George nodded to her as she opened the door for him. "Afternoon, Mrs. Rogers. I'm here to check on your air conditioner."

She stepped back and opened the door wide for him. "I'm sure glad to see you. It must be nearly one hundred in here." She led him out onto the balcony, where the A.C. unit was housed. George set his tools down and turned to her. "This is the third unit I have had to work on this week. These units have had to work pretty hard this summer. Guess they have a right to break down now and then. Too bad it has to happen on such a hot day though!" She smiled at him and he turned to his work.

Before long George came in from the balcony. "Well, I have some good news, and some bad news."

"Okay, give it to me. But be gentle!" Suzanne laughed.

George wanted to give it to her, all right, and he would be very gentle. But he restrained himself from saying so, of course. He just laughed and said, "Well, the unit is fixable and it's not going to be all that expensive. The part you need is only about $47.00. That's the good news." He stopped and waited for her response.

"And the bad news…?" she questioned.

"The bad news is, I don't have the part on hand, and will have to go pick it up tomorrow morning, so you won't have any A.C.

tonight. I'm afraid it's going to be pretty uncomfortable sleeping here tonight."

Suzanne groaned. "That doesn't sound like much fun! But what else can we do? I guess we will get through the night, and things will be better tomorrow."

"Do you have some friends you could spend the night with?" he asked. "Or maybe you could get a hotel room for the night?"

Suzanne gave a kind of chuckle and said, "No, the hotel idea is out of the question. But we do have some friends I could call. Thanks for the suggestion!"

"I hope you can work something out. It's a pity to stay here in this oven if you don't have to. I should be back here with the part about ten tomorrow. Will there be anyone here to let me in?"

"I'm not sure. Sometimes my husband is home, but lately his work schedule is changing a lot. I don't know if he is off tomorrow or not."

"Well, if he isn't here, I can just let myself in with the master key, if that is all right with you."

"Sure, that's fine."

George went back to the balcony to pack up his tools. Then he took a work report form from the side of the toolbox. He filled out a section of the report, and then turned to give the paper to Susan. She had gone to the kitchen and he saw her there, standing on her tiptoes, trying to reach something on a high shelf. George just stood and watched her an extra long moment. 'God, she's really beautiful,' he thought. Her long leg muscles were stretched taught, and her arms were extended far above her head. Her body appeared sleek and firm, made especially so in this stretched-out position. Her fingertips were just barely brushing the large bowl she was trying to get down from the top shelf.

"Here, let me help you with that," he said quietly. Before he knew it, he was standing close beside her, reaching over her, nearly touching her with the length of his whole body. Wanting to, but daring not. He reached the bowl and placed it on the counter. Suzanne smiled shyly up at him. "Thanks. Sometimes I forget how short I am! I always think I can reach up there, but I usually end up getting a stool to stand on." She had noticed his closeness, and was surprised to find herself feeling a little giddy and embarrassed. Was her face flushed? She took a step back from him and it seemed she could breathe better now.

"No problem. Glad I could help. You need to sign this form, as authorization for me to come into your apartment tomorrow." Suzanne signed the paper and his hand brushed hers ever so lightly as she handed it back to him. A surge of electricity tingled through his fingers and raced up his arm. He almost pulled his hand back at the touch, but could not. Did she feel it too? Did she notice his reaction? No. She seemed just fine, nothing unusual had happened after all.

"Okay then, I'll be back tomorrow and have this taken care of for you. By the time you get home from work tomorrow afternoon, your place should be nice and cool."

She opened the door for him and said, "Thanks again." As she closed and locked the door, he stood in the hall and looked at her signature on the paper. S. Rogers. Every letter was formed neatly and correctly, just as you would expect from a teacher. George took a deep breath and folded the paper neatly and put it in his chest pocket. This had been a very exciting visit for him. He wanted her now more than ever. How long would he have to wait? How long?

When Larry came home from the pool a little while later, Suzanne was on the phone with Melissa. Larry gathered that Lindsay would be spending the night there, due to the heat in the apartment. He went to dress and when he came back he asked, "What did the maintenance man say?"

"We need a part, which he has to pick up tomorrow morning, so he'll be here after that to fix it. Will you be home tomorrow morning? He said if you're not home, he could let himself in with the master key." Suzanne set the salad on the table and Lindsay poured ice water for everyone. While they were eating, Suzanne explained to Lindsay that she would be staying over night at Jenna's. The little girl was thrilled, just as her mom had expected. After the table was cleared, Lindsay packed an overnight bag and Suzanne drove her to her friend's house.

Melissa was concerned about Suzanne. "I don't know why you just won't stay here for the night, too," she said, but Suzanne was insistent that she needed to be home. "Do you have a fan at least?"

"Yes, we have one."

"Then let me give you another one, so you can have some cross ventilation." Melissa turned to the girls. "How about some ice cream? Wouldn't that taste good right now?" Together they went into the kitchen and Suzanne helped scoop out the ice cream. Melissa's husband Tom brought the fan up from their basement, and set it by the front door. After ice cream and goodbye hugs, Suzanne was on her way back home alone.

It was a quiet drive home, and Suzanne enjoyed the solitude. She had time to think. She was aware that something had happened this afternoon. When the maintenance man stood close beside her in the kitchen, when their bodies nearly touched, she had felt a charge, an energy surging through her. It was almost like she could have turned to him and let him gather her into his arms. Where did this strange feeling come from? A few months ago she would never have had these kinds of thoughts. True, her marriage was not the greatest, and there were things lacking both physically and emotionally. But she had never considered straying or becoming involved with someone else. She took her marriage vows seriously. A few months ago, she would have pulled herself away from any situation that was even the slightest bit improper. But instead, now here she was, rather enjoying the closeness with this stranger. And her mind was fantasizing about being with him in intimate ways.

So what had changed to make her more open to the attentions of another man? Where did these thoughts come from? Why now? And was it such a bad thing? What could be wrong with the thoughts, if they led to no actions?

But maybe there was a progression here. Maybe one thing could lead to another and then suddenly she would find herself wondering how she had arrived at another place, a place where the arms of another man were holding her and his lips were on hers.

If a journey begins with the first step, what was her first step on this trip? Suzanne was still pondering this as she parked the car and took Melissa's fan from the trunk. There was only one thing that could have brought her to this new place.

Her relationship with Paul. That had to be what had made her more open to the advances of a man she didn't even know. Not that the maintenance man had made any moves on her, really, but Suzanne had opened her imagination to the possibility that he would want to, and that she would enjoy responding. It all had to come from her openness with Paul. That was the only thing that had really changed, the only thing that Suzanne could pinpoint as being the first step on the journey.

But what was her destination? That was the real question.

As Suzanne entered the apartment, she felt a breeze blowing through the living room. The balcony door was open, and a fan was pulling air from the outside into the apartment. The outside air was slightly cooler than the temperature of the room and already it seemed that the apartment was more comfortable.

Suzanne found a note from Larry in the kitchen. "Borrowed a fan from the neighbors. Hope the apt. cools off so you can get some sleep." Then she noticed that an oscillating fan was set up in the bedroom, and with the two windows open, the room was actually almost comfortable. 'I wonder who loaned this to Larry. I didn't know he even really knew anybody in the building.'

Suzanne took Melissa's fan into Lindsay's room and set it in front of the open window. She turned it on so that it was pulling hot air out of the apartment and blowing it to the outside. 'This ought to help, too,' she said to herself.

Back in her bedroom, Suzanne turned off the lights and undressed in the darkness. With the windows open and curtains pulled to the sides, she did not want to change with the lights on, so someone outside could look in and she her. Larry might like that thought, someone watching them make love, but Suzanne was not really into that. 'At least not yet anyway,' she thought with a little chuckle. Then she stood still, shook her head and wondered why in the world she would let a thought like that slip into her thinking.

She put on a short little nightgown, one with matching panties. Then she walked into the kitchen and got a glass of iced tea. Settling in at the table with her grade book and phonics tests, she began to grade papers from the class work of the day. When that was done, she started cutting lettering for a bulletin board she was making. This was a part of teaching that Suzanne really liked, the chance to get a little creative.

After packing up all her papers and putting the bulletin board letters into a folder and packing that into her briefcase, Suzanne went to the kitchen. She rinsed out the tea glass and placed it into the dishwasher, then cleaned the salad bowls from dinner. While wiping off the counter tops, she recalled again the feeling of excitement she had felt when that man was standing close, reaching around her and nearly covering her body with his own. Had he done that on purpose, to see her reaction? Did he notice how flustered his closeness made her? Did he have any idea what she had been thinking?

Unbeknownst to her, the very man she was thinking about sat at a picnic table in the courtyard outside her building. He was watching her movements through the apartment, imagining her activities as she moved from room to room. He could never actually see her, but could only judge her movements based on the lighting changes. When first the kitchen light went out, and then the living room went dark, he knew she was headed to the bedroom. He lit another cigarette, hoping to catch a glimpse of her at the bedroom window. He waited in vain, however, and after finishing the last drag on his cigarette, he made his way to the office. Time for a phone call.

Chapter Twenty-Five

Secret Snatch

GEORGE WAS WATCHING the building the next morning, too. He knew when her husband got home from his night job. He saw Susan leave for work shortly afterwards. Then he saw the husband and another resident leave together in the neighbor's car. 'Odd,' he thought, 'I wouldn't have put those two together as friends. I've heard some rumors about that other guy. Might be trouble.'

George knocked on the apartment door, knowing full well that there would be no answer. He unlocked the door with his master key and entered her home. Fans were whirling, and there was a nice breeze flowing through the apartment. Not too hot after all. But then, he already knew that she had slept comfortably.

It didn't take him long to get the part put into the air conditioner. Before long, the unit was running properly and everything was back in order. George came in from the balcony and closed and locked the sliding door. He also turned off the fan in the living room. Then he went down the hall to check the thermostat setting on the wall. That being done, he went into Lindsay's bedroom, turned off the fan and closed the window.

He looked around the little girl's room and smiled. The room was decorated much has he knew it would be, with a Barbie doll theme. The bed was neatly made, with a pink spread and matching pillow sham, both covered with blond Barbies. The curtains were a pink and white check, and matched the dust ruffle along the bottom of the bed. There were stuffed animals and dolls sitting on a toy shelf, and a bookcase filled with children's books. On a bulletin board she had hung artwork, finger paintings and watercolors of rainbows and flowers. There was a small desk near the closet, and Lindsay had been practicing writing her name with a bold purple marker. He could see that she printed neatly, trying to match the name tag her mother had placed in the front center of the desk. George ran his hand over the nametag and smiled to himself.

Next he went into Susan's bedroom. He stood in the doorway for a moment, taking in the appearance of the room. The color scheme in this room was dark green and white, with some tans and golds. The walls were white, and there were solid green curtains at the two windows. A double bed was under one window. The bed was covered with a hunter green comforter with a forest look in the print. There were two pillows at the head of the bed, and two solid green pillow shams. The bed had no headboard, just a mattress and box springs on a frame. Rather plain, but pleasing in its simplicity. Beside the bed there was a nightstand, with a small white lamp, an alarm clock, and a telephone. On the opposite wall was a four drawer wooden dresser with a mirror above. On the dresser there was a perfume bottle, a jewelry box, and a pile of loose change. There was also a deep golden colored candle on a pewter plate. Only one picture hung on the wall. It was a print of a forest with sunlight filtering through the trees.

George took this all in with his eyes, then quickly went to work in the room. First he turned off the oscillating fan and closed both windows. Then he went to the dresser and picked up the perfume bottle. He removed the lid and inhaled deeply of the fragrance. Carefully he replaced the lid and set the bottle back down on the dresser where he had found it.

Cautiously he opened the top right dresser drawer, and was pleased with what he found there. It was her underwear drawer, and he stood quietly gazing in at her personal items. Soft pink and white panties were folded neatly and stacked on the left. In the center of the drawer were her slips, one white, one black, and one pale pink. In a small box at the back center of the drawer, she kept her hose. Most were cinnamon colored, but he could also see there was one black pair at the bottom of the box. On the right were her bras. Did he dare to touch them? Oh yes, he must. Soft, just slightly padded, one with an under wire support.

He closed his eyes and imagined her standing before him in a black bra, black panties, and black hose with a garter belt. He could almost believe she were really there. This was her room, after all, and he was looking at her intimate personal clothing items, things that had touched her and rubbed her in the most private of places.

With a sudden urgency, George reached to the bottom of the panty pile. He removed the bottom pair, a white cotton brief. Quickly he shut the drawer and reached again for the perfume bottle. Just a little spray of the perfume on the panties, and he would be ready to leave. He tucked his prize into his uniform pants pocket and turned to leave the room. Suddenly another thought occurred to him and he walked to the side of the bed and picked up the receiver of the telephone. He knew she had held that phone just a few short hours before. He placed it up to his ear and imagined her face resting there. His lips rested against the mouthpiece, and he thought about her lips being so close only a short time ago. Then he inhaled and took in a delightful fragrance, just the one he had expected and hoped to smell. For the night before, Susan had used that phone to rub herself until she had moaned with the utmost pleasure. George could catch a whiff of the smell of her lingering on the receiver. He sat on the side of the bed and breathed deeply time and again.

Suddenly the recorded voice of the telephone operator interrupted him and brought him out of his trance. "If you would like to make a call, please hang up and try again." He placed the receiver back in the holder, stood and left the room. He left a copy of his completed work order on the kitchen table, picked up his toolbox, and let himself out of the apartment, carefully locking the door after him. As he walked down the stairs, he reached his hand into his pocket, and knew that his next conversation with Susan would be even more pleasing to him than usual.

Chapter Twenty-Six

Strenuous Workout

ROBIN ANSWERED THE phone, a little annoyed at the interruption to her workout routine. As soon as she recognized the voice on the other end, however, her mood switched. "Sure Larry, you can bring it over right now." Then her mind raced and she said "But I'm in the middle of my exercise routine, and I hate to stop. So could you just bring the fan in? The front door is unlocked. Just bring the fan back here to the workout room."

As Larry prepared to go across the hall to return the fan he had borrowed, his imagination ran ahead of him. Robin, with the perfect body, was working out. She was probably stretching and bouncing and sweating and breathing deeply. What a vision! What a fantasy!

Carrying the fan, Larry let himself in to Robin and Mike's apartment. Sounds of music came from the spare bedroom, which had been turned into a work out room. Larry walked down the hall and stood watching Robin, working in rhythm to the beat of the music. She was kneeling on a bench, with her head held up but her eyes closed. Rhythmically she raised one leg, extended it high, stretched the muscle tight and pointed her toes towards the wall. Then she lowered it and stretched out to the side, nearly reaching her knee to her elbow. Next she bent her knee and raised and lowered her leg in a succession of twenty quick pumps. Then she switched legs and did the same on the other side. Her eyes remained shut as she concentrated on the pulsating music and the stretch of her leg muscles. She was, however, aware of Larry's presence in the doorway, though she gave no hint of acknowledgement.

Larry watched her with intense pleasure. She was wearing a low cut tank top, and obviously no bra underneath. With her head raised and her neck extended, Larry was free to take a long look at her breasts, which could easily be seen in their entirety. Even the hard pink nipples were visible. It was a good thing her eyes were closed. Larry licked his lips and felt himself hardening in excitement.

With every thrust of her leg, Robin's loose shorts rode up high and higher on her thighs. Larry could not be certain, but it seemed possible that she was wearing no panties at all. He moaned slightly with the thought of it, and began to stroke himself. He took a step closer to Robin, and now her face was very close to his crotch. As he touched himself more forcefully, she opened her eyes, smiled up at him, and nuzzled her head against him.

Her clothes slipped easily to the floor. She quickly removed his clothes and soon their naked bodies were entwined. The heat grew between them as their thrusting and pulsating bodies kept rhythm with the beat of the music.

"When will Mike be home?" he asked when their desires had been fulfilled and his breathing began to return to normal. They were lying on the floor, still wrapped in each other's arms.

"The hell with him," she whispered. "I want you again, right now." She moved into position on top of him, and took control.

While Larry dressed, she called Mike. Larry was very quiet, and Mike did not know he was there. "Two hours, oh no baby, that's too long. I need you right now. Please hurry home. I can't wait two hours." As she hung up she turned back to Larry. "Come to think of it, I can't even wait two minutes. Let's do it again." And once again Robin undressed him.

After Larry left, Robin removed a videocassette from the recorder, which had been running since Larry's phone call two hours earlier. She slipped the cassette into the player in the bedroom and watched with great pleasure. She enjoyed watching herself,

And she was quite satisfied with her performance in this show. It would seem that Larry had initiated the encounter, but she knew that in actuality she had set the stage and orchestrated the entire scene. Watching it, she was already planning act two.

The cassette was hidden away before Mike returned. She was in the shower when she heard him open the door. Dripping wet, she left the bathroom to go to him.

Later that night, when Larry went to pick up his deliveries at Mike's place, Robin was not to be seen. Mike explained that she had gone to bed early; she said she had had a very strenuous workout that afternoon and was really worn out.

'I'm a little worn out too,' thought Larry with a chuckle. But he kept his thoughts to himself. No telling what Mike would do if he ever found out what had happened that afternoon.

But several months later, Mike did find out.

Chapter Twenty-Seven

Guilt and Frustration

THE HOT SUMMER days soon gave way to a pleasant fall. Days were sunny and crisp; evenings were cool, with just a hint of a bite in the air. The leaves were just beginning to turn colors and some were falling. Lindsay loved to play at the apartment playground on the weekends. She gathered leaves into a pile at the base of the slide, and then took great pleasure in sliding down and landing in the leaves. Over and over she did it, and was soon joined by other boys and girls in the neighborhood. Looking out the office window, George smiled at the fun, and longed for the woman watching from the playground bench. Every time he saw her, spoke to her, or thought of her, he wanted her.

As Suzanne sat and watched the children, she thought about her latest phone call with Paul. She felt like a different person when she was talking to him. She said things, did things and thought things she never would have normally. It was so different with him. So easy to pretend that she was that kind of person. Was it easy because she was becoming that kind of person? She found herself thinking and fantasizing about being with him. Sometimes she almost felt like she knew him better than she knew her husband. She had more pleasant conversations with him, after all, and looked forward to being with him intimately, on the phone. That was more than she could say for her relationship with Larry. He was seldom home, and seldom required intimacy from her.

The only problem was, after talking to Paul on the phone, after doing with him things she wouldn't have even dreamed of a few months ago, she felt uneasy about it all. She was being unfaithful to her husband, breaking marriage vows, lusting after another man. It was a pleasure for the moment, sure, but pleasure turned to guilt when the phone was hung up. She was dealing with the guilt, yet it was so weird. Not like she had actually done anything wrong, it was just a fantasy, after all, but her mind was confused. Why should she feel bad about thinking things? If she never acted upon her thoughts, then she really hadn't done anything wrong.

But that was the problem. It seemed that Paul wanted to see her in person. He began to talk about it during almost every phone call. He talked about how good it would be to hold her, touch her, and stimulate her. How she would feel so good up next to him. How he could make her feel like a woman deep down. Maybe it was all part of the phone sex. Suzanne could not be totally sure, but she felt like he was pushing for more.

She knew she could never, never let down her guard. She could not meet him, be with him, not even if he said it was just for friend-ship. She knew where it would lead. She knew that somehow he would convince her to allow him to be intimate with her. And then where would she be? That was easy. The guilt would be based on reality then. She would deserve to feel guilty. She would have broken her wedding vows, and she would feel dirty and low. Nothing good could come from that.

So, Suzanne determined again to keep Paul at a distance. She could not take chances, not big chances, anyway. She had to draw the line somewhere. The phone calls would have to be the limit.

She could not be intimate with the real person. There was too much at stake.

Imagine, she was having a hard enough time dealing with the guilt of her fantasy life. If the fantasy became a reality, how in the world could she handle that amount of guilt? No, it just couldn't happen.

George, in the mean time, was getting more than a little frustrated. He knew that he wanted this woman. He knew that they would be good together. He knew that he had a lot to offer her, and he felt for sure that she needed him. She had gotten to him, that's for sure. Maybe it was that he saw her so often. At the pool so many days in the summer, around the complex, in the parking lot, just taking out the trash. He saw her a lot. Actually, he made a point of being near her building in the afternoons when he knew she was due home from work. And his eyes went towards the playground every Saturday afternoon, knowing that she would probably be there with Lindsay.

With the other women George had phoned and ultimately conquered, he had stayed at a distance. Usually they lived quite a ways from his home. He never had the opportunity to see them every day, to watch them get out of their cars, to see them when they didn't know he was watching. But it was different with Susan. He saw her nearly every day, and every time he saw her, he wanted her. Maybe that was why she affected him this way.

George did know that Susan would have to be handled carefully. Revealing himself to her would be a risk, but day-by-day, George knew it was a risk he wanted to take. She was definitely hot, and he needed her. He wanted to have her in the worst way. He wanted to have her in every way. And he had it all figured out, how he would convince her that being intimate with him was what she wanted, needed even. He was so sure that once she had given herself to him, she would be so hooked she would want him more and more. She would not be mad about the early deception. She would be grateful to have him in her life.

George was determined to get closer to Susan. Suzanne was equally determined not to let Paul any closer than he already was.

Their phone calls throughout the fall and into the winter were filled with sexual tension. George pushed and sweet-talked, begging for a chance to just meet her. Suzanne held firmly to her belief that Paul should stay a secret fantasy.

Chapter Twenty-Eight

A Change of Plans

MIKE CAME HOME unexpectedly early one January afternoon, and found the apartment empty. It was odd for Robin to be gone at this time of the day. But it was just the opportunity Mike needed. The next day was Robin's birthday, and he had gotten her a beautiful diamond and ruby necklace and matching earrings. With her out of the apartment, he could find a good hiding place for the jewelry.

It had cost him a bundle, but god, she was worth it. She was without a doubt the sexiest woman he had ever laid eyes on. Perfect body and unquenchable desire. Who could ask for more? They had been together for five years, and although they were not married, he felt that she was the woman of his dreams. He wanted to spend forever with her. Things looked real good for them financially right now. Business was going very well, and money was coming in quicker than ever. He was moving up in the ranks, becoming a trusted and loyal member of the organization. In fact, he was figuring to move out of this apartment, get a place with a lot more class, and take a trip to a South Sea island, maybe for a honeymoon even. There was a huge diamond ring surrounded by fifteen rubies at the jewelers. He had his eye on it for Robin. He knew she would love it, like she would love this necklace and earrings.

So he began to look for a good hiding place for her birthday present. It was while he was looking for the perfect spot that he came upon Robin's video collection. In a shoebox in the back of the closet, he found five cassettes, numbered one through five, but not dated or titled. Driven by curiosity, he inserted the video marked #1 into the player in the bedroom. Curiosity turned to rage and he threw the jewelry case across the room. His anger boiled as he fiercely paced the room. 'The god damn bitch. And him! Well, he's going to be sorry he ever laid eyes on my woman. I'll make him pay for this.'

He was jolted to his senses by the ringing of the phone. He flicked off the video and answered the phone. It was Robin. "Hey, baby, I called you at work but they said you had left early. Is everything alright?" Mike had composed himself enough to answer that everything was fine, he just wanted to get home early, and he was surprised she wasn't here.

"I went to the mall," she explained, but that was a lie. She was actually right across the hall in Larry's bed. "I wanted to get something special so we could really celebrate my birthday tomorrow, if you know what I mean." Her voice trailed off in a little giggle. Her eyes drifted to the flimsy red negligee she had purchased earlier that day. It lay in a tiny little heap on the dresser in Larry's room. He had certainly enjoyed their little celebration. But the negligee had not been worn for long, so it would be practically brand new when Mike saw it for the first time tomorrow. He would never know she had tried it out on Larry first.

"So when will you be home?" Mike asked.

"Oh, give me an hour or so," she replied. "There are still a few things I want to do first." She looked at Larry and smiled coyly. "Why don't you order a pizza for dinner? I will be home by the time it gets there."

She said good-bye and turned her attention back to Larry. Across the hall, Mike replaced the videos into their hiding place.

Then he picked up the jewelry box and carefully checked its contents. Everything seemed in perfect condition. 'Good,' he thought. 'You can't get a refund on merchandise if it has been damaged.' He placed the jewel case deep inside his winter coat pocket. She wouldn't ever think of looking there, and he could take it with him on his way to work tomorrow.

Mike went to the window and spotted Robin's car in the side parking lot. 'Does she really think I'm that stupid? Does she think she can get away with this? For god's sake, her car is sitting right out there. And I'm just not supposed to notice? So where is she, really? Did they go out together in his car, maybe get a hotel room or something?' But another look in the parking lot revealed that Larry's brand new car, a Chrysler, was sitting in its normal spot. 'A new car he bought with the money I gave him,' Mike thought with a surge of indignation. He banged his hand hard against the wall. 'So, they are probably together right now, over there in his apartment.' Rage swelled within him. 'Why, I oughta…' He began. But then Mike regained control of his thoughts. He would have to remain calm, think this thing through carefully. He needed a plan, a foolproof plan. It might take a little time, but he had time.

Mike went to the phone and ordered a pepperoni and mushroom pizza, even though he knew that Robin did not like mushrooms.

Chapter Twenty-Nine

Improvements

SUZANNE JUST DIDN'T know what to think. In the past six months, so many things had changed in her life. Larry seemed like a different person. He seemed very happy with his role as prime breadwinner. His income had greatly increased, with all the overtime hours he was putting in. He was working almost every night, yet he seemed to be extra energetic and cheerful. He was always smiling or whistling. He was making plans for the future. He was talking about his investments and how big his returns had been so far. Although he never gave Suzanne the specifics, she knew from his attitude that he was bringing in more money than he ever had before, and evidently he was investing it and making even more money from that.

Larry had taken over the monthly bill paying, a job he had detested before, when times were tough. Now he took pleasure in making money, managing money, and spending it as well. Suzanne was in the dark as to his exact income, but she was also relieved to feel like finally Larry was facing up to his family responsibilities. She was happy managing the house and Lindsay, and her class of first graders. Since Larry was taking care of the finances, she felt herself relaxing for the first time in their marriage. Larry gave her a weekly allowance, never asked how she spent the money, and was happy to give her more if she ran short for whatever reason.

He bought a brand new car in November, and made a huge cash down payment. He bought Lindsay every thing her heart desired for Christmas. He bought Suzanne an electronic keyboard and season tickets to the Kennedy Center's Classical music series. He bought her several new dresses and a winter coat. He gave her an emerald wrap ring for their anniversary in February. He was talking about buying a house in the suburbs.

So, everything was going great. Or was it? Something bothered her about the whole situation. Yet Suzanne kept herself busy with school and Lindsay, and had little time to think about the uncomfortable feeling she sometimes got in the pit of her stomach. Things seemed so right, yet there was an undercurrent of secrecy she just could not put her finger on.

Sometimes when she walked into her apartment after work, she just felt like something was different, out of place somehow. But she could never really understand why she had that feeling. She couldn't find anything obviously wrong. Anyway, she was generally too busy to give it much thought.

So despite the occasional uneasiness she had, and even though she didn't really understand where Larry's money came from, or how he invested it, or why there always seemed to be lots of it, Suzanne was happy. Life was finally giving her a break, and she wanted to enjoy it. She had never been one to look for the cloud on a sunny day. Why start now?

Larry was attentive with his gifts and generous with his money, but was spending less and less time at home. Many nights Lindsay and Suzanne ate dinner alone, and on weekends they seldom did anything as a family. Larry seemed to be drifting away on a lot of counts.

He hardly ever approached Suzanne for intimacy. It confused her at first, yet did not upset her. She had never really been satisfied by him, and had so often just gone through the motions to get it over with. It was a wifely duty, and did little to excite her. And now, even though Larry had changed so much, she had no real desire to be with him intimately. Since he had started working so much, he had not pressured her for favors nearly as much as he used to.

So that was fine with Suzanne. Yet, because of her phone relationship with Paul, she found herself thinking about sex more and more. She was becoming familiar with her body and comfortable with self-satisfaction. She had an active imagination and could fantasize herself into any situation. Just as long as she kept it all as a fantasy, and never let Paul into her real world she would be safe, and satisfied.

She had no real reason to leave Larry anyway, and felt certain that she should stay in her marriage, no matter how unfulfilled she was sexually. There was more to a marriage than just sex, after all. And they had Lindsay to think about. No, she would just go on as it was, do the best she could, and maybe things would actually get better. After all, a lot had changed in the past few months. Maybe more improvements were on the way.

Chapter Thirty

Lucky Lady

ROBIN WAS LARRY'S Lucky Lady. That's what he started calling her. Ever since he met her, that first night at Mike's apartment, his luck had turned around. He was a new man, a rich man, a happy man, and it all started that first night, when Mike offered to help him out. Well, Mike had helped him, all right, more than he would ever know. And it wasn't just the delivery job that was changing him.

Robin definitely brought him good luck. Whenever he bought a lottery ticket while she was with him, he won something, twenty-five dollars, two hundred dollars. Something. When he took her to the races, he always walked away a winner. She would help him pick the horses, and just about every race she picked a winner. Sure, sometimes they had a few losses, but overall they came out ahead. Way ahead. That's how he got ten thousand dollars for a cash down payment on his new car. A few good hunches about horses, a couple of wisely placed bets, and he had the cash. It seemed so simple.

Larry's evening job was bringing in him some nice money. Now, with Robin at his side, he spent many afternoons at the races, and was turning it into big money. 'Investments', he called it. That's how he explained the abundance of money to his wife. But it was gambling, and it was paying off. Suzanne certainly would not understand, would not approve of his taking risks with his income. So he kept his methods a secret from her. The winnings he shared with her, to a certain extent. She didn't know the half of his income, and he didn't intend to tell her anymore than absolutely necessary. He was putting some aside, investing some in actual insurances, and spending a lot on Robin. The wife didn't have a clue. She was too sweet and innocent to suspect a thing.

Of course, Robin had brought him more than just gambling luck. She had brought him a deeply fulfilled sex life, an adventure into satisfaction that he had not known to be possible. Maybe it was the excitement, the risk involved in what they were doing. Not so much that they might get caught, no, they never really thought about that. The excitement came more from the animalistic passions they felt for each other. It was like she drove him to the edge, she pushed him further and further, she took him on wild passionate journeys and he didn't ever want to come back.

Suzanne? Well, yes, he did love Suzanne. And there was Lindsay too. But Suzanne was so calm, so down to earth and everyday, so innocent and perfect. Never got ruffled, never showed much emotion of any kind. She was like a cold fish in their bed. She did nothing to arouse him, to inspire him, to drive him crazy with desire. It was just ho-hum with her. He didn't care any more if they were ever intimate again. He had Robin, and that would be plenty for most any man. Suzanne was probably just as happy to be left alone. And that's what he did mostly. He did feel it necessary every once in a while to be with her, but it was no longer satisfying to him at all. He spent as much time as possible with Robin, mostly days while Suzanne and Mike were both at work.

Robin was insatiable. She spent most of her days with Larry, and her nights with Mike. Between working out and satisfying two men, Robin kept going with cocaine and speed. Mike knew about her habit, but Larry was in the dark. All he knew was that she had tons of energy and was always ready for sex. He thought it was because she had a strong desire for him. He didn't know it was drug induced.

So Larry and Robin continued their affair, either too drugged or too stupid to see what was happening around them.

Chapter Thirty-One

One Problem Solved-
Many Questions Raised

ROBIN TOLD MIKE good-bye with a deep kiss. "I'll see you in a week," she said. Mike picked up her suitcase and carried it out to her car.

"Be sure and call me when you get there. I worry about you driving all that way by yourself," he said.

"Virginia Beach isn't all that far," she said. "I should be there in less than three hours. You worry too much!"

"Well, ok, but call me when you get there. I'll feel better."

"Okay baby. Whatever you say," Robin said with a sexy smile. She backed out of her parking space and headed south, towards the beach, the sun, and a week of vacation. The top was down on her convertible, and she was wearing her bikini with a cotton shirt over the top. Her long black hair was tied back at the neck and she had a Baltimore Orioles baseball cap to shade her face somewhat. As she drove down highway 95 she cranked the radio up loudly. The little car zipped in and out of traffic quickly. She was going well over the speed limit.

Monday morning Larry told Suzanne that he had to attend training classes in Richmond. He wouldn't be back home till Friday. When she and Lindsay left for school that morning, they had no idea that their lives would be completely changed before the end of the week.

Robin checked into her room and called Larry to tell him the room number. Then she went out to the beach to sun herself. She covered her long legs with sunscreen and also did her stomach and the front of her chest. She called a man from a nearby beach blanket and asked him if he would apply lotion to her back, which he was more than happy to do for her.

After Larry made the deliveries for the evening, he drove on to Virginia Beach, arriving just in time to watch the sunrise over the ocean with Robin. They made love in a secluded part of the beach, then went back to their room for breakfast in bed. After more love-making, they fell asleep. They had dinner at the hotel restaurant, and then drove together in Larry's car back to their apartment building. Mike was watching from the upstairs window as they drove into a parking spot. He smirked as he let the curtain fall back into place.

Larry dashed up the stairs, quickly got the deliveries and addresses from Mike and went back to the car. "He doesn't suspect a thing," he said to Robin. Upstairs, Mike was thinking the same thing.

Together, Larry and Robin made the nights deliveries. One package was undeliverable, however. There didn't seem to be any such address. They drove up and down the right street, but did not find the house number listed on Larry's delivery paper. So they decided to call it a night. They drove to the drop off point, deposited the money in the locker, and locked the leftover package in the trunk of Larry's car. Then they drove back to Virginia Beach and slept all day. Both of them were tired from the night driving and the lack of sleep the day before. Robin did insist on another round in bed before dinner, and it was another erotic episode. They showered together and then dressed for dinner.

Larry wore jeans and an orange Orioles tee shirt. Robin wore tight orange Capri length pants with a black and orange striped silk shirt. As they stepped out into the night, on their way across the street for dinner, they were hugging each other tightly and walking close together. Eyes turned to watch them. It was a sight that was hard to miss.

Most people along the street were watching the couple in bright orange. When questioned later, no one could recall what actually had happened. All they could say was that a dark colored car drove down the street very normally and then suddenly gunshots erupted from the passenger's side. The couple in orange was gunned down, right on the sidewalk, as they waited to cross the street. The car sped off, and no one could remember the tag number or even what state it was from. Someone called 911 and police arrived shortly, with an ambulance right behind. But it was too late. From the amount of blood on the street, and the gaping wounds in the woman's head and the man's chest, it was pretty obvious that there was no hope for either of them.

On the TV news that night, reporters noted that two people were killed in a drive-by shooting outside a Virginia Beach hotel. The identities of the victims had not yet been released, pending notification of relatives. An investigation was underway.

Mike was watching the news that night, but he already knew what the report would say. He was not happy. This was supposed to have been a single murder, not a double. Now, because Robin was also killed, he would surely be questioned. This was not good, not what he had arranged. Somebody was gonna have to pay for this mistake.

Across the hall, Suzanne answered a knock at her door. She was surprised to see two uniformed police officers standing there. She let them come in and asked what she could do for them. The officers informed Suzanne that her husband had been shot and killed in a drive-by shooting in Virginia Beach. She was stunned but answered, "But there must be some mistake. Larry isn't in Virginia Beach. He's in Richmond at a training conference for his job. He wasn't even in Virginia Beach."

"I'm sorry, Mrs. Rogers. We have identified him from his driver's license and other items in his wallet. You will need to come down and give a positive ID tomorrow, however." As Suzanne sank down on the sofa and began to cry, the two officers glanced at each other. This was never an easy part of their job.

"We do have some questions for you, Mrs. Rogers. You say he was in Richmond at a training conference? Could you give us any information on that, where he was staying, what the conference was about?"

"Well, no, I really don't know. Larry didn't tell me where he would be staying, just that he would be back on Friday. And it was in Richmond. I didn't ask him where."

"Do you know why he might have gone to Virginia Beach? Did he have any friends there, or relatives?"

"Nobody that I know of."

"Do you know a woman named Robin Smith?"

Suzanne thought about that for a minute and then answered, "No, I don't think so. Who is she?"

"She was also killed in the shooting. She was with your husband."

Suzanne gasped and said, "You mean they were there together? I don't know her. How do you know they were together?"

"The woman had checked into a hotel there, and your husband had the room key in his pocket."

Suzanne began to cry openly now. "So he was having an affair? I didn't know."

"What can you tell us about your husband's job, Mrs. Rogers?" The officers looked at each other again. How could this woman not know her husband was having an affair? She was being awfully vague about lot of things. Did she have something to hide?

"Well, he works in the Emergency Room at the County Hospital. He has been working there, oh, about three years now. And for the past year and a half, he has been working a lot of overtime, and long hours. He is hardly ever home." This time she noticed the look that passed between the officers.

"Mrs. Rogers, did your husband use illegal drugs?"

"Oh, no, that I'm sure of. I would have known that if he did."

"Did he have any enemies, anyone that may have threatened him recently? Any outstanding gambling debts, maybe?"

"I don't know. I really don't know. He just works all the time, and we haven't really talked about much lately. He never mentioned being threatened. And I don't think there was any big debt. He has been bringing home more money now, since he has been working overtime, and I think everything has been all paid up. We only have the car loan, and the condo Mortgage, that I know of. Larry has been taking care of all the bills for the past year and a half.

The officer closed his note pad. "That's all the questions we have for you right now, Mrs. Rogers. But we will need to remove some items from your home. Financial records, address books, phone numbers, anything that might lead us to someone who would want to do this. We could get a search warrant if necessary, but we would appreciate it if you would cooperate and give us your permission to take the things we need right now."

"Oh, sure, take whatever you need. But do you think someone did this on purpose? It wasn't just a random act? Who would want to kill my husband? Who would want to do this?" And Suzanne broke down in sobs of grief.

"That's what we would like to find out, Ma'am. We will keep you informed as we get new information. And you will have to identify the body tomorrow. Could you show us where your financial records are kept?"

Suzanne led them to Larry's desk, and the officers removed the contents of all the file drawers. They took other items while Suzanne watched through tear-stained eyes. She was shaking, and one of the officers noticed it. He helped Suzanne to sit down and asked if there was anyone she could call, to come over. She probably shouldn't be alone right now. "My parents live in Kansas, and I don't have any relatives here. I could probably call my friend Melissa. Maybe she could come over and take care of Lindsay."

"Who is Lindsay?" he asked.

"My daughter. She's asleep. I hope." Suzanne glanced down the hall.

"Would you like us to wait until your friend can get here? Or will you be all right alone till then?"

"No, thank you, I will be okay. I'll call her right now if it's all right."

So the officers loaded several boxes into their cruiser and Suzanne called Melissa, who could sense the urgency in her friend's voice and said she would be right over. The policemen returned to her door a few minutes later to thank her for her cooperation and say that if she needed anything, or thought of anything that might be helpful, she should be sure to call the prescient. When they left, Suzanne sat back down on the sofa. She was too numb to cry, too shocked to feel any pain, and very confused. She didn't understand how any of this could have happened.

As the officers got into their car, a dispatch came through to them. "We have an address for Robin Smith, and you won't believe your luck," the dispatcher said. When he read off the address, the two officers looked at each other with raised eyebrows. "And the plot thickens," said one. The dispatcher came on again and said, "The chief wants you to report back here before going to her residence. He wants you to talk to Detective Larson before this goes any further."

"Larson?" said one officer to the other as they drove towards the station. "What's that old man got to do with this?"

Melissa arrived shortly after the policemen had left. She was stunned to hear that her friend's husband had been murdered. Without hesitation, she agreed to take care of Lindsay for the next day or so, until things calmed down for Suzanne a little. Together they packed a suitcase of things Lindsay might need. Then Suzanne gently woke her daughter. She didn't want to tell Lindsay too much, or she may be upset at having to leave. So Suzanne just said that some important things had to be done tomorrow, and Melissa would take Lindsay to daycare and Mommy would see her later that day, when the important grown-up stuff was done. Lindsay was too tired to protest much, and groggily went along with Melissa.

Next Suzanne called her parents. Even though it was the middle of the night by now, she wanted to talk to them. They too were shocked, and told Suzanne they would be on the next flight out of Kansas City. They were full of questions, but Suzanne had no answers.

Then Suzanne called the principal of her school. She explained that her husband had passed away, and she would need some time off. He agreed to let her take as much time as she thought she would need. He would find a substitute for her class. He was kind and asked if there was anything she needed. Suzanne said everything was being worked out, but she appreciated his asking.

She didn't sleep a bit that night. She wandered blindly through the apartment, wondering how she could have missed the clues. Had there been any clues? What was this about drugs? Did that explain where all the money had come from lately? And who in the world is Robin Smith?

Wednesday morning it was on the news again. This time names were given, and although no motive had yet been established, the reporter did note that drugs were found in both the car and hotel room. As soon as he heard the news, Tim Simpson called Mike Santini to express his condolences. Tim also expressed his interest in taking over some of Larry's runs. Mike told him he needed to lay low for a while. He didn't want to give the police any extra reason for suspicion. Mike promised to speak with his boss about it. Someone would get in contact with Tim in a few days. Meanwhile, there would be no action out of Mike's place for a while.

George heard the news and right away he knew Suzanne would need him more that ever now. And maybe, with the husband out of the picture, she would not be fighting the guilt issue any more. She might be easier to convince, now that he was gone.

He called her almost immediately. He acted surprised when she told him the news, but then he was supportive and kind. He asked if there was anything he could do. He asked if Lindsay was all right. He asked if she needed anything. She asked him not to call until after the funeral, since she would have a lot to do, and a lot on her mind, and her parents were there with her. He agreed. He wanted her to know he understood. And he did understand. She needed some time, some space to think. He would call her when things had settled down some. "Just know I will be thinking about you," he said.

Chapter Thirty-Two

Detective Work

THE NEXT FEW days were very busy for Suzanne, yet they seemed to go by in slow motion. She had to identify Larry's body and then make arrangements for the burial service. She had to meet with the police again, and was questioned by Detective Larson. She picked up Lindsay at daycare and had to explain to her that her daddy was gone. Her parents arrived and more detailed explanations were given outside Lindsay's hearing. They were as confused about things as she was herself. The police had filled her in on some of the information they had, but it was still hard to understand.

Detective Larson had been busy, too. He and a uniformed officer had questioned Mike Santini. He was cooperative yet they did not trust him. According to him, he and Robin had a great relationship, and he was planning to marry her. He did know that Robin had a drug problem, but he wanted to help her deal with it. He didn't know she was having an affair. He didn't know she even knew the guy across the hall. He barely even knew the man himself.

Detective Larson took notes on their conversation. When they were in the squad car, Larson spoke his mind to the officer. "He's lying, every bit of it. He knew Larry Rogers very well, and he knew his girlfriend was having an affair with him. He has a solid alibi for the night of the murders, but he knew all about it. I'm sure of it. Now we just have to find a way to connect him to the murders. Let's check his phone records first, and see who he's been talking to lately."

"But what about the woman, Mrs. Rogers?" the officer asked. "Don't you think you ought to check out her story a little closer? Seems pretty strange to me that she didn't know any of her husband's business, and that she had no clue he was cheating on her with the babe from across the hall. And he had just taken out a lot of insurance with her as the beneficiary. That sounds pretty fishy to me."

"What I think is that you need to read people a little better. She is as innocent as a newborn baby. She had no clue about her husband's involvement with the drugs or the other woman. It's Santini who's the scum here. He's had a lifetime of involvement with drugs, always on the edge of being caught. So he found out about the affair, so he arranged for the neighbor to get bumped off. Whether he planned on wasting the girl, I don't know yet. But the guy's been up to no good for a long, long time. And he's lying when he says he barely even knew Larry Rogers. He'd known him quite well, for over a year, had him working the drug runs. We can prove that, and before long we will prove a lot more."

"So she's just an innocent wife here, no involvement in the drugs, no knowledge of it even?"

"Yep. Listen, I've been on to Santini for quite a while. Just been waiting for the right time to nail him, hopefully taking down a lot more of the organization with him. This murder just changes the timing schedule a bit, but we are going to get him one way or another."

*　*　*　*　*　*　*

Larry's funeral was small and simple. The casket was closed. Most of the people in attendance were friends of Suzanne's; her parents. Melissa and Tom, several teachers from school, her principal,

154

Mrs. Williams from the daycare center. Suzanne was surprised at first that at least someone from the hospital had not come to the funeral. But then she realized that Larry had not worked there for over a year, and he had not made friends with any of his co-workers. She did notice that Detective Larson was there, and oddly enough, the maintenance man from her condo complex. Both sat off to the side in the small chapel. Neither spoke to her.

The next day, after Robin's service, Mike Santini was arrested on murder for hire charges. Detective Larson had all the information he needed. And he was ready to offer Mike a deal; his life in exchange for some convincing information about the drugs he had been handling. It looked like Detective Larson would come away from the negotiating table with the names of the heads of Mike's business, and that would be just what Larson needed for that big boost in his career.

Suzanne's parents wanted her to move back to Kansas with them. They thought she needed to get away from the memories here in the city, or so they said. Suzanne was more inclined to think that they wanted to help her get her life back together. A noble thought, with only a hint of condescension. If she had not messed up her life so badly, they would not have to rescue her. Suzanne was not ready to give in to them just yet. She told them she wanted to at least finish the school year. She couldn't just leave in the middle of the year; she was committed to her students.

Suzanne did let her parents help her with one problem, however. The police had confiscated both of her cars, impounding them as evidence in the drug dealings. So she had no vehicle, no way to get to work. Her father bought her a used car, something safe and dependable, but nothing fancy. Suzanne did appreciate his willingness to help her in this way, and promised to pay him back when she could.

Her parents stayed for the next week. During that time, Suzanne found the business card for the insurance man she had met once, Mr. David Thompson. She called and made an appointment to see him, to go over the policy that Larry had taken out earlier. Lindsay stayed with Grandma while Suzanne and her father went to Mr. Thompson's office.

Mr. Thompson spoke freely with Suzanne and her father. He explained to them exactly how much income Suzanne would be receiving, and it appeared that she would be adequately taken care of. Then he told them that there was also a large sum coming to Lindsay, upon her eighteenth birthday. It was what Larry had intended to be used for a college fund.

As they left the office, Suzanne made a comment to her father. "At least he did something right for us." Her father snorted a response. "Too bad he wasn't any good to you in life." He had never approved of Larry much, and his opinion had been lowered considerably in the last few days.

Things gradually returned to normal for Suzanne and Lindsay. After her parents left, Suzanne realized that the apartment really wasn't more lonely or empty without Larry there. He hadn't been around much anyway. It was hardly any different now. Even Lindsay seemed to slip naturally into her previous routines, with barely a mention of her daddy.

By the end of the school year, Suzanne had decided that she would stay where she was. She would like to be closer to her parents, but it wasn't necessary to live with them, or even in the same town. She was doing fine on her own. She could keep on teaching at Dickinson. Everything was going to be just fine.

Chapter Thirty-Three

Revelations

MELISSA SAT AT the kitchen table in Suzanne's apartment. She was once again amazed at her friends' composure. It had been just a few months since Larry's murder, and here was Suzanne fixing banana splits, laughing and playing with the girls, chatting on with animation about their plans for the summer. She seemed so relaxed, so comfortable with her role as a single parent. Well, maybe that was understandable, really, since for as a long as Melissa had known her, Suzanne had been bringing up Lindsay pretty much alone. Not a lot had changed there. If anything, Suzanne's stress level had been lowered since Larry's death. She didn't have to worry about him exploding in anger, or being depressed or unemployed. She was more in control now than she had ever been. Even financially, Suzanne seemed better off now.

Melissa could recall a conversation she had with Suzanne here in this apartment just weeks ago. Suzanne had been almost hysterical. She had just come from the police station, where she had picked up the things that had been removed from her apartment that night the officers had first told her about Larry's death. Sitting at the table, going through things, piecing things together, Suzanne had become more and more upset. She called her friend to come over and lend her some support. Melissa had left the girls with her husband and come right over to be with Suzanne.

Suzanne had a lot on her mind. She had found evidence that Larry had been making a lot of money, all of it in cash, and there was proof that he had been gambling. There were bank deposits made in accounts she never even knew they had. In fact, there was even one account with Larry's name and Robin's name together. Now what was she supposed to do about that?

Then there were the photos, several nude pictures of Robin. What was the worst of all was that the pictures were taken right here, in Suzanne's home, in Suzanne's bedroom. How could this have been going on, without her knowing, or even suspecting? How could she be so stupid?

Melissa did her best to console her friend. She reminded Suzanne that she was not the least bit stupid, but that she had been busy holding the house together, working, and caring for Lindsay. Besides, she never liked to look for trouble. Suzanne would do whatever it took to find the best in every situation. She hadn't wanted trouble, so she hadn't gone looking for any.

Melissa suggested that Suzanne might need to talk to a lawyer, and Tom's brother Jeff could probably answer a lot of her questions. She was sure he would do it free of charge, at least an initial visit. She gave Suzanne the phone number and Suzanne promised to call the next day.

After that first visit, Suzanne took on a whole new air of independence. She felt more in control, more competent, more self-sufficient. This whole process had brought her more inner strength than she thought she could muster on her own. Jeff Anderson was a good lawyer, a good listener, and a wise advisor. He showed Suzanne how she could regain control of her finances and could assure a comfortable future for herself and Lindsay.

The change in Suzanne was almost instantaneous. She never again showed a sign of anxiety regarding her financial affairs. She got past the feeling of inadequacy she had faced earlier. She filed the past away and was ready to move on towards the future, with barely a look back except to save a few good memories for Lindsay's sake. Yes, she had made some mistakes, and she had been gullible and naive. But Suzanne had always believed that mistakes were good things, if you learned something from them. And Suzanne had learned a lot from hers.

So here she was, eating a banana split with her daughter, having a fun evening with friends, and making plans for the summer ahead. She had decided definitely not to move home with her parents. She would stay here, where she had a great job, wonderful friends, and the security of the familiar. She also had some financial security, and was looking forward to bringing up her daughter on her own. She knew she could do it.

Tonight the kitchen table was covered with travel brochures. Suzanne and Melissa were planning to take a couple weeks of vacation together. They were going to rent a cabin or a cottage or maybe even a house somewhere, they just hadn't decided where yet. Did they want the mountains or the beach? Did they want rustic or posh? Did they want peace and quiet or theme parks? Tonight was the night to get their heads together and decide. They would need to make reservations soon.

In the end they decided to head north, to a rustic resort area in New Hampshire. They would drive up in Melissa's station wagon. They would break up the trip with several fun stops along the way, including Hershey Park in Pennsylvania for the girls and an overnight visit with Melissa's cousins in New York. They would do some sight seeing in Boston, to take in some spots of historical significance. But most of their vacation would be spent in the White Mountains of New Hampshire. It promised rest and relaxation, as well as outdoor adventure. There was a lake within hiking distance from the cabin they rented. There would be horseback riding, nature programs, and evening campfires. It sounded delightful.

Suzanne was looking forward to the changes this vacation would bring. She needed some space, some fresh air, some time to clear her head. She wanted to be totally relaxed and ready to start the new school year with her thoughts fine-tuned, her goals firmly set. Lindsay would be starting kindergarten. It would be a time of new beginnings for both of them.

Chapter Thirty-Four

Summer Separation

GEORGE CALLED SUZANNE just about every day. She still thought of him as Paul, although he knew her real name now. He had learned her real name from the television, when the reporters had been talking about the murder. He had smiled to himself when he realized that she had been trying to keep something about herself hidden from him. She had not been surprised or concerned the first time he called her Suzanne. It was just natural. But he had not offered to tell the truth about himself, of course.

Since he didn't have to worry about Larry, and since Suzanne was home during the summer, he was able to talk to her much more often. Daytime calls were limited to casual conversation, however. Suzanne did not want Lindsay to overhear any intimate conversations. Those were still saved for the night. And since the murder, Suzanne had had so much on her mind, George wisely knew better than to push for phone sex just yet. She needed a little time. George, on the other hand, was starting to get impatient.

When he called that night, she told him all about her vacation plans. This vacation to New Hampshire would be wonderful, she just knew it. Just what she needed right now.

"When do you leave?" he asked.

"The middle of July," she answered. "We have to get back in time to get some school shopping done for the girls, and we have staff meetings last week of August.

"So you'll be gone in two weeks? Paul asked.

"Yes, well, fifteen days actually."

"How am I going to manage without talking to you for fifteen days?" Paul always had a way of turning the most innocent conversation into something about their relationship. "It was bad enough not getting to talk to you much during the time around the funeral. But to think of you off having a wonderful vacation, while I sit around here and count the hours until I can talk to you again – well, I just don't see how I will survive."

"Oh, I'm sure you will manage. You can always call one of your other girlfriends!" She was joking, she thought.

"You know there's no other girlfriend, baby. You are the only one for me. You know that, don't you?"

"Mmmmm, if you say so." Suzanne was starting to get that warm, cuddly feeling. She hadn't talked to him like this in a long time. And maybe she needed a little release.

"I know what would help get me through the time while you are away," Paul began. "If I could just see you for ten minutes, I could carry that memory with me while you are on vacation. If I could just put my arm around, smell your perfume, feel you next to me…" He let his voice trail off. He knew she was considering it.

"Mmmm, Paul, it is so tempting. But I don't know if it's such a good idea."

"What are you stalling for? You aren't married anymore; you don't have that for an excuse. Are you afraid to meet me?"

"Afraid? No, not afraid exactly. I just think it's too soon. I'm not ready yet."

"Too soon? How can you say that? We have been friends for over a year. We know each other very well. I care about you, Suzanne. I want to show you. You need someone, maybe now more than ever.

I could really treat you good, baby. Give me a chance. Let me come over. You need me. And baby, I sure need you."

"Please, Paul, don't pressure me like this. I just can't complicate my life right now. I don't want to start a relationship with you or anyone just yet. I just can't."

George was getting even more frustrated. "Start a relationship? I thought we started over a year ago. I have been waiting a long time, you know. And I've been very patient. You've been through some unusual and stressful times. But I've been here for you. I just want to take it further. I want to spend time with you. You owe me a chance, at least. And we could be so good for each other. I know it, and I think you know it too."

"Paul, I said no." Suzanne was feeling very uncomfortable with this pressure. But she was determined to stand her ground. "I think I know what is best for me. Right now I cannot and will not get involved with a man, no matter what. I need some space. I need some time. And if you can't understand that, well, then maybe we should end this before it goes any further."

George was silent for a moment, as if he were thinking it over. "Is that what you want?"

"Well, no, I want to stay friends, and talk to you, and all that. And maybe eventually it could go further. But don't pressure me to move faster than I am willing. I just can't get involved right now. And I really wish you could understand that."

He took a deep breath and decided to try a new tactic. This new plan formulated in his head almost instantaneously. He would be understanding, all right, and it would drive her crazy. "Okay, then, Suzanne, if you need a little space, if you want a little time, I'll tell you what we should do. I will stop calling you for a while. I will not bother you again until after you get back from your vacation. I will leave you alone, and maybe you can get your thoughts together and decide what you really want. If this relationship is to go any-where, you will be the one saying where and when. I will respect your wishes; I will give you some time. And when you get back from New

Hampshire, I will call you. I will see where we stand. And whatever you say, I will respect. Just know one thing. Every day between now and then, I will be hoping with all my heart that you will give me a chance. I will think about you every minute. I want to be with you. I think we were meant to be together. But until you feel that way too, I will not pressure you. The decision is yours."

Suzanne was touched by his sincerity. He was a wonderful understanding man. He wanted her to take her time, come to him when she was ready. And she believed him. She believed that he would respect her wishes on their relationship. She trusted him now more than ever. So George's plan was working.

Chapter Thirty-five

Truth Be Told

SUZANNE SAT ON the front porch of the cabin and listened to the frogs croaking down by the lake. It was so peaceful here. Just what she needed. Peace, quiet, few responsibilities, and a chance to unwind and think.

She was deep into her thoughts when Melissa came out to join her. She was carrying a cold bottle of wine and two glasses. She sat the glasses on the deck railing and pulled a corkscrew from the pocket of her shorts. Then she opened the bottle and poured Suzanne a glass. "You are sure quiet tonight," she said. "Want to talk?"

Suzanne took a sip of her wine. "Mmmm, that's good. Thanks." Then she looked out into the yard. "See the fireflies? Aren't they beautiful?"

"Uh, huh," Melissa smiled. She remembered the girls chasing them last night. They must have caught fifty in a jar, squealing in glee with each capture. They lit up the porch for half an hour until the girls finally agreed to set them free.

"But you aren't sitting out here thinking about fireflies, I bet." Melissa knew Suzanne had something on her mind. Maybe she was ready to talk.

Suzanne took another, deeper sip of wine. "Okay, okay. I'll talk. But first let me say that your opinion of me might be about to change. I hope this doesn't kill our friendship. I hope you don't think I am a bad girl or something."

"Keep talking, girl! I'm all ears. This might be good." Melissa was smiling at her friend, trying to make her feel comfortable talking about what might be a sensitive subject. "And what kind of a friend do you think I am, if I can't handle a little dirt about my best friend. I promise. I can take it!"

"Good thing you brought out the whole bottle of wine, though! I might not have the courage to tell you about this unless I'm half gone!" She took another drink. "It's about a man," she began.

"Good, good! Go on, tell me more!"

"Well, his name is Paul, and we have been friends for over a year. But I have never met him. We just talk on the phone." Suzanne stopped there and looked at her friend.

As Melissa listened she began to understand. "Let me get this straight. You talk with this guy, Paul, but you have never met him? And it's been going on for over a year, so that means you started talking to him while Larry was still alive. Interesting!"

"Well, it all started with a phone call in the middle of the night, while Larry was at work, you know. I think he was still working at the hospital then. Anyway, we just started talking, and he was really nice and friendly and he was easy to talk to, so I just talked and we became friends."

Melissa poured more wine in both glasses and said, "Well, that's not so bad. Or is there more?" She caught a little smile curl up on her friend's lips and knew that she was getting to the good stuff. "Come on, don't keep me in suspense."

"Well, one night, I had had a bit too much wine and I guess my defenses were down, because we started talking and next thing

I knew he had me touching myself and telling him intimate things, and pretty soon we were having sex together, but just on the phone. And since then, we do it together a couple of times a week like that. And I will tell you, just talking to him and hearing him and thinking about what he is doing and all that, well, I have had better sex that way than any time with Larry."

Melissa was intrigued. "But you never met him; you never actually had an affair with him? How could you not want to?

"It's not that I didn't want to, but I just wouldn't let myself. I was married, and I had commitments and morals. Well, sort of. But now that Larry is gone, Paul is pushing me to meet him. And I don't know if I should or not."

"Why not, for heaven's sake?" asked Melissa. "You deserve some happiness. I say go for it!"

"But somehow it just doesn't seem right. I mean, I haven't even met the guy and already I have made love with him hundreds of times in my mind. Isn't that sort of odd? I just know that if I did meet him, we would be in bed in no time, and I feel weird about that. Like it would be cheap, maybe. I just don't know what to do."

"Look, why don't you give it a try? Meet him; see how you feel about being with him then. You don't have to fall into bed with him right away. Or maybe you will want to, and what's wrong with that? You're a big girl. You know what you're doing. You can take care of yourself." Melissa was actually happy for her friend, and eager to see her move on with her life. Poor Suzanne, things had been rough on her, as far as men were concerned. If this Paul would be good for Suzanne, then she should take what happiness she could get. "I say you should go for it girl!"

Suzanne leaned back into her chair and closed her eyes. "I guess maybe you're right. I'm not married any more, so there is not that guilt to deal with. And I am entitled to a little pleasure now and then." She opened her eyes and looked directly at Melissa. "So, you don't think I'm a slut?"

"No way! But I always thought you had some little secret you weren't telling. So it's phone sex! Now I know! I never would have guessed, not in a million years! You must have some wild imagination!"

"That's what Paul says, too! But he has a lot to do with it. He can get me to relax and feel like phone sex is so natural, and there's nothing wrong with what we are doing. But even more than that, I think he really cares about me. He was so supportive when I was upset with Larry so much. He was always interested in things I was doing, and what I was thinking about. It wasn't always about the sex. That came secondary. We were friends first."

"Sounds to me like you already know you want to spend more time with him. So, when are you going to meet him?" Melissa didn't want to push her friend into something she wasn't ready for, but she sensed that Suzanne really did want this man.

"When we get back home, I guess." Suzanne giggled. "It feels like I'm back in high school, wondering how far I should let a guy go. But you're right. I am a grown woman. I can handle a relationship. I'm ready. I'm ready." Maybe she was trying to convince herself. She finished her second glass of wine and poured a third. Then she emptied the remains of the bottle into Melissa's glass. "Want some more? I'll go in and get it," she offered.

Inside the cabin, Suzanne checked on the girls, who were sound asleep in the double bed. Suzanne and Melissa each had a twin bed in a second bedroom. The cabin had all the comforts of home, but in a casual, rustic décor. There was a stone fireplace, roughly hewn wooden beams on the wall, and the furniture and accents were all in a hunting theme. Pictures of bear, moose, and fish decorated the walls. Some of the furniture was made of tree branches. Except for the running water and electricity, the cabin could have been standing here since the 1800's. Everything was comfortable, nothing was overstated. It was truly a wonderful place to get away from life in the suburbs.

Back outside, Melissa was thinking about Suzanne's recent revelations. This was all very interesting, but not too shocking. And it certainly would not affect their friendship. When Suzanne returned with more wine, Melissa gave her a big hug. "You know, your life is moving into its next chapter. And you're going to do just fine. But you have to promise to give me details. I mean, no more secrets, okay?"

"Okay, I promise!" laughed Suzanne. They talked long into the night. It was well after midnight when they finally climbed into their beds. Moonlight streamed through the window of the cabin and gave a gentle glow to the room. Just before she drifted off to sleep, Melissa whispered. "You're thinking about Paul aren't you?"

"How can you tell?" Suzanne asked.

"You're smiling," Melissa answered. And Suzanne realized that she was.

PART TWO

WEB OF DECEPTION

Chapter One

What a Tangled Web We Weave

GEORGE TOOK A deep breath and dialed her number. Suzanne answered on the second ring. She and Lindsay had been home from their vacation for three days. She was beginning to wonder if he was ever going to call.

But he did. And he was quite surprised and very pleased with what she had to say. After talking about the trip and what a great time they had had, Suzanne brought up the subject that had been in his thoughts for three weeks. "So, I did some thinking while I was out there in the woods."

"Thinking? About us?" he asked.

"Yes, about us. And about me, and what I want to do with the rest of my life. And I've decided I am ready to move on, ready to see what happens next." She was being a little vague, but she didn't want to come right out and say "ready to have a sexual relationship with you." That would have been too obvious. She couldn't do that.

"Does that mean you want to meet me? You want to take this relationship to the next level?" he asked.

"Yes, I want to meet you. Yes, I want to see what happens. Yes, I am ready to take the next step. I'm a big girl. I'm ready to move on."

"You don't know how happy that makes me," George said. "When? Where? Let's do it soon. I can't wait to meet you."

"Well, I've been thinking about that, too." Suzanne had it all planned out. She had set up some guidelines in her head. She did not want to invite him to her apartment, that's for sure. That would be too much of an invitation to jump into bed, she feared. She wanted to take it a little slower than that. But she didn't want it to be a real date, actually. She hoped they could just meet somewhere and talk. Spend some time getting to really know each other. She did not want to go anywhere with him in his car, either. She felt like she should be at least a little bit cautious. She had to be, for Lindsay's sake.

So she said, "I hope you don't mind, but I want to meet you at McDonald's!"

"Whatever you say, baby! But why McDonald's?"

"Because it is a public place, and I will feel better about meeting you there. I guess I'm not totally ready to be alone with you yet. And it's casual, a place we can talk and not have to dress up like for a date or something. I just think it's a pretty good place for meeting you for the first time."

"So, I guess this means you don't plan to let me kiss you or anything?" He said it with a little laugh, but he was more than a little agitated by her rules and regulations.

"We'll see about the kissing. But don't plan on more than that!" Suzanne was chuckling, too, only partially from nervousness.

So they agreed to meet Friday afternoon at 2:00. There were outside tables at the local McDonald's, and that's where Suzanne wanted to be. Melissa would watch Lindsay. Suzanne would need to pick up Lindsay at 4:00, so there was a time limit too. It wasn't the way George would have wanted it, but he figured he'd better go along with her wishes. No sense frightening her away.

Now he just had to figure out what he was going to say to her.

Suzanne arrived at McDonalds well before two o'clock. She ordered a diet coke and took it outside. It was a beautiful day, warm and sunny but not too hot. The sun glistened off her auburn hair. She was wearing a denim skirt and a light blue blouse tucked in at the waist. She had sandals on her feet. Her hair was pulled back with a blue headband. She had a small denim purse, which draped over her shoulder with a long strap. As she sat down at a table in the shade, her green eyes wondered over the parking lot. She hadn't asked what kind of a car he would be driving. Maybe even a Kastner's Bakery truck, since this was a regular workday for him. Or maybe he had taken the afternoon off.

She was a little bit nervous. She hoped this would work out; in fact she really wanted it to. He was such a nice man, so easy to talk to. She felt they had a real friendship. And shouldn't you be friends before you take a relationship further? Yes, and they had probably already established the friend base. In fact, it had actually moved past friendship, considering the intimacy they had shared on the phone. Now to decide if they really should move forward.

Her decision would be based on several things. Not his personal appearance, no, she wasn't looking for some great looking guy. Looks only counted to her in the area of neatness and cleanliness. She didn't care if he was tall or short, she could even accept bald and chubby, if he was neat and clean looking. She wasn't looking for Robert Redford perfection.

Even though she was nervous, she was excited, too. Deep inside she was aching for a fulfilling sexual relationship, and she did think that Paul could provide her with that. The way he talked, the things he said, the way he could make her feel and respond, wow, just thinking about it now made her imagination run wild. She gave a deep sign and shuddered slightly, trying to clear her mind of those thoughts. She had important things to think about here.

Meanwhile, George sat in his car watching her. He had been here, waiting and thinking, since she had come out and sat down with her drink. He spotted her right away, of course. He knew who he was looking for. She did not.

George knew that what he was about to do was risky. He could frighten her away completely if he didn't handle this just right. But he just couldn't loose her now. He was so close. He had worked for over a year to be with her. He couldn't stand the thought of all that work coming down to a rejection. He would have to come across as caring and concerned, apologetic and sincere, yet he also knew he would have to show some air of confidence. He did have something she needed, after all. She needed his hard body. Oh, yes, she needed him and he needed her. He was beginning to feel the excitement growing already.

George took a deep breath and got out of his car. He walked past her and smiled, then stopped and said, "Hello, Mrs. Rogers. How's your air conditioner doing this year?"

Suzanne recognized him as the maintenance man from her complex, and smiled back. "Oh, it's fine. It has been working great ever since you fixed it last summer." Something about the memory stirred a shiver of excitement deep within her.

"That's good," he said, and went on into McDonald's.

Once again Suzanne cast her eyes over the parking lot. She glanced down at her watch and saw that it was still early, ten minutes till two. Then she watched as the maintenance man came out of McDonald's with a large soft drink and walked towards her. She looked up and smiled. He asked, "Do you mind if I sit here with you?"

Suzanne smiled again, a little nervously. "Well, no, I am waiting for someone, but he isn't here yet, so sure, you can sit here for a while." She looked down and took a drink from her soda.

"I've wanted to tell you how sorry I was about the passing of your husband," he said as he sat down. "It must have been quite a shock to you. And your little girl. How's she doing?"

"Oh, she's fine. We're both fine. Life goes on, I guess. It was a real shock at first, especially as the details came out, but we're getting through it okay. Thanks for coming to the funeral, by the way. I noticed you there, but just didn't get a chance to talk to you. There weren't very many people there, but I had my family all around me, and a few friends. But it was nice of you to come." It was easy to be nice to this man. He seemed to care about what she had been going through. Once again she remembered that moment in her kitchen, when his body was so close to hers, when she had felt a quiver of excitement stir within her.

"So, your neighbor Mike is in jail, right? Are you going to have to testify at his trial or anything?" George just wanted her to know he was interested in her life.

"Well, the police say I may have to. But I guess Mike is trying to work out some deal, where he will admit to drug trafficking and conspiracy to commit murder, but be given a lighter sentence because he will also give the police information they need to arrest others in the drug ring, and the actual shooters, of course. So it might not actually go to trial, just sentencing, and that might not even happen for another year. All depends. I'll tell you one thing though. I'm sure glad that part of my life is over. It was not a pleasant time, to say the least!"

"I'm sure it wasn't!" he said. They sat in silence for a minute, until Suzanne checked her watch again.

George just watched her for a moment. She felt him looking at her and glanced up.

"It's after two," she said. "Looks like I'm being stood up."

"No, you're not being stood up," he said simply.

Suzanne looked at him curiously. "What do you mean?" she asked cautiously.

"I mean, Paul is here already. I am Paul."

Suzanne's brow furrowed as she asked, "What? What do you mean? You are George the maintenance man. What do you mean, you are Paul? And how do you know I am waiting for Paul, anyway?" This was a little strange. More than a little.

George looked steadily in her eyes and said, "Suzanne, there is a lot I have to tell you. Please, just listen. I know this is going to be confusing, but just listen. I need you to understand." He took a deep breath and plunged into his speech. "For the past year and a half, I have been calling you, pretending to be someone named Paul. When I first called you, I did not know who you were, I didn't know you lived in my very own apartment complex, I didn't know anything about you. But then I saw you and Lindsay at the playground one day, and I figured it out. When I saw how beautiful you are, I knew I really wanted to get to know you more and more, and I just didn't know how to tell you the whole truth, that I was really just your maintenance man. I care about you so much. I know what you have been going through, with Larry and the police and the murder and all that. I wanted so many times to knock on your door and hold you and comfort you and tell you everything would be alright. I just didn't know how to tell you the truth. And I didn't want to hurt you. You have come to mean a lot to me. I had to meet you, to explain, and hopefully we can move on from here. What do you think? Can you forgive me? Can we keep our friendship, and maybe go further? Please say yes. I need you, baby. I could be the best thing that's ever happened to you."

It was a long speech, and well delivered, he thought. Filled with apologies, filled with passion, hinting at his expectations but not blatantly stated. He hoped it would have the desired affect. He hoped she would understand, at least in part, and be so touched by his emotions that she would relinquish any negative feelings. But he just didn't really know how she would take the news.

And Suzanne herself didn't know what to think. Her heart was pounding loudly and she felt her head spinning. Hearing his voice, so familiar, so full of passion, brought back memories of those late night phone calls. She was full of questions, and felt more than a little anger. To think that this man had been watching her for a year, knowing where she lived, knowing what she was doing. It wasn't right. How could she have let this happen? And what should she do now?

"Friendship?" she questioned. "What kind of friendship is based on lies and deception? What kind of a man are you anyway? Why did you even call me in the first place? Was it all a lie? Do you even know how to tell the truth?" The accusations flowed forth rapidly.

"I'm telling the truth when I say I care about you, Suzanne. Please believe that. I wouldn't hurt you baby, I couldn't." He reached across the table for her hand, but she withdrew it quickly. "Can't you just relax and give us a chance? We could be so good for each other."

Suzanne heard his words, and they stirred an emotion in the pit of her stomach. She remembered the fantasies she had enjoyed; she remembered the excitement he had aroused within her. She could almost feel his lips on her now, caressing her neck, nibbling on her ears. She longed to go to him, throw her arms around him, and feel him pull her close. All her earlier inhibitions faded away quickly as she sat there, looking at him, and knowing that he desired her. It would be so easy to be swept away by him, despite the recent revelations. She felt a desire for him, an overwhelming sensation to be with him.

But there were still many unanswered questions. She had to know more. "Okay, if we are going to remain friends – and notice I did say 'if' – you have to be honest with me from this point on. I need to know I can trust you. I need to ask you some questions and you must promise to be truthful. Can you do that?"

"Oh, yes, Suzanne, you can trust me. I will tell you the truth. Ask anything you want."

"First, why did you lie about your name?"

His answer came easily. "My middle name is Paul, and I have always liked that name better than George. I was named after my great-grandfather, and I always thought of 'George' as being old-fashioned. I use Paul when I meet new people." 'Well,' he thought, 'at least it was partially true.'

"Okay, I guess. And obviously you don't work as a truck driver for Kastner's Bakery. Why did you lie about that?"

"Same reason, really. Who wants to admit they work as a maintenance man? It is not very high on the list of desirable positions. In fact, it's pretty low down there. I guess truck driving isn't very admired, either, but at least it isn't fixing toilets and picking up after animals. Maybe I have a problem with pride."

"Oh, but you are so good at what you do. You should be proud of your job. Fixing air conditioners and plumbing problems may not be a glorious occupation, but you are greatly needed and you do it well. You have no reason to be ashamed."

"That's not what my parents think. They wanted me to go to college, become an engineer, design bridges or something. Then they could be proud of me. A maintenance worker, no, they're not proud of that."

"Well, they should be. Your job is important, and you do it well. That's what counts. Not the prestige of the job, or the size of the paycheck." Suzanne had suddenly changed from questioner to supporter. George noticed the change in her and smiled to himself.

"See, you are already talking to me like a friend." He reached for her hands again and this time she did not pull away. He held her fingertips lightly with his own.

Suzanne smiled and relaxed a little. His touch felt so natural, so comforting. But she still had more questions that must be answered.

"George, why did you call me in the first place? How did you get my number and what did you want from me? It's so weird, when I think about it. I was talking to a complete stranger." She had a puzzled look on her face and she tried to remember just how he convinced her to talk to him.

"It was just like I said, baby. I am a volunteer firefighter, and sometimes after a big fire, I can't relax. There is no one for me to talk to. And I just can't sleep, and I have to talk to somebody, anybody. So I just dialed a number randomly and that's how I got hold of you the first time. It was just luck I guess, that I got to talk to the sweetest girl on earth. You were so friendly; I knew right away that I wanted to know you better. So I wrote down the number I had called, so I would be able to talk to you again."

George was really proud of himself now. It was all the truth, more or less. He was doing great. She was falling for every word. He began to stroke her fingers with his hands. "Your hands are so soft," he said in almost a whisper. And Suzanne relaxed a bit more. She watched his hands as they covered hers, and then slowly moved down the length of each finger. Then he touched each finger individually sliding his fingers around hers, slipping up and down slowly. It was like he was caressing every inch of her body, and she felt it all through her fingers. Next he pushed her fingers gently upwards and touched her fingertips with his own. Then he slid his hands down, locking his fingers in with hers. They were holding hands and she enjoyed the feel of it.

"Feels good, doesn't it?" he asked, again in almost a whisper. She smiled and nodded. "I could make you feel good all over, you know. Remember some of the things we've talked about? We could do them for real, right now. We could really get to know each other." George slid out of his seat and walked around to Suzanne's side of the table. He sat down very close to her. He whispered in her ear, "Let's go make our dreams come true, baby. I need you. I'm getting hard right here in McDonald's." And he kissed her neck and nibbled on her ear. Suzanne shuddered with pleasure and a desire surged up within her. This was crazy, she knew, but she wanted him, too.

Chapter Two

One Red Rose

IT TOOK EXACTLY eight minutes to drive from McDonald's to Suzanne's apartment. During that time, thoughts were racing around in her head. Back and forth she went, mentally regarding both sides of the picture. At first she was excited and thrilled at what was about to happen. Then the next thought would be of guilt and the wrongness of it all. Then she would go back to the anticipation of pleasures to come. Then she would fall again to the uncertainty that she should do this. It made her think of old cartoons, with the devil sitting on one shoulder and an angel sitting on the other, each whispering in her ear, telling her what she should do and why. In the end, the apparition with the pitchfork prevailed. He convinced her that she had been a goody-goody for a very long time. Now it was time for some fun.

She arrived, parked, and went to her apartment first, as they had agreed. George followed minutes behind. That way, if anyone saw him going up to her apartment, they might think it was for a maintenance call. He didn't want to arouse suspicion among the neighbors. And he wanted to give her a couple of minutes alone first, to get ready for him. She might want to put on something really sexy for him.

Suzanne did have something she needed to do before he got there. She called Melissa and asked her to keep Lindsay for a couple of hours more. Melissa agreed with no questions asked. Suzanne said "Thanks" and hung up the phone just as George knocked on her door.

She went to the door and took a deep breath. Things in her life were about to take a major turn. She licked her lips, smoothed her hair, and opened the door.

George stood in the doorway, holding out one long-stemmed red rose to her. He had stopped at a roadside vendor and bought her the rose, knowing that she loved flowers and romantic gestures. The flower had the desired effect; Suzanne smiled brightly and welcomed him into her apartment. He followed her to the kitchen, where she found a vase, filled it with water, clipped the rose stem and placed the flower tenderly in the vase. When she set the vase on the kitchen counter, George gently placed his hands on her shoulders and turned her to face him. "I've waited so long to kiss you," he said.

Without hesitancy, Suzanne lifted her lips to his. The kiss was long and explorative, one she would remember for a long, long time. When at last his lips left hers, he covered her neck with small, soft kisses. He nuzzled her ears with his nose; he nibbled her ear lobe and tongued it softly. All the while, Suzanne stood leaning into him, with her head arched back to allow him free and easy access. Her eyes were closed, and she was drifting along with the passion of the moment. A moan came from deep within her throat. His lips returned to hers, this time with an animalistic eagerness. Their tongues entwined, and George encircled her with his arms. Still kissing her deeply, his hand began to roam over her blouse, cupping her breast. This time the moan came from George. He squeezed her breast tightly and whispered, "Take your blouse off for me baby."

Suzanne took a small step backwards and began to unbutton her blouse. When it was completely unfastened, she sensuously removed it from her shoulders and let it fall to the floor. She stood there in her bra, her full breasts heaving with every deep breath. "You are so beautiful, Suzanne," he said, and took her in his arms once again. His kisses covered her neck and shoulders as he maneuvered to loosen the clasp at her back. With one quick movement, the bra fell to the floor and his mouth moved to her nipples. He gave full attention to one side with his mouth, while his hand never left the other. Suzanne was obviously enjoying this foreplay, as he knew she would.

For the next two hours, George took Suzanne on an erotic adventure. And what a wild adventure it was! Suzanne felt things she had never felt before, even with her own self-exploration. George seemed to know just what to do to make her crazy with passion. He knew what to say, where to touch, how to stimulate. There was no doubt about it. Suzanne was finally experiencing the ultimate in sexual satisfaction. She felt fulfilled, young, alive, and more aroused than she had ever been in her life. It was exhilarating, and it was exhausting.

Suzanne didn't want the magic to end.

Chapter Three

Here, There and Everywhere

THE NEXT MONTHS were a whirlwind of pleasure for Suzanne. The beginning of a school year was always exciting, but this year was even more so. There was lightness in her step, and airiness in her demeanor, a confidence in the way she held her head. George was giving her a sense of well being she had not carried with her before. He seemed to give her a little self-pride. He made her feel beautiful. He made her feel she was worth something as a woman. She was more than a good teacher and a good mother now. She was a sensual woman, a woman with needs, passions, and desires. A woman who was having her needs met and who was giving pleasure to her partner in return. Suzanne felt that at last she was becoming a complete person.

Lindsay entered Kindergarten, and was doing well. She attended class in the same school where Suzanne taught. They had lots of time every day to talk. As time went on, Lindsay met George and knew that her mother was dating him. Lindsay quickly got used to the idea of babysitters, or spending time at friend's homes, or overnight with Jenna on a few occasions. And she did not seem to mind a bit. She was a very social little girl, with lots of friends, and plenty of self-confidence. She was observant, too, and saw that her mother was happy to be spending time with George.

What Lindsay did not know was that her mother and George were not actually dating. They did not go to movies or dinner or bowling. Instead, they spent all of their time together wrapped in each other's arms. They discovered some very interesting ways and places to enact their passions. Suzanne was happy for the stolen minutes or the beautiful hours. Both were satisfying and fulfilling for her.

George had a key to her apartment, of course, and sometimes she would come home from work to find a bouquet of fresh flowers on the table. She loved his little surprises and found him to be very romantic. He left her little gifts, too; a see-through teddy, deep green to match her eyes, a sexual toy left under her pillow, a love note slipped into the pocket of her jacket. Once she found a box of condoms tucked into her underwear drawer with a note that read, "I'm already thinking about the next time, and the next, and the next…"

Lindsay seemed to like George, and did not begrudge her mother the time she spent with him. But Suzanne was still quite protective of her daughter, and did not want Lindsay to be hurt or feel left out. Lindsay was Suzanne's first concern. She made sure to spend quality time with her, and to talk with her about things other than her relationship with George. And she never allowed George to spend the night with her when Lindsay was there. All-night visits were on nights that Lindsay was staying over at Jenna's or with another friend.

George was very creative in his ways of being with Suzanne. Sometimes on their 'dates' he took her to a park, where they laid on the grass together wrapped in a blanket under the stars. George knew quite a few secluded parks and fishing holes, where they were assured of being alone.

If it were raining, they would use the back of his work van. Suzanne did not mind a little discomfort, in fact it added a little to the excitement for her. They even made love in the back of her station wagon, parked in the empty parking lot in a shopping center.

Suzanne asked him once why they never went to his place. His answer was that he had a roommate who wasn't very friendly and who was a real slob. It was the truth, after all. Suzanne never asked again.

Suzanne took walks every evening she could. Sometimes Lindsay came with her, sometimes not. George worked out a secret phone code for Suzanne. If she were going walking alone, she called his phone number, let it ring once, and then hung up. It was a signal to him that she was on her way. They would meet at the back door of his building, which opened into the laundry room. George would jimmy the door locks, and they would make love up against the laundry machines. It was quick but still very exciting. There was something to be said about the fear of getting caught. It seemed to multiply the pleasure.

One Saturday afternoon, when Lindsay was at a birthday party, George took Suzanne to a vacant apartment. The apartment was being renovated before it was rented to the next residents. New carpet had been installed the day before. George had supervised the work and made his plans. They made love on the brand new carpet in the living room, then moved into the bedroom to initiate that carpet as well.

Sometimes Suzanne took a half-day off from work, to spend the afternoon with him. During those hours, while Lindsay was at school, they could be in Suzanne's apartment. Those were good times for Suzanne, times when she could really let go, really relax, really enjoy the pleasures George was favoring her with. If they could not be together all night, then at least having a few uninterrupted hours would make up for it, a little.

On only a few occasions, they were able to be together, alone, all night long. Suzanne would arrange a sleepover for Lindsay, and Melissa was always supportive of her friend's endeavors toward a fulfilled life. George would tell his wife he was going away on a camping trip with some buddies. That is, if he told her anything at all. He was coming and going without talking to her much at all lately.

Long into the night, the lovers pleasured themselves and each other. When they were totally exhausted, they would fall asleep together. After a little rest, they would be right back at it. Suzanne particularly loved to be awakened from a peaceful sleep by slowly becoming aware that George was licking her toes. This never failed to arouse her. Then he would slowly crawl his way up her body, licking all the way up to her ears. It drove Suzanne crazy with desire.

They were insatiable and greedy for each other. Even when they were not together, Suzanne was thinking about him, what he had done to her, what he promised to do next time. He still called her every night, to say he missed her and to wish her sweet dreams.

Chapter Four

Living the Dream

SUZANNE BEGAN TO think that she was actually living in a dream. Everything was going so well. Everything was just about perfect. How her life had changed in just a few months time! She never would have imagined that she would feel so complete, so confident, and so alive. She was falling in love with George.

Melissa approved. She had met George on a couple of occasions. He was friendly and charming, had a real charisma, she thought. And he certainly did make Suzanne happy. Even Melissa's husband Tom liked him. They talked casually about the Redskins football team. They both thought the Skins had a chance for the Super Bowl this year. Tom suggested that the next time the game was on television, they should all get together and watch Anderson's house. They would provide the food, George could bring the beer. So the guys worked out all the arrangements.

Things were settling into a relaxed and pleasant pattern for Suzanne and Lindsay. There was school, homework and household chores, all the normal things a mother and daughter need to do. There were some evening visits from George, when he would stay to dinner, and play with Lindsay or talk about her day at school. They were forming a bond, not quite father-daughter, but it was evident that they liked each other. He wasn't there every night though. He knew it was important for Suzanne to have some time to herself, and some time for Lindsay. And he did have to make an appearance at his own home once in a while. He felt obligated to be there some of the time. It was like his wife was his pet. He didn't think about her much, but he did still have to feed and water her and check on her now and then.

George himself was feeling pretty good, too. He had reached his goal. He had found a beautiful, sexy, passionate woman. They were terrific together. He knew she was hooked on him. And he had to admit, he was hooked too. He was starting to believe it had gone beyond sex. He liked her kid, he liked her cooking, he liked everything about her. He wanted Suzanne to be his mistress for a very long time. She was everything he needed. He hadn't had the least desire to call another woman or even think much about anyone but Suzanne since the first time they were together. He was falling for her – hard.

As fall turned into winter, Suzanne's thoughts turned toward Christmas. This would be Lindsay's first Christmas without her daddy. Suzanne wanted to make very sure that it was a happy holiday for her daughter. She arranged for them to fly to Kansas to visit her family for the entire winter break from school. She wanted her parents to see how well she was doing, how happy she was. And she wanted to tell them about George, and how she was feeling about him. She even thought about asking George to go along with them, but then decided her parents probably couldn't handle that just yet.

Lindsay was attending a holiday party with one of her school friends when George knocked on Suzanne's door. She was expecting him, and was wearing a red negligee with white fur trim, black boots and a red and white Santa hat when she answered the door. He was so stunned that he almost dropped his load of packages. He had gotten Lindsay several things, including a big toboggan for sledding this winter. He had something special for Suzanne, too, but right now that could wait. He wanted to admire the present she was giving him.

A short while later, lying under the covers in Suzanne's bed, he rolled over and reached for his jeans, which were on the floor near the bed. He pulled a small box from the pocket and turned to Suzanne with a smile. "I got you something special, baby. Merry Christmas."

Suzanne was quite surprised to see a black velvet jeweler's box in his hand. Gingerly she reached out to take it from him. She didn't know what to expect; she didn't know quite what she hoped. She sat up in bed and leaned against the pillows. "George, what have you done? What is this?" she asked him in a shy whisper.

"Open it, silly," he said. He was watching her expression closely.

Slowly Suzanne lifted the hinged lid on the box. She caught her breath as she gazed on a ring, sparkling with red rubies, green emeralds, and shiny alexandrite stones. She stared at it, hardly able to speak. "You like it, don't you?" he asked, and she answered with a big hug and kiss. "See, not only are they Christmas colors, but they are also red for your hair, green for your eyes, and the clear alexandrites are Lindsay's birth stones. So it was made especially for you, baby."

Suzanne slipped it on her finger and it fit beautifully. She had stopped wearing her wedding ring months ago, and had been wishing she had a pretty replacement for that finger. This ring was really beautiful. "Oh George, it is just perfect. I love it. Thank you so much. This is so special." She hugged him again. He kissed her deeply and she responded by yielding to him once again.

As Suzanne dressed after lovemaking, George called her from the living room. "Baby, you've got to come out here on the deck. I've got something to show you."

The winter night was still and a chill was in the air. But the sky was cloudless, and the stars were shining with an intense brightness. "Look," George said breathlessly. "Look at those stars!"

"Wow! They are so beautiful!" Suzanne replied and cuddled into him. They stood clasped together, gazing at the wonder in the sky. "It feels like we could reach out and touch each star. They look so close and so bright." She sighed contentedly. "What a night!"

They stood in silence and shared the glorious sight. "I've got a secret," George whispered in her ear. "The stars are beautiful, but not half as beautiful as you." She raised her lips to him and they embraced in the starlight. The coldness of the night was nothing compared to the warmth that grew between the two bodies entwined on the deck. The kiss was long, deep and full of a passion that kindled a flame of desire between them once again. George's hand reached under her sweater and found her breasts entrapped in her bra. He reached behind and unhooked the clasp, then lifted her sweater up to reveal the flesh of her breasts. Her nipples were hard, both from his touch and the coldness of the winter air. He lowered his face to them and with his tongue circled each nipple. Giving no thought to the possibility of being seen, they stood on the deck engaged in this foreplay. Suzanne shivered. "You cold, baby?" he asked

"No." she whispered. "Don't stop."

His breath was warm on her chest. He kissed each breast in turn and took the nipple into his mouth and sucked like a hungry infant. Suzanne felt the tingles and contractions deep within her uterus, just like when she was nursing Lindsay years ago.

George sat on a deck chair and pulled Suzanne onto his lap. He continued to stimulate her nipples while Suzanne rocked her hips and moved rhythmically across the hardness in his pants. "Oh baby," he moaned. "You are so good." He began to thrust his hips into hers and soon exploded in a wet orgasm. Suzanne wrapped her arms around his neck and held on tight. His thrusting stimulated her as well, and once again she was excited to orgasm. Together they sat, face to face, smiling as each felt the wetness of the other soaking through their clothes.

"Incredible!" Suzanne laughed. "Even through clothes, you can make me come."

"Only one problem," chuckled George. "Now we have to get cleaned up again, and we better hurry or we'll be late getting Lindsay."

"So," Suzanne began with a shy twinkle in her eye. "Why don't we just go like this, wet pants and all? I can smell you on me, and I like that! No one will ever know. Just us." She gave his crotch a playful rub, then smelled her hand and smiled coyly at him.

George was surprised by her newfound sexual boldness. It delighted him to know that he had brought out this wildness and passion in Suzanne. She was almost as horny as he was! He pulled her close to him again, his hand reaching down between her legs, giving her pleasure once again. "Sure, baby, whatever you want." He kissed her and once again she opened her mouth and let his tongue dance with her own.

As George and Suzanne embraced, she opened her eyes and gazed up towards the stars sparkling in the sky. Dark clouds, heavy with snow, were moving in from the west but Suzanne focused only on the bright stars that were still visible. It was truly the most beautiful night.

Chapter Five

Complications

TOO SOON IT was time to pick up Lindsay at the party. George insisted on driving, since a light snow was beginning to fall and he didn't want Suzanne to have any trouble on the roads. While Suzanne went to the door and stepped inside the house to gather Lindsay and her things, George waited in the car. He had a few minutes to himself, to think about the sudden turn in his life. He knew Suzanne liked the ring, and he really wished it could have been an engagement ring instead of a Christmas ring. He could really see them married and spending the rest of their lives together as a family. Maybe he could even have a child with her. That would complete the picture for him.

There was just one little problem, of course. He was married already. Even though he didn't love his wife any more, and hadn't for many years, he couldn't just turn her out in the cold. She had nobody, nothing, without him. So, imperfect as this arrangement might be, he was just going to have to keep things at this level with Suzanne. They couldn't talk about marriage. He would have to find a way to steer her off that subject, if it ever came up. And he did think it would. She was that kind of girl. She would want to make their relationship respectable.

All he knew for sure was that he loved spending time with Suzanne and Lindsay. He really was thinking of them as his little family. He felt protective and fatherly towards Lindsay. And he felt passionate about Suzanne. If anything ever happened to her, to them, he just didn't know what he would do.

The car doors opened and a gust of cold winter wind rushed in. Lindsay sat in the back, and Suzanne reminded her to fasten her seatbelt. "Hi sweetie, how was the party?" he asked. Lindsay burst into a detailed account of the events of the party, while George gently headed the car down the snowy street. Once they got off the neighborhood streets, it was evident that the salt trucks had already gotten busy salting and clearing the major roads. He was able to drive at nearly regular speeds on the main roads. But when they pulled into their own neighborhood, driving was once again more slow and slippery.

As they turned in the entrance for the apartments, Lindsay stopped her chatter to say, "Look down there by the pool. I see ambulance lights flashing."

They looked and did see flashing lights. "That's near your building, isn't it, George?" Suzanne asked.

"Sure is. I think I'll just drop you off, and get on over there and see what's going on. Lindsay, don't you open those presents upstairs till I get back. You understand?"

"Presents? You got me presents? I'll wait, but please hurry. When it comes to presents, I'm not a very patient child!"

"Maybe not," laughed her mother. "But you certainly are precocious!"

"Huh? What's that mean?" Lindsay asked.

"Never mind, I'll tell you about it upstairs. Go on. I'll be right up." She turned to George and said, "Hurry back, okay? I'll make some hot chocolate and we can watch her open the presents." She kissed him quickly on the cheek and got out of the vehicle. He turned the car around and headed back towards home, with an uncomfortable feeling in the pit of his stomach.

He pulled up just as the stretcher was being loaded into the ambulance. He knew at once who it was. "That's my wife," he said to one of the attendants. "What happened?"

"Looks like maybe a stroke. We'll have to take her to the hospital to get it checked out. Would you like to ride along with us, or follow in your car?"

"I'll follow you. Linn County General?"

"Yes, sir. Emergency room entrance." The ambulance took off, sirens blaring and lights flashing. George went into his apartment to call Suzanne.

"Save the hot chocolate for another time, baby. I've got to go over to the hospital. My roommate has had a stroke. I'm going to follow the ambulance and I don't know how long I will have to stay. Better not wait up for me. Tell Lindsay I'll try to get over tomorrow afternoon, so she can open her presents before you fly out to Kansas. But if for some reason I can't, I'll call you."

"Okay, honey. Be careful. I hope your roommate will be okay. Drive slow, okay? And call me about tomorrow. We have to leave at three. Bye."

Although disappointed, Lindsay understood that sometimes things just don't work out exactly as hoped. They decided to have hot chocolate anyway, and watch the snow fall. Suzanne showed Lindsay the ring George had gotten her and Lindsay asked, "Does this mean you are getting married?"

"No sweetie, it's just a pretty ring he got me because he knew it would make me happy." And she showed Lindsay the different stones, and explained that the alexandrite stones were the birthstones for June, Lindsay's birthday.

Then Lindsay turned to her own presents. She shook a couple of boxes and tried to guess what was inside. One sounded like clothes, she decided, and one was very noisy. The toboggan was wrapped only with a ribbon and a bow, so that was easy. Lindsay couldn't wait for some real deep snow. George had promised to take her sledding on the big hill near the lake.

George spent the whole night at the hospital. He was concerned about his wife's health, and how much this time in the hospital was going to cost. He had some medical insurance on her, of course, but hospital bills could mount up real fast. If she needed surgery, or physical therapy, or maybe even a long-term care facility, or visiting nurses, well, he shuddered to think how much that would cost him.

Through the evening he paced in the hallway, waiting for word from the doctors. They determined that she had had a stroke, and was paralyzed on the right side. Finally they had her somewhat stabilized and admitted her to intensive care. They had tests they needed to run the next day, and she was expected to stay hospitalized several weeks, at the least. George was not allowed in the room with her for more than a few minutes at a time. But that was all he needed to see that she was hooked up to every kind of machine and monitor imaginable. She was drifting in and out of consciousness, and he didn't think she really knew he was there at all. 'So what's the point?' he thought to himself. 'I might as well be home. At least I could get some sleep.'

About four in the morning he checked on her for the last time. Then he stopped at the nurse's station and told them he was going home, they could call him if there were any change.

Halfway home, a dark foreboding feeling came over him. He didn't plan it, he didn't think it through, and he didn't formulate the thought completely. But the idea flashed into his mind and was as clear as if he had spoken it out loud. 'If she dies, everything will be perfect.' He tried to convince himself that it was not what he really wanted, but he couldn't help but admit that it was true. It was an appalling thought, but one which embedded itself more and more deeply in his mind as he neared home.

He walked numbly into his apartment. He was stunned to think that he could be feeling this way. After all, she was his wife.

They had a history. There were some good memories with her, from days long ago. But it was true, if she was out of the way, he would be free to continue his life with Suzanne. It would be wonderful to sleep with that sexy redhead every night. To do things with her whenever he wanted.

And besides, even if Helen did live through this, what kind of a life would she have anyway? She was in overall horrible physical condition, and was not stable mentally. She had absolutely nothing to live for. She was not happy, and could not function as a normal human being. Add to that a possibly lingering debilitating illness, and what quality of life did that give her? No, she would be better off dead.

George fell into an exhausted sleep. His last thoughts before sleep overtook him were, 'Lord, let her die in her sleep. We'd all be better off.'

Chapter Six

Roses and Greenery

GEORGE SLEPT SEVERAL hours, then woke and called the hospital. There had been no change in Helen's condition. They still planned to do another EKG that morning. Next George called Suzanne, showered, and went over to her place. He explained to her that his roommate was in pretty bad shape and would probably be in the hospital for several weeks.

Lindsay was excited about opening presents, so they turned their attention to her. He had gotten her several gifts, which she tore into with glee. Her favorite, besides the toboggan, was a pink Barbie sweater with a skirt and pink tights. Within minutes, the complete outfit was modeled. It fit perfectly and Lindsay asked if she could wear it on the airplane. Suzanne agreed.

After a final check of luggage and plane tickets, they headed down to George's car. He drove them to the airport. The snow had stopped in the night and the warmth of the sun was already melting what little accumulation they had received. "Looks like you should pray real hard for some good snow for us," George said to Lindsay.

"We'll go sledding at the lake the first chance we get, once you get back home."

George parked the car at the airport and helped them get their bags checked in at the counter. Then he waited with them at the departure gate. When their flight was announced, George and Suzanne embraced passionately. "I'm gonna' miss you, baby. Here, I got you something to read on the plane." He reached into his coat pocket and pulled out an envelope.

"That's so sweet, honey. Thank you. So, we have to go. I'll call you when we get there." She kissed him once more, and Lindsay gave him a hug. Together they turned and walked to their departure gate.

He really was going to miss her.

As soon as they were settled into their seats and Lindsay was seat-belted, Suzanne opened the card. The picture on the front was of a single red rose nestled in Christmas greenery. It was beautiful and reminded Suzanne of the rose George had brought to her apartment that first day. Her heart filled with joy as she read the words he had written inside for her. "You become more and more precious to me with every passing day. You can be sure that I will be thinking about you every day and dreaming about you every night while you are gone. I can't wait till you are home again, and in my arms, where you belong. Merry Christmas, Baby."

Suzanne's eyes filled with moisture. Lindsay didn't notice, as she excitedly looked out the plane window.

Chapter Seven

Those Three Little Words

GEORGE DROVE DIRECTLY to the hospital, where he made a brief visit to the nurse's station. Then he went to the chapel and sat in solitude with his thoughts. He could not really pray, he was not used to that. And how could somebody pray for someone else to die, anyway? That just didn't seem right. So he sat and thought about his predicament. Then he decided there was nothing he could do just sitting around at the hospital, so he went on home.

He settled into a routine quickly. Every morning he would call the hospital to see how she was doing. Every day the report was about the same. Little change. Then he would work his regular hours, have dinner alone, and go to the hospital for about an hour. He never stayed long; there was no point.

Sometimes when he got home, he called Suzanne. She was having a wonderful time, and had told her parents about George. They seemed happy for her, yet skeptical, just as Suzanne had expected. Lindsay was having fun with her cousins. One evening she asked to talk to George. She wanted to know how much snow they had. He told her to pray harder, they didn't have any snow left at all.

Helen improved enough to be transferred to a semi-private room. Her progress was slow, however, and she was going to need constant care. The Doctor told George he should consider a nursing home for his wife. She would need therapy and supervision. He didn't see how he could possibly afford that for her. But what choice did he have? He sure didn't want to take care of her himself, even if he physically could.

When he picked Suzanne and Lindsay up at the airport, Suzanne noticed right away that something was wrong. George seemed extremely tired and distant. He was pretty quiet for the trip home, and let Lindsay do most of the talking. When they finally got home, and Lindsay was tucked wearily into her own bed, they had a chance to really talk.

They sat cuddled together on the sofa. It was a warm and homey feeling for both of them. Suzanne thought of it as a sign of wonderful things to come. George thought of it as what would never be.

"So, what's been happening with you while we were gone, honey? Is your roommate doing any better?" she asked.

"Only a little," he said. "Looks like he needs a nursing home and therapy. And he doesn't have very good medical coverage so the bills are piling up. I'm trying to help a bit, but it isn't really my responsibility, you know? Besides, now he can't work, and there's no income so he can't cover his share of the rent…" His voice dropped off. George had prepared this little speech in his mind, but it sounded so lame, saying it now. He was just so tired of this whole mess. So many secrets, so many lies to keep straight.

"What you really need is a nice relaxing massage," Suzanne said, as she began to unbutton his shirt and rub her hands over his shoulders. He was really tense. She could sense that right away.

The back rub lead to some heavy petting on the sofa, but Suzanne did not allow him to go any further, for fear that Lindsay would wake up and see them. And although George really wanted to and needed to, he didn't think he could muster the strength anyway.

So he went home to his own apartment and dropped sadly into bed. He slept fitfully, tossing and turning, wondering what was ever to come of his happiness.

*   *   *   *   *   *   *

There was only one major snowfall that whole winter, and it came the day before Helen was to be moved from the hospital to a nursing care facility. George signed her out at the hospital, and she was transported by ambulance to the nursing home. He did not follow. Instead, he kept his long anticipated date with Lindsay at the big hill near the lake. They had a great time sledding and frolicking in the snow. Suzanne stayed at home to catch up on some schoolwork. When George and Lindsay returned, she had some beef stew cooking in the crock-pot, and fresh rolls browning in the oven. Lindsay changed out of her wet clothes. George had left spare clothes in Suzanne's closet, so he was planning to change there as well. First he took Suzanne in his arms and said, "We had a great time. I love your daughter. I love you too, by the way." Suzanne caught her breath in quickly. He had never said that to her before. When he kissed her, she kissed him back with a newfound exhilaration. When the kiss ended, she looked at him and said, "I love you too, George." They kissed again, just as Lindsay came running down the hall.

"Let's eat, Mommy. I'm starving!" Lindsay saw the smile that passed between the two adults. She was a very observant little girl.

A little later, eating dinner, George fell again into a sad silence. He looked around the table and was so content. Then he remembered his inner turmoil and felt totally miserable. How he wished he could have this life for real. How he wished Helen would just go away. Then he would be truly happy.

The next months went by quickly for Suzanne and Lindsay. They made heart shaped cookies for Lindsay's Valentine's Day party. They went shopping for spring outfits. Lindsay started talking about what she wanted for her birthday. There was spring in the air and that always brought a twitter of excitement at the elementary school. The school year was winding down.

But with George the days just crawled by. Every day that Helen remained in the nursing home was draining him, both financially and mentally. He could hardly balance his job, his obligations to his wife, and his longing to spend time at Suzanne's. He wasn't sleeping well, he wasn't eating well, he began to loose weight and his eyes were looking shallow. The only joy in his life was when he was with Suzanne. Yet he was filled with remorse then too, knowing that he could never have the complete happiness he longed for as long as Helen was alive. This double life was taking its toll on George.

Chapter Eight

Tolls of a Double Life

ONE EVENING HE went to see Helen at the home. She was asleep, and he just sat there, watching as her chest rose with heavy labored breathing. He closed his eyes and exhaustion overcame him. George fell asleep in the chair beside her bed. He dreamed that he had a big fluffy pillow in his hands and he stood over her while she slept. Her face loomed closer and closer as he bent over her. Then in his dream she opened her eyes just as he buried mouth and nose in the pillow. She did not struggle, just stared at him in panic until the expression froze on her face. In horror he watched as the flesh of her face melted away and he was left with a skull, yet the eyeballs were intact and still staring at him. He awoke with a start. His hands were shaking, but there was no pillow there. She was still breathing. God, how he must wish her dead. She's even haunting his dreams now. George rose quickly and nearly ran from her room.

He stumbled out into the night. Tears blinded his eyes as he looked for his car in the parking lot. Depression settled over him like a blanket of fog. He couldn't kill her, but oh, how he wanted to. Why didn't she just die? How much longer could he go on like this? George laid his head on the steering wheel and sobbed uncontrollably.

When he could cry no more and tears no longer blurred his vision, he started the car. What he really needed right now was a drink. Or several. He drove to a bar, one he used to go to often, before Suzanne. He sat at the counter and ordered. Half way through his second drink, he saw a woman he used to know, also before Suzanne. She sauntered sexily over to him and put her arms around his neck.

"Where have you been, Paulie?" she asked coyly. "Rosie's been missing you so bad." She planted a wet kiss on his lips and he automatically opened his mouth to her. All the old lusty feelings came back to him, all the affairs, and the wild sex, all the memories of passion with Rosie and all the other women of his past. He wanted that part of his old life back. The freedom to come and go, the excitement of a new woman, a woman without attachments. And he wanted to forget all the dark confusion he was feeling.

They ordered another drink, flirted hot and heavy, and went back to her place. It was sex just for the sake of sex, and he was extremely aroused, despite his half drunken state. Afterwards he slept for hours. He awoke with a headache and the cloudy feeling that he was supposed to be somewhere. But he had no desire to get out of bed. He just wanted to stay here, hidden from the world. He was unable to face whatever the day might hold for him. He went back to sleep.

The whole day went by, and he never left Rosie's place. He found a bottle of liqueur in her kitchen cabinet and drank himself into a stupor. He was passed out on her couch when she returned later that afternoon. She was surprised to see him still there, and thought at first that it meant he wanted more sex. Which was fine with her, until she realized he was in no condition to perform. Then she was rather disgusted, threw a blanket over his motionless body, and left for the evening. He was still asleep when she returned about midnight. The man she was with shook him halfway to his senses and kicked him out to the street.

George had his car keys in his pocket but could not remember where he had parked his car. He started wondering around aimlessly. He didn't know where he was, and he didn't know where he wanted to go.

That's the condition he was in when a police car pulled up alongside him. The officers immediately smelled the alcohol, and asked to see his identification. They drove him home, telling him he needed to get sobered up before he got into trouble.

George took a shower and did feel a little more coherent. Then he noticed the answering machine on the phone blinking. He was almost afraid to listen to his messages, and sat there in the dark for a long time, just watching the blinks. Finally he gathered enough courage to push the button on the machine.

The first call was from Suzanne. She was concerned because he hadn't called or come over that night. What night had that been anyway? How long had he been at Rosie's? George could not think clearly about time. The next call was from her too. Evidently made early the next morning, before she went to work. Now she sounded genuinely worried.

The next four messages were from the apartment managers, wondering where he was and why he had not showed up for work. The tone in each of the calls got progressively more and more angry. He sure didn't want to deal with the possibility of loosing his job. Not on top of everything else. He would just have to be sure to go in tomorrow and apologize. Make up something about Helen taking a turn for the worse. Anything to cover his back.

Then there was another message from Suzanne. It simply said, "Call me if you want to. We need to talk."

"Oh great, now she's mad too. More pressure. Just what I need."

He had to clear his head. He had to plan what he was going to say to her. He just needed a little more time. He lied down on his bed and promptly fell asleep. When he woke the next morning, the sun was halfway up in the sky. The clock said 9:15, and he was already late for work. And Suzanne would already be at school. He would have to talk to her this afternoon.

George hurried over to the office, ready to get right to work. His excuse was ready, too, and an apology for not being able to call in. They accepted it, knowing that he had been pretty distraught since his wife's stroke, yet they also warned him that he needed to get his act together, if he expected to keep his job.

He went about his usual work throughout the day, not even stopping for lunch. When Suzanne and Lindsay arrived home from school at about 4:30, he made sure he was out in front of their building. He had a chocolate bar for Lindsay, which she accepted gleefully. Before she tore it open, she looked to her mother for permission, which was granted with a nod of the head.

"I hope you don't think I can be won over by a chocolate bar," she said quietly, as she got her briefcase out of the trunk and slammed the lid down hard. He put a hand gently on her arm and looked deeply into her eyes.

"Geez, Suzanne, I am so very sorry. I went over to the nursing home that night, then stopped by a bar and ran into some old friends I hadn't seen in years. We shot some pool and drank some beer, and I absolutely lost track of the time. We ended up at Joe's place, and I passed out. Didn't even know what day it was when I woke up. And I didn't remember where my car was parked until this afternoon, so I have to get back to the bar somehow to get it tonight. Anyway, baby, I really am sorry to get you all worried and upset. And I don't blame you for being mad. You have every right to be. But please know I didn't mean for it to happen, and I promise it will never, never happen again.

Suzanne took a good long look at him and smiled. How could she stay mad at him? She loved him, and he loved her. He'd been under a lot of stress because of his roommate's illness. He wasn't thinking clearly. Mistakes were forgivable.

"We're having pork chops for dinner," she said. "Are you hungry?"

Chapter Nine

Secrets Hidden Well

SUZANNE WAS TOTALLY taken in by George. She thought her life had taken a turn for the better. Unfortunately, she was mistaken. She saw only what she wanted to see; she felt what he wanted her to feel. Once again she was being victimized by the man in her life. Only this time she didn't even know it. With her first husband she had felt trapped. She knew things weren't right but felt powerless to do anything about it. With George, she actually thought things were great, and she was willing to do just about anything to keep the relationship with him. She wanted to believe they were headed for marriage eventually. It was what she wanted more than anything else in the world. She just knew they would be happy together.

She had no idea the secret George had been keeping from her. He hid it well, and she trusted him enough to believe whatever he said. She had no real reason to doubt him. He was playing it safe, covering his tracks. Since that night when he hadn't come home, he had been extra attentive, extremely devoted to Lindsay, and insatiable sexually.

Suzanne still was not letting him spend the nights with her when Lindsay was home, but she was about to totally give in on that too. The only thing that was stopping her was the lack of a marriage commitment and an engagement ring. She felt that after they had officially become engaged, she would be more comfortable with the idea of him moving in and staying nights. They would be able to start being a family. That's how she was thinking.

On a couple of occasions, she had tried to steer the conversation towards the topic of marriage. George was able to expertly skirt the subject without making it obvious that he had done so. Suzanne was unaware that it had happened. But each time George went home more worried about how he was going to keep her, without a marriage commitment.

And then he thought, 'Well, why not? I could ask her to marry me, get her a ring even. But as long as we don't actually get married, I'm not breaking any laws. And I would get to be with her every night. Mmmm, wouldn't I love that? Since Helen is going to be in that place probably forever, she'd never find out. Yeah, I could pull that off, just fine. And as soon as the old witch kicks the bucket, Suzanne and I could really get married. Yeah, this could work.'

He bought her a ring at the Pawnshop. He put it in a brand new jeweler's box. Then he called Melissa and asked her to watch Lindsay the first Saturday afternoon in May. He said he was taking Suzanne somewhere special; he had something to ask her. Melissa was giddy with little girl excitement because she thought she knew for sure what George would be asking Suzanne. She could hardly keep the secret to herself.

The first Saturday in May was warm and spring-like. George told Suzanne to put on jeans, a shirt and light jacket, and old tennis shoes. He dropped Lindsay at Melissa's and returned to pick up Suzanne. She wanted to know what they were doing, and George simply replied, "I am taking you somewhere you have never been before, and we are going to do something you have never done before." Then they got into his truck and headed out to the lake.

Suzanne said, "So what's this? I've been here before."

"But not like this," he said as he pulled the truck up near the boat docks. Then they got out of the truck, George removed a fishing tackle box from the back, and they headed down to the docks. "I'm taking you fishing!" he said.

Once settled in the boat, George started the motor and took them out to the middle of the lake. Then he dropped anchor and set about baiting two hooks. First he showed Suzanne how to cast, and then he let her try her own. She landed her line a fair distance and he said he was impressed. They fished in quiet for an hour before she got a bite. When she reeled in the line, she found that her bait had been taken

"Okay, just reach down there and open the tackle box," George said. "I've got some more bait in there."

"You don't expect me to put a worm on this hook, do you?" she asked with a bit of mock horror in her voice.

"No, I'll do it for you. Just get me the worms from the tackle box."

That is how Suzanne came to find her engagement ring. When she opened the tackle box, there was the diamond solitaire, sparkling in its opened jeweler's box. Amidst the hooks and lures, there sat the diamond, brilliant and amazingly beautiful. Suzanne nearly upset the boat in her excitement.

So they became engaged. Suzanne joyfully showed off her ring to Melissa and Tom and called her parents as soon as she got home. They wanted to know when the wedding would be, but Suzanne told them they had not set a date yet but probably in the summer. She would let them know. Lindsay was happy, knowing that her mother was happy. She asked if she could be the flower girl in the wedding.

The school year was drawing to a close when Suzanne sat with George on the balcony one evening. She brought up a subject that she had been thinking about for a few weeks. "Honey, I was wondering how you might feel about us looking for a house to move into after we're married. I've been wishing for a garden and some space for Lindsay to play in the back yard. And I know you would like more space than just this apartment. If we have a baby, we'll need more space for sure. If we got a little house with a yard and maybe a workshop for your tools, it would be like both of us starting out fresh together. No past, no memories. And it could even be fixer-upper because you are so good at fixing things."

He agreed, and she said she would call a real estate agent who was recommended by Melissa and Tom. George went home that evening, wondering what he had gotten himself into.

The next Sunday they went house hunting. The agent had several houses lined up for them to see. George found something wrong with all of them, too old, too small, bad neighborhood, too far from work. They would just have to keep looking, he told her. He wanted their first home together to be perfect. She smiled and said she could be patient. They had all summer to find something.

Aside from the pressures he was feeling from Suzanne, the rest of George's life was going along okay. He practically forgot he had a wife.

Suzanne planned the wedding and dreamed about their new house and new life together. She was floating on a cloud of happiness. She did not know that the cloud was about to start spinning out of control. Her life was about to enter a whirlwind, like a tornado sweeping across the Kansas plains.

Chapter Ten

Whoops!

JUST BEFORE MEMORIAL Day, Suzanne went to the apartment office to pick up pool passes for Lindsay and herself. She did not know that George was in the back room. He had no way of knowing that she was in the building. She was waiting at the reception desk when she heard his voice.

He was in a conversation with someone else, another maintenance worker, Suzanne assumed. They were talking about the jobs to be done that afternoon. Then the other man changed the subject. "By the way," he said. "How's your wife doing? Is she going to get out of that nursing home and come back here to live?"

Suzanne felt the blood drain out of her face. She began to perspire as she leaned forward to hear how George would answer. What he said made Suzanne weak. She grabbed hold of the desk to keep from falling over altogether.

"She's still at the home, and probably will be for a long time. She needs round the clock care, and can't do much of anything by herself. The other night when I went to visit she was actually sitting up in bed, and was able to talk for a few minutes. But she has a long,

long way to go. One good thing, though. She is eating pretty well, for a change. No junk food. So she is loosing some weight, and she really needed to. Her blood sugar numbers are coming down a little. So, once she gets some strength and can be up and around, she should be in better shape than she was before the stroke. But it's going to be a long process. Thanks for asking about her. I appreciate it."

The office receptionist handed the pool passes to Suzanne and asked her to sign for them. Tears were stinging her eyes, and it was hard to see where to write. Suzanne did her best, then took the tickets and left the office in a blur. She picked up Lindsay, who was playing on the swings at the playground. They got in the car together and drove to Melissa's. Lindsay wondered what was wrong with her mother, but Suzanne just said she had a headache, and she needed to talk to Melissa. Melissa would cheer her up, she said.

With just one look at her friend, Melissa knew something was terribly wrong. The little girls went outside to play, and Suzanne poured out her heart to Melissa. She cried and sobbed and was eventually able to retell what she had heard in the office. Melissa was astonished, then angry, and, as always, supportive.

"Oh Suzanne, I'm so sorry this is happening to you. You deserve so much better than this. How could he lie to you about this, all this time? What a jerk! So, what do you want to do about it?"

Suzanne took a deep breath. "There's two weeks of school left. I need to get through that. And I think I want to go see this woman. I want to look at her; I don't necessarily want to talk to her. I want to see that she really exists." Then she began to cry again. "Oh what a fool I have been. Why can't I ever get a decent man? Why do I let them walk all over me? I trust too much. Maybe I need to get away from here. Maybe I should move to Kansas City, so my parents can take care of me and make decisions for me. God knows I've done a lousy job of it so far. Oh, Melissa, why do I let this sort of stuff happen to me over and over?"

Melissa cradled Suzanne's head on her shoulder and let her cry. She smoothed Suzanne's hair and wiped away the tears with a tissue.

"You're going to be okay, you know. You are better than either of those men. You deserve better. But get a grip on yourself. Make a plan. I'll help you if you want, but this is something you have to do on your own. I don't want to see you move away, but if it would help you get a fresh start, then do it! You do not have to settle for this kind of treatment. George Wiley ought to be put in jail for what he has done to you. Leading you on, stealing your heart. And Lindsay! She adores him. This is going to hurt her too."

"I don't know how to tell her." Suzanne's voice trailed off as she thought a minute. "I don't think I should, until school is over. Then we'll have a talk. I will explain it, and we will move. Somewhere. We can't stay at the apartment anyway. George has a key. I've got to get away." She was beginning to formulate a plan. It would mean a lot of changes, but it would be the best thing for her. "Can I borrow your phone, and a phone directory?"

Suzanne placed a call to the Sunnyside Nursing Home. She asked for the room number of Mrs. George Wiley. It sounded so strange to say those words. She had started thinking of herself as Mrs. George Wiley. Now, here was this other woman who was the real Mrs. George Wiley. Tears welled up in her eyes again. The receptionist's voice came back on the line. "Yes, here it is. Helen Wiley. Room 217."

"And what are your visiting hours?" Suzanne asked.

"Tonight until eight, Sunday all day. Weekdays afternoons or evenings until eight. We are really open any time for visitors. It is so good for the residents, you know. Just be sure to sign in at the front desk when you arrive, and sign out when you leave."

When she hung up, she turned to Melissa. "Want to go with me?" she asked.

They left the girls in Tom's care and drove to the Nursing home. At the front desk, Suzanne scanned the visitor's sign in a book. She saw George's name on the list several times. His visits were usually short, she noted. But he had at least been there. It was proof enough.

They went to room 217 and stood in the doorway. The woman on the bed appeared to be sleeping, although the television was on. The room was stuffy and dark, the curtains were closed and the only light came from the glow of the television. The woman was turned with her back to the door, but Suzanne could see she was a large person. She couldn't see her face, and her hair was wrapped in a scarf. Suzanne and Melissa looked at each other and turned back out into the hall.

"Okay, so she exists. I don't know what that proves, exactly, but I had to see for myself."

They drove home is silence. Melissa finally broke the quiet by asking "Now what?"

"Now, I pretend like nothing happened. I'm not going to tell him I know about his wife until the end of school. I can keep secrets, too. Anyway, when school lets out it will be all over. I will just fake it until then. I really don't want to upset Lindsay while she's still in school. And besides, I have a lot of thinking to do before I just kick him out."

For the next two weeks, George had no idea what was happening. He continued his occasional visits at the home. He kept up with his work and life with Suzanne and Lindsay. He did notice that Suzanne was not as interested in sex, but he accounted that to it being the end of the school year, and all the report cards and activities that always accompanied the final days of school. He hoped Suzanne's interest in sex would be revived when school was out and she was free to relax for the summer. He had no idea that life as he knew it was about to come to a screeching halt.

Chapter Eleven

The Truth Hurts

THE SATURDAY AFTER school was out for the year, Suzanne sent Lindsay to play with Jenna at the Anderson's house. She and George made love for the last time. She was using him, she knew, but she didn't care. She wanted one last really good romp in bed. She initiated sex in every position she could imagine. She was like a fire that just would not die. Just when it seemed the desire had been quenched, she came back for more. She was free, uninhibited, and wild. George was counting his lucky stars. He was glad he had been patient with her for the past two weeks. She had stored up a lot of energy and desire, and he was having the time of his life. He had been sure that after school was finished, she would come back to life. And this was certainly proving it. She was so turned on. And that aroused him so that he didn't want to stop either.

After hours of intimacy, they finally fell asleep. George was happy, thinking that there was a whole life of love making ahead of them. Suzanne was sad, knowing that there wasn't.

She woke early and began removing his clothes from her closet. Then she took his shaving things and other personal stuff from the bathroom. Next she took his coffee cup from the kitchen, and any thing else of his she could find. She threw it all in a box and set everything out in the hallway. The building was quiet; it was still early Sunday morning. She took her engagement ring off and held it tight in her hand. She had it only for six weeks. But a lot had changed in that time.

She shook George awake, not too gently, and told him to get dressed. They needed to talk, she said. He figured she wanted to go house hunting again. He put on his jeans from yesterday and went to the closet for a shirt. "Hey, where's my clothes?" he asked.

"That's what we're going to talk about. I put all of your stuff out in the hall. I want you to get out of my apartment. I want you out of my life. I would like it if you went away quietly. I don't want a big scene, I just want you out." She was very calm. She wasn't even shaking and her voice did not waver. She was strong and determined.

George, on the other hand, did not take the news so well. "What are you talking about?" he asked. "Why are you doing this? What's the matter, baby? Getting nervous about the wedding? We can wait awhile, if you need a little more time. You'll be okay."

"Oh, yes, I will be just fine, once you get on the other side of that door. Now leave. And here, you can have this ring back." She pressed the diamond into his hand.

But George did not leave. He sat on the side of the bed, shoulders drooping, head down. "Ah, come on. Don't do this. What's going on? I at least deserve an explanation."

"No, actually, you don't deserve anything. You are a liar, a cheat and I don't think you would know the truth if it jumped out at you. I was taken in by you, but no more. You nearly ruined my life, but now it's over. And I never want to see you again."

George knew something had gone wrong with his terrific plan. But he did not want to leave her. "I love you, baby. We can work this all out. Just tell me what's going on."

Suzanne was surprised by her coldness. She was not going to let him get to her. She was determined, and he was not going to sway her. "Love?" You don't know the first thing about love." She faced him with her hands on her hips. "I have given myself completely to you. I loved you like I didn't know was possible. But what you gave me was not love. It was lust and sex. It was lies and deception. Secrets and lies – that's how you operate. It was all about what you could take from me. I have been totally blindsided by you. But no more. It stops now. We are finished."

"But, baby, we are so good for each other. Last night proved it. You couldn't have made love like that if you didn't really want us to be together."

"As I see it, every single time we made love *you* were pretending. It's just been a big game to you. Well, last night it was my turn to pretend."

"No, no baby, that's where you are wrong. I was never pretending. I love you, with all my heart. I want us to be together, forever."

"But we can't be, can we?" She turned on him now and looked straight at him. There was a fiery anger in her eyes. "You already have a wife."

The words fell like a bomb. George felt his perfect little plan, his perfect little life, explode in front of him. He looked at Suzanne and had nothing to say.

"See, you can't deny it, can you? And you shouldn't. Because whatever you say from this day on I will not believe. Remember when we first met? I forgave you for lying to me about your name and your job, and I asked you to be honest with me. And you said you would, but that was a lie, too. You are married. You can't talk to me about love and marriage, and buying a house, and having a baby. You are already married. You lied, over and over and over. And now I know, and it will stop. You're nothing but a perverted adulterer – a real creep. And I want you out of my life."

"But at least let me explain," he begged.

Suzanne did not want to hear another word, but he felt he had to try. He hurried on. "Okay, yes, I am married. But it has not been a good marriage for a long, long time. And now she's in the nursing home, and probably is never going to get better. I don't love her, baby, but I feel obligated to take care of her. But I have needs, you know, and I need you. I have loved you since the first time I ever saw you. You are everything to me. You can't ask me to leave. I love you so much."

Suzanne wasn't falling for it this time. "You might as well stop talking, because I don't believe you any more. You have lied again and again. I will not even listen. You are married, get it? You shouldn't be here. And you should not be messing up my life. I mean it. I want you out of here right now. And don't call, or come over or anything. Leave me alone. I never want to see you again."

So George left. He was not a happy man. He piled all his things into his car and drove to his own apartment.

Inside Suzanne's apartment, she sat on the floor and cried like she had never cried before. When she thought she had cried out her last tear, she went into the bathroom and washed her face. She took a cold, wet washcloth and covered her eyes as she lay on the bed. Her bed. Big and lonely and empty. Oh, what joys she had experienced in this bed over the past months. Oh, how she would miss him. She felt like a part of her had just died. A big part. She began to cry again.

PART THREE

SUZANNE AND LINDSAY

Chapter One

Life Moves On

IT DIDN'T TAKE long for Suzanne to pull herself together. She was accustomed to taking life one day at a time. So it was time to move on, time to make plans for tomorrow.

Within the hour, she had changed the sheets on the bed and started a load of laundry. She also called Melissa, to say she would be over to pick up Lindsay before lunch time. Then she showered, put her hair up into a pony tail, applied a little make-up, and dressed in Capri pants and a cotton blouse.

Before she left to pick up Lindsay, she made one more phone call, this to Ms. Clark, the realtor who had been showing them houses. She explained the change in circumstances, but said she was still determined to move into a nice little house before school started in the fall. Ms. Clark asked no questions about George, and promised to keep looking for the perfect house for Suzanne and her daughter. "Do you still want to be in the Dickenson Elementary School district?" she asked.

"Oh yes, with two or three bedrooms, a bit of a yard, enough for a garden and a swing-set. That's really all we require. Oh, air conditioning, please."

"That's not too much to ask for. I should be able to find something for you shortly. I will call you when I have something to show you."

When Suzanne went to the Anderson's later that morning, she was already planning her future – a future without George.

*   *   *

George, however, was already falling into a deep depression. He drove to the lake and sat by the tree, pondering how in the world he would ever get on with his life without Suzanne. He crumbled up a beer can and tossed it aside. It landed in a pile with several others. Ducks at the edge of the lake scurried at the sound.

"This sucks," he said angrily, and the ducks splashed into the water. They were not used to this noisy interruption to their morning swim. "Yeah, that's right, run away," he said to them. "Everybody else does."

George dropped his head into his hands and his shoulders began to shake. He sobbed like a baby who couldn't find its pacifier. He needed Suzanne. He depended on her. She was so important to him. And now she was lost. And worst of all, he knew she was lost forever.

Not that he blamed her. He had been stupid to think she would never find out. And dumber yet to think that she might understand and forgive him. His behavior had been pretty shitty.

'But I couldn't help myself,' he thought. 'I fell in love with her. I really didn't mean to, but I did, and I couldn't let her go.' And George opened another beer.

Chapter Two

House Hunting

SUNDAY AFTERNOON, MS. Clark called Suzanne to say she had found two houses that had just been listed and might be perfect for her. They agreed to meet at the real estate office and visit the houses. After hanging up, Suzanne called Lindsay. "Honey, get your shoes on. We are going to look at some houses."

"George isn't coming with us, is he, Mommy?" She was still trying to figure out what her mother had meant yesterday when she said that she and George had decided not to get married, but that they would still be looking for a house, just for the two of them. She didn't understand how her mother's plans had changed so suddenly. But the prospect of looking at houses with yards still was exciting to Lindsay and she barely waited for her mother's answer before dashing away to put on her shoes.

"No, baby, just us," Suzanne answered, and sighed as the little girl headed towards her shoes. "Just us," she whispered.

The second house Ms. Clark showed them that afternoon was just about perfect. It didn't look like much from the outside; in fact the front yard would need a lot of work. There was a wooden fence running around the front of the house, and several pickets were broken or missing. The gate itself hung precariously from one hinge. Suzanne gave the real estate agent an uncertain look, but Ms. Clark jumped in. "I know the front of the house needs work, but just wait till you see the inside. I think you will change your mind once we look around."

And she was right. Things inside were very nice. The kitchen had new appliances and a nice sized eating area. There was no formal dining room, but Suzanne didn't have a problem with that. The kitchen opened to the living room, which was a little small but had nice natural lighting coming from a large bay window which faced the front yard. Suzanne looked around and thought that her current furniture would fit in the room. That was important, because she didn't want to have to go out and buy new furniture right away.

"This carpet would have to go," she said, half to her self. Ms. Clark looked through her notes and said, "There are apparently hardwood floors under the carpet. You could have the carpet removed and the hardwoods restored, if you would like. Most of the houses of this age were built with hardwoods, but later the owners felt they wanted to update and put down carpet. Now hardwoods are all the rage again, so people are going back to that look. You could get new carpet, of course, whichever you prefer."

"Yes, hardwoods would be nice." Suzanne went to a small window at the end of the room and noted that it looked out towards a neighbor's house. There was a row of bushes separating the yards. "Could we see the bedrooms, please?"

They walked down a hallway and Lindsay peeked her head into the first room on the left. "Look mommy, this could be my room. It's pink!"

"It sure is, honey. That's perfect for you. And here's your closet." Suzanne let her eyes wander and then said, "Yes, I think this will do just fine."

Ms. Clark opened a door across the hall. It was the bathroom, done in pink and mint green, popular colors in the 70s. "And here is the bathroom. A little dated but quite adequate. There's a little linen closet here, and a tub with a shower."

Suzanne turned to Lindsay. "Just one bathroom. Can we manage to share, Lindsay?"

"Sure mommy, we're both girls!" The ladies laughed and moved on down the hall.

"And here's the master bedroom." The room had two windows on the far wall, with just enough space in between for Suzanne's double bed. The closet was smaller than what Suzanne currently had. Without a master bath and a walk-in closet, Suzanne felt like the room was much smaller than her bedroom at the apartment. Still, they had to find a place soon. They had to get out of the apartment and away from the memories. Away from George.

"Okay, it's a little small, but I guess it will do."

"Well, let me show you the room right next door." Ms. Clark opened another door in the hallway, which revealed a small windowless room. "The previous owner used this space as an office. Of course, you could make it into a walk-in closet, if you wish, or take out the wall and enlarge your bedroom; maybe make a nice sitting area. Or you could even run some plumbing and make yourself a private bath. There are many options."

"Mmmm, yes, I guess I could," said Suzanne, but she was wondering how much a private bath would cost. More than she needed to think about right now, that's for sure. One bathroom would be fine for now.

"Now, down in the basement you have your laundry area, and mechanical room. You have your hot water heater and oil tank, as well as fuse boxes and that sort of thing. Be careful coming down the steps, it is not very well lit." The group made its way slowly down the steps. The room was open and empty, except for the washer and dryer in one corner. There were no windows in the basement, but there was an exit through an outside stairwell.

"Too bad there are not more windows down here." Suzanne voiced.

"No, but with the proper lighting, this area has lots of potential, for storage or as a family room, if you want. At least for now it would hold a little girl's bicycle quite nicely." She was always looking for the best in the home she was showing, and was trying to make a sale without sounding too pushy. "Let's go back up to the kitchen. I want to show you the nice back yard."

A door off the eating area opened into the back yard. Suzanne and Lindsay both brightened when they saw the open space. Immediately out the door was a large flagstone patio. To the left was a sunny area which had been tilled for a garden. "Good. A garden. I like that." To the right was a grassy space surrounded by tall oak trees. "Good place for a swing set right there." Along the back property line, Suzanne was thrilled to see three lilac bushes just finishing their blooming season. At the far right edge of the yard was a small shed. 'Probably for a lawn mower and garden tools,' Suzanne thought.

"And your kitchen window looks out on the back yard, so you can watch Lindsay play while you prepare dinner." Lindsay was already running around in the back yard, her arms spread out like airplane wings. She looked happy and Suzanne smiled.

Lindsay stopped at the back corner of the house and called, "Mommy, come quick. You have to see this!" So the ladies followed a flagstone path to the side of the house, where Lindsay stood gazing into a small pond. It was a peaceful space, surrounded by hostas and water cattails. There was a wooden bench sitting right under the bedroom window. "This is nice," remarked Suzanne, but she was interrupted by her daughter who was staring into the pond.

"Look! Look, Mommy! There's fishies in there! Pets for me! I like this house, Mommy. A pink room and fishes! Let's buy this house!"

Suzanne turned to Ms. Clark. "Well, you heard the boss! I think I better buy this house! I like it too. It is a little smaller that I had hoped for, but with the basement and that little office space, there is potential. And this back yard is terrific, even if the front isn't. The kitchen is just right for us. The appliances are new. There's hardwood floors under that ugly carpet. It's the right school district, the right price. What more do I need to know?"

"You do need to know that the roof was replaced five years ago, so you have a good twenty years left with it. And you have just less than half an acre. The sellers are asking a fair price. I don't think you will find any other house in this price range quite this nice. I would suggest that, if you are really interested, we should move quickly. This house isn't going to stay on the market long."

Suzanne agreed to make an offer on it that very afternoon. Two days later she got the call from Ms. Clark. The house was hers!

Suzanne called Melissa right away. Always supportive, Melissa gave heartfelt congratulations with shouts of enthusiasm. "So, when do you settle? Do you need help moving? Can we see the house soon?"

A few days later, the Anderson's minivan drove into the driveway of the house Suzanne and Lindsay would be soon moving into. As the group climbed out of the van, Lindsay asked, "Can I take Jenna to see the back yard, mommy, and the fishies?" With a nod from Suzanne, the little girls were off to explore.

Tom looked around the front yard, noticing the repairs that needed to be done to the fence and gate. "Maybe I can get over here sometime in the next couple of weeks and take care of this fence for you," he offered, and Suzanne gave him a grateful smile. He just shrugged and said, "Hey, that's what friends are for."

Once inside the house, the Anderson's were pleased with Suzanne's decision. Their own home was much larger, but this was just perfect for mother and daughter. And when they saw the backyard, they agreed with Suzanne that it was delightful. The girls were near the pond, so the adults walked over that way. They heard the little ones delightfully counting the fish. "Look, that makes eight fishies!" Jenna squealed.

Lindsay laughed and clapped her hands. "Eight fish! Eight fish! Eight fish is great fish!"

Tom noticed that the pond was right below the windows in the master bedroom, and he had a suggestion. "You know, you ought to put a fountain in the pond, or maybe a waterfall even. Then you could hear the water splashing from your bedroom. It's very relaxing to hear water at night. Peaceful, you know?"

"Oh, that would be nice. I would enjoy it, I'm sure. Do you know how to rig up a fountain? I wonder how much it would cost."

"I don't know about the cost, can't be too much. I've seen it done on TV, but I've never done one myself. Looks pretty simple. I'll check into it for you."

They walked over to the tilled area that had once been a garden. Some volunteer tomatoes were coming up and already had some small tomato fruits growing. "Check this out, my first tomato crop!" laughed Suzanne. "Next year I'll plant some green beans, and carrots, potatoes, maybe corn. This is going to be great." She looked over to the grassy area. "But the first thing we get is a swing set."

"You buy it, I'll set it up," Tom offered. He knew he would need an extra set of hands to help with that, though, and he already had an assistant in mind. 'Course, he would not let Melissa in on his plan. Not just yet anyway.

Chapter Three

Not all Secrets Are Bad Secrets

TOM AND GEORGE had tickets to an Orioles game, and Tom didn't really want to miss the game, just because George had been a jerk with Suzanne. Besides, he knew George would need a friend now more than ever. Tom was hoping that he would be able to figure George out, and get to his inner motives. Having a lawyer for a brother had taught Tom a few things, and how to ask leading questions was one skill he had picked up and used often.

On the drive up to Baltimore, they had plenty of time to talk. George was sullen at first, and more quiet than usual. Tom needed to put him at ease. "Let's get one thing straight right now, George. I think what you did to Suzanne was low and rotten. She's a great lady, and I know she loved you. That was obvious any time I saw you two together. But you hurt her bad. I don't understand how you could mislead her like that, but what's done is done. It doesn't have to change things between you and me. We can still hang out."

"Yeah, sure, thanks," mumbled George. "I kinda figured you wouldn't want me to go to the game with you today. I was surprised when you called me yesterday and said we were still on"

"Sure thing. Can't think of anybody who I'd rather go to the game with. And listen. Melissa's not too keen on me hanging out with you right now, kind of a loyalty thing, I guess. But I told her that I wasn't going to just dump my friend. What kind of a friendship would that be, anyway? She'll come around, I'm sure. She actually really liked you, but she sure is real mad right now. It'll take her some time to get over this."

"I don't blame her for being mad. I really screwed up. I never meant for Suzanne to get hurt. Things just got carried away, and I wasn't thinking about the consequences." George looked out the window next to him and shook his head. "What a jerk I am. And I don't know how I can go on without her."

Tom merged onto Route 95 headed north. "What were you thinking, man? How could you have been planning a wedding and everything? I don't get it."

"It just started out like a game, or a challenge. But then I got to know her, and Lindsay, and it felt like we were a family already. Everything was great when we were together. I had everything I ever wanted. I just felt like I was two separate people. The man I was when I was with Suzanne was the man I wanted to be. I didn't want my other life. But I just couldn't really walk away from that life and its responsibilities. That would have been way wrong."

George tapped a cigarette out of the pack. "You mind?" he asked.

"Just put the window down a bit, would you? Melissa hates the smell."

George lowered the window half way and lit up. After he inhaled deeply George turned his head to let the smoke escape. After a moment of silence he said, "I really do love her, you know? But I really messed up."

"Why didn't you just divorce your wife?"

"Oh, I wanted to, but I just couldn't do it. She's got nobody, no family, no place to go. And now, with the health problems, it just seems like I have to stick in there and take care of her. I can't just dump her, you know?"

"Yes, I guess you're right. But how could you get involved with Suzanne, being married and all?"

George stumped out the cigarette and flicked the butt out the window. "What can I say? I just fell in love with her." He was quiet while Tom found the exit for the stadium in Baltimore. "I'll always love her. I don't think that will ever stop."

Tom noted the sincerity in George's voice and was convinced. George really did love Suzanne, and although he had started out to deceive her, his feelings now went much deeper than that. "So, what are you going to do? Try to get her back?"

George shook his head. "No, she made it very clear that she doesn't want to see me again. I don't blame her."

"So you're just gonna forget her?"

"Forget her? Hell, no. I'll never forget her. I don't want to. She's the best thing that ever happened to me."

"But you aren't going to divorce your wife, so where does that leave things?" Tom found a parking lot with a vacancy sign right across from Memorial Stadium. He pulled in and followed the direction of the parking attendants.

"Well," George said slowly, "I'll just have to take it one day at a time. Maybe, in time, things will work out for us. Maybe not. But I will never stop loving her."

As they left the car and walked towards the stadium, Tom slapped George on the back. "You're gonna do okay, my friend. Hang in there. Now let's go cheer for them O's!"

On the way home, George asked Tom if he wanted to go fishing on Saturday afternoon. "Sure," Tom answered. "Oh, wait, I forgot. A friend of mine wants to put up a swing set in his backyard and I promised I'd help him. You want to help too? More hands will make the work go faster. And you know how to handle tools better than the rest of us. Then we can get out there and spend more time at the lake."

"Okay. What time?"

"I'll get back to you later in the week. He has to go pick up the lumber in the morning. So I don't know what time he really needs us. I'll let you know."

Tom did call George later in the week, when Melissa wasn't home to overhear the conversation. "There's been a change in plans," he explained. "My friend had a family emergency and had to fly out of town for a funeral. So if it's all right with you, it will be just you and me making the swing set. Can you bring your truck and we'll pick up the stuff at Home Depot? I know just what they want, and where they want it put in the yard. We could get it done while they are out of town. A great surprise for them when they get home. Okay?"

"Sure, no problem," George said. He didn't have anything else to do these days. And building a swing set might do him good, kinda like therapy.

A few days later, Tom called Suzanne to tell her that the swing set was ready for Lindsay to try out. That afternoon, Suzanne drove her daughter over to the house to surprise her. She smiled as her little girl ran to the swings. "Mommy, I have swings! Thank you!" She sat on the swing and began to pump herself higher and higher. "I'm going to the clouds, mommy!"

Suzanne sat down in the grass under the shade of a big oak tree. She sighed contentedly as she watched her daughter jump from the swings and head for the sliding board. A house, a yard, some lilac bushes and a swing set. Things were looking up. She would have to call Tom right away and thank him for helping make one of her dreams come true.

Chapter Four

Figured It Out

GEORGE WAS IN the back room when Suzanne came to the apartment office to turn in her keys. She filled out the necessary vacancy papers and thanked the lady at the desk. His throat tightened as he realized what this meant. She was moving. He would never see her again. A few minutes later he walked towards her building. He saw the moving van pull out onto the road, with Suzanne's car following. Lindsay's blond head was just barely visible, surrounded by boxes and houseplants. He stood frozen and watched them drive away.

After work, George sat numbly in his apartment. He didn't move. He didn't eat. He didn't even smoke or drink a beer. He didn't call the Nursing Home to get the latest report on Helen. He just sat.

A few hours later, his phone rang, but George did not bother to answer it. The answering machine picked up after six rings. Tom's voice spoke and broke George out of his trance. "Hey, man, what'cha doing? Wanna come over and watch the game? I can make some sandwiches or something. Melissa and Jenna aren't here. Give me a call if you get this message in time."

George grabbed for the phone just before Tom hung up. "Yeah, I'm here. Thanks, but I don't think I would be very good company tonight. I think I'll just go to bed early."

"What's the matter?"

George took a deep breath. "Suzanne moved. I saw the moving van drive out. She's gone."

"Oh, yeah, I know. She bought a little house. Melissa's over there now, helping her unpack."

"So you know where she lives?" George started to ask where but thought better of it.

"Yeah, it's a cute little house in Cloverly. I've seen it. A little small, but good enough for the two of them. It's in a nice neighborhood, and near Suzanne's school."

"That's good." George couldn't think of anything else to say. "You'll make sure she's okay, right?"

"Of course. Don't worry. Sure you don't want to come over? The game starts in twenty minutes."

"No, really, I'll just watch a little of it here, and then go to bed. Thanks anyway."

Darkness fell. The only light in George's apartment came from the television. But George wasn't concentrating on the game. He was thinking about Suzanne and how happy she must be, finally getting a house of her own. He wondered if there was a garden for her. He wondered if Lindsay had a swing set in the back yard.

Suddenly George sat upright in his chair. 'Cloverly? Did Tom say Suzanne lives in Cloverly? That's where we went to build that swing set…Small house, nice neighborhood…' Suddenly the pieces were beginning to fit together. That had to be Suzanne's new house. That swing set is for Lindsay. George reached for the phone. He had to be sure.

"Hey, Tom, I just figured it out. The swing set we built – that's for Lindsay, isn't it? That's Suzanne's new house, right?" George was both animated and agitated. "But why didn't you just tell me?"

Tom had wondered how long it would take for George to put two and two together. "I couldn't tell you, man. Suzanne moved away from you for a reason. She doesn't want to see you anymore. If she wanted you to know where she lives, she would have told you, right? And if I had told you where she lives, Melissa would have killed me! So I dropped a few hints, and you figured it out on your own. Good man!'

"Okay, but why did you want to drop those hints anyway? If you know that Suzanne doesn't want anything to do with me, why did you even let me figure out where she lives? What do I do now?"

"Do? Well, I don't suppose you should do anything. I just thought you might like to know, that's all. I know you well enough by now. I know you have done some stupid things in the past, and I'm trusting that your stupidity has come to an end. You're not going to go over there and pound on her door and force yourself on her. But I thought you'd like to know what kind of a place she's in, and see that she has found some happiness. That's all."

George was already imagining her out in the yard, pushing Lindsay on the swings, gardening, drinking a glass of wine, watching the sun set. His heart ached to share those moments with her.

"Yeah, well, I get it. And I won't do anything stupid. I've learned some hard lessons lately. Thanks for letting me know about it, though. It looks like a good house for them. I think they'll be happy there. As happy as can be… I know I hurt them a lot. I'll never forgive myself…" George's voice caught and he swallowed hard.

Tom said, "Remember, nobody knows that you know where they are. Don't blow it, okay? If Suzanne wants you to know, she can always call you. But I don't think that's going to happen any time soon. Maybe, eventually, if things change, but she needs time. Don't push her."

"Oh, I won't. I know better than to try to get back into her life right now. She doesn't trust me. And I don't blame her. I'm a real jerk."

"Cheer up, my man! You'll get through this, you both will. And who can predict what the future holds? Just don't do anything stupid."

"I won't." George said again. "And hey, thanks. You're a good friend."

George hung up his phone and went back to watching the game. Only this time he was able to focus more on the plays. His mind was definitely in a better place. He knew where Suzanne and Lindsay were. And he believed they would be happy there. It gave him a good feeling.

Chapter Five

Dream Sweet Dreams

FOURTEEN-YEAR-OLD LINDSAY ROGERS stepped lightly from the school bus and walked towards her house. She turned to wave at some friends leaning out of the bus windows. "Bye! See you tomorrow!" Her steps were bouncy and joyful. She had had a great day at school. Postings had gone up for parts in the school musical and she had gotten the part of Ermengarde in "Hello Dolly!" It wasn't a real big part, but she was only a freshman, after all, and it was quite an honor to be chosen for a part of any size. She felt great, and couldn't wait to tell her mother the happy news.

But she would have to wait. It was two more hours until her mother would get home. Lindsay unlocked the side door and went into the house. ZuZu, her calico cat, was purring at the door. She twined herself in and out of Lindsay's legs as she put her book bag down on the hall table. Lindsay scooped up the cat and held her close. "Oh, ZuZu Baby, you'll never believe what happened at school today. I got the part! I did! Me! A part in the school play, and I'm only a freshman! Aren't you happy for me? It's what I've always dreamed of. I am so happy!" She sat down in the family room and stretched out on the sofa. ZuZu purred softly as Lindsay scratched behind her ears.

Lindsay ended her conversation with the cat and got up to turn on her tape player. She turned up the volume louder than her mother would approve of, and went into the kitchen. She was listening to the sound track from Hello Dolly, as she had every waking minute for the past couple of weeks. She loved the music, and was learning all of the songs, even though the role of Ermengarde did not put her in the musical numbers. She sang along with the tape as she busied herself in the kitchen. She took a big red delicious apple from the refrigerator and sliced it into wedges. Then she scooped some peanut butter into a bowl. She took the apple and peanut butter snack outside to the front porch. Sitting on the porch swing, she dipped the apple into the peanut butter and settled in to relish the flavors. The apple was crunchy, the peanut butter was sticky, and she enjoyed the snack tremendously.

After about an hour of homework, Lindsay had finished her American History and had a good start on her English assignment. She closed her books and went to the refrigerator to see what her mother had planned for dinner. She took the chicken from the refrigerator and placed it in the oven. She cleaned two large potatoes and put them in the microwave. Helping with dinner preparations was a chore she did not particularly enjoy. But she knew it really helped her mother, and for that reason, Lindsay tried to do it diligently. Usually, her mother had done all of the preparation work; Lindsay just had to start things cooking. Tonight she would also be fixing a salad.

Lindsay was chopping celery when she heard the car pull into the garage. She put down the knife and rushed to meet her mother at the door. "Hi, Mom! How was your day? Anything special happened? Any good kiddy stories? Anything you want to talk about?"

Suzanne took a good look at her daughter. She could see the excitement on the young face, and knew that Lindsay was bursting with something to tell. "My goodness, girl! Let me at least get inside the door!" she joked. Suzanne put her briefcase on the table and took her suit jacket off before she spoke again. "My day was pretty normal, which is a good thing. But I think you must have something to tell me. So, go ahead, tell me all about it."

Lindsay took her mother's hands in her own and stood facing her. "I got a speaking part in the play, Mom! You are looking at the next Ermengarde. Freshmen hardly ever get good parts like this, Mom. Do you know what this means? I'm getting a chance to prove myself here, Mom. I'm going to do this part the best it can be done! I'm going to wow those teachers and directors and next year I'll get a bigger part, and I'm on my way! My dreams are coming true, Mom! Everything I've wanted since I was four!"

Suzanne was truly happy for her daughter. She knew how much this meant to her, how hard she was working to develop her acting skills. She hugged Lindsay firmly and said, "You sure have come a long way since you were a flower in a preschool program! Look at you now, getting parts in High School shows, and you're just a freshman. I am so proud of you!" She went to the calendar and asked, "When is the show? Maybe we could invite Grandma and Grandpa to come see you. And you know the Andersons will want to be there."

"It's the first Thursday, Friday and Saturday in November." We have our first cast meeting on Monday next week. Then Mrs. Pitkin will pass out the practice schedules. My part isn't that big, so I won't have to be at practice every night until near the end. And we'll have a couple of dress rehearsals. And there'll be a cast party the night of our last performance. I've already heard some of the upper classmen talking about what fun the parties are."

Lindsay went back to her salad makings, and Suzanne checked on the chicken. Then she went to her room to change out of her teaching clothes. She slipped on a pair of leggings and a loose fitting tee shirt. She enjoyed the comfortable feeling of the casual clothing. She caught sight of her reflection in the mirror. "Not bad, for nearly forty." She had gained a little weight in the last few years, but still looked professional and neat. She lifted her hairbrush and ran it quickly through her hair. She had been wearing it shorter now, and it was becoming. It hadn't lost its auburn glow, and still had natural highlights from being out in the sunny garden so much this past summer.

Over dinner, Suzanne and Lindsay talked more about the play. Suzanne said she was sure that Lindsay could handle the extra-curricular activities and still keep up with her school assignments. Lindsay reminded her of the promise she had made before even trying out for the play, that she would always remember that school work came first. Lindsay was a good student. She did have to work for her good grades; they did not just come easily to her. But she was dedicated and determined to do her best, and that made her mother immensely proud.

The rest of the evening went routinely for the Rogers women. Suzanne did the dishes while Lindsay finished her homework. Then Suzanne took over the kitchen table with her lesson plan books, papers to grade, and other tasks familiar to a first grade teacher. Lindsay retired into the living room to watch a little television. It wasn't long before Suzanne heard her in the bathroom, taking a shower and singing along to the Hello Dolly tape once again.

Suzanne smiled as she got up from the table to pour herself a glass of tea. She was very proud of her daughter. Raising her alone had not been easy, but Lindsay was a good girl, and had never been in any particular trouble. They were very close, like friends, but yet Lindsay knew the limits, and respected her mother's decisions on the big issues. Make-up and dating were the big topics of discussion this year. Suzanne had established the boundaries, and so far, Lindsay was following them perfectly. A light pink lipstick, thin eyeliner, and no other eye makeup. As far as dating, well it hadn't really been an issue yet. But Lindsay knew her mother would have to approve of the boy, and there would be limits as to where they could go and what time to be home, and all that. Suzanne just hoped and prayed every night that Lindsay would take things slow. She wanted her daughter to be true to herself first of all. Have a chance to discover who she was, what she wanted. Have enough self-esteem to know that she didn't have to have a boyfriend in order to have fun or to fit in. And eventually, the boyfriends could come along, and even the husband, if that's what Lindsay decided she wanted.

But Suzanne truly hoped she had shown her daughter that it was possible to be happy without being married. Marriage did not necessarily mean happiness and fulfillment. Suzanne had learned that the hard way. The only way to be happy was with a determination that came from within. Suzanne had developed that determination, and she hoped she had instilled the same in her daughter.

Lindsay came out to the kitchen, dressed in her night clothes and slippers. "Do we have anything special planned for this weekend?" she asked.

"Not really," Suzanne answered. "I need to work in the garden just a little, to get things pulled up and cleaned out before winter. Why? Did you want to do something?"

"I was thinking maybe I could invite Jenna over, maybe to spend the night. I haven't seen her since school started."

"Well, maybe we could have her whole family over for dinner Saturday, then she could stay overnight and I'd take her home Sunday. You want me to call Melissa and ask?" Although distance and time had separated the old friendships, the Andersons were still close to their hearts. Since Suzanne had bought this house, it had become more difficult to get together. It involved a drive of well over an hour one way, and with the girls getting older and all of their involvements with Girl Scouts, sports and school activities, it was pretty hard to find the time to get together as often as they wanted. There was still the phone, of course, and they had remained close friends. But it wasn't quite the same as seeing each other nearly every day.

"Okay, Mom thanks. I'm going to bed now, but could you make sure I get up a little early tomorrow morning? I want to iron my pink shirt, but I'm too tired to do it now. Okay?"

"Sure, honey. I love you. Good night."

Lindsay stooped over and planted a kiss on her mother's forehead. "Goodnight, Mom. Dream sweet dreams." It was what they said to each other every night, and it gave Suzanne a warm feeling each evening as she thought about the one who first said those words to her, so many years ago.

Suzanne poured herself another glass of tea and sat back at the table. She closed her eyes and instantly could picture him. The memory of him was as fresh as if she had been with him that very day. He was playing with Lindsay. He was sitting in a boat laughing as she discovered a diamond ring among the fish bait. He was in her bed, leaning over her, kissing her neck, giving her intense pleasure. It was like he had never left. And truly, he had never left her memory.

Suzanne opened her eyes and shook her head to dislodge the thoughts. She had to get back to these papers she was grading. School, the house and Lindsay – this was all she had time for in her life now. No need to complicate things with other thoughts.

Chapter Six

Still Keeping Secrets

IT WAS ALWAYS good to get together with the Andersons. Melissa had been such a good friend to Suzanne over the years. It seemed that they could talk about anything. Despite some differences between them, primarily their marriages, they had so many other things in common. They shared a lot of teaching ideas and often talked about children in their classes. They were able to help each other with strategies for reaching the kids having difficulties. And because of their profession, they had the same vacation schedules, so spent many days off together with their girls. In addition, they were often together at county-wide teacher's conventions or in-service training days. Yes, teaching brought Melissa and Suzanne together in many ways.

But their closest bond came because of their daughters. The friendship that started between the little girls in daycare continued through the elementary grades. Jenna was almost a second daughter to Suzanne, and Melissa felt the same towards Lindsay. Although time and distance had separated the families somewhat, the girls remained close. They had been on the same summer swim team for several years. Jenna was more of a natural athlete than Lindsay, and was now playing girl's lacrosse in high school and would be on the Jr. Varsity basketball team in the spring. Lindsay's strengths and interests were more in the area of performance arts. She was in the middle school drama club and had been in several plays and skits. Now the part in "Hello, Dolly" had her on stage in high school. She was developing her skills and abilities.

Just as Suzanne had attended several of Jenna's sporting events through the years, so too the Andersons supported Lindsay in her dramatic efforts. They were excited that Lindsay had a part in her school production, and they would be attending one night of her performance, for sure.

They discussed it over dinner Saturday evening. "We'll let you know which night we will be there," said Melissa. "Probably not Thursday evening, since we have so far to drive and school the next day. Friday might be the best for us."

"Just let me know, and I can get the tickets. We are allowed two free tickets for each night, but we can trade them off, so I can get three for whichever night you want." Lindsay added, "Friday night might be best for me anyway, because there will be a cast party after Saturday's show, and I won't be sticking around long!" She and Jenna giggled; they had already talked about what fun the cast party was going to be.

After dinner, while Suzanne and Melissa cleaned up the kitchen, Tom went out to the deck and worked on her sliding glass door. It had jumped off the track somehow, and Tom always wanted to help with little house repairs as often as he could. He was not really a do-it-yourselfer, but he did what he could to help her out. And if some project required more expertise than Tom possessed, he knew who to ask for help. Whenever George did come along to help, Tom had to be careful to arrange it for a time when Suzanne wasn't home. It took some planning, but sometimes it had to be done that way.

More than once Tom had been tempted to tell Suzanne about his continuing friendship with George. He knew that George would be more than happy to come over and help her with the upkeep and repairs to her home. Then they wouldn't have to sneak around. And he knew that George's abilities in the home repair department far exceeded his own. But he didn't want to start something going between them again, and he sure didn't want Melissa upset with him. She had told him that his friendship with George was fine for him, but that he should mind his own business as far as Suzanne was concerned. So he never mentioned George to Suzanne, and even Melissa had not told her that George still came to their house occasionally, and that he and Tom had become good fishing buddies and football fanatics.

Melissa did have her suspicions about Suzanne's true feelings, however.

When the two had first broken up, she knew that Suzanne was devastated. She also knew of the loneliness and overwhelming sadness that had come over her friend. Oh, she had tried to hide it, and tried to be strong, mostly for Lindsay's sake, but Melissa knew. She knew how deeply Suzanne had loved George, and had come to depend on him for a stability and completion of her own life. Then the truth had come out, and Suzanne reacted by expelling him from her life forever. But Melissa knew. George was still in Suzanne's heart, and could not be expelled from her memories.

Melissa was beginning to think that it was time to talk to Suzanne about George. She did not like keeping secrets from her friend, and she was thinking that there was really no harm in at least telling her that George and Tom were friends. But she wanted to wait for the right time to tell her; there was no sense in dropping the news on her out of the blue.

Tom came in from the deck. "Your door's fixed," he said, and put Suzanne's tools backing her little toolbox.

Suzanne laughed and said, "Great! Just in time for dessert. How about some apple pie and ice cream?"

"I like the sounds of that!" Tom laughed. "You keep paying me with apple pie and I'm going to have to get back to the gym."

"Hey, that reminds me, I'm thinking of joining the gym here in town. Now that fall is here, and I won't be outside working in the yard so much, and it's getting too dark to walk in the evenings, I'm thinking I would like to try some aerobics classes, and maybe work on some of those machines. They're running special beginner's registration fee right now." Suzanne cut the pie and Lindsay came in to dip ice cream for everyone. They sat at the table to eat while Melissa said, "That's a great idea Suzanne. And maybe you'll meet some muscular young hunk who will sweep you off your feet and carry you to some happy workout room in the sky!"

Suzanne chuckled, "Whoa, there, girl! All I'm looking for is a couple hours of exercise a week, and maybe I'll try to get my self back into a size 10 again. I don't need to be swept away. That is not in the picture!"

Lindsay and Jenna exchanged glances. They had just been talking about boyfriends and wondering if Lindsay's mom would ever have one again. Both of them remembered how happy Suzanne had been once upon a time, when George was in part of her life. Jenna had told Lindsay long ago that her dad was still friends with George. Jenna also said that her mom said she was not to talk about George in front of Suzanne, it might make her sad.

"Okay, okay, I get it!" said Melissa. "But yes, I do think it's a great idea to join the gym. If I were closer, I would go with you."

"No need to go to the gym, my dear," piped in Tom. "I'll give you plenty of exercise!"

"Oh, Daddy! Please!" laughed Jenna in mock horror. Lindsay groaned and they all burst into laughter.

Later that evening, when Suzanne was in bed, she heard the girls talking long into the night. She could not make out their words, however, and would have been very surprised to find that part of their conversation was about her.

Chapter Seven

Chance Meeting

LINDSAY'S OPENING NIGHT was the most exciting night of her young life. She was so happy to be acting in a high school play! Her costume was perfect, her makeup made her feel so grown up. She did her part well. She was expressive and spoke clearly. The audience laughed at her funny lines and clapped loudly for her at the curtain call. And her mom had brought flowers to present to her after the show. It was a great evening.

The Andersons attended Friday night's performance. They too enjoyed the program and congratulated her afterwards on a job well done. They all went out for ice cream afterward.

On Saturday night, unknown to either Suzanne or Lindsay, George sat in the audience. He watched the program with particular interest when Lindsay was on the stage. His eyes also searched the audience for the beautiful redhead he knew was there somewhere, but he did not see her. At the close of the show, after the final curtain call, he stood to leave the auditorium with the rest of the audience. The house was full; moving towards the exit was slow. Performers were running up to their parents and friends, squealing and shouting with ecstasy. George was jostled with the rest of the audience as he slowly made his way to the rear exit.

And then he saw them. In the back, near the door, Lindsay stood hugging her mother. She was beaming with happiness and excitement, and George felt a surge of happiness for her. Then Lindsay pulled free from her mothers grasp, held her mother's hands and began dancing and bouncing around. Her blond hair bounced freely, and George was reminded of her as a preschooler on the swing set and at the pool. He smiled at the memory. And he smiled even more when he looked at Suzanne. She was even more beautiful than ever.

As he was shuffled closer to the exit, he heard Lindsay say, "I know, Mom. I'll leave the party no later than one o'clock. And Rachel's mom is bringing me home. But she's taking three other girls home too, so don't worry if it's a bit after one. Maybe closer to two. I don't know if I'll be the first one dropped off, or what. You just go on to sleep and dream sweet dreams. I have my house key. And I will wake you up when I get in. Bye, Mom. Love you!" and she was gone, off to change her costume and head for the cast party.

George's heart took a leap at her words. 'Dream sweet dreams. Does that mean she remembers me?' George took another step forward and the crowd around him seemed to disappear. He was standing in front of Suzanne, and it seemed as if no one else in the room even existed. As she caught sight of him, Suzanne took a quick sudden breath and moved back ever so slightly. She was stunned. What was he doing here? And why was her heart beating so loudly?

"Hello Suzanne," George said softly. "She is quite the actress, isn't she? She did a great job."

Suzanne didn't know what to say. She rather stuttered, "Yes, uh, thank you. She always did love acting and dressing up." Then she stopped talking. She didn't know what she was supposed to say, or do.

George helped her through the awkwardness, as he often had in the past. "She looks so grown up. You must be very proud of her. She's lucky to have you for a mother." The crowd was dissipating, and they began to walk towards the door. "Suzanne?" he asked and she stopped and turned towards him. "Is there somewhere we can go to talk?"

"Oh, I don't know if that's such a good idea, George. What are you doing here, anyway? Did you know Lindsay was in this play? How did you find out?"

"Please, let's go somewhere and talk, Suzanne. I'll answer all your questions, really. Just not here."

"Well, I guess going some place to talk is okay. There's a McDonald's right around the corner, is that okay?"

They looked at each other and smiled at the irony of it all. "Another meeting at McDonald's?" he said. "This is getting to be a habit with us! But don't worry. I don't expect this meeting will end like out first meeting did. As much as I may wish it would, it won't."

The mere mention of their very first meeting put Suzanne on her guard. She was not going to fall for another one of his stories. She would see him this once, hear what he had to say. But she would never again allow herself to be hurt by him. Never.

Suzanne slipped into an awkward silence as they walked across the school parking lot and headed toward the nearby shopping center. She was leery of this man, a man she had once loved with all of her heart. Yet this same man had broken her heart to pieces. Only time had lessened the pain. But time could not diminish her determination that her heart would not be broken again. Never.

The silence continued as they walked the block to McDonald's. It was a chilly evening, and Suzanne was glad she had brought her heavy coat. She pushed her hands deep inside the pockets and quickened her steps slightly.

George was aware that Suzanne had put up her guard already. 'Maybe I shouldn't have made that comment about our first meeting,' he thought to himself. This wasn't turning out as he had intended. Maybe coming here, being here with her, wasn't such a good idea after all. He started talking just to break the silence. "Yes, I knew Lindsay was in this play. The truth is, Tom Anderson told me about it."

"Tom? When did you see him?"

"Well, we see each other pretty often. We've been to a couple of baseball games together, and sometimes we just hang out and watch football at his place, or mine. And he told me about Lindsay having this part in the play, and wondered if I would like to see her. And I said of course I would, so he gave me directions to the school."

"Interesting. So you are still friends with Tom and Melissa. They never told me."

"Well, I'm friends with Tom. I'm not sure Melissa would call me a friend. And I don't blame her, after what I did to you. She tolerates me, for Tom's sake, I think." He held the door for her and he asked, "Want some coffee?"

She nodded and said, "I'll go get us a table."

Suzanne sat at a small table near the window and watched as George walked to the counter. He looked older, but still had that thick dark hair, although there was maybe a hint of gray now. He was wearing gray dress pants, a light blue shirt, and a warm gray jacket. It seemed like maybe he had lost a little weight. George turned with the coffee and smiled to see her looking at him. As he set the coffee down on their table, he asked, "So, how have you been? Tom told me you bought a house. Like it?"

"Well, yes, we like it. Lindsay loves having the space. I like the yard and the garden. But there is a lot of work to it too. Tom is always over, fixing little things for me."

"Yes, I know. He sometimes tells me. And you're still teaching? That's good."

"Yes, some things never change. Still at the same school, still teaching first grade." She was starting to relax a little bit. The coffee was warming her and sitting here with George was quite comfortable, even natural after all. With only the slightest reservation she asked, "But what about you? Are you still at the apartments?"

"Oh, yea, like you said, some things never change. I moved to a ground floor apartment though. And some other things in my life have changed, mostly for the better, I think."

"Really? Like what?" she asked. It wasn't the question she really wanted to ask, needed to ask, but maybe she would get the answer to that, soon enough.

"Like smoking. I quit!"

"That is good. Congratulations. What made you decide to quit?"

"Well, it was Helen, really," he said, casting his eyes downward. "When I brought her home from the nursing home, she was on oxygen, and I couldn't smoke with the oxygen machine going, so I just decided it was a good time to quit."

"And how is Helen?" There, she had asked.

"Well, she is doing as well as could be expected, I guess. She's home now, in a wheelchair. That's why we moved to the first floor, so she didn't have to go up and down stairs. She is pretty much paralyzed on her right side. Goes to therapy twice a week. I take her. And a visiting nurse comes over three times a week, to work with her at home and be with her during the day, since I have to work. She can only be left alone for a few hours at a time." With that he looked at his watch. "The nurse was staying till ten tonight. Helen'll be in bed by now, but I should be going pretty soon."

"I'm glad she's doing better," said Suzanne. She didn't know what else to say.

George reached across the table and took Suzanne's hands in his own. For some reason, Suzanne was not sure why, she did not try to pull away. "Suzanne, I want you to just listen to me for a minute." She nodded and sat quietly. George continued, looking her directly in the eye and speaking with a passion that stirred her with emotion. "Suzanne, I still love you. I have never stopped loving you. I know I hurt you, and I can never forgive myself for that. I just hope you can forgive me somehow. I know that you have a life without me now, and I will not ask you to take me back, not now or ever. I have obligations with Helen, and I do intend to take care of her as long as she needs me to. I just want you to know that I am sorry for all the pain I put you through, and I wanted to see you, and know that you are doing okay, and Lindsay is happy and you are happy, and, well, I guess that's all."

Suzanne could tell he was sincere. She gave his hands a little squeeze. "Thank you. I did need to hear those words. And yes, we are doing okay. We are happy, I guess," Then Suzanne took a deep breath, lowered her gaze in thought, and surprised George with her next words. "But I have really missed you. We both have. I know we can never go back to the way it was, but I do miss the fun we had and the way you could always make me feel. The truth is, I think about you a lot." She smiled at him. "And, yes, I forgive you for the pain you brought into my life. Because you also brought me more love than I ever thought possible."

George squeezed her hands more tightly and said "Thanks, Suzanne. You don't know how I needed to hear you say that."

"You'd better get going now," said Suzanne. "It's a long drive back home."

They walked back to the school parking lot, mostly making small talk about Lindsay. They recalled fun times the three of them had had together and laughed at the memories. Yes, they did have some good memories.

At Suzanne's car, George helped her with the door and stood looking at her face. "It was great to see you again, Suzanne. Dream sweet dreams." He kissed her lightly on her forehead.

She said "Bye," closed the car door and started the engine. She watched George walk to his truck and realized that she was smiling. She felt happier than she had in eight and a half years.

Suzanne took a deep breath and let it out slowly, trying to clear her head and calm her emotions. She took a good long look at herself in the rear view mirror. Yes, she looked the same, but somehow she felt completely different. There was an energy flowing through her that she had forgotten had ever existed.

'Well, that was interesting,' she thought. 'I wonder what all that was supposed to mean. Well, apparently George feels a commitment to Helen. But he said he still loves me, always has loved me. Why does that make me feel so good? It doesn't change a thing. He is still with Helen, as he should be. I am still alone, whether he loves me or not. All tonight does is confuse me about my own feelings. I thought I had put all those memories aside. I've tried to forget all about him. How he could make me feel inside. The things he did to me. The things we did for each other. And now here I am thinking about all those old feelings again.'

Edging her car out of the deserted school parking lot, Suzanne tried to focus her thoughts on the drive home. She flipped on the radio, which was dialed into an Oldies station. The words and music enveloped her in a wash of memories, and she found herself wiping tears from her eyes.

The drive home went by in a blur. Suzanne's emotions ranged from joy to anger, loneliness to longing. As she unlocked her front door and went into her empty home, she was aware that loneliness was the overpowering emotion.

Maybe it was because Lindsay wasn't home yet. Maybe it was because the house seemed so quiet without her. Only ZuZu was there to welcome her home. Suzanne took her coat off, and then scooped up the cat, who began purring loudly. She had been lonely, too. Suzanne wandered restlessly from room to room, scratching ZuZu's neck as she went. 'Soon Lindsay will be off to college, maybe even married, and we will be more alone than ever,' she thought. 'It will be quiet here every night. Just me and you ZuZu."

Maybe it was because she secretly longed for the companionship of a man. Try as she would, she could not get the thought of George out of her mind. She really did miss him and she had to admit she still loved him too.

'What a fine mess I've gotten myself into!' she scolded herself. 'And here all this time, I thought I was over him. Now seeing him, just for a little while, and all that old longing comes right back. But there is no sense in it, no reason for me to even dream about us being together, being a family. It would be a waste of my energy. There must be something more I can focus on. Something that really matters. I'll just have to get these emotions under control. I've done pretty well for eight years. Can't let this one short meeting upset me, or knock me off track. There's Lindsay to think about, focus on. I'll only have her with me for a few more years. Best to make the most of it, focus on her needs and forget what I'm feeling right now. Those feelings will lead nowhere. So really, nothing has changed one bit. Not one bit. I saw him. We talked. He bought me coffee. That's it.'

By the time Suzanne had changed into her nightgown and climbed into bed, she had convinced herself that life would go on just as though their meeting tonight had never taken place. She was wrong, of course.

She slept restlessly, half awake listening for Lindsay's return from the cast party. When at last she heard a car door and then a key turn in the front door, she knew her daughter was home, and she could soon fall asleep more deeply. Lindsay stuck her head into her mother's bedroom to announce her arrival, but Suzanne was already sitting up in the bed. She reached to turn on the light and said, "So, how was the party?"

"Oh, mom, it was so awesome. I had so much fun. Thanks for letting me go. It really was great." Lindsay was excited but obviously tired too. "I've got to get to bed, mom. I am so tired. But I'll tell you all about everything in the morning. Love you."

"Dream sweet dreams, baby. See you in the morning."

Suzanne turned off the light and settled into her bed, ready for a much-needed good night's sleep. It was only minutes before she fell fast asleep. Soon dreams overtook the rational thinking of just an hour before. Reality slipped quietly into the subconscious world of dreams.

She was driving down a fast highway. Her hair was blowing in the wind. The radio was blasting out medleys from the past. She was flying, the only car on the road. She was exhilarated, excited beyond belief. Suddenly there was a bend in the road, and she was really flying, soaring off the road, over a cliff, and gliding above the treetops. She looked down and saw a church. A wedding was taking place. The bride and groom came out of the church, waving and smiling. The bride was Lindsay. She looked so happy. Suddenly Suzanne stepped out of her car and stood waving back at her daughter. Bride and groom got into her car and flew away, out of sight in no time. Then the well-wishers disappeared, and Suzanne was left standing all alone. She looked around and saw a McDonald's coffee cup sitting on a rock. It was steaming hot coffee, and burned her mouth as she drank it. But she couldn't stop: she had to drink it all, quickly. It was a compulsion; even though it burned and hurt her throat, she drank it down fast. As she tipped the cup to drain the last drops, something hard touched her lips. She shook the item out into her hand. It was a beautiful diamond ring. Bigger and brighter than anything she had ever seen before. She looked around to find the owner of the ring and saw a man out on a lake, slowly paddling his boat to the shore. He waved to her, and her feet lifted from the ground. She flew to him, and out in the middle of the lake, they embraced. The boat floated to an island and they sprawled on the beach together, and made love as the sun came up over the lake and the waves beat against the shore.

Suzanne woke with sunlight streaming through her window. Lindsay was in the shower, singing.

Chapter Eight

Journaling

WHILE SUZANNE SLEPT and dreamed that night, George walked restlessly around his apartment. First he checked on Helen, who seemed to be sleeping as comfortably as could be expected. George hoped she would sleep for the duration of the night.

As was his custom, George eventually turned on some classical music and sat at his kitchen table, writing in his journal. This writing had become an outlet for George, a way to express his feelings. He had filled several notebooks with his thoughts over the years.

At first the writings were short and curse statements, filled with pain and even anger. And he was hurting. He went through a considerable time of depression, hating himself, hating what he had done to Suzanne and Lindsay, hating Helen for not dying. And he put it all down in the journals. He was able to work through his anger eventually, and resolved to be the very best man he could, despite the rough times both behind him and ahead.

After the first year or so, George was able to focus more on the progress he was making personally. He wrote about his determination to do the right thing, to stick with Helen until the end. He wrote about her daily care routines, and her slow but steady physical improvements. As each notebook filled cover to cover, George filed them in a desk drawer. Sometimes he took them out and reread his thoughts, feeling again the sting of Suzanne's last words and marveling at his personal growth.

Yes, George had made progress. Yet, lying just under the surface, slightly disguised by his positive words, was an undeniable feeling of sadness. The loneliness was evident, and so too was a great longing. George longed to have Suzanne back in his life, hopefully as his wife, at least as his friend.

So tonight, the entry was upbeat and hopeful. He wrote about meeting her, about how beautiful she was, and how she did not turn him away. She was cautious, he admitted, but she had been civil and he had to be grateful for that. She could have turned and walked away once again, but instead they had talked, even (did he dare to hope?) seemed like friends. Yes, George was hopeful, and when he finally closed the journal and filed it away out of sight, he was smiling. Peaceful sleep came quickly.

Chapter Nine

Tragedy and Loss

IN THE FALL of Lindsay's senior year of high school, tragedy struck. The impact on the family was immediate and intense. The aftershocks lingered long after the memorial stone was engraved and placed upright in the earth. Suzanne always believed that one door was shut so that another door could be opened, but she never imagined, or wanted to even think about, the effect a death could have on her life.

It was a sparkling crisp fall afternoon, and Lindsay was on her way home from play practice. She was riding in a car with three friends. The windows were down, the music was quite loud, and Krissy, the young driver, was not as attentive as she should have been. As she rounded the corner near Lindsay's house, the car went out of control on loose gravel and skidded to the right. The right front fender of the car barely missed the mailbox at the edge of the road, but the back wheel was not so merciful to the cat that dashed out from the ditch in fear.

ZuZu, longtime friend and companion of the family, struggled for breath as Lindsay reached her side. With tears streaming down her face, Lindsay scooped the cat up and wrapped her in her sweater. "We've got to get her to Dr. Render's office," she said to Krissy. "It's near here, will you drive us?"

So the terrified little group of girls took ZuZu to the office of Dr. Marcus Render, the only veterinarian in the town. Dr. Render had treated ZuZu before, and tended to all of her immunizations and check-ups. He was a kind, elderly fellow, who knew Lindsay on sight and always asked about her school activities. He loved the pets he cared for almost as if they were his own. And he felt like part of the family.

Unfortunately for Lindsay, Dr. Render was not in the office the day of ZuZu's accident. He was starting his retirement years and had decided to take on an associate and slowly cut back on his own hours at the office. Dr. Render had gone home for the day.

Lindsay looked distressed when the receptionist told her that Dr. Render was out. But she assured Lindsay that his associate, Dr. Scott Jefferson, would take good care of ZuZu and would even call Dr. Render in if necessary. Reluctantly, Lindsay turned her injured friend over to the hands of a stranger.

Dr. Jefferson took the broken body of the beloved pet into his examination room while Lindsay made a frantic call to her mother. "Mom, you've gotta come quick." Lindsay nearly screamed into the answering machine at their house. "It's ZuZu. She's hurt, bad. We're at Dr. Render's office, but there is a new doctor working today. Please, mom, get here quick."

Lindsay's friends stayed and rallied around their distraught companion. Krissy apologized over and over for her reckless driving. There were sobs and hugs and hand holding, as well as shared tears as the girls sat together for what seemed like an eternity, waiting for either the Dr. to reappear, or Lindsay's mom to come. Her presence would take the pressure off; she could comfort them and assure them that everything would be fine. What was taking so long?

Then the exam room door opened and Dr. Jefferson came close to speak to Lindsay. He chose his words carefully. "She's been hurt badly. I've given her something for the pain, but I can't do anything else until your mother gets here to authorize the treatment. There are a few options, but to be honest, I'm not sure we can save ZuZu. Do you have any idea how soon your mother might get here? We don't really have a lot of time."

Lindsay's composure totally disappeared. Her shoulders shook as uncontrollable sobs filled the room. Even the other girls were tearful. Dr. Jefferson took in the sad scene quickly. The girls were visibly shaken by the recent events, and obviously cared about Lindsay Rogers. Someone offered Lindsay a tissue, and she wiped the tears from her eyes and blew her nose. Just then the door opened and Suzanne walked in. She took one look at Lindsay and knew that the news was not good. Then she turned towards the doctor.

Dr. Jefferson was obviously much younger than his partner Dr. Render. In fact, he looked to be in his forties, about the same age as Suzanne herself. 'Hopefully he knows what he's doing,' she thought. 'Or maybe we should call Dr. Render.'

The doctor stretched out his right hand to Suzanne and said, "You must be Mrs. Rogers. I'm Dr. Scott Jefferson. I'm sorry to have to tell you this, but your ZuZu is in pretty bad shape. She was in a lot of pain, but I gave her something to make her more comfortable. I have not taken any x-rays but I can see that she has a broken bone in her hind leg, and I believe she has some internal injuries, possibly some broken ribs, and I would expect some lung damage as well. I have to be quite honest with you, things do not look good. I'd like to take some x-rays, to determine more exactly the extent of the injuries. Then we can talk about the best treatment plan, or what other options you have. Is that all right with you?"

Suzanne nodded her consent, and as Dr. Jefferson left the room, she turned to her daughter. Lindsay collapsed into her mother's arms and sobbed. Suzanne smoothed her hands over Lindsay's hair and wiped the tears off her cheeks with her fingertips. "Oh sweetie, it's going to be okay. Don't cry." Then she turned to the other girls. "Thanks for staying with Lindsay," she said "But if you need to go now, it's okay. She'll be fine." After hugs, Lindsay's friends left the vet's office.

Again Lindsay turned to her mother. "Mom, I was so scared. It was awful. I saw ZuZu run out from the side of the road, and I just knew she was going to get hurt, but I couldn't do anything. It all happened so fast, and I couldn't stop anything from happening. I felt so helpless." And the sobs began again.

Suzanne just let her daughter cry a few minutes. They sat on a bench in the waiting room, holding on to each other, and waiting for the news from Dr. Jefferson. Suzanne was acutely aware of the fear Lindsay was feeling. She felt it too. ZuZu had been a part of their lives for so many years; she was like a family member. Dr. Jefferson had not given them a lot of hope. Suzanne took a deep breath, preparing herself for the doctor's update. She did not want to think about it, but she realized that they may have to face life without ZuZu.

It seemed like forever, but it was really just a few minutes. The examining room door opened, and Dr. Jefferson returned. Instantly, Suzanne caught a look of sadness and dread cross his face. Delivering this kind of news was never easy. He looked first at Lindsay, then spoke with Suzanne. "Well, the x-rays confirmed what I feared. She has some broken ribs, which have punctured one lung. She is having difficulty breathing. There is internal bleeding, of course." He could see the pain on the faces of the two women before him. Clearing his throat, Dr. Jefferson went on. "We could do surgery but in her condition it is very risky. She would have to be stabilized first, and I really don't think we have that much time. To be honest with you, the damage is extensive, and would require a series of operations. It could be quite expensive, and, if she made it through the surgery at all, I am not sure we could save her. I know this is hard for you, but I believe you want what is best for your pet. I think you should consider putting her down."

Dr. Jefferson knew that his evaluation of the situation was not what these ladies really wanted to hear. But it was the truth, and he did not want to give them hope if there were no hope to give.

Lindsay's grip on her mother's arm tightened and she stifled a gasp. "Mom...?"

"Lindsay, we have to do what is best for ZuZu. If there is no hope, and she is suffering, we have to let her go. She loves us and trusts us to take care of her. She depends on us to know what to do."

Dr. Jefferson spoke during the pause. "If you would like, I could call Dr. Render to get his opinion. If you would be more comfortable with his diagnosis, I'll call him right now." He left it up to the ladies.

"Please, Mom. Please call Dr. Render. He knows ZuZu, and he knows how much I love her. Please ask him what we should do." Lindsay begged her mother, and then turned to Dr. Jefferson. "Yes, please call Dr. Render." Lindsay spoke for her mother, who did not object. She simply nodded, and Dr. Jefferson stepped behind the desk to reach for the phone. Suzanne smiled reassuringly at Lindsay, who was breathing a little more calmly now.

The women listened as Dr. Jefferson spoke with the elder man. He described ZuZu's injuries, speaking sometimes in medical terms that the girls did not fully comprehend. He spoke about the x-rays, the internal bleeding, the punctured lung, and then listened as Dr. Render asked a few questions, which were answered with short responses. Then Dr. Jefferson beaconed Lindsay. "Dr. Render wants to talk to you, Lindsay," he said as he handed the phone to her.

"Hello?... I'm okay, Mom is here... I know, but... Okay, but it's just so hard... Well, if you really think so... Okay. Thank you." Lindsay handed the phone back to Dr. Jefferson and turned to her mother. "He says Dr. Jefferson is right, we need to help her this way. She is suffering and she isn't going to get better. We need to let her go. It's best."

Now that the decision had been made, Lindsay did her best to pull herself together. She wiped her eyes, blew her nose, and straightened her shoulders. She turned to speak with Dr. Jefferson. He was surprised at her composure and resolve. "Can I hold her while she goes to sleep?"

Suzanne was not surprised by the request. She knew her daughter would want to be there at the end. She knew Lindsay would not turn her back and walk out the door until she had had a few last minutes with her friend.

In the exam room, Lindsay sat in a chair with a small towel spread over her legs. Dr. Jefferson placed a limp ZuZu on her lap. Then he left the room, giving the little group some more private time. Lindsay stroked ZuZu's head and whispered softly to her. Suzanne stood behind the chair with her hands resting on Lindsay's shoulders. After a few minutes, Dr. Jefferson re-entered the room. "Are you ready?" he asked Lindsay. She nodded quietly and the Dr. inserted the needle into ZuZu's front leg. "It will only take a few minutes. When you are ready to leave, you can put her here on this table. Wrap her up in the towel if you want." He looked at Suzanne sympathetically and left the room.

And then it was over. Lindsay placed the stilled animal on the exam table and wrapped her gently in the towel. Before she turned to leave the room, Lindsay pulled the towel off of ZuZu's forehead and softly kissed her friend goodbye.

*　*　*　*　*

Miles away, another soul was about to leave its earthly body. But unlike ZuZu's, this soul was leaving without a loving stroke and a gentle kiss to the forehead. The body lay in anguish, alone and crumpled in a heap on the apartment floor. Notebooks lay open on the table, where she had sat just moments before. Empty prescription bottles were lined up on the table, along with a nearly empty bottle of Jim Beam. Loose papers lay scattered on the floor around her body. Clutched in her hand was a bourbon stained suicide note.

"Now you are free."

That's the way George found her an hour later. Her lifeless body was still warm to the touch. George sat on the floor beside her and read the note in her hand. Then he looked around on the floor. It

265

was littered with other notes she had written; most were longer than the one she had clung to at the last. He gathered the papers, stacked them in a drawer, and reached for the phone. There were things he had to take care of.

Chapter Ten

By the Script

SCOTT JEFFERSON REMOVED his lab coat and tossed it into the laundry basket in the back room. He washed his hands at the sink, straightened his tie and glanced at his reflection in the mirror. 'Looks good,' he thought. Scott turned his head from side to side, feeling ripples of tension in his neck and upper back. He shrugged his shoulders, up and down in a circular motion and felt the muscles relax slightly. 'Time for a massage,' he said to himself.

Before Scott left the vet's office, he made a call to Alexis, his favorite massage therapist. She agreed to be at his home in an hour. Scott smiled to himself, remembering the last time she had come over to give him a massage. Yes, a massage from Alexis was just what he needed after the stressful day he had just gotten through.

Scott locked the office and walked to the Mazda parked at the side of the building. As he drove home, he let his mind wander back to the two beautiful women he had met just a few hours before. Suzanne and Lindsay Rogers. Beautiful indeed. The mother, strong and supportive, luscious lips, deep green eyes, full breasts. The daughter, young yet mature, innocent yet adventurous. He sensed all of this in the short time they had been together. He imagined his own hands stroking the long blond hair. He shivered with pleasure as he thought of his fingers tracing the tear stains on her beautiful young face. He recalled the look of her ass in tight fitting jeans, and the flat stomach and firm breasts revealed by the tee-shirt she had tucked in at the waist. So casual and school-girl like, much unlike her mother, who was dressed like an uptight old maid. "Which is what she is!" He laughed out loud at his little joke. A quick look at the cat's file had revealed that there was no Mr. Rogers. Scott had also noted the home phone number, jotting it down on a small slip of paper which was now tucked inside his wallet.

When he got home, Scott had just enough time to pour two glasses of wine and light candles around his Jacuzzi tub. He started filling the tub and then walked into his bedroom to undress. He returned to the tub to check the water temperature, and then took a blue terry robe from the closet. He put it on and tried it securely at the waist. Then he took a pink robe from the closet and laid it across the foot of his bed.

When Alexis rang the doorbell just minutes later, Scott was ready for her. She smiled and kissed him deeply as soon as he had shut the front door. This was the first scene of the routine they had worked out. Everything was scripted; each scene was designed and rehearsed. She liked it that way. She always knew what to expect. His hands roamed her body, always touching her clothing, never touching her skin. Not yet.

Upstairs, she removed her clothing slowly, sensuously moving to the rhythm of the music Scott had playing. She walked over to him and allowed him to kiss her again, this time his hands grabbed her ass and pulled her as close as his robe would allow. She took his hand and led him to the tub filled with hot foaming water. She stepped into the tub, leaned back and closed her eyes. Scott removed his robe and joined her at the opposite end of the tub. When he was settled in the water, Alexis opened her eyes and smiled. She drank from the wine glass he offered her, and sat the glass on the tub's edge. Everything by the script.

The rest of the evening also went by script. Relaxing in the tub, his tense shoulder muscles warmed and loosened. When the time was right, Scott stood and stepped from the tub. He wrapped the robe around himself and went to the massage table. He dropped the robe on a chair and positioned himself head down on the table. Soon he heard Alexia's barefoot steps on the tile floor. He smelled the lotions she applied and worked into his tired muscles. Occasionally he felt her breast rub against him as she reached across his back.

When all of the muscles on his back and legs had been lotioned and lathered, Alexis gently placed a gel eye mask around his head. She whispered for him to roll over, which he did blindly. She rolled a warm towel and positioned it under his knees, to relax his legs. Then Alexis went to the head of the table and stood near Scott's face. "Now it's your turn," she said, and leaned close to him. Scott, though blindfolded, reached his hands for her breasts. He squeezed and massaged them, then sucked the nipples as she leaned over his face. As he did so, Alexia watched his crotch. The muscle there began to stiffen and stand upright. Alexis moved to the middle of the table and began to stroke his bulging manhood. She stroked and massaged until he erupted, spilling over his chest and stomach.

Alexis cleaned him with her tongue, twirling playfully around his belly button. This was the part she liked best, the point at which she knew he wanted more, but she refused to go any further. She had written the script, and he had agreed to it from the beginning. She had her standards, after all. She was saving herself for the right guy, the right circumstances. And this old dude certainly wasn't her type. He helped to pay the bills, that's all. It was getting her through college, albeit slowly.

Alexis moved to the head of the table. She leaned over him and kissed his open mouth. "Thanks Scottie," she said. "Call me again soon."

When she left the room, Scott climbed back in the Jacuzzi and sunk deep into the warm water. He heard her in the bedroom, dressing, packing oils and lotions into her bag, and removing the cash he had placed on the nightstand for her. All by the script. Her damn script. Someday he was going to throw that script out the window and direct his own scene.

But for now, this would do. He got what he needed, after all.

Chapter Eleven

Thinking About the Future

ON SATURDAY, THE phone rang. Suzanne wiped her hands on her apron and reached for the phone. She was making an apple cake for a bake sale at school. Lindsay's drama club was holding a car wash and bake sale as a fundraiser. Lindsay had volunteered to help by paring and slicing the apples. Working together, they could get the cake baked and off to the school by ten o'clock. Working side by side, they talked a little about ZuZu. They had decided that they would have a stone engraved with her name and they would place the stone out in the garden, where ZuZu had loved to lay on sunny days.

The ringing of the phone interrupted their conversation briefly. It was Melissa Anderson, calling with news of interest to Suzanne. They had gotten a call from George, and were stunned to hear that Helen had passed away. Melissa said she had no details; George was still in the process of making the arrangements.

"Hmmm, I wonder if I should call him," Suzanne asked.

"Sure, now's your chance. You guys can get back together, get married, and move on, like you've always wanted. You should call him right away." Melissa was assertive, as usual.

"Oh, I'm not sure that is a good idea. And we certainly shouldn't rush things. A lot of time has passed, you know. We have probably both changed a lot. Time does that. I think I'm a different person than I was ten years ago."

Lindsay gave her mother a quizzical look and raised one eyebrow. Suzanne shrugged and turned away. She wasn't ready to commit to a relationship with George, and she didn't know for sure if she even wanted to talk about it with Lindsay.

"I've got some news for you, too," she said, changing the subject. She proceeded to tell Melissa about ZuZu's death. "It's hard," she continued. "It's only been a couple of days, and I still expect to see her sitting in the front window, or twining in and out of my legs when I walk in the door. I looked at her food dish this morning, and just started crying all over again. I know Lindsay really misses her too. But we know we did the right thing. She was in real bad shape."

The two talked a bit longer, and Melissa ended with "You call him, Suzanne. This could be your real chance for happiness. You know he made you really happy back then, for a while. Give it a try."

"I'll think about it," Suzanne answered. But as she hung up the phone and turned back to the apple cake, she knew she would have to think long and hard if she were ever to actually call him. Maybe she would just wait for him to call her. He could surely get the number from Melissa and Tom, or even just look it up. But would he? And what would she do if he did?

"That was Mrs. Anderson, right Mom?" asked Lindsay. "What were you talking about? Sounded kinda serious…"

"Well," Suzanne hesitated. She didn't know just how much to say to Lindsay. Her daughter knew only the barest details of the break up years ago. Suzanne had been careful not to over-dramatize the split, but had tried to focus on the positives. They had had fun, they had learned a lot, they had moved on. Suzanne did have the feeling that Lindsay had always hoped, somehow, somewhere, that she and George would get back together. Similar to how children of divorced parents secretly believed the family would be whole again someday.

But as the years wore on, Lindsay seemed to understand more and more that her mother's happiness was not dependent upon a relationship with a man. At least, that is the way Suzanne had wanted to portray the situation, and she felt that she had done well. However, Lindsay didn't really know about her mother's long lonely nights since she had been apart from George. She didn't hear the sad sobs stifled so many nights into a pillow. She didn't see her mother's hands slide slowly over her unattended breasts. She didn't know that her mother had, out of necessity, stimulated herself with memories, fantasies, and her own fingers or mechanical devices. Before George, she hadn't known that she could bring herself to satisfaction. But he had sparked a need in her, and without him she was left on her own. Sometimes she was glad she had learned how to stimulate herself. It was better than no sex life at all. But often it left her longing for manly hands to caress her, real kisses on her neck and breasts, not just the memories of the past or the fantasies of what would most likely never be again.

Suzanne had let her mind drift a bit but was snapped back to reality by Lindsay's second inquiry. "Mom? What's going on?" Lindsay put the sliced apples in the strainer and rinsed them with cold water. Then she turned to her mother, waiting for an answer.

"Yes, that was Mrs. Anderson. You remember George don't you? The man from the apartments?" Lindsay nodded her head so Suzanne went on. "Well, Melissa called to tell me that George's wife had died. She thought I would want to know."

"Gee Mom, that's great!" exclaimed Lindsay, until she saw the look of shock that crossed her mother's face. "Well, not great that she died, I mean, but great that you can start dating George again. I remember he was so much fun. And he made you happy, I know that, until at the end, I mean. So now you can really get together, and you can have a man in your life again! That's so cool for you! It's just what you need!"

"Whoa there girl. Slow down, slow down." Suzanne interrupted the delightful dissertation of her daughter. "You are rushing things a little, don't you think? Who said anything about getting back together with George? And who said I need a man in my life? And how do you know so much about what I need, anyway?"

"Well Mom, I'm not blind, you know. I remember you were happy with George. I know you must be lonely without him, or at least somebody, day after day and night after night. I'm not just a kid any more, Mom. I know we women have needs. I know you put on a good front, and you act like you're happy and okay with being unmarried. But I read, you know. And I am growing up. I may not have experienced true love yet, but I know that when I do I will be happy like I remember you were. So what's the problem? Are you some kind of martyr or something, that you want to punish your-self and be alone the rest of your life? What's the point, Mom? You should go out there and get some happiness. If not George, than at least somebody. I'm not going to be around here forever, you know. And pretty soon even this little house is going to seem pretty big and empty. I hate to think about you being all alone. You need to get yourself a man."

Suzanne was stunned by her daughter's little speech. She didn't know that, after all this time, Lindsay had even remembered George, much less thought about him positively.

"Lindsay, I'm surprised at you. I would have thought that I had taught you that I don't have to have a man in my life in order to be happy. I mean, all these years, haven't we been happy? Haven't we been just fine, without a man around? We've done okay, haven't we? Where do you suddenly get the notion that a man or a husband is the key to a woman's happiness? I thought I had shown you otherwise."

Lindsay dried her hands on a kitchen towel as she answered her mother. "Yes, mom, we've been happy. We've done okay. And I know you tried hard to give me a pretty normal life even without a dad. You really did great, and I don't regret a thing, for myself. It's just you I am thinking about. I mean, one of these days I'm gonna pack up and head out to college, and then someday I'm going to move away for good, maybe for Broadway or Hollywood even, and you'll be here, grading papers and waiting for the phone to ring and sometimes I just won't call as often as you want, and you will be sad and feel lonely, and I just think it would be better for you if there was someone else in your life besides just me. I worry about you, Mom."

"Well, don't. I'll do all the worrying in this house. And right now I am worried that if we don't get back to work here, this apple cake isn't going to make it in time for the bake sale, and you are going to be late for the car wash as well. So let's just get going, and we can continue this discussion later. Or not! Now bring me the flour, will you?"

With that, they changed the subject of discussion. But both were thinking, just the same.

Chapter Twelve

Moving Forward

THE SMELL OF cinnamon and apples lingered in the car even after Suzanne dropped Lindsay and the cake at the school parking lot. They were a little late, but it would be okay. Lindsay was dressed in shorts and a tee shirt, with a sweatshirt tied around her waist in case it got chilly later in the afternoon. She placed the cake on the bake sale table and went to join the group of teens already washing cars. The weather was perfect, sunny and warm, with just a hint of fall crispness in the air. Suzanne waved as she drove out of the parking lot. She put the windows down and drove toward the shopping mall at the edge of town. Her aerobics class would start in half an hour and she would have just enough time to get to the gym and change into her workout clothes.

Suzanne enjoyed these classes. She had been going for nearly two years now, and hardly ever missed a Saturday class. She also tried to get to the gym once or twice a week, to use the treadmill and other machines. Now that Lindsay was so busy with school groups, Suzanne didn't feel the need to get home right after school every night.

Yes, Lindsay was growing up. As she had so adequately stated earlier in the day! Suzanne smiled at the thought of the morning's conversation. So Lindsay was worried about her, huh? It made her feel kind of good, yet troubled her at the same time. She didn't want Lindsay to feel too responsible for her. Lindsay had a life to live, places to go, things to do. Suzanne did not want to hold her daughter back, for any reason. Lindsay should not feel like she had to take care of her mother, like her absence would bring such loneliness and sadness to her mother's life.

Suzanne entered the gym lobby and signed in at the desk. As she walked to the ladies changing room, Dr. Scott Jefferson looked up from his workout on the rowing machine. He knew at once that she was someone he had met before, but he couldn't quite place her. Was she a regular here, someone he had noticed before? No, he didn't think so. He knew her from somewhere else, but where? The University? Not likely. She was too old to be a student, and he didn't think she was on staff. Maybe he had met her at the vet's office. Just then Suzanne came out of the dressing room, and Scott remembered.

It was her eyes that gave him the clue. Deep, dark green eyes. Her auburn hair was pulled up into a ponytail, which emphasized her eyes all the more. She was the lady from the vet's office, the one with the beautiful blond daughter, about 16 years old. They had the injured cat that had to be put to sleep. And here she was now, dressed entirely different than the other time he had seen her. That other day, she had been dressed for business. Today she was wearing a black body suit with burgundy tights and a burgundy slouch shirt that fell easily off one shoulder. He could see the shape of her legs clearly in the skin tight leotards. Muscular and firm, good shape for an older woman. Even her ass looked tight. Scott could not tell much about her stomach. The shirt also disguised her breasts, so he could only imagine she looked pretty good. A much different impression than he had gotten the other day at the office. In fact, that day he had hardly noticed her at all, just her eyes. He had a vivid recollection of the daughter, however, and the memory of that flat stomach and firm ass brought a smile to his face.

Rogers, that was her name. Suzanne Rogers. The cat was ZuZu, pretty odd name but he had seen worse. The daughter was Lindsay. He remembered that for sure, in fact he had thought about Lindsay Rodgers several times in the past few days.

Scott watched Suzanne as she joined some other women in the aerobics room. There was a huge glass wall separating the aerobics area from the rest of the gym. Scott repositioned himself on a treadmill near the glass wall so he could watch the class, and Suzanne, better.

Before long the instructor entered the room and the class began. Scott could faintly hear the music and some of the teacher's instructions. He watched as the women went through their routines, first warm-ups and stretching, then some more strenuous activities to increase heart rate. At one point the ladies used some hand weights. He noticed that Suzanne used the lightest weights available. 'She must be sorta new at this,' he thought. When they used the ankle weights, however, Suzanne chose a heavier weight and did the leg lifts and extensions easily. 'Explains why her legs look so good,' he noted to himself.

The class was winding down, and Scott planned his next action quickly. He noted that he had traveled several miles on the treadmill, although he had not programmed in too difficult a routine. He mopped his forehead with a towel and moved toward the ladies headed for the showers.

Suzanne caught his eye just then and knew that she had seen this man somewhere before. She was trying to place him, a parent of one of her past students, maybe? When he smiled at her and said "Hello, Mrs. Rogers. Imagine meeting you here." Suzanne still had not figured out who he was. He noticed her slightly puzzled expression and extended his hand. "Scott Jefferson, the veterinarian. We met this week at the office, with your daughter and your cat ZuZu."

Suzanne shook his hand and smiled back. "Oh, yes, of course. Nice to see you again. I knew I recognized you but just could quite place you. You're not wearing your vet scrubs!"

"And you're not wearing your work clothes, either. But I did recognize you. It's your eyes. You have such deep green eyes, they are hard to forget!" The comment made Suzanne blush, though she was sure he would not notice, considering that her face was already flushed from the workout she had just been through. She smiled but cast her glance downward.

"Do you come here a lot?" she asked, just to make conversation.

"A couple of times a week," he said. "I have some equipment at home, too, but sometimes I just like getting out to the gym for a change of scenery. I'm glad I decided to come out today, otherwise I wouldn't have run in to you."

Those compliments again. Suzanne wasn't used to this, and didn't really know how to react. It was flustering to her, not knowing what to say. He didn't give her much time to say anything, however, for he went on. "Are you about done here? Or is there more you want to do? Maybe we could go somewhere and get some lunch or some coffee and talk. I would like to get to know you, find out how your daughter is doing. What do you think?"

Suzanne didn't know what to say. She had not been invited out to lunch by a man in years. But of course, this wasn't really a date or anything. It was just the chance meeting of two people who would like to get to know each other better. And what was it Lindsay had said? It was time for her to get a man in her life. Well, whether that was true or not, the thought of lunch with his man did appeal to her. After all, he was handsome, established, fairly well off, and probably could keep up an interesting conversation.

Suzanne glanced at the clock on the wall. Two-fifteen. She took a deep breath, tilted her head and smiled up at Scott. "Yes, a little lunch would be nice. I need to pick up Lindsay at the school by five, so I have time. But I would like to shower first."

"Hey, me too!" Scott laughed. "But since I think they have rules about men and women showering together, you'd better go that way" he said, and pointed to the ladies shower room, "and I'll go that way." He pointed to the men's room. "Meet you back here in fifteen minutes?"

"Maybe twenty," Suzanne said with a smile.

"Fine, I'll be waiting right here. See ya soon."

They headed to the showers and Suzanne found herself feeling a little giddy and excited. She tried to talk herself out of such foolish feelings, after all it's just lunch, just talking, just… Just what? A friendship? Not even that yet.

She took a little extra time styling her hair with the blow dryer supplied by the gym. Normally she would have just gone out to her car with her hair damp from the shower. Then she could take care of it properly at home. But this wasn't normal. She wanted to appear a little more presentable this afternoon.

Scott was waiting, as promised, when Suzanne emerged from the ladies changing area. He liked the looks of the woman coming towards him, and could not wait to get to know her better. She smiled rather shyly, and he got the impression that she was not accustomed to lunches with men. Probably hadn't dated much at all lately, he figured. This ought to be interesting.

"Do you have any particular place in mind for lunch?" he asked politely.

"No, not really. Someplace with a good salad, maybe? But I don't really know where, do you?" Suzanne was a little hesitant to say that she didn't often go out to lunch, and she didn't have any special or particular place in mind.

"Well, as a matter of fact, there is a nice little café right here in this mall. We can walk there from here, if that's all right with you." Suzanne nodded in agreement. "Let's put our things in our cars, then walk on over." He offered to take Suzanne's duffle bag, but she said she could carry it herself. "Which way's your car?" he asked as he held the front door open for her. Suzanne pointed to the left and Scott said, "Mine's in that parking lot, too."

Suzanne's car was a dark blue Honda Accord. Nice enough and big enough for her needs, which were pretty basic, she figured. Safe, dependable, and good gas mileage. She unlocked the trunk and put her duffel bag inside. Looking through the windows into the back seat, Scott noticed a large zipper notebook with a sticker from Cloverly High School on its front. Lindsay's, he presumed. In the front he saw a Diet Coke can in its holder, and a pair of sunglasses on the passenger seat.

"Okay, my car is this way," Scott said and led the way to his Mazda Miata. It was a small red sports convertible, big enough for just two. Scott pressed the alarm button in his hand and the car chirped and the doors unlocked. He put his own bag in the passenger's seat, closed the door, and beeped it locked again.

"Cute car," said Suzanne. "I'll bet you have fun driving it."

"Yes, it is fun," Scott agreed as they walked back to the sidewalk in front of the gym. "Not very practical for most people, I guess. It's sure not a family car! But for just me, it's great. I have a little pick-up at home I can use when I need to haul things, like mulch or plants when I'm doing some gardening around the house. But usually I just drive the Miata."

They had reached the sidewalk that lined the stores along the strip mall. The gym was at one end of the mall, and a Sears store was at the other end. In between were a dozen or so small businesses. A craft store, a shoe store, a couple of dress shops and a jewelry store, along with a few small restaurants and an organic market lined up between the two larger anchors. Scott led the way to a bistro called Aida's, which, according to the sign on the door, specialized in authentic Italian cuisine.

They were greeted at the door by a hostess who seated them at a table for two near the back of the room. There were a few other couples dining at the bistro, but the room was practically empty. The lighting was low and intimate, even for the middle of the afternoon.

On each table was a small fresh flower arrangement. The hostess waited until Suzanne was seated and then gave her a lunch menu. Scott took his seat and thanked the hostess. Then he said to Suzanne, "They have some really great salads here. Do you like spinach?" She nodded and he went on, "Then you might want to try the spinach salad. It has mushrooms and pine nuts – really special."

"Sounds interesting," said Suzanne, but she was thinking 'Pine nuts? I've never even heard of pine nuts, much less ever tasted them.'

The waiter came by to take their drink orders, and Scott asked her if she would like a glass of wine. Suzanne declined, saying, "No, I think I'll just have a soda." Scott raised his eyebrows and asked, "Diet coke?" and Suzanne nodded and smiled, wondering how he knew that was her preference. Scott ordered iced tea with lemon and the waiter left.

Scott laid his menu down on the table and looked up at Suzanne. "So," he began, "Tell me about yourself. I know nothing but your name, you have a daughter, you like cats, and you have beautiful eyes. And I assume there is no Mr. Rogers, for whatever reason I do not know. Tell me more."

"I don't really know where to begin," Suzanne said. Just then the waiter came with their drinks, and Suzanne had a moment to collect her thoughts. Scott ordered for her, the spinach salad, and a mixed greens salad for himself. He also took the liberty of ordering an appetizer of brochette to share.

When they were alone again, Suzanne started a short dissertation on her life. "My husband passed away about ten years ago. Lindsay and I moved here shortly after that. We love this little town. I teach at an elementary school. Lindsay is a senior, has lots of friends, and plans to go to college to major in drama. It's been a dream of hers ever since she was little." It was easier for Suzanne to talk about her daughter than to talk about her own self. "She's a good girl, never been any trouble to me at all. She studies hard and gets good grades. She helps me around the house and is respectful. What more could I hope for?"

"So how is she dealing with the loss of your cat? Or would you rather not talk about it?" Scott was trying to make conversation, but wanted to be polite, too. Maybe Suzanne didn't care to discuss the pet situation. He didn't want to make her uncomfortable.

But Suzanne was not opposed to discussing Lindsay and how she was handling the death of ZuZu. "She's fine, actually, thanks for asking. It's only been a few days, but she is going to get through this. We decided to get a special marker made, kind of like a stepping stone, and put it out in the garden where ZuZu used to lay sunning herself. It will be a nice reminder of ZuZu, but not like a burial plot or something morbid like that. We will remember the good times, not dwell on the loss. At least, that's the plan."

"Sounds like a good idea. Loosing a pet can be devastating to some people, especially children. It's good to have a reminder, but at the same time you have to move on. Have you talked about getting another cat?"

"No, we haven't talked about it, but I really don't think we should. ZuZu was really Lindsay's cat. I loved her too, of course, but I think I could manage just fine without another pet. Lindsay will be off to college in just a little while, and of course she couldn't take a cat along. I don't really need the extra responsibility. So I think it's just better that we don't replace ZuZu. Now when Lindsay gets out of school and on her own, I figure she will get some kind of a pet right away. But now isn't really the right time."

Their appetizer arrived and they began to share the crusty ciabatta bread covered with diced tomatoes and delicious spices. It was wonderful, and Suzanne said so. "Mmmm, this is really good. I've never had brochette before. This is a nice place. You've been here before, I guess?"

"Yes, one of my students from the University used to work here and recommended that I come in and check it out. That was a couple of years ago, and now I come in quite a lot. They sure have good food."

"You teach at the University?" ask Suzanne. "I didn't know that. What do you teach?"

"I teach classes in anatomy and animal biology at the School of Veterinary Medicine. I've been there eight years now. I enjoy it, but what I really love is being in the office with the patients. Meeting the people, getting to know them and see the relationship they have with their pets. That's what I enjoy. Of course, there are drawbacks to office work, too. Like in your case, when there was nothing I could do to save a life. That is never easy. Even though I didn't know you, and had never treated ZuZu before, I could see that your daughter had a special love for her, and it was a hard thing to let her go. But you definitely did the right thing, and you will get through the grief and go on. Well, you must know what I mean, since you lost your husband, I mean, and you obviously have managed to get on with your life."

Suzanne shuffled uneasily in her seat. Scott noticed, but didn't question her further. The waitress appeared with their salads, and the conversation stopped for a while. Suzanne's spinach salad was fresh and flavorful, and the pine nuts added an extra zest. "This is really good. I'm glad you suggested it."

"Good. I'm glad you like it. We'll have to come back for dinner here sometime. The eggplant parmesan is really delicious, and the veal marsala, too."

"I'd like that," Suzanne surprised herself by saying to Scott. Maybe the little talk from Lindsay had already begun to take a hold of her thinking.

The lunch talk shifted to topics of interest to both of them. Suzanne learned that Scott liked to garden. He had a large back yard with a vegetable garden that kept him and half of his neighbors supplied with tomatoes and zucchini. He liked to ski in the winter and surf in the summer. He had been to Italy twice.

Suzanne talked of her love for children, her involvement with Lindsay's school activities, and the plans Lindsay was making for college. Scott asked if she was afraid of the impending empty nest.

Suzanne said that she was not really thinking about that at all yet. She was pretty sure she could handle it.

They left the restaurant an hour later, comfortable with each other and the friendship that was developing between them. When Suzanne drove into the school parking lot to pick up Lindsay, she was smiling, and wondering where this new friendship was heading. Lindsay climbed in the car, noticed her mother's smile, and said "What's up, Mom?"

"Well, my dear, let's just say that I took your little speech to heart and I have decided to move on with my life."

"You mean you called George?"

"No."

"Then what? Mom, you've gotta tell me!"

"Well, I had lunch with Dr. Scott Jefferson, the veterinarian. I had a wonderful time, and we are going to go out to dinner soon. So, what do you think about that?"

"Cool, Mom! I think you work fast!"

Chapter Thirteen

First Date

THE FIRST TIME Suzanne went to Scott's house, she was amazed at its size, elaborate décor, and overstated elegance. From the street she could see that it was the largest house in Cloverly, but it wasn't until she stepped inside that she got the whole picture of its grandness. The marble flooring in the two-story foyer echoed with her high-heeled footsteps. A crystal chandelier hung from the ceiling, casting sparkles of light through-out the foyer. To the right a stairway curved upwards and became a catwalk open on both sides, from which one could look down to the doorway or to the formal living room. To the left of the foyer, through marble columns, was a music room, complete with a baby grand piano in shiny ebony. A collection of violins, guitars, and a clarinet lined the walls, encased in glass-fronted shadow boxes. A stately harp stood in the corner.

Directly through the foyer was the formal living room. Furnished with antiques in cherry wood and rich crushed velvet, the room screamed of its expense. The polished hardwood floor was covered in part with an Oriental rug. Everything was beautiful, if a little stuffy and formal for Suzanne's tastes.

Scott had excused himself to go upstairs to change his clothes. They were going out to dinner at Aida's, as he had promised two weeks before. Before he went upstairs, Suzanne said, "Your house is beautiful. Do you play the piano?" She ran her fingers lightly over the polished black casing.

"No, the piano was my mother's. The only thing I can play is the clarinet." He nodded his head towards the clarinet on display. "And that I don't do very well." Scott noticed Suzanne's loving gaze lingering on the piano, and said, "I bet you play, don't you? Go ahead, sit down. Play while I'm upstairs changing."

"Oh, I haven't played in a very long time. But maybe, if you don't mind, I'll just sit here and pretend I remember what I'm doing."

"Sure, have fun!" Scott was already headed up the stairs. "I think there's some sheet music inside the piano bench, if you want to try it. Help yourself." Just before he went into his bedroom, he stopped, listening to Suzanne's first tentative tinkling on the keys. It had been a very long time since someone had played that piano.

When Scott came down a few minutes later, Suzanne was trying her hand at "The Entertainer." He leaned casually against a marble column so as not to disturb her. She was concentrating on the notes and the timing, and was doing a pretty good job. When the song ended, he clapped softly and said, "You're really good. Sounds like you've been playing every day for years."

Suzanne whirled around on the bench, startled by his voice and slightly embarrassed that he had been listening to her play. "No, really, I haven't played in years, except when I visit my parents in Kansas. They have an upright, not nearly as beautiful as this piano."

"I'll tell you what. You can come over and play this piano any time you want. But right now we better get going, or we won't make our reservations." He gently took her elbow and guided her outside.

As he stopped to lock the door, Suzanne said, "I always hoped I could get a piano and Lindsay could take lessons, but I just wasn't ever able to afford it. My house is a little small, too." She looked again at the large house in front of her. "Do you live in this big house all alone?"

"Well, actually this was my parent's house. But when they passed away, the house came to me. It's bigger than I really need, I know, but I just couldn't part with it. And yes, I do live here alone, but I'm hoping that will change before long." He didn't elaborate, but he touched Suzanne softly on the back and ushered her to his car. He opened the door for her and helped her in, then walked around to his own side. Before he started the engine, he said, "Oh, I almost forgot. There's something for you in the glove compartment. Go ahead, open it up."

Suzanne reached for the dash and opened the glove compartment. She took out a small white box and held it on her lap. "Scott, you shouldn't have gotten me anything."

"Well, I didn't really. Just open it, will you?" Scott started the car and maneuvered through the half circle drive and out onto the street. He watched Suzanne from the corner of his eye as he concentrated on driving.

She lifted the lid from the box and softly exhaled with an "Ohhh." She carefully removed a shiny circle of gold chain links. It was a bracelet, and it sparkled in the flickering street light. "This is beautiful. Thank you. But you shouldn't have…"

"Let me explain." Scott paused. "Go ahead, put it on. I want to see how it looks on you." Suzanne snapped the clasp shut and lifted her arm so he could see better. "Beautiful," said Scott. "That was my mother's. I want you to have it. I have all this jewelry of hers, and it feels good to finally have someone to give it to. You like it?"

"Oh, yes, I do. It's lovely. But are you sure you want to part with it?"

"Well, as I see it, I'm not parting with it. As long as you have it, and you wear it sometimes when we are together, I will see it and enjoy it too. Better than just sitting in the safe forever."

Later that evening, outside Suzanne's front door, Scott held her fingertips and raised her hand to his lips. "Thank you for a wonderful evening. I enjoy your company tremendously. And I know my mother would be pleased that you have her bracelet now."

"Thank you again, Scott. I had a wonderful time, too. Well, goodnight." She went inside the house, to find her daughter waiting up for her, eager to hear all of the details of her mother's first real date in ages.

Chapter Fourteen

Pressure

AFTER THAT FIRST date, Suzanne began to feel that her life was in a whirlwind, and that she was no longer in control. Things were happening around her, emotions were spinning wildly, and she felt powerless. She could neither run nor hide. She was like a leaf bobbing along in the flow of a river, first floating comfortably, then twisting and dancing as the current increased its pace. She couldn't stop, and there was little chance that she could control her destination. Someone more powerful than herself was in control, and she didn't even know the extent of his power.

It was rather nice, this being cared for and lavished with attention. It was a new feeling, and at times Suzanne thought she could really get used to being adored and pampered. Yet there was an underlying sense that things were getting out of control.

Scott Jefferson wined and dined Suzanne at the nicest restaurants in the area. He took her to concerts and museums. He treated her in ways that no other man ever had. He had the finances and the style that went along with it. He spent an excessive amount of money entertaining Suzanne. He showed her places she had never been; they experienced things she had only dreamed of. Her whole world was changing. And the change was rapid and overwhelming.

One weekend they traveled by train to New York City, saw a show on Broadway, and stayed in a two bedroom suite at the five-star Wellington Hotel. After the show and a delightful dinner, they spent the early hours of the morning sipping wine in front of a blazing fire in the fireplace at the suite. Scott pulled her close and told her he hoped to spend the rest of his life with her. As Suzanne turned her lips towards him, she closed her eyes. A part of her wanted to be swept off her feet, wanted to feel loved and safe and cared for. She expected his kiss to be a promise, a peaceful loving touch that would whisk away all the fears she had stored in her heart all these years. But instead, Scott's kiss was hot and demanding, and his grip on her shoulders was a little too tight for comfort. She pulled away and said, "Let's not rush things, Scott. This is just happening too fast."

Scott let go of his grip on her, and sat back. "As I see it, things are happening about ten years too slowly. You have been without a man for a very long time. And you aren't getting any younger, you know. We need to take advantage of every day we have, every second. Our time is running out." He reached for her again and forced his kiss upon her once more.

"Scott, please, you're hurting me. I'm not ready."

Once again he relaxed his grip. He put his hands up in a submissive, 'I give up' gesture, and picked up a fire poker. He leaned towards the fireplace and jabbed at the burning logs. Sparks flew up the chimney, dancing like fireflies. After a silent moment spent watching the burning embers, he replaced the poker and sat back on the sofa near Suzanne, but he did not touch her.

"Okay, sweets, whatever you want. I just thought maybe you needed me like I need you. I do have needs, you know." He deliberately moved his hand over the growing bulge in his suit pants and groped himself slightly. Suzanne noticed and her eyes lingered there just a second. But instead of being aroused, as Scott had expected,

Suzanne was actually disturbed. She felt a chill of warning crawl up her spine.

As she removed her gaze, Scott also removed his hand and placed it nonchalantly next to him on the sofa. "But I don't want you to think that's all I'm about. After all, you were the one who wanted this two bedroom suite for the night. You made it very clear that you intended to sleep in a separate room from me. I was just hoping that you might change your mind. I mean, we are two grown adults, we know what we are doing. I could only hope."

"Scott, I like you a lot. And I enjoy being with you. The things you have shown me, the places you have taken me! My gosh, Scott, I am in New York City! I never ever imagined I would be here, ever! This is a whole new world for me!" She reached across the sofa and took his hand. "I'm just not ready for the sexual involvement yet. I've had some bad experiences, and it might take a while for me to get past the past. You're going to have to be patient with me, I'm afraid. That is, if you even think it's worth it."

He leaned forward and kissed her gently on the forehead. "I'm sure you are worth it, Suzanne. I am so sure that I will wait patiently as long as you say. But in the mean time, I want to see you every day and be near you as much as I can. I have fallen in love with you, you know. And I do want to spend the rest of my life with you." He had taken both of her hands in his own, and he looked intently into her eyes. He held her gaze while he said, "I want you in my life, forever. I want to take care of you and show you a world full of things and places you've never known. I want to provide for you and Lindsay and give you the things you have gone without for so long."

Suzanne felt her resolve melt slightly with his words. His gaze was so intense, his words seemed so sincere. She smiled and leaned forward to accept his kiss. Yet there was just something needling her—call it a warning or a premonition or just a feeling of dread. Scott could give her everything money could buy. She should be overjoyed by his attention, his declaration of love. But she wasn't ready yet to say those three little words, which would, by their saying, pull her right in to intimacy, ready or not.

So she slept alone again that night, in a king-sized bed with silk sheets and the sweet smell of flowers from a fresh bouquet on her nightstand.

In the adjourning room, Scott did not sleep. Not until his hand had finished what his mind had started hours ago. He left the results of his stroking in a sticky puddle on the sheets, rolled over to the other side of the big bed, and then he slept. His last semi-conscious thought was of the maid who would change the sheets the next morning. Maybe she would be young, a high school girl with a part time job. She would smell his scent when she entered the room. She would lie in the bed and rub herself with the stained sheets. She would climax with his juices, even if Suzanne did not.

Chapter Fifteen

Uncomfortable

SUZANNE INSISTED ON fixing a big Thanksgiving dinner. Scott insisted that they eat at his house. Early Thursday morning, Suzanne and Lindsay arrived at the "mansion", as Lindsay called it. They brought a broccoli cheese casserole and corn pudding, made the night before and ready for reheating at dinnertime. Lindsay had made an apple pie, which she carried carefully inside. The turkey was thawed and ready for the oven, and Suzanne got busy with the stuffing. Before long, the rich aroma of roasting turkey filled the kitchen. Suzanne took a break from the dinner preparations to see what Scott and Lindsay were up to.

The sounds of laughter drew her downstairs to the game room, where Scott and Lindsay were playing pool. Suzanne stood frozen in the doorway for a moment, unsettled by the sight before her. Lindsay was leaning against the pool table, pool cue in hand, arms stretched outwards to make her shot. Scott stood behind her, arms encircling her young form, his chin resting on her shoulder. He had her body trapped against the table, and her rear end was pressed tightly up against his crotch. He seemed to be enjoying himself.

Lindsay, being naive, seemed not to notice the overly familiar positioning of Scott behind her. But the sight made Suzanne quite uncomfortable.

Scott noticed Suzanne at the door but made no acknowledgement of her presence. He continued with his instructions to his young student, but pulled himself away from her ever so slightly. "Now, bring your right arm back very slowly, don't mess up the angle. Then just barely tap the ball. Be gentle." Then he dropped his arms and backed completely away so Lindsay could make the shot.

And Lindsay did make the shot. The ball rolled gently into the net, and she turned to Scott with a smile. "I did it, I did it!" The two slapped their hands in a high five and Scott said, "Way to go, baby! You are getting good at this!" Then he turned his attention to Suzanne. "Did you see that shot? She really learns fast."

"You must be a very good teacher."

Scott put his arm around Suzanne and pulled her close. Lindsay turned her back to them, to set up her next shot.

"Hey, you smell good. What is that perfume?" Scott asked Suzanne.

"It's a new fragrance called Turkey with Sage Dressing. Do you like it?"

Scott nestled his face against Suzanne's neck and said, "Smells good enough to eat!" He started nibbling at her neck, which set Suzanne to giggling.

Lindsay said "You two! You're like teenagers sometimes! But it is good to see you having fun, Mom. Thanks Scott, for making my mom so happy."

Scott reached for Lindsay to pull her into the circle. "She makes me happy, too, you know. And having you both here, in my home and in my life, reminds me of how important family is to me. I am so thankful that I met the two of you. You have given me a feeling of family like I have not known for a long time." He kissed Lindsay on the forehead and turned to Suzanne. She smiled at him and he kissed her on the lips. The kiss was sweet and soft, but Suzanne pulled away, saying, "I'd better get upstairs and baste that turkey again, before it dries out. Lindsay, would you come set the table, please?"

Dinner was perfect. The table sparkled with Scott's fine china and crystal. The food was delicious and plentiful. The conversation was lively. It was a fantastic feast, with lots of leftovers and the promise of many turkey sandwiches to come.

"Suzanne, you have outdone yourself. This was terrific. I could get used to eating dinner with you and Lindsay for the rest of my life. But you can't cook this much every night, okay? We would all be headed for the fat farm!"

"You can't be done yet, we still have my apple pie," said Lindsay.

Scott groaned and held his stomach. "Oh, baby, I'm gonna have to wait a bit before I have any room for pie. Let's help your mother clear the table and we can have the pie later. Okay?"

"Well sure." Lindsay got up from her seat and started gathering dishes. "Maybe we could play some more pool after the dishes are done."

"I was thinking I would like to take a walk before it gets too dark," said Suzanne. She stood up and stretched before reaching for the bowl of broccoli. "I need to get some fresh air, and wear off some of these calories."

"Sounds like a great idea," Scott agreed.

Lindsay headed for the kitchen. "I'll pass. You two go on without me. I'll stay here and practice my pool shots."

A short time later, Scott and Suzanne headed out the door. Hand in hand they walked down the tree-lined sidewalks in Scott's neighborhood. Leaves crunched beneath their feet as they walked. The air was crisp, and the sun was already setting low in the sky. Soon it would be dark.

"Suzanne, it has been a wonderful day. I wish you could be here every day. Like a real family." They stopped walking and stood close together in the fading light. Scott's arms tightened around her, and he bent to kiss Suzanne. She lifted her face to his and accepted his kiss warmly. Walking home, she rested her cheek against his chest.

"I feel very comfortable with you, Scott, even though your lifestyle is so completely different from what Lindsay and I are used to. I'm just a simple girl, and never imagined I would ever fit in with a house like this. It's quite a change from my little house, and our slow and simple day to day life." Her voice trailed off as she slipped into thought.

"But you fit in just fine, Suzanne. And you deserve better than just a little house and a simple life. You have lived that life long enough. Let me take care of you. I want to share everything I have with you and Lindsay. I mean it."

"It's just all so sudden. I've said it before. I don't want to rush into anything. I want to be sure, that's all." They had reached Scott's driveway and Suzanne turned in. "Let's go on in, it's getting chilly out here."

"Okay, but you are changing the subject again."

"Yep, that's what I'm doing!" Suzanne opened the front door. "Lindsay, how about some pie?"

Chapter Sixteen

College Plans

LINDSAY SAT AT the kitchen table, a white envelope clasped in both hands. She tapped the envelope on the table impatiently and stood from the table to pace to the door. She was waiting for her mother to get home, but it seemed like time was standing still.

Lindsay went to the refrigerator and opened the door. She stared blankly at the contents, which had not changed since she stood looking in ten minutes before. She turned to the sink and poured herself a glass of water, which she sat on the counter and did not drink.

She picked up the letter again and considered opening it without her mother. But no, she really did want to wait. She knew how important this moment was, to the both of them. But why did mom have to be late, tonight of all nights?

The jingling phone startled her. She gained her composure and answered. "Hello? Oh hi, Scott. No, mom isn't here. I figured she was at your house... She should have been home by now. If you hear from her, would you please tell her to get home fast? I got a letter from the University, and I can't wait much longer to open it... No, no, I'll wait. But where could she be?... I hope everything is okay... Yeah, you're probably right… Okay, I'll tell her to call you. Bye." Lindsay went to the front window and looked down the street. Seeing no cars, she turned back to the kitchen and plopped down heavily.

*　*　*　*　*

Suzanne left the mall and walked briskly to her car. The chilly December wind reminded her that winter was on its way once again. She was thankful for the warm coat she had taken with her that morning. She opened the car and placed her packages on the back seat. She had bought a new dress, which she carefully hung behind the driver's seat. Scott had invited her to the college staff Christmas party, which was a pretty fancy affair. Suzanne felt it necessary to buy something new, since she didn't really have anything appropriate in her closet. Although she regretted spending so much money on a dress she probably wouldn't really wear that often, she did have to admit that she looked pretty good in it. The floor length dress was deep blue velvet, with a halter top and bare back. It came with a white lace shawl, which matched the lace on the scooped neckline. Suzanne thought the dress was beautiful but not one she would have gotten for herself if it weren't for this special occasion.

It was already dark by the time she got home from shopping. Lindsay flipped on the front porch light as soon as she saw her mother's car pull in the driveway. She dashed out of the door and was at the car before the engine had been turned off. As soon as she saw Lindsay's face, Suzanne knew that something important had happened. She quickly took off her seatbelt and opened the door. "What's the matter, honey? You look upset. Is everything alright?"

"I'm not upset, Mom. Just worried because you're getting home so late. I got a letter from Central U. and I was waiting for you to be here when I opened it."

"I'm sorry, Lindsay." Suzanne said as she opened the back door and reached in for her packages. "I had to stop at the mall and get a dress to wear for Scott's Christmas party. But if you'll help me carry this stuff into the house, we'll get right to that letter."

As soon as the dress was hung in Suzanne's closet, she and Lindsay sat together in the living room. Lindsay pushed the letter opener under the flap and cut the envelope with one quick movement. She took a deep breath and slipped the letter of the envelope. She slowly and deliberately smoothed the letter on the coffee table.

"I can't, Mom. I can't look. What if I'm not accepted?"

"Well, dear, then we will make other plans. Everything will work out, one way or another. But we will never know if you don't read the letter. So do it!" Suzanne gave her daughter a playful punch in the arm and Lindsay picked the letter up from the table.

She read aloud. "Dear Miss Rogers, Thank you for your interest in Central University of Virginia. We are pleased to inform you that your application has been accepted…" Lindsay shrieked and threw her arms around her mother. "I made it! I'm in!' She danced around the room, singing "I'm going to Central, I'm going to Central!"

Suzanne was smiling, though her eyes were misty with tears. "I knew you'd make it, honey! I'm so proud of you. We should call your grandparents. They'll be so glad you got accepted there. What does the rest of the letter say?"

Lindsay calmed herself enough to read the rest of the letter. "Well, they want a deposit, of course, to show my intent to attend. And there will be a packet of information coming to me in the summer, to select my classes and stuff about orientation week and roommates. But we have to send them the five hundred dollar deposit money within two weeks. Can we do that, Mom?"

"Lindsay, you know that we have been saving for your college ever since you were little. Yes, we can send them five hundred dollars. Now how about something special for dinner to celebrate? You want to go out for shrimp and lobster?"

"Wow! That would be great! Oh, by the way, Scott called. He asked for you to call him when you got home. Should we invite him to dinner too?"

Suzanne headed for the bathroom to freshen her make-up. "No, let's just go together, the two of us. I might not get many more chances to be with you, you know. College girls don't come home to have dinner with their mothers."

Lindsay popped her head into the bathroom and said with a smile, "Mom, I just might be home more often than you think. Laundry, you know!"

Just as they were leaving for dinner, the phone rang, and Suzanne remembered that she was supposed to call Scott. She was short with him on the phone, relaying the good news and stating that the two of them were going out to celebrate. Scott noted with some scorn that he had not been included, but said nothing.

After the brief conversation, Scott poured himself a brandy and sat in the library near a blazing fire he had laid just before calling Suzanne. He had envisioned the two of them cuddled in front of the fire, spending this Friday night necking and hopefully more. But evidently she had better things to do. Scott leaned back in the leather armchair and put his feet up on the footrest. He drank his brandy slowly as he mulled over this relationship with Suzanne.

Why was she always pulling away from him, excluding him from parts of her life? Why couldn't she just let down once and commit herself to him? He needed her body next to him in his big bed. What more could he do to convince her to make love with him? And what made her so pious and righteous anyway? She had needs too, surely. What was stopping her from sleeping with him? He had money, position, this great house, and security. It could only be good for her, a better life than she had ever had. She ought to be thankful for his attention. She should be begging to become his lover, or at least his wife. She'd better see it his way pretty soon or she just might loose out completely.

Scott finished his drink with one last gulp. The liquid warmed him all the way down his throat. He picked up his phone one more time. Maybe a massage would change his frame of mind.

Chapter Seventeen

Young and Innocent

SUZANNE DID LOOK stunning in her new velvet dress. When Scott picked her up for the staff Christmas party, he was struck with her good looks. Not that she was any model or beauty pageant winner, but she was put together quite well. And sometimes, like tonight, he felt extremely pleased to know that other men would be looking appreciatively at his date. Maybe this would be the night that she would finally lie with him. It was a boost to his ego, and he felt a rise in his pants that matched the rise in his pride.

Scott helped Suzanne wrap her lace shawl around her shoulders, then stopped to plant a long kiss on her lips. As he raised his head he noticed her flushed cheeks and breathlessness. "You look terrific, Suzanne. No wonder I love you. Just being close to you turns me on. Maybe we should just skip the party and go back to my place. I want to have you all to myself."

As soon as he said it, he knew it was a mistake. Suzanne pulled back and said, "I don't think so! Not after I spent all this money on the dress and new shoes, and getting my hair done especially for this party of yours. No way am I going to miss out on the big event."

"Okay, okay, you win," Scott said, trying to turn the tone to light and playful. "But let me warn you, there are going to be plenty of men there who would like to take you home with them. Just remember, you came with me, you leave with me. Got it?"

Suzanne laughed and said "Yes, sir!"

Just then Lindsay came up from the basement family room. "Hi Scott," she said in greeting, then turned her attention towards her mother. "Wow, Mom, you look great! I love that dress. And your hair. You better look out, Mom, all the men are going to be hitting on you!"

"That's what I was just saying!" laughed Scott. "But don't you worry; I will protect her from unwanted advances!"

"Who says I want to be protected?" joked Suzanne.

The doorbell rang and Lindsay said, "That must be Krissy. She's driving me to the game." She opened the door to let her friend into the house. Krissy was a cheerleader and was wearing her uniform. The letters CHS marched across the front of her blue top. The blue and white pleated skirt was short and loose. Her long legs were bare except for the white socks and tenneys on her feet. Her hair was pulled to each side in ponytails that bounced as she entered the room.

"Geez, you look great, Ms. R. Where are you going?" Krissy was always self confident and casual in her conversations with Suzanne, even though she did not know her all that well. She had become Lindsay's friend only recently. She had a twin sister, Kathleen, who had been in drama activities all through high school. Lindsay knew Kathleen much better than she knew Krissy.

"We're going to a banquet at the University. Oh, have you met Dr. Scott Jefferson? He is a Professor at the University. Scott, this is Krissy Feldman."

Scott extended his hand. "Nice to meet you, Krissy. My guess is that you are a cheerleader, right?"

"Right!" Krissy answered. "And I remember you. You are the vet who took care of Lindsay's cat. I was the one driving the car that hit her." She turned to Lindsay and gave her a sympathetic look. "I still feel so bad about that." Then she looked back at Scott and Suzanne. "But, hey, maybe it wasn't such at bad thing, after all. It looks like it brought you two together. Lindsay says you are practically married already. And I hear you've got a great house."

"Oh, she said all that did she?" Suzanne interrupted Krissy's speech. "Well, Krissy, you need to remember that you can't always believe everything that you hear. But Scott does have a very nice house." She quickly glanced at Scott and changed the subject. "We'd better get going, Scott. We don't want to be late." She turned towards the door and Scott reached for the doorknob.

"Oh, wait!" broke in Krissy. "Before you go, do you have a needle and thread I could use?" She lifted the edge of her skirt and studied the hemline. "I ripped out part of this hem when I got into the car. I need to sew it back before the game." She twisted the skirt to see how much would need repair, and by doing so her upper thigh was very visible, and the blue panties she wore under the skirt also showed briefly. Scott took it all in with a glance.

Lindsay spoke up, "Sure, I'll get you the stuff. Then we'd better get going too."

"Goodnight girls. Very nice to meet you, Krissy," said Scott.

"Be sure to lock up when you leave, honey," Suzanne said to Lindsay. "And you," she said to Krissy, "You drive safely, you hear?"

"Sure, Ms. R. Bye!" Krissy was still fidgeting with her skirt and barely glanced up. When Lindsay returned with the needle and thread, Krissy was sitting on the sofa with her skirt placed across her lap. "Man oh man, the doc is cute! I thought so in the vet's office, but tonight, all dolled up like that, I could barely keep my eyes off of him." She threaded the needle and twisted a knot in the end of it.

"You're something else, Krissy. Scott is more than twice your age. And here you were, practically undressing in front of the man! Have you no sense of moral decency?"

Krissy stopped sewing mid stitch and laughed. "Morals, decency? Me? What's the fun in that? And besides, I've been looking for an older, more mature man. The boys at school are so juvenile!"

She returned to the hem work with a sigh. "I can't wait for graduation, to get out of this town. To find me a man, a real man like Dr. Scott Jefferson." She stopped sewing again and her eyes glazed over in a dreamlike trance.

Lindsay reached for the skirt and took the needle from Krissy's fingertips. "Here, give me that, or we are never going to get to the game on time." Quickly she set to work.

"Okay, while you're finishing that, I'm gonna go check my makeup and hair." Krissy went to the bathroom to preen and Lindsay finished the sewing efficiently. She carried the skirt to the bathroom, just as Krissy stuck her head through the doorway.

"Great, thanks. You're the best!" She stepped into the skirt and wiggled it up over her hips. "Hey, do you think your mom is doing it with him?"

Lindsay's jaw dropped open and she sputtered in disbelief. "I don't know, and even if I did know I don't think I would be telling you. It's not any of your business!" she snapped. "Now let's get out of here!"

Scott and Suzanne were half way to the party before Scott broke the silence between them. "What's the matter?" he asked bluntly. "You seem distracted. What's on your mind?"

"I'm just thinking about Lindsay. Well, mostly I am thinking about Krissy."

Scott thought to himself, 'As a matter of fact, I've been thinking about her, too. Her long legs, her muscular thighs.' He didn't vocalize his thoughts, but the very thinking of them made the hairs on the back of his neck prickle in betrayal. Good thing Suzanne couldn't read minds.

Out loud he said, "She seems like a nice enough kid. Lots of enthusiasm and self-confidence. Young and innocent, starting college and ready to take on the world. She's typical of the kids I see every day. What are you worried about?"

"I don't know, exactly. For one thing, I'm not so sure she's is all that innocent. I'm not thrilled about the influence she might have on Lindsay."

Suzanne was deep in thought and didn't notice Scott's sudden interest. "Do you think she has been sexually active?" he asked. "Is that what you're worried about? That she will lead Lindsay down that path?

"Well, I would like to hope that Lindsay will make the right choices, if it ever comes to that. But peer pressure can be tough. I would feel much better if she spent less time with Krissy. You know, Krissy has a twin sister. And they are as opposite as day and night. I really like Kathleen. She's level headed and serious. She got accepted into an Ivy League school with a big scholarship. She's a much better influence on Lindsay, I think."

"What I think is that you worry too much. Lindsay is level headed too, and she knows right from wrong. I can't imagine her turning against everything you have taught her. She is her mother's daughter, after all." He patted Suzanne on the knee and she smiled.

"I hope you're right."

As they pulled into the banquet hall parking lot, Scott's imagination was running wild. Twins. What he could do with twins!

Chapter Eighteen

Unexpected Advice

THE ROOM WAS already crowded as they entered. Scott and Suzanne were immediately swept into the large hall, where laughter and tinkling glasses could be heard, mixed with music from the band warming up in the corner. A young man dressed in black and white approached and offered them wine from his tray. Scott maneuvered his way around the room, introducing Suzanne to his colleagues and their spouses. Suzanne chatted with each, as Scott stayed near her, often touching her back or holding her elbow. She felt the eyes of some of the men follow them as they moved about the room. It was kind of nice to be noticed.

The band was finished warming up now, and grew silent, waiting for the direction of their leader. With a "One, two, three four," they broke into a set of oldies with a big band sound. "Chattanooga Choo Choo" brought several of the older couples out to the dance floor. "In the Mood," and "Pennsylvania 6-5000" got toes tapping all around the room. Suzanne enjoyed watching the people dance. Scott enjoyed watching her smile.

"Would you like to dance?" he asked, leaning close to her to be heard above the music. The smell of her perfume delighted him. He wanted to be holding her close. He hoped that she would be in bed with him before the evening was finished.

"Oh Scott, I don't really know how to dance. I'm not good at it at all. I'd rather not. It would be so embarrassing, for both of us!"

"Come on, please," Scott begged. "I'll help you. Just follow me." He grabbed Suzanne's hand and pulled her to the dance floor. The band was playing a slow song now, and Scott put one arm around Suzanne's waist and pulled her close to him. Moving his feet, using his body to lead the way around the dance floor, he moved with Suzanne in an easy pattern. She was stiff and awkward at first, and self-conscious as she tried to match his steps.

"You're doing great!" Scott smiled at her and she began to relax. As she settled more comfortably in his arms, dancing started to feel more natural. She caught on quickly and smiled back at him.

Dancing with Scott really wasn't so hard, she decided, at least on the slow songs. The music ended but Scott kept his arm tight around her waist. His face was close to hers, and she tilted her head to look at him. He surprised her with a kiss on the lips.

Suzanne pulled back and looked around. "Scott, not here in public. What will people think?"

"They'll think I'm lucky to be kissing the most beautiful woman in the room." He tried to pull her close again, hoping for another kiss, one that would get more attention from the other people in the room. But Suzanne wiggled out of his grasp and turned to walk away. He followed her to a table, where she sat with a disturbed look on her face.

"What's wrong with you Suzanne? Why are you so cold to me all of a sudden?"

"Scott, please, don't make a scene. It's just that I don't like public displays of affection like that. You ought to know that about me by now. I don't know these people, and I don't want them thinking things about me. I just don't feel comfortable with that kind of behavior."

"Okay, well now you just listen. I wish you would relax a little. You are so high and mighty, you can't let go and enjoy the moment. Always thinking about your reputation, what looks right, who's thinking what." Scott's voice was full of tension and he was struggling to keep the volume down. "I'm going to walk away now, and give you some time to come to your senses. When I get back, I should hope that you will be ready to act like a mature woman, not a self-righteous goody-goody." Scott turned and walked quickly away.

Suzanne was trembling. His words had stung and stunned her. How could he dare to speak to her like that? What right did he have to pressure her into something she didn't feel comfortable with? Didn't he respect her feelings at all? Suzanne stood and walked to the bar, where she asked for another glass of wine. She needed something to calm down her anger. Yet she was determined not to let down her guard. She was resolved to stick to her guns about this.

Scott walked toward the back of the banquet hall. As he made his way through the crowd, he spoke to several people. He had many friends on the faculty. Fortunately, it seemed that none had witnessed the difficulties he had been having with Suzanne.

Professor Evans, head of the biology department, shook his hand and said, "Hey Scott, good to see you! Happy Holidays!"

"Same to you Bill. It's a pretty nice party, isn't it?"

"Sure is. I see you have a lady with you this evening. Someone new? I've never seen her before."

"Well, actually, we've been dating a few months. Her name is Suzanne Rogers. She's a first grade teacher. Come on over, I'll introduce you to her." Scott glanced towards the table where he had left Suzanne, but she was not there. "Oh, wait, she must have gone to the ladies room or something. I don't see her now."

"That's okay; I'll catch up with you later. I see my wife has been cornered by Dr. Henderson's wife. She's trying to recruit Eileen for some fund raising committee, I'll bet. Excuse me while I go rescue her."

Scott laughed and watched as Bill moved towards his wife. Eileen Evans was a shapely blond, well preserved for her years. But Scott went more for the younger women. And just at that moment, a much younger woman caught his eye.

It was Alexis. He was surprised to see her here, dressed in a black skirt, a white shirt, and a black bow tie. She had a silver platter of hors D'oeuvres balanced on her right hand, and smiled bewitchingly as she sauntered towards him.

"Hi Scottie," was all she said. Her voice was low and sultry. His imagination kicked in immediately. He remembered her hands on him, her breasts dangling over his face. "I bet you'd like a little nibble, wouldn't you?" she purred seductively.

He took a cracker topped with crab dip from her platter and popped it into his mouth. Swallowing, he smiled and said, "That was good. Do you have anything else for me?"

Alexis giggled softly. "You ought to know, baby." She licked her lips slowly. "Hey, I saw that little scene with the red-head. What's up? She turn you down?"

"Yeah, well, she'll come around." Scott changed the subject. "What are you doing here, anyway?"

"Trying to make a little extra money, obviously. I have expenses, you know. So I answered an ad for help at a catering company, and here I am." She smiled with a twinkle in her eye. "You wouldn't know how I could make a little more, would you? I mean, I could make you forget the red-head troubles, and you could make my night a bit more profitable."

Scott could not resist an invitation like that. Alexis led the way down a secluded hall and opened a door that led to a library. She sat on a leather sofa and Scott stood in front of her. Alexis unzipped his pants and reached in. Her mouth was hot and eager, and it wasn't long before Scott totally forgot about Suzanne. He thought only about the wet full lips surrounding him, the moaning sounds of pleasure that came from deep within Alexis's throat, and his shaking knees as he released himself into her mouth. He withdrew his handkerchief from his jacket pocket and wiped the sweat from his face as Alexis swallowed and smiled up at him.

Alexis took the handkerchief from him and dabbed it on her lips and chin. Then she folded it neatly and slipped it back into his breast pocket. "Very tasty. Thank you so very much. I didn't know I was so hungry." She gave his cock a quick kiss, tucked it away, and zipped Scott's pants. Then she held out her hand. "I believe you have something for me."

Scott took out his wallet and placed a twenty dollar bill in her palm. Alexis raised her eyebrows and remained with her hand outstretched, with a pouty expression on her face and a tilt of her head. Another twenty was added and she closed her fist, then tucked the bills into her bra. "It's been a pleasure, a real pleasure," she said, and left the room, swaying her hips rhythmically as she exited.

Scott tucked his shirt into his pants, straightened his tie, and took a deep breath. He certainly felt better. Now to find Suzanne and hopefully talk some sense into her. She was really being difficult tonight. And Scott was getting sick of her rigid moralistic behavior. This woman needed to be brought under control, and soon. He needed a physical commitment, now.

Suzanne was deep in conversation with two women near the bar. Each had a glass of wine, and Suzanne was smiling. The conversation was animated, but as Scott approached, the women turned to look his way.

"Hi," said Suzanne. She turned to her two friends, "Ladies, this is Dr. Scott Jefferson. He is a veterinarian and teaches veterinary science at the University. Scott, these are some old friends of mine, Penny Seacrest and Monica Craig. You may know their husbands. They are on the staff here at the University too. Penny and Monica both had children in my first grade class several years ago."

Both women spoke briefly with Scott, and he acknowledged that he know both of their husbands. After a little more small talk,

Scott smiled at Suzanne and took her by the elbow. "If you will excuse us, ladies, my pretty friend and I are headed for the dance floor. It was a pleasure to meet you."

When they were safely out of ear shot, Scott said, "So, see, you do know people here. Feel better now? I mean, it's obvious that you fit in well with these people. They would be happy to know that you are getting what you so desperately need from me."

His words had an effect of Suzanne, an effect that Scott had not anticipated. "That is so crude, Scott! Is that all you ever think about? Are you so perverted that you have to bring sex into this conversation? Can't we just have a nice evening? Meet people, talk to people, dance a little? Why do you have to always be on me, pushing for intimacy? I'm tired of the pressure, Scott. I need some space."

Scott decided it was time to change tactics. "Hey! If you want space, then space you shall have. Go! Chat with your friends. Have a great evening. I'll catch up with you at dinner. Then we'll leave. Or do you want to just go now? I'll get your coat."

"Oh Scott, don't be ridiculous. We don't have to leave so soon. No, I wouldn't do that to you. We need to stay for the dinner. You have people you need to talk with. This is important for your career." Suzanne was feeling confused. She didn't really want to be here with Scott, the way he was acting, but she didn't want to ruin the evening for him either.

"Fine, said Scott. "We'll stay for dinner. But you very obviously don't really want to be with me tonight. And I don't mean just sexually. I don't know why, but you are acting very up-tight tonight. More than usual. Well I'm not going to let you bring me down. I'm here for a good time. If you have a problem with that, then that is your problem, not mine. Now if you will excuse me, I have people to see. I'll see you at dinner. I guess you will have to sit beside me. Hope that doesn't offend you." With that he turned abruptly and walked back to the bar. Drink in hand, he walked to a group of people and joined their conversation.

Suzanne walked quickly to the ladies room. There was a lounge area just inside the door. Several overstuffed chairs offered a quiet retreat from the noisy crowded banquet hall. She collapsed into the closet chair. Her hands were shaking and she was breathing heavily.

She picked up a magazine that was laying on the end table near her. Using it as a fan, she cooled herself and tried to exhale slowly. She felt heat building from deep inside herself, and imagined steam spewing from her ears. This night sure wasn't turning out the way she expected. How could things have changed so quickly?

'It's all this pressure from Scott,' she thought to herself. 'Why does he get to me so strongly? Why do I feel like I need to run away from him, every time he mentions sex and commitment? He is a good catch. Any woman would be lucky to share his life. His house is fantastic, his lifestyle is comfortable. He can take me to great places and I'd never have to worry again about how much something costs. I could live an easy, stress free life. But is that what I really want? Isn't there more to a marriage than financial security?'

Suzanne knew the answer to her own question. She stood and walked to the mirror. Looking herself in the eye, she said softly, "So maybe you need to get out of this mess."

"Excuse me?" questioned a voice from behind her. Suzanne jumped a little, and smiled as a young woman exited the toilet area and walked to the sink to wash her hands.

"Oh, I'm sorry. I didn't know anyone was in here. I guess I was talking to myself." Suzanne watched as the woman wiped her hands on a towel and glanced at herself in the mirror.

She was surprised when the woman started to unbutton her white blouse. "Sorry, I didn't mean to scare you," the young woman said. Without a thought about Suzanne watching, the woman reached her hand towards her bra cup and withdrew several twenty dollar bills. She smoothed them out on the counter and counted the money to herself. When she realized that she was being watched, she said, "My tips so far tonight. But the night is young, and I still have time. I'm trying to make enough for a car payment. A girl's gotta do what a girl's gotta do." She folded the bills and put them into a small black handbag. Then she reached her hand into her bra and lifted her breast to adjust its position. She did the same with the other breast then giggled and said, "There. That's better, don't you think? Lift and separate, you know. Creates more cleavage, and that gets the attention of the men. They all like cleavage, you know." She buttoned a few buttons on her blouse, leaving several buttons at the top undone. She loosely tied her black tie around her neck. "Wish I didn't have to wear this. It really detracts from my look." She tucked her blouse into her short black skirt. Suzanne now recognized her as one of the waitresses from the party.

"I saw you earlier, with that good looking Professor," said the waitress. "Looked like you were upset about something. Take it from me, sweetie, no man is worth getting that upset over. Be true to yourself. Don't let a man turn you into someone you don't want to be. Just because he has balls and a penis, doesn't mean he has the right to push into your hole if you don't want him to. Men? They all think they are God's gift." She reached into her bag for a lipstick and began to apply a thick red line to her full lips. "He was pushing you for sex, wasn't he? I can always tell. And he wants to control you, right? He may have the looks, and probably lots of money and a big house, but honey, it takes more than that. If you don't feel, you just don't feel it. Take charge, and don't let him take what you aren't willing to give." With that, Alexis puckered her lips in the mirror, kissed the air, and flounced from the room.

Suzanne was stunned. Like a whirlwind this young woman had blown across her path and created a tornado in her thinking. This was crazy! The woman had hit the nail on the head. It was all true, everything she had said. It was an affirmation of what she had been thinking earlier. Maybe it was a sign.

At dinner, Suzanne sat beside Scott and tried to make the best of the situation. She smiled at his jokes, chatted comfortably with those sitting at their table, and appeared to be having a great time. There was a short program after the dinner, and Scott slid his chair close to hers and put his arm around her shoulders. Suzanne did not pull away.

Scott smiled smugly to himself. He just knew she would come around. That little talk he had with her must have opened her eyes. It was about time.

Driving home that evening, they talked about the food and the music, but not the argument they had had. Scott didn't want to recreate the nasty scene, and Suzanne didn't quite know how to voice her feelings. She needed some time to think things through. She wanted to word things just right. Now was not the time.

Chapter Nineteen

Christmas is Coming

AS THEY NEARED her house, Scott said, "So, do you and Lindsay want to come over Christmas Eve and spend the night? Then we can have Christmas morning together. Open presents and everything. Have a nice breakfast. Like a family."

Suzanne turned in her seat towards Scott. "I was thinking that I would like to have this last Christmas morning with Lindsay. She'll be off to school next year, you know, and everything is going to change. I really just want this last Christmas morning for the two of us. I know you understand."

Scott bristled inside but tried to remain calm. "Well, okay, if that's the way you want it. You're in charge."

Suzanne smiled to herself, thinking about the advice of the young waitress. "Take charge," she had said, "and don't let him take what you aren't willing to give." Suzanne was not willing to give him her last Christmas morning with Lindsay.

"Well, can I at least come over and give you your presents?" he asked.

"Sure? Why don't you come over Thursday afternoon? We can exchange gifts, maybe have some eggnog. I like to make a cherry turnover treat for Christmas. It's tradition at our house.

"Okay. Say about four o'clock then?" Scott pulled into her driveway and turned off the car.

"Yes, that's fine." Suzanne reached for the door handle. "Thanks for taking me to the party tonight. You don't have to walk me in. See you Thursday." With that, she was outside and the car door slammed shut.

Scott watched her walk across the porch and open the front door. 'Damn her,' he thought. 'There she goes again, pushing me away. What is with this woman?' He turned the key, backed the car out of the driveway, and headed for his house.

Lindsay was waiting up for her mother. She wanted to hear all about the big party. But Suzanne was not in a very talkative mood. She said she was tired and wanted to just go to bed. They could talk about it in the morning, she said. But Lindsay looked carefully at her mother. There was more about her demeanor than just fatigue. Something was wrong.

Suzanne did not sleep well that night. Every time she closed her eyes, vivid pictures flashed through her mind. She imagined herself in Scott's bed, under him, struggling to breathe. She saw herself dressed stylishly, attending parties, traveling the world. But under her beautiful gown was a ball and chain holding her captive. She rolled over onto her other side and tried to get the images out of her brain. It did not help. She heard the voice of the waitress in the bathroom. What had she said? 'If you don't feel it, you just don't feel it.' Rolling onto her back, she stared through the darkness up at the ceiling.

"What am I going to do?" she whispered to herself. "I'm just not feeling it."

Suzanne sat up on the side of the bed. It was then that she realized she was hot and sweating. Fumbling in the dark, her bare feet found the slippers she knew were there under her bed. Suzanne stood and padded towards the bathroom for a glass of cold water.

As she turned from the sink, her gaze fell on the framed picture hanging on the wall. A red rose surrounded by Christmas greenery. As her fingertips gently stroked the rose petals through the glass, Suzanne was overcome with grief. She felt that her heart was carrying a great weight and she could hardly breathe. Tears rolled uncontrollably down her cheeks and she sobbed quietly. Taking the picture gently from the wall, Suzanne carried it into the living room. She slipped the back off the frame and removed the card that she had kept for over ten years. George's words of love, written that Christmas so many years ago, stirred her heart. She sat on the sofa hugging the picture close to her heart and cried. She felt very alone.

Chapter Twenty

Christmas Conversations

THE NEXT FEW days went by slowly, as the days before Christmas usually do for children. But for Lindsay, the time was passing slowly because she felt a sadness in their home. Although her mother seemed busy with the usual holiday preparations, there was a distance in her eyes. While cookies baked in the oven, Suzanne sat and looked out of the window. She watched the leafless trees blowing in the wind. Lindsay watched her mother.

"We need some Christmas music, Mom. I'll get the records. We can sing while we decorate the cookies." She left to find the holiday records and when she returned, her mother had a smile on her face. She was determined to make this holiday a good memory.

Suzanne looked through the stack of records. "What do we want to hear first? How about this one?" She lifted a record from the pile and showed Lindsay 'David Seville and the Chipmunks.' "This used to be your favorite. Remember?"

"Of course I do! I used to run around the house singing like the Chipmunks. It drove you crazy!" Lindsay put the album on the record player and started the music. "I love Christmas, Mom. You always make it so special."

Suzanne smiled and took the powdered sugar from the pantry. "You melt some butter in the microwave okay? Let's get going with this frosting. We've got to take these cookies over to the homeless shelter by three o'clock." Every year since they had moved into their house, Suzanne made sure that their Christmas included doing something for the less fortunate. Sometimes it was buying items for the Angel Tree in the mall. Sometimes it was gifts for children at the orphanage. This year they had decided to help with a holiday party at the homeless shelter.

Christmas Eve brought a visit from the Andersons. They had a nice but simple dinner followed by a gift exchange. Drinking eggnog as they sat around the decorated Christmas tree, Suzanne said, "You know, our little girls have really grown up. No more Barbie dolls and coloring books. Now we're doing make-up and driving and off to college soon. Here's to our everlasting friendship through good and bad, ups and downs, always and forever!" She raised her eggnog mug in and toast and the others joined in.

"Always and forever!" they chorused together.

The next morning, Lindsay was up before her mother. She turned on the tree lights, put Handel's Messiah on the record player, and took her stocking down from the peg where it hung. Inside she found some small items, nail polish and pens, dental floss and hair ties. There was also fruit and candy, and near the toe of the stocking, Lindsay found a small white box. Opening it, Lindsay gasped. Two shiny diamond earrings rested on black velvet.

"You like them?" Suzanne asked from the doorway where she had been watching her daughter.

Lindsay jumped up from the couch and hugged her mom. "I love them. They are beautiful. Thanks Mom."

Suzanne hugged her daughter tightly. "I thought you would, sweetie. They are going to look so good on you."

Lindsay went into the bathroom to put in the earrings. She came back in to model them, smiling broadly. "I love them, mom. Thank you so much!"

Suzanne kissed her on the tip of her nose. "You are sparkling. Your ears and your eyes and your whole beautiful face! Now, let's get on with the other presents."

They sat near the tree, sharing a wonderful Christmas morning. To Suzanne, it was bitter-sweet. She knew things would never be the same after Lindsay left for college. It was an exciting new venture for Lindsay, but left Suzanne feeling empty and sad. She tried to shake the feeling, but it was hard.

That afternoon, Scott stopped over at Suzanne's house and delivered gifts to the girls. He didn't stay long. They opened the gifts while sipping eggnog, but the mood in the room was one of distance and discomfort.

It was beginning to snow when Scott left the house. Lindsay looked out of the window and remembered a snowy day long ago, when she had spent hours sledding down a big hill on her new Christmas toboggan. She said, "Mom, let's go take a walk in the snow. Then we can come back and have hot chocolate with marshmallows."

Bundled in coats, hats, and boots, Suzanne and Lindsay left the house arm in arm. They walked around the neighborhood, looking at the Christmas lights and yard displays, watching snow cover the grass and begin to pile up on the tree branches and fence posts. It was beautiful, still and quiet except for an occasional passing vehicle.

"Mom, is everything alright? You seem so quiet lately, sorta distant. What's the matter?"

"I don't know, honey. I'm sorry, I don't mean to be distant. I guess I'm thinking about you, how quickly you've grown, how our lives are about to change. I'm so proud of you, going off to Central, making a grown up life for yourself. It's what I have always wanted, but now that it's almost here, I guess I'm already missing you!"

"I know things are going to change, Mom, but I will still be around a lot. And it's natural, you know, for kids to grow up and eventually move away from their parents. I know it's the way you actually want it to be. You don't want me living with you forever!"

Suzanne hugged her daughter and tried to change the mood with a smile. "You're right, of course, it is what I want. You have a whole wonderful life ahead of you. You can make anything of yourself you want. It's a brand new chapter of your life, and you get to make choices and plot out your own destiny. I know you are excited, and I'm excited for you. Just don't forget me, okay?"

"Oh Mom! Of course not!" Lindsay bent down and scooped up a handful of soft snow. She tossed it high in the air and watched it fall, scattered by the wind.

"Remember when George took me down that big hill on my toboggan? That was so much fun! We did it over and over. I never wanted to quit, even though I got wet and cold. He made me stop when I started shivering so bad I could hardly talk. Then we went back to the apartment and you had hot chocolate waiting. That was a great day."

"It was, wasn't it?" replied Suzanne wistfully. Then she slipped into silence as they trudged along, snow crunching beneath their feet. That was the first day George had said 'I love you.' Remembering still brought a flutter to her heart.

Lindsay broke the silence. "Do you ever think about George, Mom?"

"Well, yes honey. I do. Funny thing is, I've been thinking about him a lot lately. He was important to us, to both of us. I can't forget the good times we had together. But so much of that time was based on a lie. I just can't forget that either."

"You know, I used to think that we were a family, the three of us. I mean, I knew he wasn't my real daddy, but in a lot of ways he was even better. I don't remember having so many good times with Dad. But with George, it was so natural to think of us as a family. I used to just feel like we were all supposed to be together."

"I felt like that, too, Lindsay. But it was all based on deception. At first anyway. That's what he said. It was all a game to him, but then he fell in love with me, and he loved you too. Then it got complicated."

"Did you love him?"

"Yes, I loved what I knew of him. But as it turned out, there wasn't a lot I actually did know about him. And when I found out…" Suzanne shrugged.

"Can you forgive him for lying to you, and hurting you?"

"Yes, actually, I already have. Do you remember the night of your cast party after "Hello Dolly"? George was there to see you in the play. I didn't know it till after the show. We talked for a while, and he explained a few things. It was nice."

"Wow mom, you mean he came to watch me in the show? You never told me."

"I didn't want to confuse you or start you thinking that he was getting back into our lives. Nothing changed, after all. As a matter of fact, he came to all of your other shows as well. He was one of your biggest fans!"

Lindsay was quiet as she processed this new information. "So, why don't you get back with him, now that the circumstances have changed? I know that Melissa told you his wife died. Why didn't you call him as soon as you found out? And you could have been really happy again. You could be married to him right now! All this time, we could have been a family again"

"Like I said honey, it's complicated. I didn't feel like I should call him right away. He needed time to grieve, to get his thoughts together, and to move on with his life. And then suddenly, there was Scott, and I got involved with all that. Another complication." Suzanne's thoughts drifted away, and Lindsay noticed the silence.

'I probably shouldn't get into this,' thought Lindsay. 'But I have to know what's going on. I have to be sure my mom will be okay when I leave for college.' She took a breath and asked, "So, can we talk about Scott? He seems to make you happy, most of the time. But sometimes I can tell you are confused or upset. Like today. And I don't think you were just thinking about me going off to college. I think you are confused about Scott."

Suzanne squeezed her daughter's hand. "Oh Lindsay, you are wise beyond your years. You always have been." She laughed. "Talking with you about Scott makes me feel like I'm a teenager talking to my school girlfriends about boys and dating."

"But Mom, if you are confused about him, you do need to talk to someone. Maybe Melissa would be better, if you think. But you need to talk it out."

"You are probably right." They walked on a bit, both deep in thought. Finally Suzanne opened up to Lindsay. "You're right, I *am* confused about Scott. Sometimes he makes me very happy. He certainly has a nice home, and can give us a good life with all the luxuries we might desire. He can take us places, we would never have to worry about bills and expenses. That would be a nice change for both of us. But true happiness doesn't depend on money. And there's just a feeling I get from Scott, like he isn't all he seems to be. I don't want to be fooled again. My track record with men isn't very good, and I don't want to make another mistake because I have been naively blinded to the truth."

"Then you are smart to be cautious, Mom. Just because Scott can give us a lot of stuff, that's no reason to think he is the best choice for a life partner. You have to have more than money to make a great relationship."

Again Suzanne smiled at the wisdom of her daughter. She went on. "Scott keeps pushing me for a deeper, more intimate relationship. I'm just not ready to jump into that. He can be very persistent, though. And angry when he doesn't get his way."

"He's never hurt you, has he? I mean forced you to do something you didn't want?" Lindsay was concerned. She hadn't ever noticed signs of physical abuse, but she wanted to be sure.

"No, of course not." Suzanne answered quickly. "I didn't mean that. But he does make some demands on me that I don't feel comfortable with. And when I say no, it makes him sulk or get angry with me. That's what happened at the Christmas banquet. I just can't get this ominous feeling off my chest. Something just isn't right.

"So, what do you want to do about it? Maybe you need to take a break from him and have time to think."

"Once again, you have some great advice for your dear old mom! I think you are right. I need a little time to think."

They turned and went back towards their home. The little house was lit brightly with Christmas lights shining through the windows. It was a warm and welcoming sight. The travelers shook the snow from their coats, removed their boots, and went into their house, ready for hot chocolate.

Later that evening, Suzanne sat alone with a glass of wine, watching from the living room window as snow began to fall once more. Occasionally a car would drive by slowly, snowflakes swirling in the headlights. More often, she saw no movement in the world outside her home. The wind picked up and the snow piled in the corners of the window. This was going to be quite a storm.

Except for the whining of the wind, the world was silent. Suzanne was alone with her thoughts and her mind turned, as it had so often in the past, to memories of George. 'Lindsay was right,' she thought. 'I really was happy with George. He gave me so much hope, so much to live for. I've never felt that way since. Oh, I've managed my life just fine, and both Lindsay and I have adjusted to this life we have. It hasn't been all bad. But I miss that closeness we had, how we could talk about anything. He could make me laugh and he taught me things I didn't even know about. And then there was the sex. He could make me feel things I hadn't felt before. I miss that, how he could touch me so deep down inside. Yes, I miss sex. And doing it by myself takes a distant second to his touch.'

Suzanne stood and walked to the kitchen to pour herself another glass of wine. 'Maybe I should go take a hot bath,' she thought, and smiled to herself, remembering how she had shyly spoken to George about her self stimulation so many years ago. Back when she was so inexperienced. Back when George was Paul to her. Suzanne shuddered, remembering how confused she had felt when 'Paul' had first revealed his true identity. And yet she had so quickly fallen under his spell. She was so vulnerable then. Needy. Lonely. Even though he had tricked her, she had wanted to give the relationship a chance.

Suzanne leaned her forehead against the window pane. The coldness felt good at first, but soon chilled her until she shivered and pulled away. She went back to the couch and pulled the afghan down across her shoulders. She took a sip of the wine and snuggled back onto the couch, resting her head against the arm and stretching full length, then pulled herself into a bent leg position. She closed her eyes and continued her reflection.

Despite the deceptions, Suzanne believed that they had been good together. George had really brought out the best in her. The best sexually, but more than just that. She felt relaxed, confident, and even powerful when she was with him. It was a wonderful feeling, a completion. He was the missing piece that she had been looking for, longing for. But now, without him, she felt disjointed. It went beyond loneliness. It was a hole, a void, a cavern that Suzanne had not been able to fill, even though she tried.

She had tried by pouring herself into Lindsay. That was not a bad thing. They had a wonderful relationship. But it was soon time for Lindsay to be out on her own and then what? Things between them were bound to change, at least a little. She would have to let go. That is what was best for Lindsay, but it was best for Suzanne as well.

Work filled the void, but couldn't give her the same feeling of completeness that she had had with George. She still loved the challenge of teaching first grade. She still knew that she was making a difference in the lives of the children in her classes. She wanted to keep teaching for many more years, and could imagine no other life for herself. But was it enough? With Lindsay gone to college she pictured herself alone, grading papers or developing unit plans, alone, night after night. There would be no one to share the day with, the successes of a lesson plan, the joy of a child reading, the growing confidence of a shy child. Who would she talk to about all those things?

Scott? Honestly, he never really seemed that interested in her work. Oh, he might listen patiently while she tried to share an event, but usually he was more anxious to talk about his day, not hers. And his was a different world. The University, his upper-class friends, even his ostentatious home, it was all too much. She just didn't feel comfortable. She didn't fit.

No, Scott certainly was not filling the void. In fact he was actually making her feel insecure and fearful. Not good. There was just too much tension between them. He was not the answer to her loneliness.

Maybe Lindsay was right. Maybe she needed to take a long break from Scott. Maybe permanent. Maybe she should call George. Maybe.

Chapter Twenty-One

New Hire

KRISSY FELDMAN NEEDED a job. And she knew just where she wanted to work. She got out of her car and strolled into the vet's office. She walked confidently to the receptionist's desk and announced, "I'm here about your job opening."

Mrs. Zondra Lewis looked up from behind the desk. "Okay, here's an application to fill out. When you are finished I will look it over. Here's a pen." She went back to her work as Krissy took a seat. Krissy crossed her legs and started to fill out the form.

Zondra had worked for Dr. Render as his office assistant for six years. She loved her job, and had run things efficiently. It gave her a sense of pride to know that she did her job well. But a car accident a year ago had left her with a back injury that required her to work only part time. She had cut her hours down to evenings and Saturdays, leaving her time to rest and attend therapy sessions during the week. And now, with another baby on the way, it was necessary to take a leave of absence for several months.

Zondra glanced at the picture of her daughter that was clipped to the corner of the desk calendar. Brianna was four and the light of her life. Her smile radiated from the picture. Her dark hair hung in bouncy ringlets around her face. Brianna attended preschool three days a week. She loved books and puzzles and dress-up. And she was all excited that she was going to be a big sister.

This pregnancy had been hard on Zondra. Physically, it had taken a toll on her back and the extra weight and strain was making it more and more difficult to work. Sitting was painful, and standing was even worse. Her doctor had recommended less stress for the remaining three months of her pregnancy. Much as she hated to leave her job, even for a few months, it was necessary.

Krissy stood and walked to the desk, handing the application form to Mrs. Lewis. "All right Krissy," she said, glancing down at the completed paperwork. "I see here that this would be your first real job, other than babysitting. And you are still in high school?"

"Yes, Ma'am," Krissy answered politely. "I'm a senior. And I haven't had a real job before because I have always been so busy with cheerleading. But now I need to work, because it's time for me to look ahead past high school. I have always liked animals, and I am good with meeting people and stuff."

"Well this job requires more than just a love of animals," Mrs. Lewis was quick to point out. "You would be answering phones, making appointments, checking patients in and out, as well as tallying up the receipts at the end of the day. How are your math skills?" Mrs. Lewis noticed Krissy cringe slightly.

Krissy was beginning to feel uncomfortable. Math skills? She really didn't want to admit that she had squeaked through Business Math with a C minus. But maybe, if she really tried, she could learn how to balance the receipts. Kathleen might be able to help her. She was really good with math.

Just then, the door to the examining room opened and a man came out with a beagle on a leash. The dog strained to reach Krissy and sniff at her leg. Krissy knelt down to rub the brown and white head that was nuzzling between her legs.

"Buster, stop that!" exclaimed the man with embarrassment. He pulled at the leash and Buster retreated. They walked to the desk and Mrs. Lewis took his paperwork, excused herself from Krissy for a moment, and began to process his bill for the visit.

Dr. Jefferson appeared at the door. "Zondra, we need to make an appointment for Buster in two weeks," he said, then turned to Krissy. He recognized her immediately as one of Lindsay's friends. But what was her name? The one with the great legs, the cheerleader. "Well, hello, young lady. What brings you here today? Do you have an animal with you?"

"Hi Dr. J." Krissy said brightly. "No, I came in to apply for the receptionist job." She nodded toward Mrs. Lewis. "We were just talking about what I would have to do."

"Okay, great. Well, are you available to work evenings and Saturdays? I thought you were busy with school things." He looked at her pretty young face and smiled. "And these hours would really cut into your high school social life. Not much time for dating or partying."

Krissy giggled. "Oh, Dr. J., I don't party that much! And I don't date those boys from school anyway. They are so immature. I'm getting ready to go to college so I have to get serious and make some money. I can party later!"

Buster and his owner left the office and Dr. Jefferson turned to Zondra. "That was the last patient for the day, wasn't it?" Zondra nodded. "Then why don't you just finish up here and you can leave for the day. I can do this interview, and you can get home early to rest."

"Thank you. Dr. Jefferson. It would feel good to get my feet up for a while. I'm just about ready to go, just have to input this last receipt and total up the day's income." She handed Krissy's application to the doctor, and he scanned the form and quickly found her name.

"Why don't you come back to my office, Krissy, and we can finish the interview there."

"Sure, whatever you say, boss!" giggled Krissy. Zondra raised her eyebrows and Dr. Jefferson caught the look of dislike that crossed her face. He smiled and shrugged as if to say "Kids!" They went through the hall to his office. He left the door ajar slightly and offered a chair to Krissy, who sat facing his desk, leaning forward eagerly.

"So, when can I start?"

Scott chuckled. "Not so fast, girl!" Let's talk about your responsibilities and your qualifications first. This is an important job, and whoever we hire has to be able to handle it. When Mrs. Lewis comes back in six or seven months, I don't want her to have to deal with someone else's incompetence." He looked over the application more carefully. "So you have never had a job other than babysitting, and you don't have any work references."

"No, but I did put down Mrs. Rogers for a personal reference. You know you can trust her opinion, and she knows me pretty well."

"Yes, I know she does. And I do trust her opinion." He was thinking back to Suzanne's conversation about Krissy just a few weeks earlier. Something about not being quite as innocent as she might seem at first. So maybe it was time for Scott to find out for himself.

"What do you think are your qualifications for this job?"

"Well, that's easy! You want somebody at the front desk who is cute, and that's me!" Krissy was certainly not shy. Scott raised his eyebrows and Krissy laughed. "Seriously, I'm more than just a pretty face! I am friendly, I can handle the phones! I talk on the phone all the time! I can set appointments and I'll figure out the billing part. I learn quickly, when I put my mind to it. And I'll do whatever I have to, to make you happy. You'll see!" She flipped her hair and looked at him in a playful seductive manner.

Exactly what did she mean by that?

Scott thought for a moment and then asked, "Since you don't have any references, except for Suzanne –Mrs. Rogers –what do you think your high school teachers would say about your qualifications?"

"Most of my teachers know that I try my hardest. I never just give up. I always ask for extra help if I need it. I try to get what they say. I don't get discouraged, I just try again. I have a good attitude. I have fun, no matter what. Not that math was exactly fun, but I know if math is required for this job, then I will work till I get it right."

"So, you're saying you might have trouble with the bookkeeping part?" Scott heard the front door close and knew that Zondra had left for the evening. He was alone with a very attractive and obviously flirtatious young woman.

"Yeah, but I will get help and I will get it, eventually." Krissy hoped she wasn't sinking her own ship. She had to turn things around to a positive resolution. "Dr. J., you can ask anyone. They will tell you I am flexible, I will try anything, and I want to please. Those are my best qualifications. Oh, and I learn quickly. Please give me a chance to prove myself to you. You won't be sorry, I promise!"

"We would need you every day after school and Saturdays eight till noon. Can you do that?"

"Sure, usually I sleep in on Saturday, but if you want me here by eight, then I'll be here. I do have a little problem with every evening though. I have to cheer for basketball games, that's every Thursday until the end of March. Would that be okay?" She gave him a sweet smile, and Scott found himself wanting to see more of that face.

"Thursday just happens to be the evening we close early, at five instead of nine. So I could probably get the day shift person, Nancy, to cover a few extra hours that day.

"So does this mean you're giving me the job?"

"We'll give it a try. Can you come in Saturday to work with Zondra for a little training? You would be paid for training hours, of course."

"Oh, yes, I will be here. No more sleeping in for me! I have a job now!" She clapped her hands together like an excited child. "Oh, by the way, what are you paying me? I don't even know."

"We will do minimum wage, since you have no experience yet. If you stay six months, we will have a review and there might be a raise. No promises of course."

"Okay, sure. Are there any fringe benefits?" she asked, tilting her head to the side.

"Do you mean benefits?"

Krissy giggled in a self-conscious manner and nodded, but Scott got the feeling she knew exactly what she was suggesting. "Sorry, Krissy. There are no benefits for part time employees. As far as fringe benefits, well, I have a great pool, as you know, and you would be welcome to schedule pool parties with your friends. How's that?"

"Oh, Dr. J. that's just great! I love swimming! It would be awesome to get to use your pool any time I wanted! I could work on my tan. And swimming is great exercise, you know. It will really keep me in shape if I can get to the pool several times a week. Thank you, that's so great!"

"Well, let's not jump in just yet, okay? It's only February! Might be a little cold!"

"Gosh, I know. But just wait till I tell all my friends. This is so cool!"

Scott stood and walked around his desk. He was already imagining the scantily dressed teen girls soon to be lounging around his pool. Might be a very interesting summer.

Krissy stood next to him and took his hand with both of hers. "Thank you so much for this chance. I will be so good, you'll see. You won't regret having me around. We'll be a great team!" Again Scott wondered if Krissy was aware of the double meaning behind her words. Again, he was pretty sure she knew exactly what she was suggesting.

They walked towards the front office. Scott placed his hand gently on Krissy's back as he ushered her towards the door. She turned and stood with her body very close to his. He could smell the scent of her shampoo as she looked up at him and smiled. "Thanks again, Dr. J. You won't regret this, I promise."

Krissy left and Scott exhaled deeply. What a whirlwind interview that had been! It left him breathless. She was certainly lively and excited. This was an interesting turn of events. Scott turned off the lights and locked the front door, then went back to his office, picked up his cell phone, and entered Krissy's number in his contact list.

Chapter Twenty-Two

Resolved

JUST THEN THE office phone rang, and he answered quickly when he saw Suzanne's number on the caller ID. This was an unexpected surprise. Although Scott had called her often in the last month, she always seemed busy and was short with him on the phone. It had been a while since they had really talked, and they hadn't been together since Christmas. She was probably calling to apologize for the way she had been treating him. At least she should be sorry.

"Hi Baby. It's so good to hear from you. I've missed you." Scott settled back in his large desk chair. He was still spinning from his encounter with Krissy, and he let his hand fall onto his lap, where he gently rubbed his arousal.

"Are you busy?" Suzanne asked. "I was wondering if we could talk."

'Ahh, I knew it,' Scott thought. 'She's finally ready to admit she wants me.' He hardened even more. Aloud he answered her, "I'm done at the office," I could come right over to your house."

"Well, actually, I'm right here in the parking lot. I see that the lights are off in the front office, but your car is still here. Could I come into the office?"

"You're right out in the parking lot? Sure, come on in. I'll meet you at the door." They both hung up and Scott thought, 'Wouldn't this be cool, to take her for the first time right here on my desk?' He walked to the front office and unlocked the door.

Suzanne took a deep breath and got out of her car. Her palms were sweating and she had a queasy feeling in the pit of her stomach. But she knew this was the right thing to do.

"Hi Suzanne, you look great! I've missed you," Scott said as he opened the door for her and bent to kiss her. Suzanne turned her cheek to accept his kiss, and immediately Scott felt the coldness. 'Some things never change,' he thought.

He led the way to his office, and she did not speak until they were seated across the desk from each other. "I need to talk to you, Scott. I have been doing some serious thinking and I have come to a conclusion." She looked down at her hands which were clasped tightly in her lap.

Scott just looked at Suzanne. He waited for her to continue. Somehow he already knew what she was going to say.

"This just isn't working out for me Scott. I don't feel like myself when I'm with you. I need to stop seeing you. I am just not feeling it with you. You are a wonderful man, smart and good looking and you have a lot to offer to a woman. But I am just not that woman. Thank you for all the places you have taken me, for showing me a different kind of world. But it's just not the world for me. I need to be true to myself."

There. It was out. Suzanne sat in silence for a few seconds, and then stood to leave as she realized that Scott was not saying a word. When she reached the office door, he finally spoke. There was a hint of anger in his voice

"You're making a big mistake, you know. You are getting older and the chances you have of meeting your Mr. Perfect are getting smaller by the minute. You'll never find a man who can offer you what I can. And you have been so cold and distant you haven't even really given me a chance. This whole time, your mind has been closed. Maybe you don't even know it, but you've got problems, Suzanne. You can't relax with a man. You are such a tight-ass. You don't know a good thing when it stands right beside you. I tried. But no, you wouldn't even give me a chance. I could stand here and beg you to let us have more time to work through our differences, but you know what, I don't think you're worth the trouble. You'll never come down off your high and mighty pedestal. I could bust my butt trying to make you happy, but it wouldn't do any good. So go. And have a great life without me. Long and lonely and cold and sexless. So be it."

Suzanne remained composed, even though his words were hurtful. She would not stoop to his level. She would not shoot back at him. She spoke softly. "That just goes to affirm my feelings, Scott. You just don't know me at all. You have no idea of the passion that lies within me. But I don't feel it with you, Scott, and feelings that have to be forced can't ever be real and deep. I've learned that." She reached into her purse and pulled out a small white box. "Here," she said, and placed the box on his desk. "It's your mother's bracelet. I'm giving it back to you. Good-bye Scott."

She took a deep breath and turned the doorknob. It felt like the weight of the world had been lifted off her shoulders. Her step was light and easy as she headed out to her car. The sky was dark and the stars seemed to be shining brighter than they had in a very long time. Suzanne smiled. Despite the chilliness of the night, she felt warm, way deep down inside.

Inside, Scott was fuming. He walked around the office shaking his head and mumbling to himself. After a few minutes, his anger subsided sufficiently and he let his thoughts drift towards his new employee. Krissy Feldman might be just the distraction he needed.

PART FOUR

SECRETS OF LOVE

Chapter One

Kissing Practice

PRACTICE FOR THE spring play was underway. This year they were doing "The Sound of Music" and Lindsay had the lead of Maria. She was both excited and a little more nervous than usual. The role required quite a lot of singing, so she had both lines and music to memorize. Practices were every day during drama class, but as the show dates drew nearer, they began to practice just about every evening after school.

Suzanne bought Lindsay a used car so she was able to get herself to and from school. She was a careful driver, always wearing her seatbelt, always using caution. Lindsay's best friend from drama class, Kathleen Feldman, sometimes came home with Lindsay after school, so they could work on their parts together. Kathleen had the part of the Mother Superior, so they had a few scenes together. Kathleen also had an excellent singing voice and was able to give Lindsay some practical hints about the music, breathing and phrasing advice which helped Lindsay to feel more and more confident about her role.

Driving from school one afternoon, Lindsay asked Kathleen, "So what's up with Krissy. I haven't had much of a chance to talk with her lately. I never see her anymore."

Kathleen nodded. "I hardly ever see her myself. She got a job, you know. Working almost every day after school, and even on Saturdays. She's never home. But she's lovin' the money. Last week she showed me a bunch of new clothes she bought, and some CDs."

"Cool! So since you are twins and wear the same size, that means you've got new clothes too, right? She'll share with you, right?"

"Well, actually we do wear the same sizes, but the stuff she bought just isn't my style. We're really different, you know. She goes for short skirts, low cut and tight tops. Not me. Give me longer, looser, and more modest. We're twins in looks, not in attitude."

"Like I'd never noticed!" Lindsay teased. "Where is she working?"

"At that vet's office, you know, the one that took care of your cat after Krissy's car hit it." She gave Lindsay a sideways glance, curious to see the reaction this news would bring. She knew Lindsay's mom had been dating the vet, and she knew that Lindsay had spent some time at the vet's house. She also knew that Lindsay hadn't mentioned him in quite some time.

"Oh, that's cool. I didn't know." Lindsay pulled carefully into traffic. "I wondered what she was up to. Does she like the job?"

"She likes the money, that's all I can tell you. Like I said, I never see her much. Hey, are you ready for the kissing scene? We're supposed to practice that part this week, you know."

Lindsay was blushing slightly and laughed nervously. "I know. It is going to be interesting. At least it's a good thing Conner is so cute!"

"Admit it; you're glad he is your leading man, aren't you?"

"Well, sure. He is cute and everything. But he's really nice, too. I think he's as nervous as I am about this kissing thing. I just hope it doesn't look all awkward."

"You'll just have to practice a lot!" Kathleen giggled and so did Lindsay.

Conner England was playing the part of Captain Von Trapp. He was tall and handsome, with dark brown hair and bright blue eyes. Lindsay had secretly had a crush on him for quite some time. He too was a senior and they had been in drama classes together since they were freshmen. They had done small skits together, but this would be the first time they had both had leading roles in the school play.

Before practice one evening, Connor came and sat next to Lindsay. "So, tonight's the night!" he announced, and Lindsay knew what he was talking about without it even being said. It was on her mind too. He playfully put his arm around her shoulder. "It's no big deal. Just pretend you're kissing your boyfriend."

"I don't have a boyfriend!" Lindsay exclaimed before thinking. It was almost like telling him that she had never kissed a boy, which was the truth but not what she wanted him to know.

Connor reacted in mock shock. "What? No boyfriend? How can that be? You're so cute. I would think you have guys drooling after you! Who could resist?"

Lindsay giggled at his silly act. "I guess I'm just particular. The right boy has never come along."

"Before now, you mean. You never know. I might be the man of your dreams. You might even like kissing me! We'll have to see, won't we? This play might be the beginning of the rest of your life. Who knows?" Connor reached out and took Lindsay's hand in his. He bent his head and kissed the back of her hand. Then he turned and walked backstage. Lindsay was left breathless.

The drama teacher brought her back to earth when she called for the rehearsal to begin. Practice went well. Lindsay had learned most of her lines, and was remembering the blocking they had practiced previously. As the practice drew to a close the teacher dismissed all of the actors except Lindsay and Connor. They were going to rehearse the love scene without an audience.

The scene required Maria to be shy and even a little backward when the Captain confessed his love to her. Lindsay played the scene perfectly, and when Connor touched her chin to pull her lips up towards his own, she felt a surprising flutter in the pit of her stomach. She smiled shyly at Connor, and their lips met for the first time.

"Okay, that was great. Just the feeling I was hoping for," the director complimented. "Let's try it once more." The actors parted to take their places and the scene began again. This time Lindsay was a little more confident.

Connor noticed the difference and smiled at her when the scene was over. "See, I knew you'd like it! Can't wait for the next practice!"

Lindsay drove home in a slight daze. She still felt the pressure of his lips upon hers. She wondered if it was anything more than an act in a play. The fluttery feeling in her stomach made her realize that she was hoping for more.

Chapter Two

Don't Loose That Number

SUZANNE PICKED UP the phone and took a deep breath. 'I'm ready for this' she said to herself. 'It's the right time.' She dialed George's number and waited for his voice to answer. For the one hundredth time, she went over what she was going to say.

"Lindsay's school play is coming up in a few weeks and I know you like to watch her. So I was wondering if you would like to meet me there. Maybe we could sit together." It sounded so lame. Why were her hands sweating?

The phone rang and rang, then the recorded operator voice came in and announced that the number was no longer in service. "Great. Now what?" she said out loud as she hung up the phone.

She was startled when the phone rang almost immediately. She picked it up and said "Hello?" It was Melissa.

"Hi Suzanne, you must have been right by the phone."

"Yes, I just put it down before you rang. Kind of scared me!"

"Oh, sorry. Hey, I was just calling to ask when Lindsay's next play is. I need to get the tickets lined up."

"That's so funny. I was just thinking about the play tickets myself." Suzanne pictured George sitting next to her. She told Melissa the play dates and Melissa said. "Okay. I'll Check my calendar and see which night would be best for us. Is Lindsay excited?"

"Of course. She's singing the music morning, noon and night. And she's talking a lot about a boy named Connor who has the male lead. I think she likes him."

"Really? Are they dating?"

"No, they just spend a lot of time together at rehearsal. I think she would like it to be a little more than that, though. I met him at school the other night. Good looking kid, much taller than her. And he seemed polite. Lindsay's first crush."

"They are growing up so fast. Look how quickly time is going. They will be in college before we can blink."

"Don't remind me."

"Which brings up another subject." Melissa went directly to the main purpose of her call. "When are you ever going to call George?"

"Are you some sort of mind reader? As a matter of fact, I was trying to call him just before you called me. But the number is disconnected."

Never one to beat around the bush, Melissa said, "I've got his new number right here. Get a pencil and write it down." Suzanne did as she was told, and repeated the number back to Melissa. "Yes, that's it. He moved just a few weeks ago. I'm glad you finally came to your senses. Now call him. Bye."

Suzanne chuckled as she replaced the phone. Melissa could be so pushy sometimes. Before she could dial the number, there was a sound of a car in the driveway. She walked to the door when the bell rang. It was Connor.

"Hi, Ms. Rogers. I was driving by and wondered if Lindsay was home?"

"Why, yes she is, Connor. Would you like to come in? I'll go get Lindsay."

Connor took a seat in the living room and Suzanne went down the hall to Lindsay's room. Peeking into the room, she saw that her daughter was applying a little pink lipstick. Her hair was pulled into a bouncy ponytail and her cheeks were flushed. "Hi honey. Did you know that Connor was coming over?"

"Not until I saw him pull into the driveway. Do I look okay? I wonder why he's here."

"Why don't you go out and ask him? And yes, you look fine."

Lindsay took one more glance in the mirror and walked into the living room. "Hi Connor. What are you doing here?"

Connor stood when he saw her. "Just driving by and I knew this was your house, so I thought maybe we could practice some more. I'm having trouble remembering my lines in that scene at the beginning. I thought maybe we could go over it a few times."

"Okay, I'll go get my script. Mom, is it okay if we go downstairs and practice?"

"Well, sure, that's fine."

Lindsay went to her room for the script and Suzanne turned to Connor. "Would you like something to drink? I've got some Cokes in the refrigerator."

"Yeah, thanks, that would be great." Connor took two cans of soda and followed Lindsay down the stairs. Suzanne closed the basement door and went back to the phone. She sat a moment, thinking of her daughter downstairs with a boy. Yes, things were certainly changing fast.

Chapter Three

Phone Call

GEORGE WAS IN his garage, putting away tools. His new job as a heating and air conditioning repair man was keeping him pretty busy. It had been a month since he left the apartment maintenance position. His many years of experience had gotten him several job offers and he had accepted a position as lead technician with Hinkley's HVAC.

He was renting a small house and had almost finished unpacking. George wasn't surprised when he heard the phone ringing inside the house. He and Tom had planned to get together to watch a ball game on TV. George didn't hurry into the house. He could call Tom back in a few minutes. Just a bit later, when George went into the house, he glanced at the phone and noticed that there was no message waiting.

He was in the bathroom, washing his hands, when he heard the phone ring again. Expecting to hear Tom, George was surprised to hear a female voice speaking on the answering machine. Quickly he turned the water off and grabbed a towel, but he was not able to reach the phone in time.

Three times he played the message recording over before he sat down and exhaled. Suzanne! She called him! She sounded wonderful, her voice just the same but yet different at the same time. Her words ran through his mind… "Hello, George, this is Suzanne. Lindsay is going to be in the senior play in a couple of weeks and I was wondering if you would like to watch her. I really don't like leaving messages on machines. Maybe you could call me back?" Then, as an after thought, she gave him her phone number, not knowing that he had long ago committed her number to memory.

George dialed the number immediately. His voice was strong and clear, despite the loud heart beat rumbling in his chest. The phone rang three times before Suzanne answered. "Hello," she said and George answered simply "Hi."

A moment's silence lingered between them before they both started talking at once. "I'm glad you called back!" she said, while his words were "It's really good to hear your voice." They laughed and George let her speak. "I just hate talking on answering machines. It makes me nervous."

"Yeah, I know what you mean. So, what play is Lindsay in this year?"

"She's got the lead in "The Sound of Music." Would you like to come and watch her?"

"Of course. I haven't missed one yet. She always does so well. "The Sound of Music?" Doesn't that have a lot of singing in it?"

"Yes, and she's been practicing for weeks now. Learning all the music has been a new challenge, but she likes it. I'm sure she will be great."

"I have no doubt! When is the show?"

Suzanne checked her calendar just to be sure. "April 15, 16 and 17. That's a Thursday, Friday and Saturday."

"Well, I'm free on any of those nights, of course. Will Tom get me the ticket, like he usually does?"

"Um, well, he could if that's the way you want to do it. But, well, I was thinking…" Suzanne's voice trailed off, and George had to prompt her to go on. She took a deep breath. Something about this conversation made Suzanne realize that it was just possible that her whole world was about to change.

Finally she got the words out. "Well, I was wondering if maybe this time you would like for me to get the tickets, and then maybe we could sit together for the show." There, she'd done it.

"I really would like that, Suzanne." George knew he could not hide the smile in his voice. "It would be wonderful to see you again, and to sit with you watching Lindsay in her last school play, well, yes, I would love it."

"Good," Suzanne sighed. "Which night would be best for you?"

"Well, should we keep with our tradition? I always go to the Saturday night show, and then we talk a little afterwards at McDonald's. Three years running. In fact I always look forward to that, as much as I look forward to seeing Lindsay in the play."

"I know. Me too"

"But maybe opening night would be better. I've never seen an opening night show, and this would be my last chance. And besides, Thursday comes two days sooner that Saturday."

Suzanne giggled slightly and knew exactly what he was thinking. And now that the plans were in the making, Suzanne didn't know if she could wait until Saturday either. Or even Thursday, for that matter.

"Okay, let's make it opening night. The show starts at 7:00. Do you want to meet me in the lobby?"

"If that's what you want. About 6:45 okay with you?"

"Sure, that's good. Well, I guess I'll see you then." Suzanne didn't want the conversation to end but she knew she couldn't go on forever.

"Okay," George said and then quickly added, "I'm sure glad you called, Suzanne. I think about you all the time."

Suzanne hesitated before saying, "I think about you, too. It will be good to see you again. Bye." And she meant it.

Chapter Four

A Little Friendly Advice

TO LINDSAY, TIME was just flying by. Her days were filled with classes and schoolwork; her evenings were filled with rehearsals and Connor. The time she spent with Connor left her giddy with excitement and smiling all the time. She even found herself daydreaming sometimes in class, doodling little hearts in the margins of her chemistry notes. Then she'd pull herself in and focus on the task at hand. She never let her thoughts get out of control, but just seeing Connor in the hall could quicken her heartbeat. This was certainly a new phase in her life.

She couldn't help but wonder if this connection she was feeling with Connor would be all over when the final curtain fell. Was all his attention just because of their parts in the play? Maybe Connor was just spending all this time with her because he thought he had to. Maybe when the play was over 'Connor and Lindsay' would be over too.

Lindsay wished the clock would slow down. The days were going by too fast. She wished the play would never come, because then it would be over, and what then?

Suzanne, on the other hand, felt like the days were just crawling by. Opening night could not come soon enough. She began to think about what she should wear. Maybe she should get her hair trimmed, maybe colored to cover up some of those pesky gray hairs she was beginning to notice. Looking through her closet, Suzanne realized that she hadn't been shopping for herself in a while. Maybe a trip to Macy's was called for.

Suzanne called Melissa after school one evening and suggested a shopping trip and lunch in town. They met at the mall on Saturday and both women were prepared for a day of dressing rooms, mirrors and decisions. Suzanne told her friend why she was looking for a new outfit, and Melissa was thrilled. "You called him! I'm so glad. You should have done it months ago, before you got involved with Scott. I never did like him much. But George, well he has proven himself over and over. This is a good thing!"

"If it's so good, why do I feel nervous about being with him? I mean, I want to, I really, really want to. But I feel like I have to be so careful with him. I just don't want to rush in and then be sorry later."

"Hey listen!" Melissa scolded her. "You have waited a long time. You are not rushing into this. A lot has changed in the last ten years. Changes for both of you. Changes for good, I think. Just relax. Remember the good times. You were so happy with him for a while. And now that he is moving on, and you are too, maybe it's time to start thinking about moving in the same direction. It couldn't hurt to just think about it. Give it a try. You might be surprised. You once said you thought George was your destiny. Maybe he really is."

"I know. I felt that way once. But then so much happened, and I felt so betrayed. It's hard to just forget all that."

"Yeah, I get that. But that was then, now is now. Start over. Give it a chance."

"Well, that's sort of what I'm doing, you know. I mean, I called him. I asked him out. I made the first move. Now we will just have to see how it goes." Suzanne picked a dress off the rack, held it out to Melissa and asked, "How about this one?"

"Great, if you want to look like an old maid. Why not this one? Much more stylish." Shopping continued until Suzanne had chosen a classic black dress with an animal print jacket. Melissa convinced her to also buy a pair of heels and a purse to match.

"Wow, I'm not taking you shopping with me again!" Suzanne laughed as they left the cashier's counter. "I spent way too much. I never would have gotten the shoes or the purse if you hadn't been here!"

"But face it, honey, you need those shoes. You only wear flats at work, and these little heels do make your legs look great. You'll thank me later, wait and see!"

"I'm sure you're right. You usually are! So where should we go for lunch?"

"Somewhere with a big juicy burger. Not fast food. I'm totally starving."

By the time their shopping excursion was over, Suzanne was even more excited about the upcoming event. Just a few more days now.

George was in town, too. First he got a haircut, then he went shopping for a new shirt and ended up getting two, with a new pair of pants as well. He decided his boots needed polishing. He washed his truck. He wanted everything to be perfect. This was as nerve-wrecking as his first date in high school. Would Thursday ever get here?

Chapter Five

The Curtain Goes Up

FINALLY THURSDAY DID arrive. The day dawned as any other, and closed with a sense of finality. A chapter was ending. But surely a new chapter was about to be written.

George was waiting in the school lobby as Suzanne arrived. She looked fantastic, better than he had even dreamed. She seemed more self-confident than she had been a year ago. Something had changed.

She was still as beautiful as the first time he had seen her, at the apartment playground so many years ago. Yes, her hair had darkened to a deeper auburn, almost brown with a few lighter highlights. She had aged, but more towards a maturity, not like she looked that much older. Ten years was a long time, but she had taken care of herself, that was obvious. The body looked toned, her legs were fantastic, and that smile, oh that smile.

Suzanne did smile as she found him in the crowd and walked towards him. Her heels clicked rhythmically on the tile floor, and her hair bounced ever so slightly as she moved across the lobby. "Hi! Have you been waiting long?"

"No problem. I've only been here a couple of minutes. Besides, it was worth the wait." George smiled down on her. "You look terrific."

Slightly embarrassed, Suzanne smiled and looked down. "Thanks. Well, let me get the tickets." She turned toward the ticket booth but George caught her by the elbow. "I already got them. Our seats are right near the front."

"Oh, okay, well, great! Let's go!"

As they made their way down the aisle to seats up front, Lindsay was watching through a crack in the stage curtain. She smiled to see them together. Her mom looked so happy. And that new dress was awesome. Lindsay watched as George stepped aside to let her mother go in first. Suzanne stopped, looked at her seat number, and turned towards George. He leaned forward and whispered something in her ear, and Suzanne smiled broadly. She bent slightly and picked a single red rose off of the seat, then turned toward George. Lindsay was able to lip read her words as Suzanne said "Thank you," then touched the rose to her nose and took her seat. George sat too, and leaned over to speak again in Suzanne's ear. She looked up at him and nodded.

Lindsay felt a hand on her shoulder. It was Kathleen, dressed already for her role as the Mother Superior. "So that's him, huh? Your mom sure looks happy. Did he just give her a rose?"

"Yeah, sweet, huh? I remember he used to bring her roses a lot, back in the day." Lindsay turned from the curtain. "Are you ready for this? I'm so nervous! Hope I can hit those high notes on "Doe A Deer."

"You'll be fine. You warmed up, your breathing is good, you'll do just fine. Trust yourself. You know what you're doing up there!" Kathleen tucked some of her hair in place under her headpiece. She saw Connor approaching from behind Lindsay and said, "Here comes lover boy!"

Lindsay blushed and turned towards Connor. He reached for her hands and said, "You ready? We're going to be great, you know. We're a perfect team." He leaned forward, kissed her on the forehead, and moved further back stage. Lindsay let her breath out slowly. She had not even been aware that she had been holding it.

The orchestra music started and everyone took their places. Soon the lights went dim and the show was under way. Half way through the first act, George reached for Suzanne's hand and held it until intermission.

The play went well. The music was stirring, the acting superb, and the kiss sent sparks of electricity through the audience. At curtain call, there was a standing ovation when first Connor and then Lindsay took the stage for their bows. Suzanne was beaming at her daughter, and George was clapping enthusiastically.

George held Suzanne's elbow as they maneuvered through the crowd towards the auditorium exit. Several times the press of the crowd pushed Suzanne back into George and she felt the strength of his arms, as well as the warmth of his body as she leaned against him. She signed deeply, and hoped he hadn't noticed.

But George did notice, and he liked having her so close to him again. Even in a crowd, even jostled and pushed along with the flow of the mass exiting the building, it felt damn good to have her close.

They waited together in the lobby for Lindsay to appear, dressed in jeans and a nice blouse, ready to go home. Lindsay walked shyly up to George, not sure whether she should shake his hand or give him a hug. His warm smile relaxed her immediately, and Lindsay decided a quick hug was appropriate. "Hi, George. It was nice of you to come see the show. Mom told me that you have been coming every year. That's cool."

"Yes, I've been to every one of your shows. You certainly have become a terrific actress. Grown up a lot, too. Kissing boys now, I see!" George teased her and chuckled to see her blush. He put his arm around her shoulders and said, "Seriously, you were great! Lots of improvement from your days as a flower!"

Lindsay giggled. "You remember that?"

"Well, I heard about it when you were little. Your mother described it so well I felt like I was there." George looked at Suzanne. "You hungry? How about we go get something at McDonald's?"

Lindsay jumped in before Suzanne could answer. "Mom, Connor just asked me if he could drive me home. And he wants to go to McD's first. Would that be okay?"

"Well, sure hon, just don't be out too late. There's school tomorrow you know."

Suzanne looked at George and said, "Maybe we should find somewhere other than McDonald's tonight. I think a lot of the kids are going to be there. I know a coffee shop down the road a bit. Would that be alright?"

"Sure, whatever you want." He turned to Lindsay and said, "Really, you were wonderful tonight. I'm so glad I got to see you again." Lindsay hugged him tightly this time and said, "It's good to see you , too. Don't be a stranger, okay?" With that she was off, calling over her shoulder "I won't be late mom. I might even beat you home!"

They drove to the coffee shop in George's truck. Suzanne gave directions and for a while they just watched the traffic signals and spoke only when necessary to maneuver through traffic and find a parking space. When George took the key out of the ignition, he turned to Suzanne and said, "I'm so glad you invited me to watch the show with you. It was great seeing Lindsay. She's a beautiful young lady. And you can tell you've raised her right. I'm just sorry I missed so much. I'm sorry about a lot of things."

Suzanne didn't know what to say, so she chose the safe subject first. "Yes, she is a good girl. She's respectful, responsible, takes school seriously, and she really does love acting. Did you see how many people in the audience were wiping tears out of their eyes? She really got to them!"

They laughed and George said, "So, how about some coffee? Or would you rather have tea?"

"I think it's a night for hot tea."

They sat at a quiet table in the corner. The waitress brought tea, coffee, and some blueberry scones George ordered. They talked about things like old times. School, the house, George's new job, Lindsay's plans for college. Time slipped away and most of the customers left the café. Suddenly Suzanne was aware of the lateness of the hour.

"Oh my, look at that!. It's nearly midnight already. I need to get home. I'll never be able to get up in the morning." She stood to leave, and George took her hand as they left the café. There was a little spring chill in the air, and George pulled her close to him and wrapped his arm around her waist as they walked to his truck. He opened the door for her, then went around to his side and started the engine. "Let's see if we can get back to the school without getting lost in the dark!"

Suzanne picked the red rose up off the seat of the truck, where it had lain while they were at the café. "Thanks again for the rose. You must know how much I love them."

"Yes, of course I remember." He pulled out of the parking lot and headed towards the school. "Suzanne," he said, "It's been really great seeing you again. I was wondering, if it's alright with you, could we do it again soon? Go out, I mean." He glanced her way and saw her looking straight ahead. Did that mean she was upset? She seemed sorta stiff and quiet.

After what seemed an eternity to George, Suzanne drew a deep steadying breath. "I would like that," she said softly. "There's a lot we have to catch up on."

"Great! When? How about Saturday?" His enthusiasm made Suzanne chuckle.

"Saturday is the last night of the play. I really don't want to miss it, since it's her last show. I know, I know, it's obsessive, but I always go to all of the performances, every show. I never want to miss one. She'll be gone so soon and I probably won't get to see all of her shows in the future, when she's at college. So I don't think Saturday night is good. What about next week, next Saturday?"

Disappointed, George sighed, "Really? That long? I don't know if I can wait till then."

Again Suzanne chuckled. "Well, that's the best I can do! Sorry! You could call me though. If you want."

They had reached the school parking lot, which was deserted except for Suzanne's car and just a few others. After turning off the ignition and unfastening his seatbelt, George leaned close to Suzanne. "I would like that, very much. I have missed talking to you. There is so much I want to tell you. So much. So I'll call you, you can bet your life on it!" He put his hand on her chin and lifted her face towards his. Suzanne closed her eyes and he leaned in closer.

With a sudden unexpected move he planted a kiss on Suzanne's forehead. She opened her eyes, surprised, but smiled. Her heart was beating rapidly. Maybe she really did want him to kiss her, really kiss her, but she was also glad that he was moving slow. They had a lot to talk about. George opened her door for her and walked her to her own car. "I'll call you tomorrow. Dream sweet dreams." As Suzanne drove towards home, she glanced down at the one red rose laying on the car seat beside her. One perfect red rose. Perfect.

Chapter Six

The Honest Truth

AND HE DID call. Both Friday and Saturday, before they left for the school, George called to wish Lindsay the best. He didn't talk long, just long enough for Suzanne to know he had been thinking about them. Just long enough for her to hear the familiarity in his voice. Just long enough for her to long for more time to talk.

Sunday morning, Lindsay slept in late. Suzanne decided to let her sleep. She had been keeping long hours during rehearsals and needed her rest. It had been quiet late when Connor brought her home after the cast party. Her last cast party as a high school student.

It was a beautiful morning, so Suzanne took a cup of tea outside to sit under her oak tree and enjoy the spring breeze. Tulips were starting to bloom and the tips of her stargazer lilies were poking their way up through the warming earth. She watched as a pair of bluebirds explored the bird house that was attached to a pole in the back yard. Yes, it was going to be a beautiful day.

She took a sip of tea, closed her eyes, and leaned back to rest her shoulders against the bench. Resting so, her peace was disturbed by the ringing of the phone. Suzanne reached into the pocket of her sweater and pulled out the cordless phone she had brought outside with her. "Hello?"

"Hey. Whatcha doin'?" George asked.

"Just sitting outside watching the birds. Lindsay's still sleeping. All these late hours left her pretty tired."

"Did she get home late last night?"

"It was after one. Connor brought her home from the cast party. I was awake, of course. They sat outside on the front porch quite a while before she came inside. She's been asleep ever since."

"So, is she serious about this fella?"

"He's her first boyfriend. And they haven't really been dating, just doing all these play rehearsals. But I know she likes him. And he's been over here a few times. Seems like a nice guy. I've known his parents a little from school functions. I think Connor is a good student. I know he's planning on college, just don't remember where."

George was quite for a moment, then went on, "So you're sitting outside in your backyard?"

"Yes."

"Would you like some company? I could come over, if that's ok?"

"Well, I guess that would be fine. Do you want some breakfast?"

"Naw, don't you bother with that. I'll bring something over. We can sit outside and eat, if you want."

"Sounds nice. Got a pencil? I'll give you directions."

"That's okay. I know already. Just make some coffee, okay? See you in about half an hour."

Suzanne clicked the button on the phone. 'He knows already?' she puzzled. 'Well, maybe Tom told him where we live. Guess I'll go make that coffee.'

Lindsay was still asleep when Suzanne peeked in on her a few minutes later. Coffee was perking and she had set out some paper plates and forks, not knowing for sure what George's idea of breakfast would be. She stepped into the bathroom to comb out her hair when she heard his truck pull into the driveway. A little lipstick, a quick glance of satisfaction, and she was at the door to let him in.

George looked comical and off balance as he struggled with a picnic hamper and a large plaid blanket. He said, "We're going to have a picnic in the backyard," jerked his head towards the side of the house and started around like he knew just where he was going. "Grab your tea and coffee and meet me out back."

Following his instructions, Suzanne met him in the backyard. He had already spread the blanket on the grass and was kneeling to unpack the picnic basket. He stood and came to help, taking the tea and coffee thermoses she had prepared. She bent to put the paper plates and two mugs on the blanket and started to sit down. George touched her arm before she could sit.

"Thanks for letting me come over this morning. I just couldn't wait another whole week. I had to see you. I have to talk to you. I miss you so much." He pulled her close and once again Suzanne thought he was going to kiss her, but she was wrong. He hugged her tightly and stroked her hair, then said, "Let's eat!"

"Okay! Let's see what you have in there." Suzanne started to reach into the basket, but George intercepted. "Here, let me do it. I brought some fruit, and a little yogurt dip, and some pastries fresh from the bakery." He placed some strawberries and grapes on a plate, then opened a package of blueberries and found a couple of kiwi rolling around in the basket. With a knife he had brought along, he deftly peeled and sliced the kiwi and arranged it on the plate. He opened the yogurt dip and found a spoon. He arranged the pastries on a separate plate and sat them all in the center of the blanket. Suzanne watched in contentment. "There," he said with satisfaction. "Now for the coffee."

Suzanne poured him a steaming cup and also some tea for herself. They both sipped the warm liquids and sighed. "Nice," she said softly. "Very nice."

"Okay, listen, before we start eating, I have a lot I have to tell you. I have to get this all off my chest – something I have been keeping from you for all these years. And now is the time to confess it all. I want no more secrets between us. We can't even think about what might happen between us in the future until you know all this I have to tell you. No more secrets, ever again, and I want to start right now to tell you all. It's important, very important to me, that you hear all this."

"You're scaring me, George. What are you talking about?" Suzanne sat her tea cup down. Her hands were shaking.

"Well, it's about this house. I've been here before. In fact I've been here lots of times. You never knew, but I want you to know now."

Suzanne furrowed her brow and asked, "What do you mean? When?"

"It all started with Lindsay's swing set. You know how much she always wanted her own playground, while we were living at the apartments? Well, Tom came to me one day and asked me to help him build a play set for a friend of his. So I helped him – did most of the work myself, to tell you the truth. You know what a klutz he is with power tools." He laughed at the memory. "Anyway, I didn't know it at the time, but the play set was for Lindsay and we built it right here in your back yard. And when I found out, weeks later, that this is your house and that it was Lindsay's play set, it felt good to me to know that I had helped to make her happy. And I imagined you out here playing with her, pushing her on the swings and stuff. It helped me. It made me happy."

"Really? I never knew that. Tom never told me." She paused and thought for a minute. "It's kinda sweet, actually. And Lindsay was so happy when she saw the play set for the first time. We spent hours and hours out here. So I guess I should say thank-you. I always did wonder about Tom's sudden interest in handy man stuff. Just thought he was trying to help."

"Well, there's more. Here, do you want some grapes?" He handed the plate of fruit to Suzanne, she took some grapes and said, "Go on."

"Well, I guess the next thing was the broken fence and gate in the front of the house."

"You mean you helped with that too?"

"Yup. And you know those rose bushes?" He paused and reached for some more berries. "Planted them with my own two hands. I knew how much you love your flowers, specially roses, and I wanted you to have some growing right away. I trimmed your lilac bushes and sometimes just raked leaves. Anything to help out a little. I didn't care that Tom got all the credit. I just wanted to be sure you were happy."

"I never knew. Never suspected." Suzanne looked at him with wonder.

"I didn't want you to know. I didn't want you to think I was stalking you or something like that. But I did want to think that, in some small way, I was helping you find happiness here."

"And I have been happy here, George. Partly because of the playground and the roses. Partly because I was just going on with my life and doing okay. Lindsay was my life. We did alright."

"I know. Tom kept me up to date with things. He helped me in other ways, too. Always there to talk to, always helping me keep it together. He's a great friend. We went fishing a lot, and talked and went to ballgames, too. Melissa wasn't too keen on the idea of us being friends at first, but as long as I left you alone, and let you heal without me interfering, I guess it was alright with her."

"Actually she told me just recently that you and Tom have been friends. But she didn't tell me anything about you planting those rose bushes."

"That's because I don't think she knew anything about it. Tom was pretty good about keeping it just between us. I think she got a little suspicious after a while, though."

"What do you mean?" Suzanne looked at him quizzically.

"Well, I guess she started hounding Tom to put in a water feature with a fountain and plantings, and everything and he really doesn't have a clue." He chuckled and poured another cup of coffee.

"Wait, you mean you did that, too?"

"Well, yeah, I put in the fountain and fixed up the waterfall. The pond itself was here already, but I just added a little to it. I liked to think about you lying in your bed, listening to the water splash, and just feeling all peaceful and calm. Did it work?"

"Well, yes, I used to love to listen to the water. But I never dreamed that you had built that waterfall and everything."

"Yup, that was me. Now I guess I really ought to get over to Melissa and Tom's house and help him put in a pond for her. She's been waiting for him to get around to it, and I know he can't really do much without me! Not that I'm trying to sound like superman or anything, but that guy has five thumbs on each hand!"

"Oh, now wait. He has done things around the house. I've seen him. He fixed my sliding door when it was off the track."

"Yeah, but who do you think taught him how to do that, Norm Abrams?"

Suzanne laughed and realized that she hadn't laughed so comfortably in a very long time. She looked at George and touched his hand. "Thank you for doing all that for us, for me. It was very thoughtful. You took real good care of us."

George laced his fingers in with Suzanne's. "I want you to know that I thought about you every day in the past ten years. I thought about how I had deceived you and hurt you. I thought about what a wonderful woman you are, and how I destroyed what we had. I never meant to. Things got crazy. It's like I was living two lives. The life I had with you was the life I really wanted, but it was built on so many secrets and lies."

George put his fingertips under Suzanne's chin and raised her face. He looked directly into her eyes and spoke from his heart. "Those days are over now. I've gotten some counseling, did some soul searching. Things are different now. I am different now."

He reached down and took both of Suzanne's hands on his own. "Suzanne, I want to start again. To do it right. I was hoping maybe you want that too."

Suzanne noticed his sincerity and also noticed the feel of his fingers linking in with her own. He stroked his thumb across the back of her hand, tracing little soft circles. She felt the warmth and gentleness of his touch. She took a deep breath and looked directly into his eyes. "You did hurt me. I've told you how I felt about that, and I've already told you that I have moved on and can forgive you. I couldn't stay bitter. It wasn't healthy for me, or for Lindsay. And now I think I've built a wall around myself. I am determined not to be hurt like that again."

George slid his body closer to her, and put his arm around her shoulders. "I'm so sorry Suzanne. I need you to know that. I understand about the walls. It's going to be hard. But I can promise you honesty and truthfulness. No more lies. No more secrets. I only hope you can come to trust me again. I hope you can try."

She laid her head on George's chest and signed. It felt good to be this close to him again. It felt right. The emptiness in her heart was filled with his presence. The sun was coming out from behind the clouds of her life and she felt warmed by its rays. The future was full of potential. "I want to try. I really do want to," she said softly.

George squeezed her tighter. "Thanks. That means a lot to me." They sat together for a long moment, and Suzanne began to smile.

From inside the house, Lindsay watched out the kitchen window. She smiled too.

EPILOGUE

THE BACK YARD had been a bustle of activity all morning but now things were quieting down. The guests were taking their seats, quietly whispering to each other as they waited for the ceremony to begin. Soft music from a string quartet, all friends of Lindsay's from college, filled the backyard with beautiful harmony. The weather was perfect for an outdoor wedding, not too hot, just a light breeze.

Looking around at the friends gathered to celebrate the occasion, Melissa Anderson gave a sigh of happiness. "You okay?" asked her husband Tom. "Absolutely," she replied. "Everything's perfect."

Inside the house, Suzanne gave her daughter one last hug before taking her place near the door. "This is it!" She raised her hands to cradle Lindsay's face and smiled, then gave Lindsay a quick kiss. "I'm so happy. You look beautiful!"

"Thanks Mom. You look great too. This day is everything I have ever dreamed of. Thank you so much! You're the best. I love you!"

"I'm so proud of you, Lindsay," said Suzanne, beaming with joy. "College, a career you love, and now a fine man to spend the rest of your life with. I can wish you nothing but happiness."

George came up behind Lindsay and laid his hands on her shoulders. "Ready, honey?"

"Let's see. Something old – that's Mom's Christmas Ring. Something new – that's my dress and everything. Something borrowed — that's this necklace from Jenna. And something blue — that's my garter. I've got my flowers, I memorized my vows, and everybody's here. Yup! I'm ready!"

"You sure do look beautiful, Lindsay. Almost as beautiful as your mother. And so grown up! It's hard to believe. You're not the little girl I built that swing set for, are you? I'm so proud of what you have become."

"Don't make me cry, Dad," said Lindsay, dabbing at her eyes. Then she threw her arms around him. "I love you. Thanks for all this. And thanks for making Mom so happy."

George moved back to look Lindsay in the eye. "Your mother and I just hope that you and Brad will be as happy as we have been. There will be hard times, that's for sure. But remember this day, how in love you are, and always remember to be honest with each other. That's the most important thing. No secrets." George glanced at Suzanne and saw her smile back at him. He took a deep breath. "Now, are you ready to do this?"

"Oh, yes, I am so ready!"

The processional music was cued and the grandmothers were seated. Brad's mother was escorted to her seat, then Suzanne took her place. Two bridesmaids entered on the arms of their escorts, followed by Jenna as maid of honor. The groom, Brad, came to the front, looking both nervous and sure of himself at the same time. The onlookers stood as the Wedding March began. All eyes turned towards the door as Lindsay, the beaming bride, walked down the path on the arm of George, her father.

From her spot on the front row, Suzanne Rogers-Wiley smiled and could hardly keep tears from welling up in her eyes. She watched as George proudly walked forward with Lindsay at his side. Lindsay looked so happy, eager for what changes were to come. Her life was turning a new corner, and the future looked bright.

George caught Suzanne's gaze and gave her a wink. He reached with his free hand and touched the boutonniere pinned to his lapel, a single red rose. Suzanne winked back, softly touched her red rose corsage and smiled. Quite possibly, this was the absolute happiest day of her life.